Sor

No family celebr... ...ltrys of
Texas. Every year, ...bration
and gifts (always h... ...ily. But
the twentieth birth... ...a Daltry child is a special event.
When a Daltry turns twenty years old, Grandmother Minerva (a great fan of classical mythology) assigns the young
one a "labor," in the tradition of the twelve labors of Hercules. Only three aspects of Minerva's challenges are predict-
able: the labor will last one year, it will help to build her
grandchild's character, and it will not be easy . . .

The Ladies' Man by Lorraine Heath
Oldest son Hercules must quit ranching and be the town
schoolmarm for a year . . .

The Wallflower by Linda Francis Lee
Shy daughter Persephone must spend a year in New York as
a debutante . . .

The Matchmaker by Debra S. Cowan
Lovesick Cupid has one year to find a husband for a comely
girl . . .

The Flirt by Rachelle Nelson
Flirtatious Venus must spend a year in the company of a
blind man . . .

The Tomboy by Mary Lou Rich
Atalanta has to learn to cook, dance, and be a lady . . .
Available in February 1996

The Perfect Gentleman by Elaine Crawford
Atlas must put away his lists and take out a popular
widow . . .
Available in April 1996

The Flirt

Rachelle Nelson

JOVE BOOKS, NEW YORK

THE FLIRT

A Jove Book / published by arrangement
with the author

PRINTING HISTORY
Jove edition / December 1995

ISBN: 0-515-11768-4

A JOVE BOOK®
Jove Books are published by The Berkley Publishing Group,
200 Madison Avenue, New York, New York 10016.
JOVE and the "J" design are trademarks
belonging to Jove Publications, Inc.

PRINTED IN THE UNITED STATES OF AMERICA

10 9 8 7 6 5 4 3 2 1

To David

"I know you, I walked with you, once upon a dream . . . " Thank you for walking with me through ten years of dreams. I love you.

And to Melinda Metz, my first editor, with deepest appreciation and gratitude for your blind faith.

Acknowledgments

This book could not have been possible without the contributions of my Daltry Sons and Daughters Sisters or my friend and fellow author Maureen Child, who saw my voice before I did.

Prologue

EVERYONE IN PARADISE PLAINS, TEXAS, KNEW WHAT APRIL 30 was. Venus Daltry made sure of it.

Therefore it came as no surprise to Minerva Daltry each time the recently installed door gongs set off a cacophony, and on the threshold stood another of Venus's suitors, with stars in his eyes and a garishly wrapped gift tucked under his arm. Every year was the same. Every eligible bachelor within fifty miles flocked to the ranch to wish her granddaughter a happy birthday. Minerva didn't know why she had expected 1884 to be any different.

Of course, madness and mayhem had ruled the ranch for weeks, Minerva admitted. Each member of her growing family had been racing about the expansive and often redesigned house, searching for a secluded corner in which to construct a special token for Venus on this important occasion. Saws grated, hammers banged, glue speckled the carpet runners down the hallway, and heavenly aromas filtered in from the kitchen.

Even now two of her grandsons were hunched over in the doorway of the parlor, either spying on their sister or making a frantic effort to finish the gift they planned to give her at suppertime. Minerva suspected the latter as she drifted toward the young men on silent feet.

"That's not his name, I'm telling you," Cupid insisted. "If you're gonna make the list, then make it right, or I'm not putting it in the box!"

"And I'm telling you, that is *too* Nate Trumball!" Atlas argued in a harsh whisper. "He moved in from Taylor County. If you didn't have your head in the clouds over your bride all the time, you might notice when Paradise gets a new resident."

"What are you two disagreeing about now?" Minerva inquired, folding her arms over her plump bosom.

Cupid and Atlas started at the sound of her reedy voice, then bowed their heads, looking more like naughty boys than grown men. "We're working on Venus's birthday present," they answered in unison.

"Well, do so from someplace other than the parlor doorway else she'll hear you. Then you will have been sneaking around trying to surprise her for nothing."

"Yes, ma'am."

"Yes, Grandmother."

Shooing the young men off, Minerva took up her post in the wide doorway, a silent chaperone. The elegant parlor was practically bursting at the seams with suitors. Minerva had made it clear to Venus that a Daltry's twentieth birthday should be nothing less than a private affair. But as usual, Venus had chosen to ignore custom. As if the household weren't in enough of an uproar, the endless stream of devoted callers was adding to it. And, of course, in the midst of them sat Venus, the glow on her peaches-and-cream face making her look lovelier than ever.

Minerva watched Venus graciously entertain the dozen or so coat-and-string-tie gentlemen with frivolous banter. A bemused smile came to Minerva's lips. Besotted fools all of them. She clicked her tongue and shook her head with pity. Not a face was unfamiliar; at one time or another every one of the lovestruck swains vying for Venus's attention had approached her son for his daughter's hand in marriage. Even when Odysseus withheld his approval

at Venus's request, they returned again and again, unde-
terred, unable to resist her granddaughter's allure.

Minerva could hardly blame them, though. Venus had
that effect on people, most especially on men. The soft
Southern drawl she imitated from a Georgia-born woman
in town enchanted them; her cherub's smile or a flutter of
her tawny lashes scrambled their wits. And her legendary
beauty and coquettish charm could have persuaded any
one of the young men to leap off a cliff if Venus desired
it.

The problem was that Venus knew it. Minerva loved
her granddaughter dearly, but she was aware how Venus
perpetually took for granted that her angelic looks would
get her anything she wanted.

Her lips twitching, Minerva had to admit that they did.
The extravagant gifts lavished on her already today were
visible proof that her slightest whim would be honored.
The oval serving table in front of the settee on which
Venus posed prettily overflowed with a mountain of
presents and torn paper and trailing ribbons. Small velvet
boxes holding radiant trinkets littered the floor at her
feet, along with dainty gloves and gossamer shawls, cut-
glass perfume bottles and marabou fans.

Well, things were about to change for her capricious
grandchild, Minerva reflected. Venus was the fourth in a
new generation of Daltrys to carry on the twentieth-
birthday tradition; two brothers, Hercules and Cupid, and
one sister, Persephone, had already preceded her. Minerva recalled the tasks she had given each of them to
complete before their next birthday. They had endured
the depths of anguish and the heights of euphoria during
their year-long quests, but for their endeavors, Minerva
had rewarded each of them with a prize worthy of their
achievements.

And now, it is my beloved Venus's turn. Minerva knew
that the labor she had chosen for Venus would not be
easily accomplished, for Venus had been doted on exces-
sively all her life. However, beneath her granddaughter's
frivolous veneer lay a strength of steel, tempered with a

generous and loving heart. It just hadn't been given a chance to flourish.

But once Venus discovered her capacity to love, Minerva hoped she would find a prize greater than anything money could buy.

Sanford Buchanan was just the man to help her.

One

VENUS DALTRY'S EARS BUZZED AND THE EXCITED SMILE SHE'D been wearing for months slowly crumbled. She reread the words printed on the vellum card in her hand, hoping that her feverish anticipation of the moment had made her jumble the letters. But a third inspection of the card proved her eyes weren't playing tricks on her.

Venus darted an incredulous look at the old woman who sat watching her expectantly from the far end of the supper table. The silence thickened in the candlelit dining room as the other members of the family also sat on pins and needles. Her admirers had long since been ushered from the house, since the designation of a Daltry's labor was strictly confidential.

And at that moment, Venus was grateful.

It meant that only the handful of Daltrys present would witness the tantrum she was about to throw.

"You can't be serious, Grandmother!" Venus cried, springing out of her chair.

Unruffled, Minerva Daltry retained her usual serene expression. She clasped her lined hands together upon the lacy tablecloth and cleared her throat. "I know you've been overwhelmed with gifts today but I also know how

you adore them. That's why I wrapped your labor in a
pretty box instead of announcing it as I usually do.
Clever, eh?"

As if disguising it in colorful paper would soften the blow?

"What's it say?" her father asked, his mild Texas drawl
distinctive.

Her mouth slack, her eyes wide, Venus passed the note
to her right. *Let him read this rubbish for himself!* Odysseus took the card in his burly hand. From his flannel
shirt pocket, he withdrew silver-rimmed spectacles and
curved the ear stems around his ears. His gunmetal-blue
eyes, a physical trait Venus had inherited on a softer
scale, scanned the paper. There was a slight pause, then
his belting laughter rumbled through the spacious room,
as if to twine around the golden leaf pattern of Minerva's
wallpaper.

"Don't keep us in suspense," Jane Daltry urged her
husband. "Read it aloud so all of us can hear!"

Complying, Odie rose to his tremendous height, still an
impressive figure in his middle years. And though he had
surrendered his place at the head of the cluttered maple-
wood table for Venus on this special day, there was no
question that this man ruled the ranch—succeeding
Grandma, of course.

He brought his mirth under control long enough to
recite, " 'My darling granddaughter Venus. For your
twentieth-birthday labor, I assign you to travel to Nevada
with a dime novelist and assist him with his writing.' "

Odie's eager audience nearly shook the rafters with
their robust laughter. Venus felt scarlet color flush her
cheeks. She glared at each one of her brothers and sisters
who sat around the oval table, slapping the surface and
rattling the dishes and holding their convulsing bellies.
"What's so blessed funny?" she hollered, rounding on
them.

Across from her, C.J. tilted his fair head. "You were
laughing just as hard at me three years ago, sis."

Venus pressed her lips into one flat line. That had been
different. In spite of his name, "C.J." being an abbrevia-
tion for "Cupid," her older brother used to have terrible

luck with love. So when he'd been given the labor to find
a husband for the town shrew, she hadn't been the only
one in the family to think it comical. C.J. finding a mate
for Lizzie Colepepper? When he suffered as much—if
not more—misfortune as the shrew? A labor that outlandish deserved a bit of buffoonery!

But hers . . . there wasn't a darn thing laughable
about it!

"I recollect you tittering at me, too, little beauty," her
eldest brother, Lee, chimed in. His rope-roughened
hands cradled the back of his head and his solid weight
tipped the chair he sat in onto its rear spindled legs. With
that dimpled grin slashing his carved features, he was a
near replica of their father while Venus possessed
Mama's Nordic fairness. With a teasing note, he went on.
"I also remember feeling pretty horrified at first, but I
hope to Zeus my face wasn't as puckered as yours is
now!"

"Worse!" C.J. said. "Who could blame you, though?
Trading ranch work to teach a schoolroom filled with
monsters in short pants would horrify anyone!"

Appalled that her face might display the unsightly lines
of "puckering," Venus forced her features to relax, lest
the condition become permanent. But when the conversation veered to the unconventional teaching methods
Lee used before the original schoolmarm was able to
regain her stolen position, Venus's expression trans-
formed again to one of vexation. Certainly she bore a
fondness for the schoolmarm—she and Meredith were
sisters-in-law now, after all—but she didn't give a fig
about hearing Lee and Meredith's happily-ever-after
story. Land's sakes, her own life was crumbling!

Venus crammed the lid onto the box she'd just opened.
"We aren't discussing *your* labor, Hercules Daltry, we're
discussing mine." Venus scowled at her brother. "In comparison, yours and C.J.'s and Persy's were easy! At least
y'all weren't being sent to some wasteland people have
scarcely heard of!"

Ignoring the jeers of disagreement from her elder

brothers and sister, Venus swung back to her grandmother, her eyes flashing. "What if I refuse?"

A penny dropping on the hardwood floor would have
sounded like a thunderclap in the ensuing hush.

Then, all spoke at once.

"What?"

"No one has ever . . ."

"A Daltry doesn't . . ."

"That isn't an option!"

Minerva's hand rose in the air and an uneasy quiet
settled over the room. "Venus, why would you refuse
your labor?"

Venus stomped her slippered foot against the braided
floor rug and folded her bare arms across her satin-and-
lace-covered bosom. "Because I don't want this task. I
want another one."

There. Now Grandma would pick something more suitable, Venus figured smugly.

"Oh?" Minerva raised one faded brow. "And did you
have anything special in mind?"

Venus made an airy gesture with her hand and pretended to ponder the question, when in fact, she had
made a mental list months ago. "Well, you *could* send me
to the Continent and make me purchase gowns for im-
porting. I read in *Light and Shadows of New York Life* that
they've designed the most divine ball gowns in Paris that
cost only five hundred to one thousand dollars each. With
my elegant taste and personable charm, I'm certain I'd
have no trouble finding buyers here in America!"

Minerva's tranquil expression encouraged Venus to
continue. "Or I could take the train to New York like
Persy, and make my debut!" Paradise Plains' idea of a
debut was a barn dance, and Abilene, though evolving
from a tent town to a more cultural environment, still did
not boast the sophisticated facilities of New York society.
Venus wasn't as shy as her elder sister, either. A social
debut in a big, glamorous city . . . fancy balls . . .
wealthy men all dying to meet a lady with her beauty and
charm. . . . And in her spare time, she could go *shopping*! She'd dreamed of visiting that department store,

R. H. Macy & Company, ever since Persy had told her about it.

"Or you could have me marry within the year as Lee and C.J. and Persy all have done," Venus suggested demurely. "Surely I could persuade *some*body to make little ole me his wife." The truth was, she could arrange that by tomorrow and complete her task in record time! The hardest choice she'd have to make then would be whose proposal to accept. She'd received a dozen this month alone! And though she hadn't given any of them serious consideration before, she might do so now to fulfill the labor and get her prize. She could think of worse fates!

Such as traveling to the ends of the earth with some ten-cent writer . . .

Minerva was clicking her tongue and shaking her head, though. Venus absently followed the motion, her manicured brows scaling her forehead under her wispy bangs. "Those are not labors, Venus," Minerva pointed out. "Those are desires. What inner growth could you possibly attain by achieving something that comes as natural to you as breathing?"

"I don't need inner growth!" Venus protested. "I'm perfect just as I am!"

"Ve-nus." Minerva dragged her name out patiently while she twiddled her thumbs. "I always put a lot of thought and deliberation into the tasks I choose for my children's and grandchildren's twentieth birthdays. Tasks that will challenge their personalities, test their fortitude, and expand their horizons.

"For you, I decided on the last of the twelve labors of Hercules. Do you remember that one?"

Venus cocked her hip out. Of course she remembered it! Every child born into the Daltry family was weaned on Greek and Roman myths. Grandma shared her obsession with everyone in shouting distance whether they were interested or not. And the story of how the god Hercules had been given twelve difficult tasks as penance for killing his own wife and children during a curse of madness enthralled Minerva most.

Rolling her eyes, Venus droned, "Hercules had to go

into the lower world and bring the three-headed dog Cerberus back to Hades, god of the dead, without using any weapons."

Minerva's rosy face wreathed in a self-satisfied grin.

Venus wrinkled her brow. "What does fetching a dog have to do with helping a writer?"

"I will expect you to have figured it out by your next birthday."

"It doesn't matter to you that my entire social life will be disrupted? Evan Bollinger has invited me to the dance Maybelle is throwing to celebrate Mrs. Bennett's fiftieth birthday, Garrett Moore has asked me to join him on a picnic Saturday, Clay Masterson to dinner Saturday night, and the charity box social is to be held on Sunday after church to raise money for new hymnals. I promised the Twins I'd be there, and that I'd decorate my basket with a blue bow to match my eyes so they'd bid on the right one. And that's just *this* week's schedule!" Venus sighed dramatically. "I declare, how would any of them survive the disappointment if I canceled?"

A wry grin tugged at the corners of Minerva's mouth. "I'm certain they will recover eventually."

Staring at those faded gray eyes as they took on the glimmer of wet silver, Venus shook her head with wonder. She probably should have noticed Grandma's mind taking a wander ages ago; she'd always been a little eccentric. And yet, Grandma had duped them all into believing her odd character somehow normal. Even dear, departed Grandpa had condoned her quirky nature. In fact, it wouldn't have surprised Venus at this point to learn that he had encouraged it. And if there were those who didn't find her character normal, then at least they viewed it as endearing.

But Venus now acknowledged the painful truth. Her beloved grandmother, her father's mother, was—quite fully—a pickle short of a full peck. It was the only explanation for the nonsense spilling from the old woman's lips.

Dime novelists. Dogs. Hades. Land's sake, Venus thought dismally, *why'd she have to fall off her rocker to-*

day? This is my *day,* Venus lamented. *The day I've been anticipating all my life!*

From the moment she had woken this morning until suppertime, it had taken the weight of every cumbersome petticoat she owned to keep her from floating. Odie had led her to the honored seat at the head of the table to receive the homemade gifts from the rest of the family— another Daltry tradition. A feast of her favorite dishes had been laid before her. Venus had recognized her sister's gift, for no one else in the family possessed Persy's culinary skills. The beef tips in mushroom sauce and the lemon custard had tasted like ambrosia. Next she tore off the wrappings of a cosmetic pouch of cowhide made by Lee, tried on a newly woven straw hat from Mama, fingered the smooth pebbles of a heart-shaped box from C.J. that contained files on all her beaus from Atlas, and sniffed a sachet of wildflowers dried by Atalanta.

Then, it was time for Grandma to announce the labor.

Three brothers, two sisters, her mother and father looked on, their curiosity as strong as Venus's own. They, like herself, had heard the stories all their lives, of how aunts, uncles, even Daddy when he'd reached twenty years, had been given a task to perform within a year's duration. And if the task was successfully completed by the twenty-first birthday, Grandma Minerva gave a spectacular prize for a job well done.

The twentieth-birthday tradition was just a drop in Grandma's bucket of oddities, Venus now realized. In retrospect, she wondered if maybe Minerva's penchant for naming all the children after the gods and goddesses of ancient lore should have been the first indication. In addition, there was her penchant for Greek designs, and her passion for trinkets of the Greek and Roman cultures, and her obsession with legendary acts of heroism.

It never occurred to Venus that they'd humored a bedlamite all these years. Nor that they were just as guilty of indulging her as Grandpa.

Until now.

Dazed by her discovery, Venus's vision swam as she stared at the table centerpiece. In the midst of a bouquet

of her mother's beloved flowers, the twenty flaming can-
dlewicks placed there in recognition of Venus's age became a macabre dance of orange tulips on fat, waxen
stems. The conversation around her rang hollow in her
ears, as if she were standing at the bottom of a well and
sinking deeper.

Mentally, Venus grappled for a thread of rationality to
pull her from these suddenly irrational depths.

The prize.

Yes. She licked her rouged lips, tasting the dry, bitter
flavor of cosmetic coloring she always wore. Her mind
began functioning again, focusing on the very real evidence that, no matter how unhinged Grandma seemed to
be, her promises bore fruit.

Daddy had gained the ranch, Lee received a library,
Persy had her little house with the white picket fence, and
C.J. was gifted with his gilded mirror. They all got their
prizes.

And Venus wanted hers—whatever it happened to
be—because gifts were tokens of what she loved above all
else—winning.

She just didn't want this labor.

"Grandma," she said, trying to reason, "what do I
know of"—land's sake, she could hardly utter the
word!—*"dime novels*? I don't even read the lurid books,
much less have any idea how to write them."

"You will not write them. Sanford Buchanan, the
nephew of a very old, dear friend of mine, creates his own
stories. You are only to help him gather information and
take notes while you travel with him."

This crazy idea of going to Nevada with some writer
seemed to be locked in the old woman's mind, regardless
of how absurd or how many protests Venus issued.

Land's sake, where was Nevada, anyway?

Frowning, Venus tugged on a curl dangling over her
shoulder. She needed to gather her thoughts. Find some
other course of action since Grandma wasn't being
swayed. If she gave in now, she might as well kiss her
popularity goodbye.

Venus released the curl and nibbled on one of her

manicured fingernails. Weren't these supposed to be her prime years? The time for her to enjoy a variety of beaus before finally settling down with one lucky fellow? Of course, she hadn't yet decided *which* one to settle down with. There were so many to choose from, after all. And even though she felt confident that any man would wait the year—an entire lifetime if she asked him to—for her return, there was the chance that he might find another bride . . . if only to ease the heartache of her absence.

No, she mustn't be forced to choose which of her beaus to ask to wait for her. In haste she might settle for the wrong one. A decision of that magnitude took time.

Besides, how would she *survive* without her social life?

Venus shook her head vehemently. That thought was too dreadful to consider! *No, there must be a way to change Grandma's mind.* If there was anything she'd acquired from Minerva Daltry, it was perseverance!

Venus contemplated her options while her gaze flicked to each member of her family. Atlas, the baby of the family at sixteen, sat adjacent to Grandma, his gray eyes at half-mast as if mapping out another list inside his all-too-serious brain. He'd be no help. About all he'd offer was an inventory of pros and cons, nothing very convincing.

Across from him Atalanta slouched in her chair as always and gazed out the divided panes of the window overlooking the corral. In spite of the fourteen months that separated her brother from her sister, Venus never failed to think how easily Atlas and Allie could pass for twins. Other than the obvious differences between boy and girl, they looked very much alike, with the same short brown hair—Allie's was curly—and the same facial features.

Venus dismissed her younger sister though, since Allie probably wasn't listening anyway. Allie always had her head in the clouds.

She looked next to C.J. and Lee, who sat paired off beside Atlas. They wore their usual teasing smirks as if they were enjoying every second of her discomfort. That meant that counting on her normally protective brothers

was out of the question. They were too honorable to dispute Grandma's dictates.

Venus then glanced to her right at Persy, who scraped
crumbs of birthday cake from the table into her hand.
Her sister positively glowed with happiness since her marriage to Jake Devlin and the subsequent birth of their
first child, Diana. Venus guessed all she'd get from Persy
was a lecture on the necessity of optimistic thinking.

And Mama seemed completely unaffected by the dilemma, Venus noticed, watching her pat her mouth delicately with an embroidered napkin. And Daddy . . .

Daddy! Of course!

Knowing his weakness for a lady's tears, Venus thrust
out her lower lip in a pretty pout and willed moisture into
her big baby-blue eyes. He'd always been her champion.
Surely *he'd* come to her rescue! "Daddy?"

Of all her relatives, he'd be the one most aware of how
far around the bend Grandma had gone. Minerva was his
mother, after all!

But it slowly dawned on her that Odie Daltry was going
to ignore her plight, too. His strapping shoulders quaked
under his black suspenders. His index finger and thumb
framed his squared jaw and clefted chin; his elbow rested
on the table's edge beside his empty plate. Sawdust still
speckled his dark brown hair from wood-carving earlier
in the day and his eyes, a shade darker than her own,
were alight with humor. They stayed fixed on her while
his head swung back and forth.

He was tellin' her no without saying a word.

Stunned, Venus turned to her mother. Jane tilted her
slender neck to the side and the blond braid circling her
crown drooped over one pearl-adorned ear. "Sweetheart,
you've never minded traveling before. Why are you so
against it now?" she asked.

Venus cast Jane a skeptical glance. "Ma-ma, there's a
big difference between a jaunt to Abilene twenty-five
miles away with the boys as chaperones, and taking off
for parts unknown with a total stranger! What will people
say? My reputation will be ruined!"

"We will simply tell people you are off broadening your

education. They will accept it, and it will not be a false-
hood," Jane replied, unconcerned. "And as for Sanford
being your escort—Mother Minerva trusts him. She
wouldn't send you with a disreputable person."

Oh, yes, the paragon of the printed word.

Didn't anybody care that some tragedy might befall
her? Did they even care that she would soon have to
leave? Why, she could wind up a spinster before ever
returning home! An ugly, wrinkled old prune nobody'd
want again, forsaken by her family, forgotten by her
friends . . . Her throat tightened.

In desperation, she balled her hands and cried, "Why
do I have to do *this* labor?"

"You don't, Venus," Minerva said. "I will not force you
to accept the assignment. Whether you accept it or not is
your choice."

Venus's relief proved fleeting.

"But you might consider this: if you decline the assignment, you forfeit the prize."

"Forfeit the prize!" Venus echoed. "But I'm your
granddaughter! It's my right!"

"No, it's your privilege and it does not come freely.
You must earn it just as all those before you have earned
theirs."

Oh, this was getting worse and worse, she thought dismally. *Earn.* What a foul word! It meant *work.* Why, she'd
never been required to work a day in her life! What was
the sense? All she had to do was beguile someone else
and they did it for her. She asked; she received. It was
that simple.

Except with Minerva.

If there was one person on earth with a stronger knack
for persuasion than her, it was her grandmother—an egg
shy of a full dozen or not.

Suddenly, Venus wanted to kick herself. Why had she
wasted so much energy contesting this labor? She'd just
get someone else to complete it while she found herself
some isolated sector of the world to hide for a year!

Concealing her glee, she lowered her lashes and

sighed, feigning surrender. "I guess I have no choice but to accept the labor you've given me, then."

Minerva cast her an amused look and said, "Perhaps we should make sure you understand the rules, Venus. You must perform the labor yourself. You must not include anyone else, nor will you be allowed to speak of your task with anyone outside the family. And lastly, I must receive a detailed report of your progress by the end of every month by telegraph. A breach of the rules will declare the labor null and void and the prize forgotten."

Venus fled the dining room in tears. Real ones.

Two flights of stairs later, Venus found refuge in the bedroom she shared with Allie. Odie had a love of making things out of wood, and if his inventions saved space, he was doubly eager to pull out his tools. Therefore, the beds in the girls' attic room were designed to hide in the walls. Except, only one of the beds was folded neatly into their niches; Venus's remained open and mussed. In her opinion, organization wasted time and energy better used for more important matters.

She hurled herself onto the ready mattress, kicking her feet, punching the layers of ticking. The knitted wool coverlet printed with blue stars inside pink squares absorbed her shrieks.

"She hates me! She truly must to give me such a dreadful task!" Venus sobbed. "And for what?" She punched her ruffled pillow and a puff of feathers exploded from one end. "To help some idiot write trash stories?"

She screamed into the damaged pillow wadded between her arms and fluttered her feet wildly while her tantrum ran its course.

When next she lifted her head, the horizon had swallowed the sun and dusky shapes of furniture lining the walls were being kissed by shadow and moonlight. Land's sake, she felt drained, as much from waking so early as from the chaotic day.

And to think she'd had such great expectations this morning. Why, her family's reactions when she'd shown up in the dining room an hour after sunrise had been worth the sacrifice of her beauty sleep! Poor Daddy. He'd nearly choked on his ham steak. Mama had nearly swooned, and Allie had glanced out the window, swearing hell had frozen over.

But nothing, at that time, could have dampened Venus's spirit. It was her birthday. Supposedly the most wonderful birthday a Daltry experienced.

They'd all misled her, though. Daddy with his stories of his labor, and Lee and C.J. and Persy with their stories. But Grandma was by far the worst, Venus decided. Making her believe she would embrace this dreadful labor with enthusiasm.

Venus rubbed an errant tear from her gritty eyes as she sat up, then lit the kerosene lamp on the stand beside her bed.

A book lying on the pink and white doily caught her notice.

"Where'd that come from?" Venus said to herself. It hadn't been there this morning. She was sure she would have seen it. And neither had she noticed it upon entering a short while ago.

Tentatively, she grasped the paperback novel between her thumb and forefinger and turned it over. The binding was crisp, unbent, as if never opened. Once more she turned it over then scanned the front cover. *Adventures of the West* was printed in bold lettering across the top, *New York* emblazoned in the upper right-hand corner. And under the nameplate there was an issue number and volume. Below that, the title, *Smoke Screen in Abilene,* arced over a picture of two cowboys looking warily over their shoulders while pressing a branding iron to the flank of a prone calf.

Uninterested, Venus made to set the book aside when the name of the author at the bottom of the facing caught her notice. She stared at it until the letters blurred, her breath trapped in her chest.

Buck Buchanan.

Buchanan.

Sanford Buchanan.

It had to be.

Venus flung the book across the room with all the rag-

ing fury her tantrum hadn't released. It bounced off the
papered walls, onto the chest of drawers where she had
placed the heart-shaped box with files on her beaus from
C.J. and Atlas.

Allie chose that moment to venture into the room.

Venus fell back onto the pillow, wishing she didn't have
to share a room with her sister. She and Allie had very
little in common, and though they'd tried, Venus didn't
understand Allie's nature, and Allie didn't understand
hers.

But it didn't stop the rail-thin seventeen-year-old tomboy from plopping on Venus's bed. "You're mussing up
my coverlet with your dirty britches, Allie."

"No more than you've mussed it with that gook you
wear on your face."

Jaw dropping, Venus scrambled off the mattress and
raced to the brand-new vanity table Daddy had built into
the corner beside her dresser. "Oooh!" Venus wailed.
"Look what they've done!"

Because of Grandma and that . . . that *dime novelist,*
her face looked like something painted by a drunken
cowboy! Fat rivulets of black kohl ran from her eyes down
her cheeks, tracking through blotched face powder. The
coral lip rouge she had ordered in newly invented stick
form and artfully applied on a continuing basis throughout the day was so smeared, her mouth appeared twisted
and twice its tempting size.

With a kiss-printed hanky used a dozen times before,
Venus scoured at her lips.

"Seems to me you've had a day full of surprises," Allie
remarked, rising from the bed to investigate the book
lying on the bureau.

"Some I'd rather do without," Venus muttered out of
the corner of her mouth, still scrubbing at the mess
Grandma had caused.

"Well, I think you're lucky."

"Now, how did I know you'd say that? What's lucky
about traipsing across the country with a writer who can't
even write?"

"Where'd you come up with that idea?"

Venus leaned closer to her image. "Why else would I have to take dictation? The man must be illiterate—or just plain lazy—or he'd be able to take notes himself instead of requiring a secretary."

"Maybe he's rich. Rich folks don't like to work. It's more convenient to hire someone else to do that sort of thing for them."

Venus hadn't thought of that. Yes, her family had wealth thanks to Grandpa, but Grandma never squandered it on luxuries such as servants. She claimed each of them were perfectly capable of seeing to themselves and flaunting the Daltry wealth would only make them look petty. Then, glimpsing the novel Allie was perusing, Venus decided her own conclusion seemed more plausible. "I seriously doubt he's got a penny to his name. Besides, where would he have gotten it? Everyone knows that dime novelists are little better than vagabonds with high hopes."

Allie shrugged then wandered to the window. "I still think it's exciting. Do you know what kind of horses are bred farther west?"

"The smelly kind."

"Mustangs, Thoroughbreds . . ." Suddenly, Allie's enraptured prattle ceased and she gasped, "Lord have mercy! Venus, come look!"

Venus sighed. If she didn't look, Allie would pester the daylights out of her. She rose from the carved wooden bench and glided to the window, smoothing slick white cosmetic remover across her face.

Venus reached the sill dividing Allie's tidy side of the room from her cluttered side then knelt one knee on the paisley-cushioned window seat. The third-floor vantage point afforded her a pinnacle view of the mile-long dirt road that formed a horseshoe in front of the house. A frame barn and stables set on foundations of stone stood to the east of the main house, and behind them, Venus knew the bunkhouse would be alive with light and rowdy noise as the ranch hands gambled away their hard-earned pay in card games.

Off the western curve of the drive a few paces from the

front porch, the whitewashed stones of Grandma's gazebo glowed in the moonlight, outlining Odie's Greek-
temple design of ivy-cloaked pillars and fountains. And
beyond, shapes of the smokehouse and pantry shed were
barely discernible beneath a canopy of trees.

Venus searched the familiar vista for whatever held her
sister spellbound, and spied two figures on horses approaching the hitching rail in front of the lantern-lit
porch.

Venus blinked with surprise. The fella riding the chest-
nut horse might have just left a Sunday meeting, he was
so gussied up. Bowler hat, brown tweed coat over a clash-
ing red and green checkered vest, and slightly creased
trousers. Venus judged the man to be decades older than
her father; his hair was the color of dead ashes and his
face bore more grooves than a phonograph disc.

Unimpressed, her gaze slid to the right, to the other
rider.

"Isn't he glorious?" Allie breathed.

Venus's mouth dropped open and she stared at Allie as
if she'd just put on a dress. Her sister's silvery-gray eyes
couldn't *possibly* be lit up for the stranger! He looked as
though he'd narrowly survived a cattle stampede!

"Those have *got* to be the sleekest muscles I've ever
seen!" Allie exclaimed.

And Venus gripped the windowsill, sure she was about
to swoon. Was everybody in this house diving into the
deep end of a shallow pond? First her grandmother, now
her baby sister . . .

Land's sake, there was nothing *sleek* about him! In fact,
he was the most beggarly-looking man she'd ever laid
eyes on. How Allie could rave about muscles was beyond
understanding. Venus glimpsed long ole legs clad in
washed-out denim, threadbare at the knees, flanking the
horse's girth, but the rest of his body was concealed by a
faded almond duster.

Unaware of her sister's bafflement, Allie gushed on.
"And that powerful structure . . . firm, lean flanks I'd
bet my last dollar would beat the wind in a race!"

Venus shook her head. Allie's brain must've been

baked by the sun today. Sure, the material of his pants strained over his roped thighs but no one could ever accuse her of drooling over a man's flanks like her sister was doing!

"And the lines of his face! Now *that's* impeccable breeding!"

Venus rolled her eyes, wondering if maybe she should notify Mama that her youngest daughter was careening around the bend in Grandma Minerva's wake.

The stranger wouldn't know a higher class of people if he was standing on a cloud. Venus never claimed to be a genius, but then, it didn't take one to see that this pitiful man would feel as comfortable in a social setting as a mouse in a snake pit.

Black bristles sprouted like scorched weeds all around where she knew a mouth should be—but wasn't—and meshed with longer black hair topped with a frontier-style hat. The ragged brim curled upward on the sides but the front brim hid what night shadows did not.

"Lord, I'd sell my soul for a stud like that!"

Venus's eyes nearly popped out of their sockets and she clapped her hand over her sister's mouth. "Atalanta Daltry, such language!"

"Well? I would!" Allie asserted, shoving Venus's hand away. "That's the finest damn horse I've ever seen!" She tossed her short brown curls. "And I'll tell you something else, too. I'm gonna ride that gray, and I'm gonna rub it in Hal's face till he's pea-green with envy."

At that announcement, Allie marched from the room, leaving Venus staring agog at the firmly closing door.

She swore the flames of embarrassment were going to burn her alive. She should have known better than to assume Allie was talking about something other than the horse under the stranger. If it didn't have four legs, a mane, and a tail, her sister simply wasn't interested. And only Hal Anderson, the son of a neighboring rancher and Allie's best friend, seemed to understand her tomboy-sister's obsession with the dull animals.

Then again, Venus reasoned, her sister was too inno-cent to understand how useful men could be—if managed properly. Venus had discovered this wonder during her thirteenth summer just after she'd passed her comprehensive exams to graduate from school. That was when Andrew Grimes began following her about town as she attended her errands. And she had learned that the more she ignored him, the more ardent he grew, using any means to capture her devotion. Venus always recalled that period of her life as "the summer of her first diamond."

Since then, her jewel casket had overflowed with trinkets bestowed on her by smitten swains, eager for the slightest sign that she might consider them worthy of her attention.

Venus pressed her nose to the window, and peered again at the stranger, her breath fogging the pane. She wondered what there was about him that triggered this mysterious fascination inside her. *He's awful rugged,* she told herself. Not at all the type of man she'd look twice at on the street.

Of course, she didn't suppose she'd be looking twice at any man for a while. As soon as the blessed writer showed up . . .

Her meanderings ceased and her vision became distorted. Shimmery. As if she were crying. Only she wasn't crying . . .

She was stunned senseless.

It's him! Venus didn't know how she knew it—she just did. The wild and woolly creature dismounting at the porch was Grandma's ten-cent writer.

Venus groaned in agony. It looked as if the days of diamonds and devotions had come to a skidding halt. Like it or not, ready or not, her labor had begun.

Two

"YA COULDA CLEANED UP SOME, YA KNOW," ZEB BUCHANAN grumbled, swiping at the trail dust coating the one suit he'd ever purchased as they approached the three-story house.

"Will you quit badgering me? I'm here, aren't I?"

"She's gonna think I had ta hogtie ya and drag ya in the dirt behind me, though!"

"She won't be taking her eyes off you long enough to notice me." Besides, Sanford thought, *he* wasn't the one trying to impress Minerva Daltry with a liberal dose of bay rum and spiffy new duds. He'd only come this far out of his way because he'd given his word to help Uncle Zeb. And although he questioned the wisdom in agreeing to bring some wet-behind-the-ears tenderfoot on a research trip, Zeb had rarely asked a favor in all the years they'd ridden together. Sanford hadn't been able to refuse this one; he owed his uncle too damn much.

Actually, he *had* wanted to stay in Paradise Plains a little longer—at least, long enough to sponge off the trail dust that had settled in every pore and crevice of his body. But he didn't try explaining that to Zeb. Or anything else, for that matter. A sensible conversation with the man had been impossible ever since the letter had arrived in their base point of St. Louis—the letter from the old man's former sweetheart, Minerva Daltry, inviting Zeb for a visit.

The two had been in occasional contact over the years, but this last letter . . . Sanford chuckled to himself. Honestly, harnessing Zeb Buchanan had been like holding the wind captive. Minerva would write and tell him about special events in her life but she obviously hadn't been ready to mix her past with her present. Until a couple weeks ago, that is. Her letter, faintly scented with an unidentifiable fragrance, had sent Zeb into a whirlwind with her offer of home and hearth if he accepted her summons to Texas where she lived with her youngest son and his family.

They made the trip in three days, Uncle Zeb choosing to ride a train for the first time in his life. Upon reaching the whistle stop in Paradise Plains, a little town five miles away from the Daltry ranch, Zeb had raced to Sally's barbershop for the full treatment while Sanford alone ordered the abundance of supplies needed for the lengthy trip west he planned.

A man named Hank had barely gotten the provisions strapped to the extra horse Sanford bought in town when Zeb came clattering out onto the boardwalk, slicked up and eager to finish the last leg of their journey.

Sanford shook his head ruefully. There had been no time for his own spit and shine unless he wanted to be left behind in a foreign town among strangers—which he didn't.

Besides, he wasn't about to miss this reunion for the world.

The iron-shod hooves of Zeb's steed ceased striking against compact dirt, and Sanford's horse, Ranger, followed suit. Sanford used the respite to doff his hat and dab at the moisture on his forehead with his sleeve. Lifting his face to the mild evening breeze, his nostrils were assaulted with the sharp odors of horseflesh, warm soil, and fresh sawdust, as if someone had recently been sawing wood.

Then, a sensation of being watched made the back of his neck prickle and Sanford paused with his arm over his brow.

Before he could distinguish the source, Zeb yelled, "Whatcha doin', boy? Waitin' fer the cows ta come home?"

Sanford shrugged off the feeling and replaced his hat on his head. It was probably someone marking their arrival, he surmised. He swung his leg over the pommel and slid to the ground. He gave Ranger's quivering neck a fond pat, silently commending his pet for holding up so well throughout the harried train ride and the frenzied pace from town to the Daltry place. Sanford then slapped his battered felt hat against his trousers, raising a cloud of choking dust, and ruffled the hair sticking to his scalp. Securing Ranger to the hitching rail was unnecessary, as the stallion had been trained long ago not to stray. Neither did the faithful steed need his reins trailing on the ground as some horses did. He simply obeyed commands by instinct alone.

"Are ya comin'?"

Sanford shook his head and his wandering thoughts returned to his irritable uncle. By nature, Zeb was a man of few words. But when he did talk, his manner simulated that of a ship captain—loud and masterful. It tickled Sanford, since Zeb was no bigger than an average twelve-year-old boy, spare of manly height and build; and yet, when he demanded, Sanford knew to comply. More than once while Sandford was growing up, Zeb had dragged him around by the earlobe to exert his authority.

And though Sanford was now thirty-two, he did not doubt Zeb would revert to a discipline scrapped for many years.

Striding at his uncle's heels, Sanford listened to Zeb's footsteps as they changed in pitch, from a solid *phlat* on packed earth to a hollow clacking as they mounted plank steps. The stairs leveled off to an even platform and Sanford stood behind his motionless uncle. Seconds passed and nothing happened.

Well? Is Zeb going to just stand here chafing at the bit, or knock on the door?

Sanford opened his mouth to speak but Zeb beat him to it. "Back up, boy, yer crowdin' me."

Raising his eyebrows, Sanford stepped away. "Here?"

"Farther. Yer so dad-blamed tall, she'll see you afore she sees me."

Sighing, Sanford retreated two more paces. "Is *this* far enough?"

"Farther."

Sanford arced his head in exasperation. *Ah, hell.* Nonetheless, he withdrew . . .

He had no way of stopping himself. The heel of his boot lost purchase and slipped off the edge of the un-railed porch. He floundered like a windmill in a tornado for balance that evaded him, and just as he was about to fall, Zeb's name tore from his throat.

A gnarled, leathery hand shot out and seized his elbow and yanked him to safety. "Didn't mean fer ya ta stand in the rosebushes," Zeb scolded.

"You could have warned me!" Jesus, his heart was thundering in his chest!

"Well, shoot, ya woulda figured out they was roses the minute the thorns pricked ya in the rear."

That wasn't what he meant and he was sure Zeb knew it. Still, Sanford chuckled. "Thanks a lot!"

There had been times when Zeb's tendency to leave him to fend for himself hadn't been funny, though. Or harmless. Like the day that falling tree had nearly crushed him in a Wisconsin lumber camp. His logger's story had been months past deadline while he recovered from a concussion and a couple cracked ribs. He thanked luck alone for sparing him a split skull!

Then there was the time he'd stabbed himself in the foot with a pitchfork doing research on that Kansas farm for his Jayhawker piece. Naturally, Zeb just scolded him for not paying attention even as he patched the bloody prong-holes.

And most memorable of all, Sanford recalled with a shudder, was the time he'd trespassed into a black bear's den in northern Louisiana. An enraged mama protecting her cubs had chased him halfway across the state before Zeb's skill with a shotgun finally ended the pursuit. They'd been provided with a healthy meat supply, though.

Zeb always made some wisecrack over the "mishaps" but Sanford knew how much his uncle cared about him. Otherwise the old coot would have let him rot in that Mississippi orphanage nineteen years ago instead of taking him under his wing.

He'd been a belligerent little cuss the day Zeb found him, Sanford recalled with a bittersweet smile. He'd been sitting on the chipped marble steps of that crumbling plantation-house-turned-orphanage. The other kids were playing ball with a wad of fabric and a board. Listening to their cheers and lighthearted laughter, he'd tried not to care that he was being left out again. He had cared, though. And if any of those children would have bothered to look beyond his resentful scowl, they would have seen a lonely kid wishing they'd spare a few minutes to teach him the rules of the game.

But not one of those orphans seemed to think him capable of learning; neither did Mrs. Wilkens give him credit for grasping even the simplest tasks. The war widow possessed a kind heart, having taken him—along with a dozen other waifs—into what the Battle of Buzzard's Roost had left of her home. Sure, he appreciated the roof over his head—his home was gone, the lands confiscated—however, Sanford knew that he could not endure another year of being cosseted and babied by her. But there was nowhere else to go, and no one left to give a damn—except an old river rat who shared his name.

If Zeb hadn't shown up that day, Sanford was convinced that all the fight, all the ornery determination to be as normal as possible again, would've drained right out of him.

He had so much to thank his father's brother for. Not just for rescuing him from a stagnant fate, but for teaching him the fundamental skills of everyday living. For treating him like a human being, a boy entering manhood. For easing the grief in his heart over the loss of his father at the close of the Civil War. For helping to heal the wounds inflicted on his then scrawny body after the Yankees had stolen his horses.

For just being there, at his side, for nigh onto twenty years unfailing.

Sanford swallowed the lump obstructing his windpipe. He owed Zeb his life. And if it came down to it, Sanford would give it to him, too.

Yet all Zeb had ever requested was a little time off from their constant travels to visit with a woman he'd fallen in love with almost fifty years before and had never forgotten. A new assistant was even to be provided for him while Zeb renewed the old relationship, a grandchild of Minerva's, eliminating the need to put his work on hold.

Sanford wondered again about the grandchild due to help him with this current book. Zeb's details were oddly sketchy. All Sanford had been told was the grandchild was young and healthy, could read and write, liked to travel, and craved adventure. Such a lack of information gave his imagination free rein. For all he knew, he might be stuck with some green-as-a-seasick-sailor school pup.

Still, the debt he owed Zeb was too great for objections, despite the reservations he harbored in trusting a stranger with any facet of his career or his life.

"I shoulda wore my blue shirt." Zeb's scratchy voice snapped Sanford from his reverie. "Minerva always liked me in blue."

Sanford swallowed again then coughed into his hand. "It was missing a button."

"Why didn'tcha sew one on?"

"I used the last one on your red shirt."

"But I hate the red one. Gol-durn thing gives me a rash."

Sanford closed his eyes. Nerves were giving the old river rat a rash, not the red cotton. "Just knock on the door." He couldn't believe Zeb was as jittery as a June bug in August! And all because he was about to come face-to-face with the true love he hadn't seen since before Sanford was a gleam in his daddy's eye.

Sighing, Sanford supposed if he were in Zeb's boots, he'd be just as rattled. Of course, he had no intention of winding up as such a pathetic case because he was never going to fall in love. Women were not part of his grand scheme and never would be. He was a writer—always on the road searching for interesting people and places to incorporate into his stories. It was no kind of lifestyle for the gentler sex.

Women wanted stable homes and hearths and men they could depend on. And Sanford avoided those restrictions like the plague. He detested anyone tying him down, depending on him—especially a female—which was why he and Zeb got along so well.

"Oh, no," he groaned suddenly, hearing the rustle of paper. "Uncle Zeb, you aren't bringing out Minerva's letter again, are you?"

"I jist wanna make sure she wants me to come."

"*Why* would Minerva have sent the letter if she didn't want you here?"

"But what if she ain't 'spectin' me *today*?"

"Uncle Zeb, you're stalling. We both know she said April thirtieth. I'm positive she'll be expecting you." In fact, Sanford deduced, it was probably Minerva herself watching from the house.

"But are ya sure this is the Daltry spread?"

Sanford clenched his teeth. His patience was wearing thinner than a Rebel boot. Sure Zeb was nervous—but this was ridiculous! "The man at the mercantile said to go five miles up the north road, and when we see the wooden fence with the big 'Circle D' at the arched top, we've reached Mount Olympus."

"Why do ya s'pose the townsfolk call it Mount Olympus?"

"Just knock on the damn door!"

"Humph. Ya don't hafta jump down my throat an' bite my innards!"

Before Sanford could come back with a worthy retort, Zeb sucked in his breath then blew it out between his

lips. His courage fortified, he not only hammered upon
the door loud enough to wake the dead, but he also got a
hold of a metal rod and beat it against something that
sounded suspiciously like kettle lids. The various pitches
vibrated through Sanford's body, from his toes to his
scalp, making him wonder why in creation someone
would have such an unusual—and deafening!—calling
device when a bell or knocker should be sufficient.

Adding to the din, the porch boards creaked like a
seesaw. Sanford's lips twitched. The old geezer couldn't
be still a minute.

The screech of a door swinging open made him perk
up his ears. A sudden tenseness seemed to hold time
captive and Sanford knew the man he looked upon like a
father had just come face-to-face with the woman he'd
adored his entire adult life.

Aware that this could take a while, Sanford relaxed
against the sturdy vertical beam supporting the porch
overhang and felt the sharp angle dig into his spine. He
hooked his thumbs into his front pockets and kept a respectable distance from the reuniting couple.

No words were spoken between Zeb Buchanan and
Minerva Daltry, yet there was a powerful force in the air.
Sanford couldn't quite identify it. Awe, maybe. Or ab-
sorption.

Either way, it was private.

So he stayed silent and motionless until Zeb called for
him.

The sound of crinkling paper reached Sanford. He pictured Zeb wordlessly handing the cherished missive to his
sweetheart. A soft *oh* drifted on the dusky breeze and he
sensed the faceless woman's smile.

The quiet became more intimate, then. Sanford grew
uncomfortable. He shoved his hands into his back pockets and scuffed his boot along the wooden porch floor.
What would it be like, he pondered, to love someone
enough to wait fifty years for her? Was there really such a
thing as everlasting love? Was there really a woman out
there for every man? If so, he hadn't found the one for
him. But if there was, and he did find her . . .

Damn it all, Sanford thought with disgust, Zeb and Minerva were planting foolish sentiments in his head. He wasn't looking for that.

Occupy your mind with something other than the two lovebirds, Sanford lectured himself. And yet, neither did he want to waste any more time wondering about the stranger he'd promised to bring on this trip.

He decided to think about his stories. They could usually keep him busy for hours. Resting his head against the post, Sanford envisioned the character he'd invented after meeting a real-life card shark. Real people were the best inspiration, he firmly believed, for most of his ideas came from people he'd encountered in his travels. Of course, he gave them other names and fictitious lives and wrapped up their turbulent adventures with a satisfying ending.

All right, he thought, *I've got Slick Drayson, the clever gambler, as skilled with the ladies as he is with the cards. He's won a Nevada saloon from a greedy hustler who doesn't take the loss kindly. Upon hearing the hustler is out for his blood, Slick employs the help of one of his enamored ladies to sneak him out of town . . .*

After that, Sanford drew a blank. He wanted to get Slick from St. Louis to Nevada. A lot of silver mines were being played there and he wanted the saloon sitting on top of a mother lode, making it valuable enough to kill for. That would give the hustler a motive for being on Slick's tail. That left conflicts to be concocted between beginning and end. But he'd used just about every dangerous scenario he could think of in his other books. Fresh ideas were what he needed. A new plot that would still land Slick in a heap of trouble before he finally claimed the saloon he'd rightfully won.

Sanford stared at the nothingness surrounding him, trying to weave goal, conflict, and resolution into a page-turning tale.

Girlish giggles broke his concentration, bringing him from his imaginary world to present reality.

"Bucky-boy," Zeb called, "come on over and meet the woman who done stole m'heart 'most fifty years ago."

"Zebuelan Buchanan, you'll make him think I'm some sort of thief!"

Sanford smiled. Obviously nobody but Minerva Daltry got away with calling Zeb by his full Christian name. Sanford glided the pads of his fingertips along the fresh paint of the lumber wall as he ambled toward the couple. "I wouldn't think any such thing, ma'am."

Though introductions weren't necessary, Zeb did the honors anyway. "This here's my nephew Sanford—my brother Jed's boy. Only I call 'im Buck 'cause when he was little he strutted 'round like a male deer durin' . . . uh, well, I mean he was a proudful sort."

Zeb elbowed Sanford in the ribs, eliciting a grunt. "Take off yer hat!"

Sanford swept the covering off his head, smoothed his hand down his trouser leg, then held his hand out to Minerva. When she placed her soft, fleshy fingers into his palm he felt the warmth of rings and riches. Absent was cold recoil and snobbery; present was simple and sincere welcome.

"He has a right to be proud. So do you, Zebuelan. You raised a fine-mannered young man."

Sanford kissed her knuckles and felt his heartstrings being reeled in like a fishing line. He thought he understood now why his uncle was so enamored with this woman. Her voice was pleasant as a fall morning and she exuded a kindness he really didn't expect from a lady of her station.

Of course, Uncle Zeb had bragged so often about her that Sanford wondered at his surprise. Hadn't he been told that she was a courageous woman with fierce loyalties to her large family? Hadn't he been told that, although her late husband had left her with a vast cattle empire, money was of no importance to this lady of moderate tastes? But Sanford rarely formed impressions based on words; his judgments stemmed from intuition and experience. And both were validating this woman's steady character and unprejudiced heart.

In his mind, he saw Minerva as Zeb had when he first met her, and by adding five decades to that mental picture, saw her as she must be now: hair of rich, sweet chocolate now changed to a rich silver, eyes as light and lively as a dove's wing in flight, figure and features now stout yet displaying the regal bearing of a lioness . . .

But what he liked most was that she seemed to accept the fact he wasn't like normal folks.

"I'm so happy you've agreed to bring along company on this trip, Sanford," Minerva said.

"It's the least I can do. Bringing your grandchild along saves me the headache of trying to hire someone to take Uncle Zeb's place. After everything he's done for me I suppose he deserves a little holiday. I wouldn't be where I am today if not for him."

"From what he's written to me over the years, you've come this far thanks to your own determination. He boasts about you so."

To further Sanford's embarrassment, he felt a blush steal into his cheeks. He'd always hoped Zeb was proud of him, but since the old coot never said either way, a sliver of uncertainty had imbedded itself in his soul. But confronted with the truth, he felt a bit of shame for the ounce of doubt he had carried around. "Well, he's the person I get that determination from—among other things. He has taught me a lot over the years. I can't say I was always grateful for his methods, though," Sanford admitted.

"Felt like kicking him in the seat of his pants now and then, did you?" Minerva said.

Sanford chuckled at her refreshing candor. "That's a polite way of phrasing it, yes, ma'am."

"You're not alone, Sanford." Minerva wedged herself between them and, hooking her arm through each of theirs, guided them toward the front door. "But now I'll have the opportunity we both missed and I'll make sure to give him a swift boot for you, too. Meanwhile, my family is waiting in the parlor."

The screen door bounced shut behind Sanford as he entered the house. The coolness of the entryway gave him the impression of a cavern, and Minerva confirmed that the ten-foot-high walls in the hall were paneled from ceiling to midpoint, while the rest was stone. The echo of boot heels told Sanford the floors were hardwood and he could smell the sweet beeswax that had been used to polish them.

A weak aroma of salt and fried beefsteak came from farther down the hall, indicating a kitchen or dining room to his left. The strong odors of cattle and sweat trailed from a room to his right, suggesting someone had recently returned from a pasture or barn.

Minerva's skirts tangled around Sanford's legs as she directed them to that room. They stopped just inside a doorway wide enough for all three of them, and the blending of male and female voices from within ceased.

Sanford felt every eye in the room lock on him. He shifted his weight from one leg to the other and crumpled his hat in his hands.

They can tell, he thought as prickles of panic crept into his veins. *And they're either shocked or appalled or both.* Then Sanford wondered why in the hell he cared *how* Minerva's family reacted to him. They were strangers after all, and he figured if there was anything he'd grown used to, it was strangers staring at him and conversations dropping in mid-sentence as he entered a room.

But to his dismay, he wasn't as used to it as he'd thought. And it took all his willpower not to plant his hat on his head and tilt the brim down low. But he figured such a course of action might call undue attention to his deficiency. Or more important, he might insult Minerva by donning his protective headgear inside the house.

Well, as Uncle Zeb always said, if folks didn't cotton to him just because he was a mite different, then it was their problem.

The memory prompted Sanford to square his shoulders and assume his mask of indifference.

Minerva introduced him and Zeb to her son Odysseus and his wife, Jane, and their children Atalanta and Atlas. She expressed her regret that the rest of her grandchildren could not be here to meet him.

It didn't bother Sanford. This wasn't *his* social call, just a detour to collect his temporary new partner.

Minerva led him to a nearby chair. Sanford ran his hand along the twilled upholstery and lowered himself onto the cushioned seat. Odysseus welcomed them to the Daltry Ranch and a floral-scented Jane set a cup of coffee on the table next to him.

The flavorful brew tasted of a hint of cinnamon and as Sanford sipped at it, more to keep his hands occupied than out of thirst, the tension seeped from his neck. The voices around him rose once more, conversations and topics overlapping.

Sanford deferred questions about their travels to Uncle Zeb, preferring to listen instead.

After what seemed forever of trying to guess which person had volunteered to make the journey West as his adventurer-in-arms, he was no closer to an answer than when they'd first gotten the letter. He could dismiss Odie and Jane immediately, for Zeb had informed him his helper was a grandchild. That left Atlas, who might have been a candidate if he hadn't mentioned attending a Chicago college in September, and Atalanta. Although she was a vivacious young girl inclined toward trekking across the wilderness, Sanford did not believe Zeb would be so cruel as to match him with a female of any age, regardless of their shared affinity for horses.

Well, hell, Sanford cursed to himself in confusion. Who was he supposed to take with him? Who was the avid frontier lover, the earnest scribe willing to trade luxuries of civilization for a few months of brotherhood with the land?

It struck Sanford that he was being kept in the dark, figuratively speaking. Not one person exhibited the courage and grit necessary for the job, nor did anyone show an interest in joining him as Zeb promised. A major detail was being withheld.

And it was beginning to irritate him.

Zeb sat beside him in another chair and Sanford leaned over to tug on his sleeve. Not one minute more was going to pass without him knowing just what in blazes was going on.

Just then, Sanford sensed a presence in the doorway at

his back. At the same instant, a strong gust of perfume blew into the room, curling around him like a flowering vine, nearly smothering him with its potent scent.

Abruptly Sanford stiffened. Dread careened through him; recognition of a blue blood hit him with the speed of a runaway locomotive.

No! he mutely screamed. *Uncle, you wouldn't do this to me!* Yet, hadn't he had that feeling of impending doom the instant he smelled the perfume?

"Well, well. I see your guests finally made it, Grandma."

That voice. It was a stranger's voice yet so familiar. Sanford clenched his eyes shut. *That voice!* So feminine, so breezy. Oh, Jesus. He'd never heard this particular one . . . although he'd heard similar ones. Mocking him. Making him feel inferior. Or worse, like a little boy in need of coddling.

Sanford relied heavily on gut feelings—the one twisting his vitals now told him that Zeb had done the unthinkable this time. *Of all the low-down, dirty tricks . . .*

His uncle, the man he trusted, had saddled him with a female.

But not just any kind of female. The most dangerous kind. The kind that talked as if she were made of fragile spring blossoms and smelled as if she bathed in bubbles of riches.

The kind he'd avoided since . . . since the Confederates lost. Since he had lost . . . everything.

She'd been taught since childhood that a grand entrance commanded attention, but some things just came naturally. Venus swept into the parlor with an inborn grace many of her friends spent hours and fortunes perfecting. She held her floral damask gown aloft, the lacy hem fluttering around her trim ankles, the narrow train dusting the fringed border of Grandma's Greek alphabet carpet.

"There you are, Venus," Minerva reproached.

"I hope I haven't kept everyone waiting," Venus cooed, though she knew she had. Purposely, too. Tardiness was a fashionable habit for a lady. Labor or no labor, she was *always* a lady. Nothing or no one would take that from her, Venus vowed.

Unless she wanted them to, that is.

Scanning the room, she noticed her daddy and brother and Grandma's guest already standing, but the other man, the saddle tramp she assumed she must accompany, took his sweet ole time getting to his feet. His sorry hat was clutched in his hand and his coat was missing, revealing a butternut-dyed shirt and brown vest, the leather sporting more cracks than a parched creekbed.

But when he did stand, Venus could not speak. Land's sake, he didn't seem so tall sitting on his horse, she marveled. *Or* so big! But without the duster hiding his physique, she could see that the man towering a good head and a half above her was not one who shirked manual labor. She'd taken great pains to keep her own figure fit and trim, but in comparison to him, she felt *runty*!

No, there was nothing sleek about him, she decided when he turned to give her a frontal view. In fact, he was the most bulging individual she'd ever seen in her life! His biceps strained his shirtsleeves and she hoped he never planned on buttoning his vest since the edges would have a heck of a time meeting over his muscular abdomen. His expansive chest was level with her nose and the vee of tanned flesh visible at the opening of his unfastened collar held her riveted.

Her insides were growing mushy and she couldn't seem to catch her breath. Her only coherent thought was, *A body like his belongs to a Roman god.*

Long seconds ticked away before she forced herself out of the trance. She moved her gaze upward, beyond the thick cords of his neck, passed the length of mussed dark hair falling over his ears and frayed collar. She'd been deceived, though, in thinking his hair plain black—it was brown. But not ordinary brown. In the soft light of whale oil lamps scattered about the parlor, the wavy strands looked like veins of copper in a tarnished gold mine—if such a thing existed.

And nearly hidden by a beard and mustache of the

same shade were his lips. Salmon-colored and firmly
pressed together in a shapeless line, but lips all the same.
Above them, his nose bore a small bump on the straight
bridge. Rather than detract from his appearance, it lent
him strength of character.

Reaching his eyes, she found him staring at her. Venus
stared back while her belly slithered to her toes. *Land's
sake, a girl could look into those sultry brown depths forever
and still hope for longer.*

They reflected nothing, though. Not his thoughts, not
his emotions. Actually, nothing about him hinted at what
he felt.

Venus was accustomed to striking men dumb, yet this
man . . .

He exuded an untamed aura that both attracted and
repelled her. Something virile. Dangerous.

And what those mysterious, drowsy, bone-melting eyes
did to her insides . . .

Bless my soul, Venus thought upon further reflection,
*he's got potential! A little grooming . . . a decent frockcoat
and cravat . . . why, he could be darn-right handsome!*

Perhaps this labor wasn't going to be as dreadful or
dreary as she'd first assumed.

Venus dangled her hand in front of that diamond-in-
the-rough face. "Mr. Buchanan, I'm Venus Daltry. Your
new assistant." She wore her coyest smile, gave her lashes
their most darling flutter, and her practiced Southern-
belle accent would put even Maybelle's genuine inflection
to shame.

But he did not kiss her hand, nor did he shake it. In
fact, he completely ignored the offer altogether.

All he did was stare at her.

*Well, I've been known to paralyze men before but this is a
little unnerving!*

Letting her arm fall to her side, Venus glanced about
the room. Why, *everyone* was staring at her! Self-
consciously, she patted the coiffed blond spirals that were
pinned at her nape so they cascaded flirtatiously down
the sheer lace of her back. Every strand seemed to be in
place. Well? she wondered. Was her kohl smeared again?

Her lip rouge smudged? "Why are y'all looking at me so strangely?"

As if her question spurred them to action, Atlas and Allie made excuses and filed out the doorway. Mama's hands trembled nervously as she rearranged the silver coffee set on the bow-legged center table and Daddy pretended deep interest in the designs he'd recently carved in the fireplace mantel.

With increasing perplexity, Venus silently sought answers from the elder Buchanan, who averted his face, then Grandma Minerva, whose serene countenance gave nothing away. Finally she turned once more to Sanford, as if he—of all people—could explain her family's odder than normal behavior.

Yet all he did was stare at her!

It was becoming quite unnerving the way his eyes never left her. The man's boldness bordered on rudeness. Venus pursed her lips and fixed him with a challenging gaze.

It was then that she noticed the absence of light in those sinful brown depths, the complete lack of movement . . . of dilation . . .

The utter vacancy.

Land's sake, what is wrong *with this man?*

There wasn't a male alive who didn't show *some* reaction to her. To her uncommon beauty. To her captivating smile and her misty blue eyes. And there was no denying he was a man—under all that coarse clothing and rumpled veneer. Nor could anyone dispute that she possessed exceptional looks; that fact had been drilled into her since she had learned to flash her dimples at the tender age of two!

So what was so different about Sanford Buchanan that her pale gold hair, delicate features, and shapely figure could not produce the response she'd come to expect? Was he the first man immune to her beauty?

Venus scoffed at that notion. A man would have to be blind not to—

She sucked in a gasp.

Swinging toward his companion, she whispered, "He can't see?"

At the elder Buchanan's helpless shrug, Venus closed her eyes in despair.

Peachy. Just peachy.

She would have to travel through godforsaken territory with a *blind* dime novelist.

Three

In the dead quiet, Sanford's voice rang out clear and true. "No, he can't *see*. But he can hear!"

More silence met his statement and the shame was almost tangible.

Sanford curled his fingers into his palms, wishing Zeb's neck was in his hands so he could wring it.

Better yet, Venus Daltry's neck. The gall . . . the pure indecency of mentioning his disability . . .

And acting as if he weren't in the room! As if being blind affected his hearing . . .

Hell, that's not what bothered him. So what if she told the whole county he was blind—he didn't care. It was the repugnance behind her shocked words that disturbed him. Then, to treat him as if he didn't exist . . .

Why hadn't Zeb told him his assistant—the reading-writing-eager-to-make-his-mark-in-the-world-lad—wasn't a lad at all, but a damn *lady*?

No. He couldn't blame her. Not entirely. He was used to shock. And to repugnance.

But he could blame Zeb. Entirely. For his duplicity and his damn selfish ambitions.

It was only through sheer force of self-discipline that

Sanford maintained his composure. As a guest in some-one's house, he would avoid making a scene. He seethed, though. Inside, where no one else was allowed. Not Zeb, who had deceived him in the worst way. Not Venus, whose alarmed reaction galled him but was no less than he expected. And not the collective group of Daltry adults watching this farce unfold.

But two minutes alone with his uncle . . . Oh, if Zeb were wise, he'd steer clear for a while.

"There's been a huge misunderstanding, Mrs. Daltry," he finally managed, schooling his features and keeping his tone even. "*Someone* neglected to inform me your grandchild was a girl—"

"Well, nobody told *me* you were blind, either," Venus cut in, "so that makes us even." There was movement in the air before him and Sanford pictured the tiny thing standing in front of him slicing a wide arc with her hand. "But that's beside the point."

His forehead creased and he thrust his hip out and planted his fist at his waist. "What exactly *is* the point?"

"The point? Well, it's . . . it's that you're going to Nevada and need an assistant. I need to see the country but require an escort."

Sanford wanted to argue that he didn't need anybody, but it would be a lie. As much as it stung, he couldn't research and write his books without aid. There was no use denying facts. Admitting the truth to himself was one thing, but he sure as hell didn't have to admit them to anyone else.

Then, as if realizing there might be more to the job than she'd declared, Venus haltingly asked, "Ah . . . just *what* would I be assisting you with?"

She sounded so leery that Sanford might have laughed if the situation wasn't so infuriating. She probably reck-oned he needed help dressing and undressing, probably believed he wasn't even capable of walking alone or feeding himself. She sure wouldn't be the first to hold those notions.

Zeb answered for him. "Not much, little lady. Just keeping a record of the surroundings—people, places, activities. And when Buck tells his story to ya, ya just write it down."

Sanford ground his teeth and trapped a growl of outrage in his throat.

"Well, that doesn't sound so hard," Venus quipped. "Now that everything is out in the open and we both understand our duties, we can get ready to leave."

She made it sound so easy. So uncomplicated.

It was that asinine logic, that ignorance, that gave Sanford more insight into her nature than her perfume and her lilting voice and her nerve-wracking scrutiny of him. As if he were an indentured servant on the auction block and she a judge of his worth as a human being.

He'd endured enough appraisals of that ilk to know he wouldn't tolerate any more.

"There is more to my trips than simply taking notes and strolling across the western frontier, *Miss Daltry,*" Sanford said, suppressing the anger mounting inside him.

"Ah, Sanford dear," Minerva intervened, "why don't I have Jane show you a room. I'm sure you must be weary after traveling so far . . ."

"No, thank you, ma'am," he declined with strained politeness. "If you'll just direct me to the door, I'll be on my way—"

"To check his horse!" Zeb quickly supplied. "Buck here frets 'bout that animal of his more'n a mother hen." Sanford felt bony fingers grip his arm. "And if it don't make no trouble, we'll grab our winks in the bunkhouse with the other men—no slight intended, Odie."

"None taken," Odie said.

Not waiting for Minerva to argue the plan, Zeb ushered him outside, collected the horses from the hitching rail, and led Sanford across the yard to the stables. "Mighty p.o.'d at me, ain'tcha, boy?"

Sanford didn't trust himself to speak. Furious strides carried him down a corridor strewn with sweet-smelling hay and old lumber and oiled leather. A few penned horses nickered at him in greeting.

Near the rear of the stable, Sanford kicked up dust motes and hay particles with his agitated pacing. Eventually he brought his temper under control and laughed bitterly. "If I wasn't convinced you'd completely lost your mind, I'd knock some sense into it."

"Hah! You ain't that big yet."

They both knew he topped the old geezer by nearly a foot and doubled him in strength, but it had been an ongoing joke since Sanford was young. However, he was in no mood to play word games with his uncle, not when he'd been deceived so unscrupulously.

He scrubbed the back of his neck with his nails. "I can't believe you had the gall to pawn a woman off on me. Worse, one like *her*!"

"Whatcha mean, 'one like her'?"

"You know I cannot abide . . ." Abruptly, Sanford stilled. "Where are you, you scheming old river rat?"

"Sittin' on a hay bale in front of the last stall watchin' ya make an ass outta yerself. Yer throwin' a temper tantrum like a spoilt young'un insteada actin' like the man I raised ya up ta be."

Sanford ignored the insult as he sought his uncle's location. "She was wearing silk, wasn't she?"

Feigning stupidity, Zeb said, "I don't know. Somethin' shiny with big ole sunset-warm flowers all over it an' ruffles at the bottom."

Sanford imagined the color pink, not quite grasping the elusive shade, but feeling it instead. "And the house. I know it's big because I heard an echo. I bet it's filled with nice things."

"Well, it ain't no palace but Minerva's husband left her in fine shape an' Odie is doin' right by her. They ain't eatin' off the floor or usin' crates as chairs if that's whatcha mean."

"That's exactly what I mean." He had detected the newness, the modest finery. And no dandelion-root coffee for that house, but choice beans served in fine china cups. He did not begrudge the Daltrys their wealth, only the social standing that wealth afforded. And he detested the pompous characters that social standing produced. Characters like Venus Daltry, who sat in her high gilded throne, looking down her nose at the less fortunate. Characters like Venus Daltry who never lifted a manicured finger her whole life and whose idea of work was dressing herself in the morning.

Sanford wiped his hand down his face as if the action could erase his fatigue, his soul-deep disappointment in the man he considered more than a father, more than a mentor, more than a steadfast friend.

"*You* know," Sanford said with a calmness he did not feel, "that if you had told me she was a lady, and came from a fine family, and lived among fine things, I never would have agreed to take her along." He grew more passionate. "But you were so damned intent on impressing Minerva by accepting her offer of her grandchild as my assistant, and freeing yourself of me for a while, that you didn't have a lick of concern as to how I would feel about the arrangement. And you used my sense of loyalty against me to get me to agree without revealing all the facts!"

"Dad-gummit, Buck, I'm ashamed of you!"

"*You* are ashamed of *me*?"

"Thought ya said ya could hear!"

"I heard perfectly. I just can't believe my ears!" With both hands clamped on his hips, Sanford said, "What have I done to shame you?"

"Yer shyin' away from a challenge. Ya ain't done that since you was a young'un trippin' at my heels."

"A challenge!" Sanford bellowed. "You consider this . . . she . . . I . . . you . . ." Infuriated, Sanford sucked in a breath of air then proclaimed, "She won't be a challenge, she'll be a pain in the ass!"

Sticking the knife in deeper, Zeb defended Venus Daltry. "She ain't so bad."

"That's easy for you to say!" Sanford gestured wildly. "You're not the one who has to drag her along! You'll be here spooning with Minerva while I'm worrying if I'll live long enough to write another book!"

"Ain'tcha exaggeratin' a mite?"

He sighed with frustration. "You were there. You heard her. She thinks this is going to be a pleasure outing." He shook his head. "She has no common sense and no concept of the perils we might encounter because it's obvious even to *me* that she's never set foot outside her sheltered little world. It doesn't take a genius to guess what kind of traveling partner she'll make."

Zeb chortled. "A lot pertier one than me, I'll say that!" His voice went to taffy. "Hair mellow as sweet butter, eyes soft as a night'ngale's song, and more curves than a mount'n pass . . ."

"I don't give a damn what she looks like—I won't take her!"

The air went frigid. Icier than a Montana winter.

He had disappointed Zeb, his only breathing relative, his sole comrade. Not even any of his botched attempts at adapting to a world that spared no room for a cripple caused him to feel as shut out as the stillness that followed his statement.

Sanford tried not to care that he'd let his uncle down, but the small and lonesome kid deep inside him cared. Cared very much.

He longed to take the refusal back—but he couldn't. Because he meant it. Venus Daltry, princess of Paradise Plains, would not join him on this—or any other—research trip. Yes, he had promised. But in his opinion, a promise made under false pretenses wasn't worth spit.

Zeb's knees creaked as he rose, reminding Sanford of his uncle's advancing years and the sacrifices this man had made for him.

"You listen to me, Sanford Joseph Buchanan. Of all the things I done learnt you, honor was the most important. Without it, a man ain't no man a'tall. And I gave my word that you'd take Minerva's grandchild with you so's me an' her could have a nice long visit. Weren't no conditions, just my word as a man. As a *Buchanan.* And I don't aim ta break it on account o' my brother's son needs me ta hold his goddamn hand the rest of his life."

The firm words and his usage of God's name in vain delivered a punishing blow to Sanford's pride. "I didn't say I wanted you to."

"Then tell me what's got you so dad-blasted twisted."

Sanford braced himself, determined to stand his

ground in this matter. Make Zeb see the folly of making a promise without even consulting him. "You know what kind of life I lead. It's hazardous and unpredictable, trying for even the most competent. How often have we crossed paths with death together and escaped by the skin of our teeth? How often, in spite of our vigilance, have we been hit broadside by calamity?"

"Is you fergettin' who taught you the ropes?"

"Not for a second. But you had climbed those ropes before . . . knew how to get down. I never had to worry how you'd fare . . ."

"Yer skeared!" Zeb charged suddenly. "Yer plumb fearful ya cain't keep her safe!"

"Quit bending my words!" Sanford argued, clenching his fists. His chest heaved with helpless fury. *"Nothing* . . . has scared me since the day I awoke without my sight. I have faced raging rivers. Wild boars. Prairie fires. For damn sure I'm not afraid of a little girl!"

"Ya tryin' ta convince me? Or yerself?"

He was trapped between the proverbial rock and a hard place. Honor warred with rebellion, debt with denial, loyalty with common sense.

Sanford stood alone in the stables, hanging his head between arms outstretched and locked at the elbows, his hands curled over the top of a stall door. His sensitive fingertips dug into the grains of wood. All his one hundred ninety pounds were balanced on one leg while the other leg crooked at the knee.

A female assistant.

He slugged the flat, grooved boards then thrust himself away, flexing his stinging fingers. Why was Zeb being so difficult? Sanford wondered. The old coot wasn't stupid; he knew that it wasn't just the danger. Sanford avoided entanglements with women. Ladies. Females. Hell, all of them! Period.

Since the hot summer night that Yankee incited the horses to stampede out the barn, Sanford had learned there were only two kinds of females. The mollycoddling kind that fussed over him and did for him until his stom-

ach churned, and the other kind, the ones who scorned
him because a blind man didn't meet up to their standards.

The first kind he had appreciated for a time. It had
been one of them, a nurse coming home from the war,
who had found him broken and bleeding in the dirt, the
side of his head bearing a swollen mark from a spooked
steed's hoof. With Jed off fighting and Sanford not knowing when he'd return, the nurse had conveyed him to
Mrs. Wilkens's home where later he received word Jed
was never returning—not to him, anyway.

The bitterness festering inside from the ruthless soldier
and his father's involuntary abandonment compounded
each day he was forced to endure Mrs. Wilkens's sappy
intonations. *Sanford, do you need help eating? Sanford, let
me rebutton your shirt. Sanford, the leash on your arm is
there so you will not stray and get lost . . .*

The bile remained in his throat until Zeb found him a
year later. And in their travels he had encountered others
like Mrs. Wilkens. He'd also met up with the second kind;
the ones who wouldn't spit on him if he was on fire. The
high-society misses and matrons who thought him beneath them, whose noses were so far in the air that if it
rained, they'd drown. The ones whose most strenuous
tasks were choosing which tea to attend and which gown
to wear. Yes, they contributed to charities—even to or-
phanages and schools for the "unfortunate"—but it was
more out of socially ordained righteousness than true interest. None of them would be caught dead actually
working in the institutions, for fear they'd contaminate
themselves.

Venus Daltry fit into that category.

He had heard the repugnance in her voice. She'd recovered from the shock quicker than most folks but it
didn't change facts. Venus, like so many others, seemed
to think his condition was contagious. A disease rather
than the result of an accident.

And yet, she had still insisted they leave together. Why,
when she was obviously offended by him?

Sanford shuffled toward Ranger and fondled the

coarse forelock of his mane. Well, he had news for Miss Daltry. He didn't know what her game was, but he wasn't playing. Games were for children.

"What am I going to do, Ranger? I have already promised Uncle Zeb I'd take Minerva's grandchild, but that was before I knew 'he' was a 'she.' "

Ranger shied away from his touch.

"Oh, you're upset with me, too, huh?" Sanford batted at the horse and missed. "Well, consider this, you uppity stallion, *you'll* be stuck with her same as me!"

As usual, he was left to extricate himself from a mess.

Sanford lowered himself onto the hay bale vacated by his uncle and pondered his predicament. The problem lay in his promise to Zeb, he determined. He was bound by his *own* word. His *own* honor. Zeb might not believe it, but Sanford felt just as strongly about the Buchanan name.

Mulling it over, he figured the only solution was to convince Venus Daltry to forget her crazy notion of seeing the West. If she pulled out, he wouldn't be breaking his commitment—she'd break it for him and he'd be let off the hook.

All right, now that he'd devised a solution, how should he carry it out? Consequences always followed an action. Rashness risked unfavorable results . . .

Sanford slapped his hands on his thighs. He'd be honest with her. Simply tell her he didn't want her along. Why would anybody want to be where they weren't wanted? Sanford knew he sure didn't.

He stood, aiming to discuss his decision with Venus and get it over and done with. Then immediately afterward he'd nose around Paradise for another assistant so he could be on the trail again. No sense in sticking around. A story was due to his editor next summer and he'd hardly started it.

But Sanford hadn't taken two steps when the door ahead squeaked open and the subject of his thoughts "yoo-hooed."

Sanford cringed.

"Are you in here, Mr. Buchanan?" Venus called.

I wish I wasn't. He turned away, attacked by a sudden case of cold feet. *Yer skeared.* Cursing to himself, Sanford mutinously took a step, then stopped. Let her come to me, he thought. Better that than go through the humiliation of stumbling over something to reach her. "I'm in the back," he called.

Hopefully, she had arrived at the same conclusions as he and that's why she sought him out.

She closed the distance between them, bringing with her those fancy fumes and light, swishing fabric. A vision of her gliding across hay stems formed in his mind, against his will. Palomino hair and figurine-doll features. Dainty yet shapely in all her sunset silks.

So damn feminine. So damn dangerous.

Sanford fought the unwelcome impact that proximity to the opposite sex occasionally inspired. Yet he found it harder than usual to calm his quickening heart rate, to control the sudden rush of blood through his system.

"My trunks are all packed. You can load them onto the wagon anytime," Venus decreed, her vowels broad and softly rounded. Her speech was different from that of the other Daltrys . . . it sounded almost contrived. And yet, it was more like song than speech. The novelty of it whetted his appetite for soft flesh and sweet nothings . . .

Sanford whipped around once again, hoping she hadn't noticed how his chest swelled—among other things. "Are your trunks going someplace?" His hands trembled as he busied them with Ranger's bridle.

It was the woman-factor affecting him, he reasoned, blaming months of abstinence. Given the length of time since his last indulgence, it seemed only natural that his body would respond.

Except . . .

Lusting for a woman might be legitimate; lusting for a lady was lethal.

"Why, they're going with me, of course," she answered. "And since I'm going with you, I'll guess they'll be going with us!"

The bridle bit set in the horse's mouth, Sanford advanced to Ranger's back. His hands met bare hide instead of saddle. *Damn Zeb!* He ducked under Ranger's regal neck. Sanford searched by touch for the equipment only Zeb could have removed, and responded to Venus's claim. "I'm making this trip by horseback, lady. I don't go anywhere without my stallion."

"And I don't go anywhere without my wardrobe. I'll handle the rig, you handle the horse."

Sanford kept one hand on the stall while the other glided through the air.

He finally located the saddle draped over a sawhorse near the hay bale where Zeb had been sitting and his suspicion was confirmed. Beside the worn leather seat also awaited his collection of pouches, bedroll, and blanket, everything he needed to get the hell out of here.

After he took care of one minor detainment.

Sighing heavily, Sanford addressed her. "Miss Daltry, under the circumstances, I think we'd both be better off if you stayed here and I found another partner."

"Why? Because I noticed you were blind?"

The corner of his lips twisted in a wry grimace. "That's not exactly a secret."

"It was to me."

Obviously. Her surprise had been as genuine as his. So they both boasted manipulating relatives. It made no difference. Sanford snatched the woven rectangle blanket then gave her his full attention. "Listen, it was no more my idea for you to join me on this trip than it was your idea to be escorted by a blind man. I'm certain you can see the absurdity of such an arrangement."

"Absurd or not, we each have something the other needs. You scratch my back, I'll scratch yours."

"Scratch my . . ." Hell, he didn't want to go near her with a ten-foot pole much less join forces! "Hear me out. I can't take the risk of having an inexperienced female along. Logging my stories is only part of the job. There's rough territory between here and Nevada and I need someone who has some knowledge of coping with adverse conditions." He flipped the blanket onto Ranger's back and smoothed the wrinkles. "You," he tossed over his shoulder, "are by no means the man for the job."

"I'm pleased you noticed."

Sanford raised his eyebrows. That had been easy! "Then we are agreed?"

"That I'm not a man? Yes. That I'm not qualified? No, I don't agree."

Bracing his fist on his hip, he challenged, "All right, Miss Daltry, tell me what an *arroyo* is. Or a *mesa*. And can you treat a snakebite, snare a rabbit, or tie a bowline knot?"

She giggled; he tensed. "I've been tying bows since I donned my first pinafore. And everyone knows an arroya is a contest between men riding bulls and *mesa* is Spanish for *house.*"

Sanford blew an exasperated breath between his teeth. "Exactly my point. You know nothing outside this little world you live in and, because of that, you are a danger to me." *And yourself,* he added silently. "The last thing I need is some pampered, ignorant princess tagging along, causing me headaches."

Swift and fierce, she closed the gap between them and poked her finger against his chest. "Let's get something straight, mister. I am not ignorant! Yes, I was joking about the arroyas and the mesas. Living in Texas all my life, of course I'd be familiar with what they are. As for snakebites and such? Well, I don't claim to know all there is in the world but I'm willing to learn—which is more than I can say for you, you narrow-minded mule's behind!" Her sweet breath came hot and heavy as she continued. "And I'm not pampered! Ambitious, maybe—I see something I want, I go after it and don't give up till it's mine instead of waiting for it to come to me . . ."

She jabbed him in the chest again. "Just who in Hades do you think you are to judge me, anyway? You" —*poke*— "don't even know me!" *Poke.*

The lush perfume tickling his nose and the fingernail repeatedly driving into his chest coupled to make him crazy. Sanford seized a wrist of tender skin and frail bone and tempered his grip. "You're wrong," he snarled. "The minute you walked into that room I knew you. I know you don't rise out of bed until noon. I know if your food isn't done to perfection you send it back. I know that homespun has never touched your flawless skin and I'd stake my life that you've never been denied a single thing in your life."

He shook her wrist free from his grasp. "Guess what? There's a first time for everything." And he pivoted on his heel, hoping she'd take the hint and leave.

But she didn't leave.

"You think you've got me all figured out, don't you?" Sarcasm plain as a Kansas prairie laced her voice. "You think I'm some spoiled brat and this is just some little whim."

"I'd say that sums it up nicely."

"And I'd say you've got a chip on your shoulder the size of Texas."

Sanford rubbed his chin wearily. The week's growth of bristles needled his fingers but shaving was the least of his worries. "Miss Daltry . . . Venus . . ." he implored, his voice sounding as tired as the rest of him. "Do us both a favor. Find another fool to take you on your adventure."

Venus stubbornly crossed her arms. Given a choice she would rather tell Mr.-Holier-Than-Thou what to do with his quills than tolerate such callous treatment. But Grandma had insisted she go and talk to Buchanan. Try and soothe his wounded ego.

Venus had balked, believing that when the man had walked out of the parlor, clearly enraged, she would be assigned another labor. After all, she could not very well perform the one she had been given if Sanford refused to take her west!

Grandma shattered that notion. The terms were specific and inflexible: Venus was told she must travel with Sanford Buchanan, help him write his blessed book, and return within one year. Minerva said if she made concessions for one child, she'd have to make concessions for all the others and the tradition would eventually become trivial.

So unless Venus persuaded Sanford to allow her to accompany him, the labor was lost—as was the prize.

It seemed that's all she'd been doing today—trying to

get people to change their minds. It was becoming very tiresome, too.

How was she going to convince this obstinate, prejudiced barbarian to change his mind? she wondered, watching as he settled padding onto his horse's back over the blanket, his deft, precise movements mildly impressing her. She hadn't met a man who didn't leap at the chance to spend a single day with her—much less three hundred and sixty-five! Land's sake, some had even been inspired to brawl for the honor!

But Sanford Buchanan, lowly dime novelist that he was, wanted nothing to do with her. It wasn't very flattering. In fact, it was downright insulting!

If he could see, Venus knew her beauty would have him bewitched into doing anything she desired.

But he couldn't see, she acknowledged. Therefore she'd have to rely on more devious means.

She curled her lips into a pout.

Moisture sprang readily to her eyes and for good measure she gave a loud sniffle.

He paused for a moment—a fleeting moment—then turned and reached for the saddle set on its perch. "Don't try that ploy with me," Sanford warned. "It won't work."

Venus stewed. Not only was he sightless, but he was heartless, too.

His fingers skimmed over the leather seat and found the backrest. Venus considered her options. As his hand closed around the pommel and he hefted the saddle onto the gray's back, another idea was born. The biceps nearly splitting the material of Sanford's shirt pleaded for her touch. Venus yielded to the call and laid her hand on the taut muscle.

Goose bumps skittered down her spine. She ignored the sensation and smiled slyly. Then she rose on tiptoe and whispered into the bold curve of his ear, "Please, Mr. Buchanan? I won't be any trouble."

Over his shoulder, Sanford narrowed his eyes in the direction of her face, then at her hand on his arm, then at her face again, the line of his vision only marginally off.

Venus's smile turned smug. She'd known he couldn't resist her once she used her charms. No man was immune to them for long. Some of them just thrilled at being chased, but she always caught them in the end.

He leaned his head close and whispered back from deep in his throat, "Do you think to seduce me, Miss Daltry? Are you willing to sacrifice your innocence to gain my consent?"

Her smile faded. Venus stared at him, astonished that he dared to use such lascivious words. But her tongue felt so thick in her mouth that she could not speak, not even to demand he remember his place.

And when he folded his hand around her fingers, and stroked each digit, chills raced up her arm. Wickedly, he added, "And if so"—he licked his lips suggestively—"do you think you're woman enough to bear the consequences?"

The amused slant of his mouth kindled a rage inside she hadn't imagined herself capable of feeling. Mock her, would he? Venus yanked her arm away and spat, "To Hades with you, Buchanan. I wouldn't go to Nevada with you if I was dying of thirst and you were carrying the last bucket of water on the planet. I'll just go alone."

Spinning around, Venus marched down the passageway between the stalls. She'd never wanted him for a labor anyway; she'd only gone through all this trouble for the prize.

"And if you run into outlaws, what will you do? Throw your gloves at them?" Sanford taunted.

Without breaking stride, Venus tossed her head defiantly. "At least I'd see them coming!"

Four

THE BLOOD DRAINED FROM SANFORD'S FACE AND HE WEAVED IN place.

He used to dream of regaining his sight. Of seeing something—anything!—besides the unrelenting darkness.

Zeb had taken him to doctor after doctor in the years subsequent to their pairing up. All had said the same—no hope. Too much internal damage. Extensive blow to the cranium. No hope.

No hope.

Sanford's gut wrenched.

They'd told him he was lucky. It could've been worse. He could have been killed. Or paralyzed. But they *had* their sight. They hadn't lost it. *Lucky,* he thought mockingly. To lose that sense . . . it had been like dying or being paralyzed in its own right.

None of them had understood, though. How could they? Not just the physicians. People in general. Venus.

Sanford swallowed heavily, trying to gather his riotous thoughts. He remembered wishing just one of those people could walk in his shoes for a while—cruel as it seemed—so they might feel his pain and bitterness. So they might understand the devastation of having all the light snuffed out of their world. So they might stop dismissing his loss as if it were a mitten or a penny—a material possession that could be replaced.

He didn't wish anymore. Or hope. Or dream.

Several years ago when he had finally accepted the darkness, he had also accepted the fact that people understood only what was comfortable. Blindness was not comfortable. It was distressing and frightening and no one wanted to associate with it when they didn't have to.

He gulped down another thick breath. Well, Venus didn't have to, either.

Her heels ceased clicking on the straw-strewn wooden floor and her gaze on him was penetrating. "Mr. Buchanan, I . . . I didn't . . ."

He had already sensed her regret for blurting out the tactless comment. But he didn't want her pity or her apology or whatever it was she was having such difficulty expressing. If nothing else, deep down inside Sanford respected her blunt honesty. It was a rare trait in one of her persuasion.

Concealing his anguish, he rounded on her. "What are you so all-fired determined to go to Nevada for? And why with me?" Sanford gestured to his eyes. "*These* don't work. I have to live with it. You don't."

"But I *can*. My eyes will help you, and your experience will protect me."

He refused to consider the ramifications of that statement. Not now, while the old memories were so fresh. "You still haven't told me why."

"Because my grandmother—" She paused in mid-sentence as if reluctant to divulge her reason. Then she sighed. "My grandmother has agreed to finance my . . . h-husband-hunting trip."

The last was said weakly.

"And if I want my pr—inheritance, I have to find a husband before I turn twenty-one next April."

"You can't find a husband in this area?" Paradise Plains had abounded with menfolk today when he'd passed through.

"Not one I want to spend the rest of my life with. And I've heard there is a shortage of women farther west."

Grudgingly Sanford admitted that there was, although more were coming every year. Still, something did not ring true. But the persistence in Venus's voice when she mentioned setting out without him disturbed him. His blood ran cold at the prospect of her trekking across the wilds on her lonesome.

She could be trying to manipulate him, he conceded. It could be just another attempt to get her way. Like her tears and her touches and her nerve-tingling whispers.

Yet . . . what if she was serious—and Sanford suspected she was.

Ah, hell. Venus wouldn't last a day on the frontier by herself!

It's not your problem, an inner voice asserted.

But if she did take off alone . . . and something happened to her . . . it would be his fault for breaking the promise to Zeb. But if something happened to her while she was in his care . . . it would still be his fault.

He was damned if he did and damned if he didn't.

"All right, you win," Sanford relented. "But you'll do things *my* way, got it?" he added sternly, pointing to himself with his thumb. "I have a job to do and I won't have some helpless princess interfering with it."

"I wouldn't dream of interfering."

"You'll write my story on paper exactly as I dictate it."

"Word for word."

"And I won't make allowances because you're a female, nor will you treat me differently than you would any other man."

"Perish the thought."

"*And* if you can't learn a few basic survival skills, your fanny'll be back on this ranch faster than you can shake a finger. Do I make myself clear?"

"As a windowpane!" Which sounded more like "hallelujah" to Sanford. Then, after a moment's hesitation, Venus asked, "Will you be teaching me these . . . survival skills?"

Sanford perceived she didn't mean to be critical, just

curious. "I think I can manage. You have until dawn to fit into saddlebags what you're taking—like it or not, I'll not drag a damn wagon behind me. If you're not ready, I ride out of here without you."

"Everyone's waiting outside, Venus. Are you ready?"

Venus gazed longingly at her gowns, all meticulously folded and wrapped and lying in the trunk she was not allowed to bring. She buried her face in her hands and wailed, "Allie, I can only fit three—*three!*—into those silly bags! That's hardly enough for one day!" Oh, Zeus, she couldn't believe she was actually doing this. Leaving her treasures behind, taking off for parts unknown with a stranger. But she'd gotten him to agree to take her along. That's what counted. Now she still had a chance to earn her prize. She hadn't lost it after all.

But her clothes . . . her beautiful clothes!

She whirled around and clasped Allie's roughened hands between her own. "Do something for me, Allie. See that no one fusses with them, please?"

"Cupid has outgrown them and Bubba gave up wearing them last summer."

Venus looked at Allie through watery eyes and laughed weakly at the jest. As if C.J. or Atlas, whom most of the family dubbed "Bub" or "Bubba," would fill out her gowns as well as she did. Then Venus dragged one of Allie's brown curls through her fingers. "You grew up when I wasn't looking."

"It happens to the best of us, Vee." All too quickly, the tender moment fled. Uncomfortable with displays of emotion, Allie cleared her throat and pulled her hands away, then shoved a bulging potato sack into Venus's arms. "Here. I put a snack in here and my own cache of jerky and biscuits, along with a coffeepot and a sack of beans. If you want milk, you'll have to supply your own cow."

"Thank you, Allie. He didn't say anythin' about food." Venus glanced at the watch pinned to her bodice. "I guess it's time . . ."

"I picked the gentlest gelding in the corral for you,"

Allie said. "Bubba has him saddled, and I think he's made a list of commands for you since we know it's been a while since you've ridden."

Venus wrinkled her nose as she tied the ribbon to the hat Mama had made for her. She was actually going to ride on one of those smelly creatures. Land's sake, the depths she'd sunk to! "I'd best get going before I change my mind. I'm already having second thoughts." She snatched the saddlebags and the drawstring cowhide bag holding her cosmetics. With Allie at her heels, Venus hastened down the stairs.

At the threshold of the front door, Venus paused. She stored the sight of every room in her mind. No doubt when she returned, Daddy would have made more changes, possibly would have added another room . . .

Life would go on without her.

Minerva stood by while Odie and Jane said goodbye to another of their daughters. She'd been apprehensive about her choice for Venus's labor. After all, it was highly improper to send a young maiden off alone with a virile bachelor, regardless of how honorable he'd been raised. Yet, seeing her granddaughter evolve from a beautiful child into a stunning young woman and observing the effects that knowledge had on her, Minerva knew she could not have chosen a more apt task.

As she awaited her turn to speak with Venus, she looked her fill of the strapping man she was entrusting her granddaughter to. Zebuelan, too, was sharing a few parting words with his nephew. He had told her a great many things about Sanford, both in his frequent letters and during the hours of the evening as they reminisced. Although Sanford's loss of sight at such a tender age had presented him with many obstacles to overcome, he had become quite an extraordinary man for his persistence. Stronger, wiser. But for all her pride in his achievements, Minerva also found comfort in knowing that he would not be tempted by her granddaughter's outward beauty as so many other men before him had been.

Perhaps he would succeed where she had failed. Make

Venus realize that appearances could often be deceiving.
Teach her the true value of love and commitment.

Odie and Jane stepped aside and Minerva approached
her granddaughter. Venus sat upon a light brown horse
with a mane as pale as her hair. *Always so much a lady.*
She hoped Venus would learn that at times, she was *too*
much a lady. And too much a child. Life had so much to
offer, if only she'd open her eyes and see it. Under that
frivolous exterior lay a good heart and a deep passion—if
only Venus would set them free.

"Child." Minerva addressed Venus. "Have courage.
Never doubt your own abilities." Venus's misty blue gaze
landed on her and Minerva felt the sting of tears herself.
"I'll await your reports."

Venus nodded stiffly.

The soft command "Lead, Ranger" echoed in the still
morning.

Minerva slapped the hindquarters of Venus's horse,
then dabbed at her watering eyes.

What a pair they make, she thought. *He so dark and
rugged, she so fair and dainty.* Minerva's fears that she had
made a mistake were set aside. In her heart, she knew the
next year would bring about changes in Venus, changes
that would give her granddaughter a whole new outlook
on her life and her future. And if Minerva's meddlesome
matchmaking efforts came to fruit, Sanford would learn
that not all women were cast from the same mold.

Ten paces out, Minerva spied Venus sawing on the
reins. The gelding stopped. Venus's parasol snapped open
above her head.

Zeb chuckled at her side. Minerva joined in as she
observed what appeared to be an argument between Venus and Sanford. Venus looked at the gelding's rear end
in horror, then patted it once. She nearly lost her precari-
ous seat when the sorrel began to trot.

Again, ten paces later, Venus sawed on the reins and
the horse went still.

Minerva and Zeb shared quizzical looks as she rum-
maged through the bag hanging from the pommel.

Good goddesses! Minerva silently exclaimed, thinking

her rheumy eyes were playing tricks on her. But Zebuelan's hoot of laughter validated the sight.

Venus was spraying her horse with perfume!

Venus couldn't recall a morning passing so quickly yet
so slowly in all her born days. Waking at the first gleam of
sunrise had never been one of her favorite activities, and
saying her goodbyes to her family proved harder than she
had counted on. Even to Grandma Minerva, whom she
still resented for forcing this ridiculous task upon her.

Once she and Sanford had gotten the hooves to hoof-
ing, though, Venus wished for just a little more time to
memorize Daddy's craggy face and Mama's delicate man-
nerisms, Atlas's sober way of walking and Allie's crude
way of talking, and most of all, Grandma's gentle smile as
she told her "happy trails," for Venus had the feeling
she'd never look at them through the same eyes again.

Sanford rode beside her on his big gray beast. A pack
horse, connected by rope to the saddle Venus perched on,
brought up the rear of their procession, his bulky load
waving with each step.

Venus would have much preferred the comfort of a
buggy or well-sprung wagon if their transportation had to
be primitive but she held her tongue. Yesterday had worn
her out—Buchanan's arrival, her own anxiety, the tooth-
and-nail battle getting his permission to begin "the labor
that almost wasn't" . . .

It was too blessed early for another argument.

"Miss Daltry," Sanford said, stroking the brim of his
hat. "Did anyone ever tell you that perfume is supposed
to be dabbed on, not poured on?"

He had to start right in, didn't he? Venus scowled at him.
"I only sprayed enough on him to abolish the smell."

"On *him*? Him who?"

"On *him* this creature you dictated I ride."

"You sprayed your horse with perfume?"

Venus heard the baffled amusement in the question
and felt obligated to defend herself. "The smell of horse
is disgusting and I don't want the stink clinging to my

clothes. If I must sit on one of their wretched backs I will at least strive to make it bearable."

"I can guarran-damn-tee you that *that* is hardly an improvement!"

"I'll have you know that a gentleman gave me this fragrance for my birthday. It is a very expensive import from Paris."

"He should have left it there."

Was it just her? Or did Buchanan find fault with all ladies? Land's sake, he could use a few lessons in charm from C.J. or Lee! "If you don't like it, don't smell it."

"That's easier said than done, princess. When I lost my sight, my other senses became more acute. A sort of compensation, I guess. But there are times—now for instance —when I wish my nose wasn't this keen."

"So plug the blessed thing," Venus muttered under her breath.

"I can also hear better than most."

"Oh, and I suppose you read minds, too."

"Only when there's a thought worth reading."

"Then read this . . ." Venus stuck out her tongue.

To her disgrace, he chuckled. "That's not a thought, that's an invitation."

Venus felt a blush steal into her cheeks. For a blind man, Buchanan saw entirely too much.

She wasn't completely naïve, due to her vast collection of suitors. Most often, though, the men she found physically attractive shared no common interests with her. And those with mutual likings wound up leaving her feeling empty as a hole-riddled bucket with their kisses.

Somewhere out there in the wild blue yonder existed a man who appealed to all her emotions. And he'd accept her just the way she was. Changing her ways to please a man was out of the question. He'd notice when she fixed her hair a certain way and when she wore a flattering dress. He'd notice when she was unhappy without her having to tell him and buy her special presents without her having to point them out. And he wouldn't give a care for her family's wealth. Instead, he'd be rich in his own right.

Yes. Somewhere out there was her ideal mate; the one who'd see her love as a gift, freely given, not a trophy; the one who'd be as good a father as her own to the children she hoped to eventually bear; the one who'd delight in the things she accomplished and support all her dreams . . .

Venus admitted her standards might be a little high. But she'd always gotten what she wanted in the past. She saw no reason to settle for anything less.

And just because she hadn't found the man yet didn't mean she wouldn't. She'd just keep searching for him.

So, in a sense, she *hadn't* lied to Buchanan when she'd told him why she needed to go West. The thought eased her conscience. Maybe she hadn't confessed the full truth, but the terms of the labor forbade anyone outside the family learning of the tradition.

Venus suspected Grandma wanted it kept mum that she was missing a hinge on her barn door. Honestly, Venus would rather that skeleton be kept in the closet, too.

"Venus!"

Jolted by the shouting of her name, Venus yanked on the reins. "What!"

Then she noticed Sanford had halted near a patch of yellow-centered fleabane growing wild alongside the road. His head was angled and his hand was planted on his hip, obviously annoyed.

"Where have you been? I've called your name ten times!"

"I wasn't listening!"

"I noticed. Would it be too much trouble to listen now? I'd appreciate an update on where the hell we are!"

She couldn't resist. "Why not use your 'acute senses'?"

His body went limp and he looked even more aggravated. "That's what I have you along for—to give me visual descriptions. Remember?"

"Oh, very well." Venus lowered the parasol shielding her milky complexion from the sun's freckling rays and scanned the area. "To the north of this road is grazing land that belongs to my family and to the south is our neighbor's land."

"What does it *look* like?"

"The land or the Moores' house sitting on top of the hill?"

"Everything," he said. But his lips didn't move.

"The land is flat mostly but has a few hills and is covered in green grass. But the Moore house is grand! It is a two-story brick building with four white columns on the front veranda and lots of pecan trees surrounding it. In the fall we can open one of the windows and simply reach out and pluck them from the limbs. Of course, this is spring so the nuts have hardly begun to grow, but I still have tea with Amy Moore. And she and her husband, William, do host the most marvelous barbecues. Why, at their gathering last month, I wore two pairs of slippers clean through dancing all night—"

"I think I've heard enough."

"—but because my gown was a divine claret velvet—all the rage in Europe, my modiste assured me—"

"Miss Daltry . . ."

"And I only had the two dyed-to-match pairs of slippers, I had to leave before dawn . . ."

"Miss—Venus . . ."

"And Garrett—that's Amy and William's son—was simply *heartsick*—"

"Venus!"

"Wha-at?" she cried, sorely vexed at his constant interruptions.

"Just stick to relating what I want to know!" he wailed.

Venus lifted her chin. "Humph!" Land's sake, he was a bore. What did she care about drab ole buffalo grass stretching from here to infinity when there were more exciting things to talk about?

She'd bet her bustle *he'd* never been invited to such a prestigious gathering. No, according to Grandma, he spent all his time visiting places far and wide. Places Venus had only dreamed of . . .

Now *there* was a topic she wouldn't mind discussing! And he'd have no reason to yell at her either since they'd be talking about him. And didn't men love to talk about themselves? Besides, she thought, she'd be spending the next year with this man—a virtual stranger. Didn't she have the right to know something about him?

"I gather you've seen lots of interesting sights, haven't you, Mr. Buchanan?" she initiated.

"Not lately," he answered drolly, spurring his horse forward.

Falling into a matching gait, Venus could've kicked herself for her bad choice of words. In the stables yesterday she'd also been unnecessarily—and unintentionally—cruel. Making the same mistake twice didn't seem very wise given the fact that they were awful close to her home and he could easily send her back.

Even so, she was curious about him. And the matter of his sight—or lack of it—had simmered in the back of her mind for most of the night. Now questions boiled. Since she'd broached the issue in a roundabout way, she decided not to mince words. "How long have you been blind anyway?"

He seemed to expect her query. "Since I was thirteen."

"Thirteen! Why, you were just a little boy!"

"There weren't any little boys in the war."

Venus deduced he meant the War Between the States. "One of our hired hands lost his leg in a battle. Is that how you lost your sight?"

She missed the stern setting of his jaw. "I was too young to fight."

"Then how did—"

"Your first lesson of survival, Miss Daltry, is don't pester a man about his past," he exploded. "Some don't take kindly to nosy prying."

Venus stared at his severe expression. Land's sake, he possessed a fuse shorter than a Chinese firecracker! "Pardon me. I didn't realize it was such a touchy subject. I just thought that since we're partners, I deserved to know a few things about you."

"Then spare me and don't think."

Venus bristled at the arrogant remark. Questions continued to churn within her but his display of quick temper warned her against posing them. Instead she said, "Well,

I'm not as secretive. You can ask me anything and *I* won't bite *your* head off. Go ahead. Ask me anything."

"Don't you ever shut up?"

She did then! Honestly, she thought *she* was grumpy in the mornings!

They lapsed into silent discord.

And Venus grew bored.

With nothing better to do than listen to the steady clop of iron-shod hooves making contact with the earthen road, she studied Buchanan. He'd forsaken the duster in deference to the bright warmth pounding on their backs. His nankeen-clad legs loosely flanked the gray and his sturdy black leather boots were lax in the triangular steel stirrups. The ease with which he rode showed he was a person who spent a vast amount of time in the saddle.

Unlike herself.

She'd been on the sorrel less than an hour but already her body ached with the strain of staying erect; Buchanan's rocked smoothly with his steed's motion.

Venus tried massaging the stiffness settling in her lower back and encountered the barrier of whalebone under her waist-fitted jacket.

The morning advanced and her aches spread. A cramp had developed in her right knee. Allie had tried telling her that western saddles were not designed for riding sideways but Venus seldom listened to her little sister's advice. Sitting astride was hardly ladylike. Furthermore, she doubted her bustle would retain its saucy bell-like shape stuffed between the cantle and the quilt serving as a bedroll.

Venus glared with envy at Buchanan again. Between his shoulder blades, sweat dampened the dingy white of his baggy pleated shirt. Otherwise, he appeared numb to any discomfort. In fact, he looked downright relaxed. He'd rolled his cuffs up to his elbows, uncovering muscled forearms sprinkled with bleached-brown hair that contrasted with his suntanned skin.

Venus tore her eyes away and placed her hand to her rolling stomach. Either she had been in the sun too long or the liberal dose of perfume was taking its toll on her, too. She was feeling kind of queasy all of a sudden. And light-headed.

"I want to stop now, Mr. Buchanan."

He whipped around. "It's barely noon!"

"But I'm dizzy."

"Then loosen your corset strings. Or better yet, take the contraption off."

"How do you know I wear a corset?"

"The way you talk. Breathless like."

He sounded disapproving. "Well, I won't take it off. For you to suggest such a thing is bold and disgraceful."

"Suit yourself." He shrugged. "Just don't blame me if you keel over in a swoon."

"Then you aren't goin' to stop?"

"Unless the horses need rest, not until nightfall when we make camp."

It figured. The horses received more consideration than she! "Won't you even break for lunch?"

His hand disappeared into his saddlebag and pulled out a thin strip of shriveled meat. He offered it to her.

"What's that?" she asked, frowning.

He grinned. "Lunch."

Venus snatched the piece of jerky, sulking as she nibbled on the tough beef. *My prize better be well worth this suffering.*

Over the course of the next few hours, Venus's replies to his questions were stilted and undetailed. She couldn't feel the nether part of her leg anymore and the base of her spine, she swore, was permanently imbedded in the saddle. A crowbar would not be able to pry her out of it.

She shifted now and then and wished she had the courage to stand in the stirrups as Sanford did periodically. But the way her luck was running, she'd lose her balance and wind up getting a gander at a very unpleasant side of her horse.

Venus sniffed delicately. If they'd ridden the South Pacific train out of Paradise like normal, civilized human beings, she wouldn't be suffering this torture.

Of course, Buchanan wasn't normal. Nor was he civilized. She even doubted he was entirely human.

He was a dime novelist, after all.

Finally, her endurance reached its limit. "Mr. Bu-chanan, I must insist we stop."

"We've had this conversation already."

"I know. And you were unreasonable."

"I'm still unreasonable."

"Then you go on ahead. I'll catch up."

At last, he reined in. His head slumped on his broad shoulders and a gusty sigh burst from his lungs. "Are you happy now?"

"Not quite." She was too sore to garner any triumph from winning this round.

Sanford simply scowled at her.

"Well?" she demanded. "I'm waiting!"

"For what?" He rested his hand on his corded thigh.

"For you to pretend you're a gentleman and help me down."

"I told you I'd make no allowances because you are a female. Get down yourself."

Her face flooded with angry humiliation. "I can't."

"It's not that far to the ground. Just jump."

Almost inaudibly, she whispered, "I'm stuck, Mr. Bu-chanan."

His slender brows came together with confusion. Then he swung his leg over the gray's neck and slid to the ground, letting the reins trail in the sandy soil, making a mockery of her predicament.

His cautious steps brought him around the sorrel's head and he stood in front of her. Venus shrieked when his hands landed on her thigh, inches from the most inti-mate part of her body. "How dare—"

"Hush." Briskly, his fingers followed the separation of her body and the saddle. "What the . . ."

His left hand found her shin above the high casing of her kidskin boot and moved up to where her leg crooked around the saddle horn. His bark-colored hat tumbled off his head as he buried his face in her thin woolen skirts and groaned.

Stunned, Venus gazed at the thick whiskey strands of hair draping across the union-blue of her dress. No man had ever dared such a liberty! Yet, with his bare head dropped in her lap, his breath scorching her skin under folds of cloth and numerous petticoats, and despairing noises filling Venus's ears, he looked . . . vulnerable.

Venus's heart ceased beating. Of its own accord, her arm raised itself, her fingers hovered above his skull, the urge to comfort him so powerful she felt helpless to obey.

Then he wailed, "Why me?"

And the impulse fled. Venus pushed him off her leg. "Just get me down."

"I should leave you up there. Maybe it'll teach you a lesson on how to ride a horse. Thought you'd at least know how to do that considering you live on a damn ranch . . ."

He continued ranting to himself while he freed her numb leg from the saddle horn.

Caught off guard, Venus pitched forward. His arms shot around her waist, and his solid weight took the brunt of her fall.

In his tight embrace, Venus went stock-still. The sight of his parted lips, mere whiskers away, caused her heart to sink to her belly.

Bless my soul, she marveled, *he's going to kiss me!*

Five

SANFORD STILLED, UNABLE TO MUSTER THE WILL TO MOVE.

It was as if by holding Venus Daltry, he also held time. Trapped it, froze it. With a fresh spring wind and a bluejay's flight.

He breathed in the scent of her. Not of her cloying perfume but the softness of woman beneath.

He felt her. Nearly every inch. With her arms locked around his neck, her body melding to him from chest to knee, he learned a whole lot more about Venus than he wanted. He knew where her breasts swelled under her ribbed corset, where her waist tapered in, then flared out again, where the tapes of her bustle wound around her hips, and where her thighs connected to her pelvic bones.

He experienced a swift and forbidden birth of longing. A powerful craving to know what she looked like beyond mellow, sweet butter hair and nightingale-song eyes. Blond-haired and blue-eyed described too many women.

Was Venus's skin as smooth and unmarked as he suspected? Were her cheekbones high or low? Her eyebrows thick or sparse, her lashes long and sweeping or short and dense? Was her forehead wide or narrow? Her jawline as

stubborn as he perceived? Or daintily pointed? And her
lips, full and hot? Or bowed and warm?

Jesus, he was suddenly hungry for the sight of her. For
a picture of this sassy, I'll-get-my-way-or-else goddess to
carry in his memory . . .

Hungry for a taste of her. Flower-petal skin, no-
nonsense mouth.

Caution fled and reason deserted him. His head drifted
forward, his lips parted, seeking the honey of Venus. Of
the one woman who had somehow managed to slip past
the wall of cynicism he so carefully guarded. The one
woman who had managed to stir to life something dead
inside, buried during his tender years. The one woman
who had managed to get close enough to . . .

Close enough to make him forget how dangerous her
gender was to his sanity.

Sanford jerked back and released her quickly, stricken
that he could forget who he was and who she was and
why he had avoided her kind for nineteen years. And
Venus stumbled against that godawful, gardenia-reeking
horse, her arms falling away.

Sanford cried out when an object lanced the corner of
his eye. His fingers shot to the puncture, coming away
with a sticky film he knew to be blood. "What the hell was
that?" he bellowed.

"It . . . it was my . . . my parasol."

"Your parasol," Sanford repeated tonelessly. He
turned from Venus, wiping a clammy palm down his face,
hating the fact that his hand shook. "You're carrying a
parasol, riding sidesaddle on a western seat, and wearing
a birdcage on your butt." His laugh mocked himself more
than Venus. "I knew bringing you was a mistake."

"What is that remark supposed to mean?"

*It means I've got to be one hell of a lonesome old fool if a
prissy, conceited, apple-of-daddy's-eye lady can arouse me.*
Sanford tucked his chin against his collar and a weary
breath slid from his lungs. "Never mind. Just get my rifle
off my saddle."

With detectable fear, Venus cried, "You don't plan on
shooting me for getting stuck on my horse, do you?"

Sanford grinned despite his aggravation. *There* was an entertaining idea! It sure would solve his present problems—some of them, anyway.

"Because if you do," she declared, "I'm not about to fetch the weapon for you!"

"No, Miss Daltry, I'm not going to shoot you." Sanford brushed away the wayward fall of hair tickling his eyelids. "But while we're here, the horses can rest and I might as well teach you to shoot. You'll never know when you'll have to protect yourself."

Her moment's delay suggested uncertainty. If she thought to trust her safety entirely to him, then he had a few disparaging words to offer. He had a hard enough time keeping his own carcass unmolested. But Venus surprised him with obedience. One footstep sounded louder than the other as though she limped along, and her occasional moans grew fainter the farther she moved.

Sanford steeled himself against feeling any sympathy. She might not be used to riding now, but she'd toughen up after a few days. She had to.

With grim purpose, Sanford strode to the pack horse. His foot struck an object in his path. Sanford halted. He bent down and ran his hand across the gritty, weed-patched sand. His hand knocked the familiar felt of his hat and his brows knitted together. When had he lost his hat? Usually he was so sensitive to change . . . had to be for his own safety . . .

Venus. He'd been distracted with her, by her. His fleeting attraction had been a *dis*traction.

Ah, hell! Didn't his body bear enough scars from past preoccupations? Hadn't Zeb warned him over and over not to let his mind wander—not even for a second? That, for him, mistakes of that order could prove fatal?

Sanford's neck went limp and he let the base of his head slump backward onto his shoulders. He closed his eyes, cursing her, cursing himself.

Then he plopped his hat back onto his crown and proceeded forward with renewed caution. Damn, in the future he must be more careful! More guarded. And *never* could he let Venus Daltry divert his attention again.

He treasured his life—what there was of it.

Sanford located the cache of extra bullets in one of the oil-treated burlap sacks. As an afterthought, he also grabbed a palm-sized tin and dropped it into his shirt pocket. Better to loan Venus salve for her soreness than listen to her gripe until her body adjusted.

At the same moment he turned, Venus approached. But it wasn't the blast of floral scent that arrested him . . .

It was the menacing nudge below the gun belt draped around his hips.

Sanford froze, a slender tube steely and cold as death positioned at his groin.

In less than twenty minutes she had caught him unawares twice.

Fear clutched Sanford's middle with vicious talons when Venus just stood there, poking the rifle barrel against his front pocket. A vision formed of Venus, sulky and indifferent to the threat she presented. And that made his situation more critical. One reckless move . . .

"Venus," he croaked. "Move the gun. *Slowly.*"

Detecting a strained edge to the normally commanding tone, Venus's glance shifted from the stain on her cuff to Sanford's ashen face.

Then her gaze lowered and she saw what had caused his alarm. The long brass-bound weapon she cradled in her arms happened to be pointing at a very susceptible region of his body. Shamefaced, Venus swung the barrel aside and planted the oak stock against the ground. "Sorry."

He said nothing; he just sweated.

When her gaze fixed on him once more, Venus wondered why he so intrigued her. So what if she saw promise in his scruffy looks? So what if those drowsy, liquor-brown eyes of his summoned thoughts of cozy fireplaces and cupid arrows? His bossy manner rubbed her the wrong way. Nice words were not part of his vocabulary and getting a compliment from him would be like pulling a molar. She found she missed the gallant worship of her multitude of beaus.

No, all he thought of was shooting and traveling and writing silly books no one with an ounce of taste dared read. Oh, yes, she added silently. She must not forget his determination to make her into the "ideal survivalist."

More bewildering was her own reaction to his nearness, now and before. She was glad he hadn't tried kissing her, she mentally insisted. Why, that beard of his would no doubt scrape the skin clean off her face! So why, then, had disappointment lodged in her belly when he'd spurned the opportunity? It made no sense!

Venus wondered if maybe Grandma Minerva's daffiness was catching. And maybe she'd caught it. She wouldn't welcome a kiss from a man of Buchanan's ilk.

No, Venus speculated, watching him blot sweat from his brow with a faded kerchief. The type of woman who suited his character was the kind that slaved over a campfire cooking wild game on a spit. Blistered her poor hands riding and shooting at his side. And, God forbid, dressed in *calico*.

Land's sake, it gave her hives just thinking of such an existence!

And yet, when he touched her next, his palm on her wrist sent a shock wave clear to the bone. Shaken by the force and mystery of the sensation, her limbs refused to move.

She stared at his seeking fingers as they trailed down the back of her hand. Those fingers, long and lean, the nails clipped short. That broad hand, the knuckles etched with lines, such a dark contrast to her own light skin.

Her mouth went dry as shorn wool.

Suddenly her hand was empty and Sanford had possession of the rifle. "*Never* point a loaded firearm at a person unless you intend to shoot them," he scolded. "You just shaved ten years off my life!"

She wanted to make some wisecrack, but her brain had gone to seed.

"Let's get these horses off the road."

Buchanan gathered three sets of reins then laid his

forearm on her shoulder. The instinct to race ahead, to flee from his presence as if he were black sin itself, nearly overwhelmed Venus. One thing restrained her; her promise to act as his eyes.

A measure of self-control returned as she led him through knee-high, feather-topped grasses. Underfoot, purple Tahoka daisies were ground into the earth. Venus stopped a safe distance from the road. Once her tutor left the reins to dangle, the horses bowed their regal heads and munched on grama grass.

"There are a variety of positions to shoot from," Sanford instructed without preamble. "Standing, like so . . ." He lifted the rifle to his shoulder socket and spread his legs. "Or squatting . . ." He bent his knees in demonstration, resting one on the sandy turf for balance. "Or lying prone." He stretched out on the grass on his stomach.

Then he sprang back to his feet. "Which way do you prefer?"

Venus pursed her lips. "A lady does not lie in the dirt."

"Then don't be a lady, Miss Daltry. Be a woman. A woman does what it takes to survive regardless of convention or what is considered proper. Even if it means 'lying in the dirt.' "

"I prefer to stand," she said haughtily.

"Good choice." He couldn't handle her being a woman anyway, Sanford thought. As a lady, she was easier to withstand: stuffy, selfish, exasperating.

But Venus Daltry as a woman . . . heaven help him. His glimpse into that aspect of her had been brief but incredibly disturbing. It still staggered him when he pondered how close he'd come to kissing her.

With a curt shake of his head, he stepped away from Venus, not trusting his roguish tendencies. "Put the stock against your shoulder as I had it."

"It's heavy. Why can't I use your pistol?"

"One shooting lesson at a time. Master the rifle first. You'll get used to the weight." Sanford braced his hand under the raised barrel of the gun to hold it steady. His other hand remained stiffly at his side. "Now, view your target through the sight at the end of the barrel and squeeze the trigger," he told her, removing his hold.

"What am I shooting at?"

"At anything out there."

"There's nothing but grass and sagebrush."

"No trees? Fenceposts?"

"Well, there is one tree way yonder, a short, crooked thing with bushy branches."

"Possibly a post oak. Aim for the lowest branch." Hastily, Sanford added, "Oh, and watch out for—"

Crack!

"—the kick," he finished lamely.

But Venus didn't care. Excitement rushed through her veins, a burst of victory so pulsing, she thought she might explode like the smoking weapon in her grip.

She leaped to her feet, unperturbed by her smashed bustle or the hazel stains on her rich blue skirt. "Did I hit it? Did I hit it?"

"I don't think so. The bullet whizzed skyward."

"Ohhh," she wailed plaintively.

Sanford chuckled. "Try again. With a repeating rifle, reloading after each shot isn't necessary. You just pull down the lever behind the trigger guard, cocking it, then fire afterward. Repeat the process until you run out of cartridges."

Venus missed the branch over and over, and grew frustrated with her failure to hit the distant target. But a hunger for the dynamic thrust of speed and might, a lust to absorb the weapon's authority motivated her to continue until her hands went numb and her shoulder burned and her bottom sustained bruises from falling.

Finally she exhausted the round of ammunition. Sanford retrieved the gun, and while he reloaded it, he explained, "Remember that shooting at an object is not the same as shooting at a person. So when you sight your target—in this case, the tree branch—pretend it's someone you hate. Picture the person in your mind. The blood. The guts. All the gory details. That way if you ever fire on a human being, your conscience won't get in the way of defending yourself."

"But I don't hate anyone," Venus protested, a bit disturbed by his advice. She wasn't sure she was capable of such an intensely negative emotion, not even for Sanford Buchanan.

"Then pretend you do. The idea is to get used to a means of defense and its consequences."

She gazed at his implacable face with awe. "Can you take a life so pitilessly? Without remorse?"

"If I have to, yes," he said matter-of-factly. "And don't look at me as if I'm some kind of monster. There is time for remorse after the deed—when I'm still in one piece to feel."

Venus moved her head from side to side. "You have a frightening sort of logic, Mr. Buchanan."

"I cannot control my will to live—it is inborn—an instinct predominate in most people who have no yen for dying." He pushed the rifle toward her. "Take your best shot, Miss Daltry."

Suddenly disgusted and beginning to feel the effects of the drill, Venus deferred. "No, thanks. I think I've hurt something." She brushed her hand across her backside, making contact with her damaged bustle. She twisted around. "Bless my soul, I've ruined my dress improver! And my gown . . . and—oh, darn it. I broke a nail."

Sanford's smile faded. Venus knew it without looking, in the same way she knew when a cloud passed over the sun and left the world dim and chilly.

"Do it again until you hit that mark. When you are involved in a life-or-death situation there won't be a damn soul concerned about your clothes or manicures."

Venus winced at the cold disdain in his voice. Unbidden tears welled in the corners of her eyes, blurring his rigid form as he sought his horse with uncanny instinct.

His moods confused her. In the blink of an eye he switched from blue skies to black thunder. Venus stroked the plate of brass connecting butt to barrel, her heart feeling stomped on. She replayed the last few minutes in her mind, trying to piece together clues to what had prompted his outburst. Was he angry because of her awkward aim? Or because she wasn't a mirror image of his sadistic, perfectionist self?

That didn't seem fair, she thought, swiping her tears away. She came from a genteel environment where her days were spent with tasks befitting a lady: needlework, correspondence, teas, dress fittings, dances . . .

Blowing harmless tree branches into the next county had never been penciled in to her schedule! Allie's maybe, but not hers!

The more she thought on it, the more she decided that her younger sister would have been better suited for this labor. Yet Allie's twentieth birthday wasn't for another few years. And, Venus reminded herself, she had accepted—both Grandma's labor and Buchanan's silly conditions.

But as she watched him whisper into the gray's fuzzy, perked ear, outrage began to simmer inside her. When the animal reared his majestic head then swung it from side to side, she saw Sanford caress Ranger's neck with a calming hand. It appeared the ill-tempered author demanded obedience from everyone!

Well, she might have agreed to learn his silly survival skills but she did not have to abide his domineering ways. A man had never been allowed to boss her around before. She was not about to permit it now!

Venus sucked in her cheeks and looked at the rifle she held. Hit the mark, huh? She'd like to see Buchanan hit the blessed thing. That would teach him not to expect the impossible!

Then, a wicked smile gradually spread from cheek to cheek. What a delightfully daring idea!

Venus lifted her chin. "Buchanan? If you want the tree dead, *you* kill it!"

He looked startled by the challenge, jerking in her direction and cocking his head. He recovered swiftly, though, and as grim strides carried him to her side, Venus wished her tongue would stop running ahead of her common sense. But she refused to cower. She stood boldly, holding the rifle at the uppermost end of the barrel for his searching fingers to find.

If Sanford did anything uncertainly, it was walk. He took slow, measured steps and used his hands as feelers. Nothing moved but legs and hands.

Except now.

He seemed to know exactly where she stood, precisely where the rifle dangled, for he stole it from her hand and jammed it against his shoulder. "If that tree was a number on a clock face, what number would it be?"

The brusque question took her by surprise. Even so, Venus judged the position of his aim and the target and said, "The three."

And before she could say "Zeus," a half-dozen shots exploded through the field, the echo lingering long after Sanford lowered his arm.

Stunned, Venus heard nothing above the ringing in her ears, saw nothing but the result of his rapid fire through wisps of smoke—a drooping oak limb.

Wide-eyed, she gasped, "How did you *do* that?"

"I practiced," he drawled. And she thought she caught a flicker of pleasure in his features, but it disappeared too quickly to be sure. "Now if I can do that," he continued, "*you* can do that."

He'd issued his own challenge.

She took the rifle numbly. "Mr. Buchanan?"

He paused in the act of turning away.

"You . . . you weren't picturing me as that tree . . . were you?"

A full-blown laugh was his reply, and when the quaking sound ebbed, he whistled for his horse. Then, he threaded his hand through a strap of the dutiful animal's bridle, and Ranger led him to where the other horses were hobbled.

Venus sighed and continued with her lesson until her arms were dead weights and so quivery she could no longer hold the weapon to her shoulder. Soon after, Sanford deemed it time to head out again. She still hadn't managed to shoot with any direction but she vowed to match Buchanan's accuracy one day. Her brothers would never let her live down the pitiful fact that a *blind* man could beat her!

As she approached the sorrel, she found herself facing a more immediate dilemma, though: how to mount the beast. The last thing she wanted was to get back in that saddle after the morning's misery, yet neither did she relish walking. Choosing the lesser of two evils, she opted to ride and called to Sanford for a leg up.

His hand already gripped his own pommel and his foot rested in the stirrup. He gave her a look of annoyance. Nonetheless, he came to her aid, boosting her onto the fragrant animal with as much care as he might give a sack of potatoes.

Venus cried out as she threw her leg over the opposite side of the horse's girth, sitting clothespin as the saddle intended, yet feeling as if she were splitting down the middle.

She closed her eyes against the raw pain. But once they were under way, she discovered the indecent position was less perilous than her earlier seat.

She led them on a westerly course. Ranger followed the lazy pace, his hot, horsey breaths blowing against her right thigh the entire four miles they traveled along the wagon ruts. Then one of the many creeks branching off the Clear Fork of the Brazos River cut into their path and Sanford leaned forward, effectively halting the steed.

Weariness lay on Venus's shoulders like an iron mantle. If Sanford wanted to stop for the night, then she was not about to argue—this once, anyway. She'd caught herself nodding off in the saddle twice so far. Any place flat to rest her aching bones sounded like heaven—even if it was a patch of dirt beside a bug-infested stream.

Sanford dismounted with an ease she envied and began unloading gear from the pack horse. "I'll take care of the horses while you gather wood for the fire."

Venus dragged herself off the sorrel. "You gather the wood. I'm washing my face then going to sleep."

"Not so fast, princess. We made a deal—unless you'd rather forget it," he taunted.

Venus glared at his smirking face. "Not on your life." Oh, *God,* she wished this year were over with!

She scanned the area around the site. Sword-leaved

bases and center-shooting stems of yucca plants abounded, the top flowers a pale delight against the monotonous green grass. She recognized the pecan trees and a smattering of oak, but not a broken limb or twig littered the ground. Even she was aware that green wood did not burn.

"Mr. Buchanan, unless you claim log-birthing in that bag of powers you carry, we're out of luck for firewood."

He dropped his bedroll and the sack containing cookware. "This is cattle country. Cow chips make sufficient fuel and the sagebrush makes good tinder."

"Cow chips!" Venus cried. "Do you mean *dung*?"

His lips twitched and he nodded.

"I'd rather drink turpentine than touch animal droppings!"

He shrugged. "Fine. Freeze, starve, and become coyote bait, then." Suddenly he cupped his ear. "Oh, I think I hear them yowling out there now."

Venus growled epithets as she dug for her gloves and fetched the disgusting dried patties strewn across the turf.

His amusement continued to gall even after Venus filled her stomach with charred biscuits and smoked ham. She settled down into her thick rosebud-printed quilt, sucking on her burned finger.

Disparaging thoughts of Buchanan faded as her eyelids drifted shut. The twilight of sleep started to claim her, and Venus succumbed, growing lighter, lighter . . .

Sanford's cultured voice and a painful thumb against her hip destroyed the peace. "All right, take this down. 'Slick Drayson raced out of Cottonmouth Bend like the hounds of hell were nipping at his—' "

Venus's eyes snapped open. "Hold it." She flipped onto her side and spied a thin leather-bound journal, a bone-stemmed quill, and a small jar of ink scattered near her pallet. "What are you doin'?"

"Chapter one. Okay— 'Nipping at his heels. The summer sun blazed on his bare head—' "

"I'm suppose to take dictation after the day I've put in?"

"That's what I have you along for. Where was I? Oh.

'Blazed on his bare head, so hot his ebony hair felt afire.'"

He rambled on. Venus heard about a man named Slick clutching a pouch of winnings and a deed to a saloon to his chest as he made his escape from a foul hustler named "Gunns" Murphy. But she refused to listen to a word.

She flung the quilt over her ears, pressing it there with her arms. Buchanan was surely a quart short of a full keg if he expected her to write his silly story now! She was exhausted! Why, she hadn't been able to dredge up the energy to brush her hair—and if she must forgo *that* priority, what in Zeus's name made him think she could pick up a pen!

He could . . . stuff his quills where the sun didn't shine for all she cared!

Stubbornly, she blocked out the sound of his voice. He'd get the hint eventually.

And a few minutes later when he asked, "Are you getting all this, Miss Daltry? Venus?" Her name on his lips was the last she heard.

Six

SANFORD LAY ON HIS THIN BEDROLL WITH HIS HAT TIPPED OVER his face. The pesky little gnat had fallen asleep on him. He felt no rancor, though. His spirits were still soaring from his earlier success at scoring the tree. Venus had dared him purely out of spite—he banked on that—but it didn't stop the warm gush of pride flowing through him even now.

He had impressed her. Not intentionally, but he had. Maybe that shouldn't mean much since Venus Daltry was simply his business associate and student, and her opinion of him wasn't going to change how he felt about her. Yet, it felt damn good to be able to show off and have somebody—a woman—notice.

Even a tender-footed society priss slumbering six feet away.

Rarely did he hear commendable words regarding skills he had strived so hard to perfect. Not that he needed them, he convinced himself, yet he preferred them over condemnations and platitudes.

Or in Zeb's case, nothing at all.

She certainly wasn't Zeb, though, he thought as he listened to the gentle rise and fall of her breathing. And the lack of raucous snores had nothing to do with the difference.

His thoughts started tripping over each other. On one hand, he admitted that she had fared pretty well for their first day out. They hadn't covered as many miles as he had hoped, but neither did he want to break her before they'd truly begun this trip.

And yet, he didn't feel safe with her. Probably wouldn't for some time to come—if ever. Today's training was mild compared to what he had in store for her. His brow creased and he clasped his hands under his head. So much left to teach her and so little time to do it. For both their sakes.

On the other hand, in order for Venus to learn the proper skills, he could not avoid being close to her. Not as close as when she had landed in his arms, but close enough to make him uncomfortable. He might have control over his mind—he was able to distance himself from her—but his body . . . there arose a problem. A very obvious one.

Against his will, Venus Daltry evoked natural, manly needs in him. Over the years he'd grown used to denying his carnal desires. A few minutes of satisfaction wasn't worth the keen emptiness he always felt afterward. But building a relationship with a woman held even less appeal; a relationship needed a stronger foundation than lust. For it to survive, there must be love and faith and security. Since he had none of those to offer, he found it a fruitless effort to pursue one.

Knowing this, why, then, did he have such a difficult time controlling these spontaneous and unwelcome physical responses around Venus?

He crossed his legs at the ankles and shifted on his thin bed, the cool night air his only blanket. Even now her curves and swells and satin voice haunted him. Played havoc with his bloodstream and heart rate.

She was neither bordello whore nor lusty woman, but elite lady born and bred. And of the females he had encountered in his lifetime, those were the ones he had the least appetite for.

Maybe his neglected needs were to blame for Venus arousing him. And if that was the case, then they'd just have to remain neglected. He had more pressing matters to concern himself with, such as living long enough to write the book he had contracted to write.

He chewed his lower lip, catching a few whiskers with flesh. First and foremost—thanks to an impetuous promise—was preparing his inexperienced assistant for their journey. Shooting, hunting, reading signs, gauging weather changes . . .

Then he needed to plot Slick Drayson's story. Hell, it wasn't even titled yet. His mind had been too occupied in dealing with his disrupted life!

No more, though, he resolved. His goals set, he figured come morning he could put into motion accomplishing them. And hope he survived until then.

"Wake up, Miss Daltry. It's time to ride."

She wished he *would* have shot her. A quick killing would have been more merciful than this slow, painful torture Buchanan seemed bent on putting her through.

Venus rolled onto her stomach, swallowing an agonized moan. Every muscle burned with pain. She lifted her hand weakly then let it fall, the action costing more agony than she could bear. "Go away, Sanford," she mumbled, ignoring formality.

He didn't go away. He wedged the toe of his boot between her hipbone and the quilt and flipped her over.

"Ow!" Venus cried, rudely awakened by invisible daggers lancing every battered muscle in her body. She lay on her back a moment, struggling for a calm breath, blinking back tears. "That *hurt*," she finally whimpered.

"You'll be sore for a while but lying there just makes it worse." Casually, he tossed a small round tin to her.

Venus waited for it to land on the quilt, then slid her hand over to the container. "What's this?"

"A liniment for your muscles."

She pried off the cap and swerved away from the lethal odor. She was certainly awake now! "It smells like the salve used on horses!"

"It is."

"You expect me to rub horse liniment on my body?"

Either he didn't hear or pretended not to. His back was to her, his hands gripping his lean denim-clad hips, and he sniffed the air. Then he stooped to run his hand over the ground.

Unsympathetic rat! Venus couldn't imagine *moving*! Her legs were raw and bunched, her bottom felt like a chopping block, and her shoulder ached as though it had been clamped in a vise all night. She chanced a dreaded look at it . . . and noticed a hideous purple bruise marring her creamy skin. The sight was enough to compel her to apply the noxious salve.

"We need to hit the trail," he said, rising. "We'll have rain by tonight."

Glancing at the clear, cloudless sky, Venus then awarded Buchanan a skeptical look. *The whole world is daft!*

Nonetheless, as soon as she had smeared the greasy paste over her limbs, she struggled to her feet. Her pained groans were broken by plenty of mild curses as she tripped and tangled in snares of her own making. "Blessed blankets . . . stupid petticoats . . . darn buttons . . ." Finally redressed, she squared her stiff shoulders.

Then she went completely still and inhaled a hiss when Buchanan ordered, "Next time, don't get up until you have checked your body and bedroll. Could be there's a snake curled on or near you for heat."

Ignoring her thunder-stricken gasp, he forged on, "And make sure you shake out your boots before putting them on in case a critter is hiding inside. After you've dressed, pack up your gear, saddle your horse and remove the hobbles—"

"I thought Lincoln freed the slaves," she muttered, but did as she was told, not willing to test Sanford's threat to send her home if she didn't pull her weight.

He lingered over a robust-smelling cup of coffee while she set to work. The moment she finished breaking her back loading the saddle onto the sorrel, though, she al-

most wished he would send her home—prize or no prize.
Where she found the strength to tighten the cinches, load
the packs—to simply walk!—she didn't know. But some
part of her was stubborn, proud, and loathed the notion
of failure.

And she knew, *knew* that whatever she must endure,
whatever Sanford-the-master threw at her, whatever
sorry conditions and pitiful inconveniences awaited her,
she'd grab them by the horns and wrestle with them until
this labor was done.

Her list of chores completed, Venus then stood beside
the sorrel and began her morning ritual. She scrubbed
her face until every last speck of grain was erased and her
cheeks glowed with health, and she brushed her teeth
until they were as lustrous as pearls.

Now all she had left was the artwork upon the clean
canvas of her features. Let Sanford bluster and bluff to
his heart's content, she thought scathingly. Nothing or no
one stopped her from her daily grooming.

"Aren't you ready yet, Miss Daltry?" Sanford demanded. "I'd like to get moving sometime before noon!"

"I'll be through in a minute." His reflection in her
pocket mirror cocked his hip to the left and yanked on
the frayed brim of his hat.

"You said that ten minutes ago. What's taking you so
long?"

"Ah'm pottin' on mah akah."

"In English, please!"

Venus closed her mouth and rolled her cherry-red lips
together. Her appearance did not meet her usual standards of perfection but it was the best she could achieve
under the circumstances. "I said, I'm putting on my
makeup."

She capped the stick of lip coloring and tucked the
metal tube into the cosmetic bag hanging on the sad-
dlehorn. Her wood-framed pocket mirror and powder jar
joined the collection of various cosmetic brushes, pencils,
glass vessels, and cleansing tins. Then Venus began counting aloud the strokes she applied to her hair with a silver-
plated brush.

Sanford merely gaped at her. "You're joking, right?"

"I never joke about preserving my looks." Not when she spent such a vast amount of time and money for the very best in cosmetics! Her choices ranged from creams to keep her complexion clear and moist and flawless, and soft-hued powders to bring out her most attractive features—namely the glorious shower of gilded hair and the bewitching blue of her eyes.

Sanford spread his hands wide. "But there's no one out here to *see* you!"

"True," Venus conceded. There wasn't a soul in sight and Buchanan, well, he had no sight at all. If he did, he might appreciate the care she took with her beauty. "Even so," she went on haughtily, "I expect we'll run into people at some point. And I won't be caught looking like a hoyden when we do. I *do* have a reputation to maintain."

He fell into a sullen silence, whisking his hat off his head and gazing toward the sky. Venus bent at the waist to reach the underside of her hair with the flat-bristled brush. *Thirty, thirty-one, thirty-two . . .*

The next thing she knew he was standing in front of her. Venus parted the golden curtain of her hair to peer up at him through her long, kohl-tinted lashes.

Dark brown strands of hair whipped against his beard, catching and holding before being torn away again by the wind. His stance was that of a warrior. And his bearded visage looked fierce.

Grandma Minerva would liken him to Mars.

A sensation of foreboding trickled through Venus. Her namesake, Venus of the myths, had taken the Roman god of war as one of her lovers.

Venus quickly twisted her locks into a rope, coiled it about her crown, and stabbed pins in place. That comparison didn't sit well at all! Sanford Buchanan was a labor—not a lover!

"Venus . . ."

She rose and shut her eyes as if the action would make him disappear. Make this sudden too-stuffy-to-breathe feeling go away.

But land's sake, the way he said her name—VEE-nus instead of Vayn-IS, like her family and friends—sent her heart to thumping like a happy dog's tail.

And she wished he wouldn't stand so close, smelling of fire smoke and coffee grounds and fresh washed denim, as if the odors had been weaved into his simple attire. It didn't seem fair that he could look this clean, this confident first thing in the morning when she herself needed at least an hour of fussing over herself before she felt ready to face the world.

At length, she asked, "Yes, Mr. Buchanan?" Amazing how calm her voice sounded, she marveled, considering her quivery nerves.

"Let's dispense with the formalities." He flashed his teeth with false amiability. "Other than cosmetics, what else did you pack?"

One glimpse of that wicked smile and those fluttering eyes made Venus wonder why he had such interest in her belongings. "Just essentials . . ."

He shut his eyes and muttered, "That's what I'm afraid of." Opening his eyes again, he angled his head. "Mind if I . . . ?"

Venus wanted to refuse, but Sanford was strong-willed enough to do as he pleased with or without her consent. Opting to give him permission rather than have him ransack her packs, she stepped back. "Be my guest."

His hands slipped under the flap of the left saddlebag slung over the sorrel's back. Venus wrung her hands. He withdrew a palmful of ruffles and his shoulders slumped. Wary, Venus swallowed the lump in her throat.

He rubbed the embroidered taffeta hem between his fingers then fished for another—this a wad of silk. Then a filmy fabric, the fine lawn of her chemise. "What's this?"

"My clothes," she replied dumbly.

He nodded, yet on his face was an expression of lazy resignation.

Rolling her eyes, Venus squeezed between him and the pack and withdrew one gown. "This is silk." She slapped his hand upon the sleek material then stole it back and shook it free of wrinkles. "Watered silk to be specific

. . . my evening gown . . . a mite rumpled but pressed it is divinity itself. It is cut to lie delicately off the shoulders, has a sloping heart-shaped neckline and a draping train. Blue is my best color, and in this gown, I put to shame all other girls."

Venus laid it in Sanford's limp arms and grabbed another soft bundle. "And this is my afternoon walking dress. It's a rather bland shade of puce but the vertical burgundy stripes flatter my figure and the saucy cream bow fits delightfully over my bustle." The third she stared at pensively. "I hope I didn't ruin this morning gown. It has the most darling crepe rosettes on each tier of flounce but they are the dickens to unsquash . . ."

Venus paid no notice to Sanford's dumbfounded look. Fashion was what she lived for! And now that she'd begun listing her treasures, and he waited patiently for each detail, she was unable to stop. He certainly could be an attentive listener when he so chose!

She dug deeper into the bag, eager to show him her necklaces and earbobs and all the other accessories she'd brought to complement each dress. She tossed aside the canteen Allie had stuffed in there, on a quest for more baubles. Scooping her finds into Sanford's arms atop the gowns, Venus squealed in delight with each new find.

And when she emptied the one saddlebag, she rounded the sorrel to investigate the other bag. *That's* where her ribbons were hiding! And her scented soaps . . . the extra bustle she'd packed . . . two ankle-length petticoats . . . a small pouch containing items for her female cycle . . . the coin purse Daddy had pressed into her hand before leaving home . . . "Why, I'm ready for any occasion!" She clapped her hands in glee.

His face grave, his tone dark, he asked, "What about a funeral?"

Seven

THE TYRANT BURIED HER THINGS.

Venus argued. She cajoled. She snatched things from his hand and he snatched them back again. Nothing she said or did dissuaded him from his purpose. Mute frustration ate at her as she salvaged what she could from the hole before he tossed in another spadeful of dirt. Clods of sandy clay landed with a hollow thump upon her possessions—upon her spirit.

On the brink of hysteria, she shouted, "What gives you the right to destroy my possessions?"

Sanford leaned against the shovel handle and thumbed his hat toward the back of his head. "If I wanted to destroy them, I would have burned the heap—or dumped them in the creek with stone weights. Think of this as . . . internment." He grinned at his own reasoning.

But Venus was in no mood to be reasoned with. "You are the meanest, lowest bully I've ever had the misfortune to meet!"

The insult barely grazed him. All he did was sigh deeply then continue shoveling. "Think of me what you will but we made a bargain. Your saddlebags should have been stocked with survival gear."

"In my world this *is* survival gear!"

"Well, you're in *my* world now, princess." Using the sole of his boot he stomped the area tight. A bend in the creek marked the grave's location. "As soon as we happen upon a store, we will outfit you with durable clothing, camping supplies, medical kit, and the like. And harsh as you may think me, maybe the day will come when you'll realize I'm doing you a favor."

Venus held angry tears in check. A favor—ha! He'd buried her beautiful clothes! Her jewelry, her ribbons . . . and anything else she had not succeeded in wresting from his thieving hands. And he'd even pocketed her money pouch so she could not replace the items behind his back! "Why didn't you just stick me in that hole, too? You've made it perfectly clear that you think I'm as frivolous as my belongings."

He attached the shovel to the pack horse. "Because, Miss Daltry, I think there's hope for you yet."

Venus stared at the fresh mound of dirt for long minutes, her lips quivering, giving no indication she'd heard him. *He's going to pay for this,* she swore. Her gaze darted to the azure sky, to the fingers of autumn-squash light fanning from the eastern sun, to the new shoots of grama grass struggling for a place between stringier roots of buffalo grass. Maybe this was Buchanan's world, but what was wrong with bringing a little bit of hers along?

Nothing, that's what, she told herself.

She considered waiting for him to ride off, as he sometimes threatened to do, then digging everything up. But a dread of him discovering her deed, then truly destroying the expensive and good-quality items dampened that idea.

To Hades with him! If he thought to control her every action with brute strength or intimidation, he'd soon learn he was wasting his time. She had not gained her level of popularity by being submissive. And she wasn't about to start surrendering to a man's whims just because he ordered it. Labor or not, there was a limit to her tolerance.

Venus grabbed hold of the saddle horn and crooked

her leg as far as possible. It took two tries and plenty of hopping around on one foot before she got her boot to catch in the stirrup. Thank heavens he hadn't seen the spectacle she made of herself before she had managed to swing her left leg over the sorrel's rear. It would give him something else to taunt her about.

Adjusting her skirt to conceal her ankles, she glowered as he mounted his stallion in one fluid motion. *Show-off.*

Well, at least he hadn't gotten his grubby hands on her cosmetic bag. That was some consolation. If anything happened to her beauty products . . . Venus shuddered. Without the artificial aids she used to enhance her looks she would be like . . . a diamond without its luster! Satin without its sheen!

Without her cosmetics, why, she'd be absolutely . . . dull! Venus shuddered at the thought.

For reassurance, she clutched the brocade pouch to her bosom as if the bottles within were children and she their protective mother. Then Venus fished inside for her perfume bottle. The delicious essence of gardenias flavored the crude odor of horseflesh as she gave the gelding his daily fumigation.

"Oh, not that again!" came Sanford's bellow. "Those fumes just wore off!"

With a sly glance and a smirky grin, she squeezed the cloth pump and squirted Ranger with a healthy dose, too. Silently, the second civil war of the century was declared.

Sanford ran his hand down Ranger's mane. The horse heeded the mute command to press on slowly. At the base of the rise, Ranger pawed the ground once, the signal for cattle in the area. That in itself did not alarm Sanford. The two backward steps warning him of humans close by did.

Under ordinary circumstances, he supposed, mere caution would be stirring in his gut. But the presence of the lady at his side awakened an anxiety that coiled around his vitals. In spite of his resolve to expose her to the same experiences as he would a greenhorn lad, he could not suppress the beliefs his father had instilled in him before his death: that the gentler sex should be protected and sheltered from danger at all costs. Knowing he could not possibly live up to his father's idea of what made up an honorable man, Sanford repressed his grief.

Venus was offered the chance to back out but she had insisted on coming along; therefore she had to learn to depend on herself. And if danger awaited them, then he figured this was as good a time as any for her to gain mettle.

And as he listened to the scuffing sound coming from his right, his tongue cleaved to the roof of his mouth. He identified the mild grating noise—Venus was using the respite to file her nails. *God knew, she needed mettle.*

Again, a stroke of mane directed the horse forward. Plaintive lowing greeted Sanford at the top of the hill. He twined his fingers through Ranger's mane in case the situation called for a fast getaway. "What's down there?" he asked Venus.

The scuffing sound ceased momentarily. "A bunch of cows." She resumed filing.

His eyes shut with exasperation. Why'd she have to be sulky now? Then again, she'd been in a sour mood all morning, ever since he had disposed of her frivolities. Apparently, she was the type to hold a grudge.

Sanford wished she'd picked a better time, though. "I know there are cows. I can smell them. I can also smell singed hair and hot irons. What I don't know is if it's safe to hail the camp or if we should be running for our lives."

"Of course it's safe—unless my brother plans on running you down with his lariat!"

Sanford shook his head in confusion. "Your brother?"

"Lee. He and a group of his men are down by the chuckwagon—eating lunch from the looks of it. In fact, he's just spotted us and is heading our way. Yoo-hoo, Le-ee! Just wait till I tell him what you did to my things, Sanford Buchanan."

Sanford brushed off the empty threat. Brother or no brother, Venus was in his care until this book was written. How he dealt with her was his business. Besides, he was too busy grappling with the news she'd imparted to worry about an unknown relative avenging the loss of her clothing. "Are you telling me that we've been traveling for a day and a half, and we haven't even left your family's spread?"

"Not hardly. Although this is technically Hercules's land, he is still a Daltry, and the Daltry lands extend all the way to a couple miles this side of Abilene."

Sanford flexed his jaw in vexation. Sure, knowing they weren't wandering into a den of rustlers or a gang of bandits was some relief. But Venus could have told him that right from the start and spared him the anxiety! By damn, that was her job! To inform him of his surroundings so he could make preparations accordingly.

But, no. If he didn't ask the exact question, he didn't receive an exact answer. It was never this way with Uncle Zeb. Zeb anticipated his needs before Sanford knew he needed them!

What an idiot she probably thought him. And though he didn't give two hoots about how Venus regarded him, the unfair judgment rankled. Especially when he'd strived all these years to prove to an ignorant society that his blindness didn't affect his mind. That was one of the advantages of being an author. The anonymity. Folks who read his books were privy to nothing but his writing style unless he chose otherwise. If they didn't like his books, it wasn't because of a personal aversion to his body's disorder—it was because the story did not suit their preference in reading material. He could deal with that. What he couldn't deal with were people who considered him less of a person—less of a man—because he lacked the use of his eyes.

Not everyone held the same preconceived notions, he conceded. But what of this . . . Lee? The oldest son, he remembered, whose given name was Hercules. The name itself denoted invincibility. Confidence. Control. A man with a name like that probably didn't have a trouble in the world, Sanford surmised. Probably never had an obstacle to overcome. So what kind of reception would he receive from this faultless brother?

As the advancing hoofbeats halted, he figured he was about to find out.

" 'Lo, Venus," Lee called, out of breath. Then, inhaling deeply, he remarked, "Gardenias this time, huh?"

This time? Sanford supposed his bewilderment showed, for Lee confided, "She's forever dousing the livestock with perfume. She's been doing it since she was five. One year, our whole remuda reeked of Lily of the Valley."

In her defense, Venus said, "Mama wouldn't let me use her rose water."

"Well, stay away from my herd. I don't feel like giving two hundred head a scrub down. Neither do I believe the cows are hankering to have their faces powdered again."

"Land's sake, Lee! I was only eleven at the time and Persy wouldn't let me practice on her!"

Hercules chuckled from deep in his throat and told Sanford, "You can't imagine what a nuisance she can be."

"Ohhh, I think I've gotten an idea," Sanford quipped, feeling an instant rapport with Venus's brother. He held out his hand in greeting. "Sanford Buchanan."

The returning grip was sure and smooth. "I suspected as much. I'm Lee Daltry. It's great to meet you. Grandmother told us she was expecting you, and though I wish I could have stuck around to welcome my favorite author, we had a few late-born calves to brand. But I'm glad for this chance to tell you how much I enjoy your novels. My son Jimmy is also a big fan of yours."

"Thank you. I appreciate hearing that readers are pleased with my books."

"Actually, you have my wife to thank. She gave me *High Stakes Gambler* as a birthday gift a few years back and I've been addicted to your Adventures of the West ever since. I admire your dedication to your work."

As always, an abundance of acclaim suffused his face with heat. He steered the subject away from himself. "Well, running a ranch of this magnitude is no easy task, either. I hadn't realized you Daltrys owned such a big backyard."

A note of pride crept into Lee's voice. "This land was acquired when it was still Comanche stomping grounds.

My father expanded when the call for beef sent the price per head soaring after the war. Each of us own a share in it but, of course, our prizes don't come freely; we have to earn them. Don't we, little beauty?"

Venus's glare pierced Sanford in the back, but the reason for it was not clear to him.

"Now that the railroad has come to Paradise, we don't drive the cows to market anymore. But if you'd like to experience a true trial drive, we'll arrange one to Abilene —Texas, that is."

Though his creative wheels whirred with possibilities, Sanford knew he'd have to decline Lee's generous offer. The New York Publishing House wanted another gambler's story for the series since *High Stakes Gambler* had profited so well a few years back, and he needed to submit the manuscript by next summer. The odds were already against him with Venus as his assistant.

Sanford shook his head. "It's damn tempting, Lee, but I'm under deadline. Another time?"

"I'm open," Lee cheerfully agreed. "But you will come down and grab a bite of grub before stealing my sister away. We've just started dishing it up."

Sanford paled a shade and old dreads resurfaced. Venus acted feisty—bordering on hostile—when they were alone. How would she act among company? Would she leave him to fall on his face and thereby embarrass him in front of Lee's men? Or worse, would she fawn all over him as if he were a helpless cripple?

He mulled over the invitation and the possible consequences of accepting. Unable to invent a refusal without insulting Lee's hospitality, Sanford reluctantly accepted. He'd just keep his guard up.

Venus scowled as she made a few minor repairs to her appearance before greeting the throng of dusty men lolling around the chuckwagon. She adjusted the wide brim of her hat and retied the ivory velvet bow beneath her chin. Then she brushed at the fine coating of clay turning her crisp union-blue jacket a ruddy orange. When a mild wind kicked up another spray of dust she wondered why she bothered trying to make herself presentable.

The spicy aroma of stewing peppers, onions, and beef mingled with the smell of charred hickory and pungent male sweat and, not to be outdone, cow patties. She wrinkled her nose. There was nothing refined about roundup.

Yet, wherever men abounded—be it an elegant soiree or a rustic campsite—a beautiful lady was appreciated. And the burden to provide the treat lay on Venus. The expectation had been drilled into her almost from the instant she decorated a cradle.

Bathed in compliments and attention beginning at an early age, Venus had learned that her looks made her special. Plain girls didn't receive undivided focus or intense popularity. Plain girls didn't receive much at all.

Not even love.

She slipped easily into her role of debutante as the ranch hands bypassed their boss and raced toward her like a pack of famished coyotes. She grinned coyly as dozens of arms jostled each other for the honor of helping her dismount.

"I take it you boys remember my sister," Lee said.

Lee's amused statement barely put a dent in the din of "Howdy, Miss Venus!" and "Y'all look mighty fetchin' today, Miss Venus!" and "What's a lovely lady such as yourself doin' in the mire of the low pasture, Miss Venus?"

The chorus was music to her ears. It seemed ages had come and gone since she'd last been sought with such enthusiasm.

Then, Lee introduced Sanford. "This is Buck Buchanan."

They let her go instantly. Her wobbly legs scarcely touched ground before the collection of cowpokes evaporated.

Venus stared with amazement. Why, they were acting as if Lee just announced that the Good Lord Himself was in their midst! Venus gained her footing. Forgotten and abandoned, she leaned against the sorrel with her arms akimbo and her mouth slack. Crushing battered Stetsons

to soiled shirtfronts, all eight men regarded Sanford with
awe.

Even Angus, the cook, paused from scraping slop into
a bucket to gawk at Sanford. Nothing or no one aroused
Angus's interest!

"I done read ever' book ya wrote, Buck," Old Willy
boasted, balancing his spare weight on his one natural leg
rather than the wooden substitute, a souvenir of the war.

"*Call of the Badge* was my favorite," Red O'Ryan said.
"That ole Marshal really gave them yahoo train robbers
what-for in the end." His shaggy russet head bobbed with
glee.

Venus had no idea that Red could even read!

More shouts rose from the gathering. Venus listened
intently to the praise directed at Sanford. Apparently, every man working the low range recognized the name
Buck Buchanan.

No doubt he was grinning like a cat in a fish pond, too,
she thought, throwing him a sulky glance. But when her
eyes locked on him, her surprise was palpable enough to
taste. He did not bask in the adoration at all! In fact, he
remained sitting stiffly in the saddle with his hat so low
over his eyes his face was nothing but haggard felt and
whiskers. And his hands clenched the reins so tight she
expected his fingertips to puncture his knuckles any minute.

Bless my soul, Venus marveled, *he looks scared!*

The sight surprised her. She'd seen nothing but arrogant confidence radiate from him since the moment he'd
topped the rise to the ranch.

Inexplicably, a tide of protectiveness swelled inside Venus, drowning her irritation at being deserted. From nowhere soared a compelling need to hide him from the
idol worship turning him to stone more effectively than a
glance from Medusa the monstrous Gorgon. But a man
of his size would not fit into her pocket or under her
fitted jacket, and mirrors fended off evil only in mythology . . .

Quickly, Venus gathered her wits and called, "Land's

sake, what does a lady have to do to get fed around here?"

Lee guffawed when the men once more scrambled to her side, begging her pardon. Then her brawny brother winked at her for the swift maneuver that stole their attention away from Sanford. The gesture proved she had not imagined Sanford's reaction; Lee had witnessed it, too.

But clamped between sweat-dampened, cotton-clad shoulders, Venus had eyes only for Sanford as she was half carried to the tailgate of the chuckwagon. His body was rigid as he dismounted. Lee moved beside him so that their shoulders touched, guiding him without making it obvious to any of the men not bedazzled by her flirtatious smile. Of course, they all were, so her worry was for naught.

Even so, questions filled her mind as Sanford seated himself on a crate Red provided. What had come over him? Had it been the unexpected rush of the crowd? The frantic motion?

Venus closed her eyes in an attempt to experience whatever it was he felt. She felt nothing but a need to open her eyes. *It must go deeper than that.*

Venus fanned her pleated skirt around her own crate while Angus placed two bowls of chunky stew on the makeshift table. Nobody seemed to notice how Sanford hovered over his meal, or how he tried to grasp the spoon without fumbling for it, but she did. And if she didn't know better, she'd think he was concealing his blindness from the starstruck men standing by.

His unease increased. Venus sent an imploring look to Lee, who stood behind Sanford. Once Lee summoned the men away so the two could eat in peace, they left, although grudgingly, and gathered their discarded dishes off the ground. Granted breathing space, Sanford visibly relaxed. And when the tension seeped from her body, Venus realized she too had been held in talons of anxiety.

Sulphur permeated the air as cigarettes were lit around the bend of the wagon, a respectable distance from her ladylike sensibilities. She continued to watch Sanford out of the corner of her eye. He broke a chunk of bread and dipped it into the stew. With his spoon he scooped chunks of meat and vegetables onto the crust.

Halfway to his mouth, his hand paused. "Don't worry, Venus, I'm not going to embarrass you," he jeered.

Venus sucked in her breath and nearly choked on a pepper. She pulled her hanky from the braided cuff of her sleeve and wiped her mouth. "What do you mean?"

"You're staring at me as if waiting for me to miss my mouth or dribble broth down my shirtfront."

Calmly she stuffed the hanky back in place. "I didn't think you would."

"Then what were you thinking?" He dared her to answer.

"Well . . ." Venus folded her hands in her lap, startled at the way they trembled. He tore off a bite of bread with his teeth and chewed, his lips drawn tight. Again, she tried picturing him without the bushy beard and mustache. He had such a nice smile; what a shame to hide it under all that dark hair. One thick brunette brow arched when she hesitated. "The truth?" she asked.

He swallowed then taunted, "Noooo. Be as deceitful and dishonest as possible."

Deliberate or not, the ridiculous request lightened the mood. Venus propped her chin in her hand and leaned close. "I was wonderin' if you ever shaved."

It was his turn to choke and she could swear a blush was creeping into his cheeks. But with all that hair it might have been a reflection of sunlight through the burnt-gold strands.

"When I find a reason to shave, I'll do it," he groused.

Venus straightened, wondering why she had given this grouchy hunk of leather and denim an ounce of compassion. He certainly didn't know the meaning of the word. Her lips compressed into a thin line, she pushed her meal away, no longer hungry.

At that moment, one of the seasonal drovers approached the wagon with a faded copy of *Wrangler on the Run* secured between his lean fingers. His youthful freshness seemed so out of place amongst all the livestock and weathered drovers that he drew her attention. His bleached blond hair, topped by a brand-new black Stetson, and fine features with peach fuzz for facial hair made him look more like a choirboy than a cow-tender. Only his bowlegged walk marked him as a drover.

Shyly, the cowboy halted between Sanford and herself. In the depths of his doe-brown eyes Venus glimpsed sad wisdom—as if the worst sort of tragedy had matured him beyond his years. Her heart ached for him.

Sanford set his spoon and bread down and slowly raised his head. Venus thought Sanford mirrored her anguish, except Sanford's had flashed on his face rather than in his eyes before he schooled the inward pain.

"Uh, sir, I'm a roper. That is . . . uh . . . I lasso calves for brandin' an' tell the ironman what mark to put on its flank."

"I'm aware of a roper's duties," Sanford said gently.

The boy dropped his gaze to the book in his hand, then focused on Sanford again. "This was my pa's, rest his soul . . ." His deep drawl broke with emotion then resumed with bold strength as he composed himself. "He woulda been plumb tickled ta meet ya, sir. He read everything ya ever wrote." He shot the hand holding the book forward. "Would ya . . . would ya honor him by puttin' yer mark on it?"

Sanford stared blankly at him. After suspended moments, the boy began to fidget.

Then it dawned on Venus that Sanford had no idea an object was dangling in front of his nose. A novel of his own creation waited for his signature. No smell, no noise alerted him of its existence. Sometimes Venus forgot how important these clues were to him. Most often his incredible instinct alone disguised his physical limitation.

Neither did the choirboy-cowpoke seem to realize anything was amiss.

A soft spot in her heart held her back from revealing that the infamous Buck Buchanan was nothing more than a blind dreamer; whether for the hopeful roper's benefit or Sanford's she didn't explore.

Instead she contemplated how to subdue the mounting

tension. Sanford sat too far away for her to kick him
under the tailgate. And shoving the book into his face
would be the same as slapping him across the cheek . . .

She remembered the tree branch. How Sanford had hit
it with the mere relation to a clock face. "Why, Sanford,
isn't that flatterin'?" Venus cried. "The boy is takin' time
off his *noonin'* to ask for your autograph!"

The bit of stress she put on *noonin'* clicked. The lift of
Sanford's eyebrows was so slight, the skitter of surprise
across his face so brief, she might have missed the reactions had she not been looking for signs he'd gotten her
veiled message.

When he stretched his arm out and received the book,
Venus felt pretty darn proud of herself. Laying it on the
tailgate, Sanford peeled the cover open. "Got a pen
handy, partner?"

Beaming, Venus withdrew the bone quill and ink bottle
she kept in her skirt pocket to jot notes as they rode, and
tapped the items discreetly against Sanford's thumb.

Suddenly, her smile slackened. What if she'd made a
mistake? What if Sanford couldn't write, not even to sign
his name?

She held her breath as he uncapped the small jar and
dipped the steel tip into the black fluid. Using his index
finger as a guide, he scribbled *Buck Buchanan* on the
inside cover.

And Venus's lungs deflated.

Sanford returned the book to its owner and the two
chatted a moment about the wrangler in the book accused of rustling his boss's herd, and how he proved his
innocence by catching the real thieves.

Once she and Sanford were alone again, the clanging
of Angus's pots became painfully loud. At length, Sanford
said, "You didn't tell him I was blind."

Venus shrugged. "It must've slipped my mind."

Lee came and fetched him, deferring any reply he
might have offered. It relieved her to see he appeared
much more at ease. Grabbing Ranger's reins, Sanford
persuaded the stallion to perform a few tricks for the men

while they swapped bawdy tales so outrageous, none could possibly be true.

Venus wasn't in any hurry to carry on with her brutal frontier training. She pulled her crate beneath a square of shade cast by the wagon and watched as Sanford lay flat on the ground, feigning injury, while the horse dragged him with his teeth.

Land's sake, he's an enigma, she thought, fanning herself with her hanky. Superior yet susceptible. Mighty yet meek. What was it about this dime novelist that inspired such wholesome devotion?

And what was it that she found so magnetic about the man? Perhaps his powerful structure had a bit to do with it, for she approved of a man who took care of his physique. And though she preferred a clean-shaven face, she'd become accustomed to his whiskers; they suited his rugged ways. Yet it went further than his looks. Sanford dared to challenge her in a way no one else ever had, challenge something deep inside her she did not recognize.

Lee and Sanford laughed freely at something her brother said, unheard over the distance, and Venus's heart squeezed at the open sound. They strolled to where she sat like old friends rather than strangers thrown together by fate's whim. Sanford's hand was tucked in Ranger's bridle strap, and with the horse guiding him, his steps were more confident.

He should laugh more often, she thought. His whole being glowed, as if someone had lit a candle inside him. He didn't laugh much around her, though. Or with her. At her, yes, which was probably why he'd done it now, but not with her. He just yelled. And gritted his teeth. And sighed. A lot.

Stopping a few paces away, Lee grasped her hand and tugged her to her feet. "I'd best get back to work, sis. These calves won't brand themselves and I still have a day's worth of gathering strays before I can return to Meredith and the kids." He bent to kiss her forehead. "Quit giving Buck guff and listen to him. Do what he says and this year'll pass quick as a whip flick."

Venus finished brushing grass from her hems long enough to grimace at Sanford, who stood nearby, his idle hand shoved into his back pocket. "Tattletale. I suppose you forgot to mention how rotten you've been treating me."

He gave her a boyish grin that tripped her heartbeat and then he shrugged noncommittally.

Lee ruffled her bangs. "You're such a stick-in-the-mud."

Venus slapped his vest lightly. "What is with y'all? You sound just like Mama and Daddy and Grandma—as if you trust him, too!"

All traces of brotherly banter vanished. "I trust this man with your life, little beauty."

And Venus knew how dead serious her brother was. Lee used that private pet name he had given her so long ago when he wanted a point taken to heart.

Lee swaggered off then, chaps slapping, spurs singing.

Trust Sanford? He should have asked her for the moon; that she could probably manage. But place her faith in a man who accepted things only on his conditions . . . who thought of her as a spoiled pest, a frontier simpleton . . . who might leave her behind at the slightest provocation . . .

How could she trust a man like that?

Venus realized her thoughts had wandered. Her gaze flitted to Sanford. No doubt he'd heard the exchange— had probably read her mind again too, she guessed, flushing guiltily—but he said nothing either way.

Instead he urged her to locate the other two horses. Dampness weighed heavily in the air and he told her they needed to find a campsite before the rains fell.

The warning of nasty weather had become more pronounced in the last half hour, Venus noticed. As she gathered her sorrel and the burdened brown pack horse, slow-moving gray clouds thick as clabber had drifted in, making it harder for the sunshine to peek through. Wonderful, she thought, on top of everything else she had to tolerate, she had a good dousing to look forward to before day's end.

Obscene calls to the cattle faded behind the hills to the rear as the mounts covered ground. Venus detected a hum of excitement about Sanford while they rode.

After ten minutes, her intrigue got the best of her. "All right, Buchanan, fess up."

He turned in the saddle and said, "Did you know there's a town southeast of here called Babyhead?"

Her eyes flew open at the animated question. "Honestly, who told you that?"

"The man they call Red."

"That bowlegged Irishman?" Venus shook her head with pity. "Sanford, I hate to be the one to dim your candle. Red may have lost his brogue, but he's plenty full of blarney."

"Even tall tales grow from a seed of truth," he insisted. "According to him, the Comanche killed a white baby back in '50 and mounted its head on a pole on a mountain to discourage settlers from settling on the mountain. It didn't work, though. They built a town there anyway and named it and the creek Babyhead after the mountain."

Venus curled her lip in disgust. "I've heard enough. That's a gruesome story."

"But it has all the elements of a great plot." He grinned. "And I think it's worth investigating."

Now? They had to go to Nevada! Fulfill her labor!

"No, but someday. I'm going to find this place and verify the facts and maybe gather enough information to write a book on it."

Venus rolled her eyes. "Honestly, you'll go anywhere for a story."

"Research is important for accuracy. I won't write about something I know nothing about. I want to sell books, but I also want a reputation as a reliable author. Do you know how many men and women have been lured West by dime novelists who tend to romanticize events and deeds? And when disillusioned folks sell everything they own, they come out here and learn it's not all glorious sunsets and heroes on horses as they've read, but grueling work and monotonous days."

"But you're a dime novelist." Had he forgotten that? she wondered.

"I consider myself a storyteller. I base my tales on truth, which in many cases is more enthralling than raw fiction."

"You just said people read fiction to escape from truth. How can what you write be enthralling?"

"Ahhh, that's the secret, Venus. Hook them with characters they can relate to and root for, put them in a wild setting, and make them triumph against all odds. *Those* are the stories that sell—be they dime novels or classic works."

Venus contemplated everything Sanford told her but still didn't understand. She guessed that's what set her apart from the common world, though. She had loftier aspirations than living a romantic life through someone else's words. She led a romantic life of her own—in truth!

Or did. Until Sanford Buchanan came along.

She would again, though, she vowed. Then she'd really give him something to write about!

"You don't think very highly of what I do for a living, do you, Venus?"

Her answer was immediate. "Not as highly as Lee's men, obviously. Dime novels rank right up there with sand on my teeth and smelly horses. You may have gained some popularity with your ten-cent books, but looks like mine are what legends are made of."

"What poetic vanity!"

"You don't believe me? What of my namesake, Venus? Or Aphrodite? Or even Lady Godiva, the famous wife of the Earl of Mercia, if you're not familiar with mythology?"

"I'm afraid Lady Godiva's looks weren't what made her outstanding. I believe it was her lack of apparel and the fantasy of being the white horse she rode that caused people to remember her." Sanford chuckled, paying no attention to her intake of breath. "Did you ever consider how long the illusion of beauty lasts?"

He gave her no chance to reply and Venus was almost thankful since anything she said would probably come out in a stutter after his brazen comment over Lady Godiva's nakedness.

"Beauty is temporal, princess. Any day it can disappear."

How well she knew, Venus thought, cringing. The suggestion had caused her untold agony in recent years, with every new line and blemish that developed on her once flawless face. The hours of pampering she awarded herself were little insurance that she'd have her fair, angelic youthfulness forever. So for now, she hoarded her moments of praise and adulation, aware and dreading the day when all she'd have were memories.

"However," Sanford continued, "wisdom is eternal. It never fades. It is chiseled in stone and printed on paper and spoken of for generation after generation."

Land's sake, this was a depressing topic! And yet, their differing viewpoints caused lively debate. Venus was not about to surrender gracefully. "I see." She grew passionate in her own defense. "You are convinced that brains are the answer to everything while beauty is worthless?"

"Not worthless. Superficial. Where do you think beauty will get you out here?" He swept his hand in a wide arc. Again, he didn't wait for her answer. "I'll tell you where—six feet under with a daisy blanket, that's where. I'm just hoping you'll learn before it's too late."

Never in her wildest nightmares could Venus imagine the lengths he'd go to prove his point.

Eight

THE DAY HE NEARLY DROWNED HER MARKED THE DAY VENUS concluded Sanford was trying to kill her.

They had reached the Colorado River after three days of miserable travel. She might have considered it a pleasant morning had she been in an appreciative frame of mind, for the weather held fair after what seemed an endless deluge of spring rains, but Venus was in no mood to give thanks for the fine climate.

Sanford had been playing a stupid game of "Indian attack" all last night. Venus lost count of how many times he jarred her awake, then gave her less than a minute to throw herself onto the sorrel's bare back and race pell-mell across the soggy countryside. And just when she thought she'd finally be able to get in a decent wink, dawn broke.

So while Sanford waded into the rusty water atop his horse without a qualm, Venus remained mutinous on the eastern bank. Her temper already sore, the last thing she wanted to do was humor Mr. Survival by plunging into water thick enough to chew.

"It's not deep here, Venus," Sanford said. "Just flick the reins. The horse will get you across."

No, it wasn't deep, she conceded, but it looked about as appealing as a flooded chicken coop. The current that lapped at Ranger's belly and hid the stirrups cupping Sanford's boots teamed with debris and floating sludge.

She pursed her lips defiantly. "Thanks to you, my wardrobe is severely limited. This is the only decent gown I own and my father paid a fortune for it. I will not ruin it walking through a mud puddle—not for anybody. Least of all for you." Bad enough she'd been forced to don evening raiment for a morning jaunt!

Impatience tainted his gusty sigh. "Why must you always be so damned difficult? It's only water! You and that animal of yours have needed a bath since we left anyway!"

"Not in a cesspool, we don't!" she countered, not entirely denying her need for a good get-in-and-soak bath. Neither she nor Sanford had been afforded the privacy or facilities to do much more than sponge off in creeks. Every now and then, they would find a watering hole out in the open, but Venus didn't dare take advantage of the pools. What if someone saw her bathing in the nude? "Look, mister, I will make this as clear as possible so you don't tax yourself trying to understand a lady's tastes. That water is disgusting. I don't aim to waste another outfit on account of you. Already I've lost four gowns, eight petticoats, one bustle, and virtually all my underclothing. What you didn't bury isn't fit for the rag bin—"

"Are you still having a fit over your skirt catching on fire, even after I'd warned you time and time again not to stand so close to the kettle when cooking over an open fire?"

A growl erupted in her throat. He *had* to rub it in, didn't he? But worse than the destruction of the blue traveling dress was the beating she received after yelling Sanford's name when the flames began roasting her shins.

The incident had occurred the evening after they left roundup, yet Venus recalled it vividly. And a blush crept into her cheeks at the memory of how Sanford had tackled her to the ground to beat the fire out with his bare hands, unintentionally multiplying the bruises on her legs produced from riding. She had been touched by his hero-ism, his concern for her welfare, his offer of salve for burns she had not sustained.

But her opinion of him took a drastic turn the moment she told him she hadn't been hurt; he'd cussed at her then. Rebuked her for not listening to him in the first place. Threatened that next time, she might not be so lucky as to come out unscathed.

So much for being a gallant hero.

She decided that maybe the pummeling hadn't been as unintentional as she'd thought.

And before crawling into her bedroll that night, she had traced the scorched edges of her skirt panel with her finger. She denied being hurt by his scornful words. Her tears, she told herself, were for her beautiful clothes. Nothing more.

Down to one article of clothing since the burial and the fire, she clung to this last vestige of her former life. Venus tilted her chin and declared, "I won't cross that river and you can't make me." To punctuate the statement, she folded her arms, crushing the ivory lace decorating her pointed bodice.

The wicked glow on Sanford's face as he wheeled his horse around and advanced toward her shook her bra-vado. A sinking feeling lodged in her stomach the closer he came, murky drops splattering everywhere with the pressure of Ranger's hooves hitting the surface. And though she quaked inside, she didn't so much as flinch once he reined in beside her.

His empty gaze found her, and he settled his elbow on his thigh, rested his bristly chin in his closed hand.

For long moments, Venus watched him, wary and won-dering what fate awaited her for her disobedience. She held her breath.

The squawk of a hawk above was the only sound heard in the stillness as Sanford's blank stare bored into her, arresting her, holding her prisoner.

Those sinfully sensuous eyes, half-masted and arro-gantly rich, the color of fertile soil, stirred an emotion inside that Venus didn't want to examine.

Attraction.

He was bold, discourteous, and primitive. A saddle tramp who wrote sordid novels. And yet, she felt a compelling tug in her breast, familiar, but of a depth beyond the familiar.

She forgot her gown, forgot the naturally polluted river, forgot her own identity.

And when he reached out his hand, of its own volition, hers met it. No reservations, no hesitations.

The rough pad of his thumb stroked her tapered fingers as if treasuring the texture. She wished her skin was softer, as it had been before the sun and heat had taken its toll. The lotions she used thrice daily were little help. But he seemed not to notice the calluses on each digit. Instead his touch savored the feel.

Disconcerted, Venus licked her lips. The coloring she had applied this morning tasted gritty. Like Texas itself.

What would Sanford's mouth taste like?

His lips were firm and even, with defined borders, the upper denting in the middle, the lower an appealing crescent. They didn't appear chapped, because he protected his face often with the bandanna slung around his neck, but neither did they glisten.

The thought struck her that he'd taste spicy, exciting. Strong. Like Texas, too.

She recognized his voice through the cloud of her musings and a moment passed before his husky words registered.

"Don't you know I could make you do anything I want?"

Venus nodded dumbly, forgetting he couldn't see the movement.

He could. Right now, using that seductive voice and his soothing touch, he could make her dye her hair red. Walk through a mud puddle. Read a dime novel. Yes, anything. He needed only ask.

But he didn't ask.

His hand came down on the sorrel's rump. Hard.

Dulled and witless, Venus didn't comprehend what

he'd done until the horse she sat upon bolted and her neck snapped backward.

Belatedly, Venus screamed.

Sanford's smug chuckle died the instant he heard the splash following Venus's alarmed squeal.

"Venus?" He hastened Ranger back into the river, his blood curdling. He'd only meant to teach her that he couldn't be suckered in by a childish tantrum—not have her thrown!

"Venus!" he cried again. What if she'd gone under? What if the current swept her away? He had no means of estimating the river's size except Ranger's judgment. Nor could he know the power of the current where she had fallen. All he knew was they'd received two days' worth of steady rain, the river had swelled, and mud sucked at his horse's hooves.

And though he could guess where Venus had landed by gauging the distance between the bank and the splash, and the magnitude of the noise, if she was beneath the surface, how would he find her?

A keen slash of agony sliced through his middle.

Damn his eyes!

His private darkness had never been this petrifying. This icy cold. His heart froze solid in his chest.

Frantic, he urged Ranger, "Find her, boy!"

The animal nickered and pranced forward. A second later the water broke and the air filled with sputtering coughs. Ranger took two more steps ahead and arched his neck and Sanford jumped from the saddle.

Venus screeched again, fell again, and came up—again—hollering, "Get away from me, you blasted beast!" And Sanford's knees buckled with relief.

He assumed that Ranger, believing he'd found her, had upset her balance.

Sanford reached out, thinking of nothing but wrenching her into his arms and assuring himself she was, indeed, all right. In one piece. Unharmed.

"What are you trying to do, Buchanan? Drown me?"

Her flippant query checked his impulse and the air went static.

Venus gasped, "You *are,* aren't you?"

Sanford, still lingering in a whirl of emotion, couldn't grasp what she was saying.

"That's what this is all about, isn't it? You're trying to kill me!"

His throat felt as if it were lined with sandpaper. "That's absurd."

She went on as if he hadn't spoken. "Now it all comes together! First you try to beat me to death, then you try to burn me alive, and now you try to drown me!"

She was serious! She honestly thought he was attempting to do her in! "Venus, if I killed every female who got on my nerves, you'd be part of an extinct species and I'd be a wanted man." He tossed his arms wide. "I'm trying to keep you alive!"

"Oh?" From her tone he could imagine her standing with her arms crossed and her foot tapping a rapid, silent beat on the mucky riverbed.

A clear picture of Venus formed in his mind, a soaking wet, skin-and-bones princess who'd had her throne swiped out from under her. It came as a shock that, of all the fuzzy images he'd tried over the years to bring into focus, hers needed little effort. He saw her, in all her adorable muss, her precious makeup smeared and her sunshine-warm hair in sopping disarray and muddy rivulets streaming down her outrage-flushed cheeks.

And something twisted inside him. Something tender, vulnerable. Something caged since he had entered his manhood years.

Sanford suppressed what he considered a weakening will as Venus continued her outlandish allegations.

"What about when that bullet almost put a hole smack between my eyes?" she demanded.

Sanford recalled the incident two days past when Venus had been practicing her shooting. "You blame me for *your* hitting a rock because of lousy aim?" He couldn't believe she would blame *him*! "How was I to control the bullet's ricochet?"

"And what about yesterday, when you left me stranded in the middle of godforsaken country without food or water?"

Ah, hell, not that issue again! "We were in a cow pasture; you were supposed to follow my tracks! If you had listened to directions and taken notice of your surroundings, you would have found me lying in that gully not fifty feet from where you were wandering around in circles, crying over the broken heel on your boot!"

He didn't bother explaining—for the third time!—that even had the horses not been fully stocked with filled canteens and provisions, she was in no jeopardy. They had been a scant quarter mile off a well-traveled road heading into Sweetwater.

Obviously, Venus could not be reasoned with and he . . . he was still recovering from the jolting impact of almost losing her to the Colorado, which, under normal conditions, was dry as an Englishman's wit.

She proved his theory with her next claim.

"Just admit it, Sanford Buck Buchanan! You want me dead!"

He clenched his jaw and swung away from her, longing to end this discussion. That was the most ridiculous thing he'd ever heard Venus say. And Venus said a lot of ridiculous things. "I want you to learn to survive."

"Even if it kills me, right?"

Debating her while standing in bone-chilling water was not getting him anywhere, he concluded with a weary frown, except to the nearest doctor if either of them came down with pneumonia. And if that happened, Venus would add making her ill with lung fever to her list of fabricated notions.

Plastering a smile on his face, he said, "Think of it in these terms, Venus. Riding with you will be much more bearable now that the stench of that perfume you wear has washed off."

She growled. It was his only warning before a big gob of mud smacked against his back and slithered down between his shoulder blades.

Astonishment was added to the gamut of emotions

he'd endured the last ten minutes and thwarted the step he was about to take toward his horse.

Sanford jerked in Venus's direction. So she wanted to play dirty, did she?

A grin stole across his face as impulse seized him.

Sanford reached into the water and, cupping his hand, filled his palm with sludge.

"Wh-what are you doing, Buchanan?"

"Turnabout is fair play, princess." And he let the handful fly.

He knew he'd hit his target when Venus screeched, "My hair!" Adding with menace, "Why, you . . . filthy . . . low-down . . . *mudslinger!*"

She pelted him with another packet of slimy river-bottom mud.

Again, he matched her toss, and she cried, "Ooooh, you're going to pay for that one!"

The threat evoked in him a carefree playfulness he'd forgotten how to feel. For nineteen years, he'd spent so many waking hours alert and studious under Uncle Zeb's gruff hand that such frolicking had become a distant memory, like a souvenir of bygone days stored in an attic trunk.

He felt young again, for the first time since the war, dodging the mud balls Venus flung his way. And his sole concern was to splatter her before she splattered him.

He cared about nothing save Venus's daring and his own reclaimed youth and the bountiful gladness of being alive. Here. Now. With her.

She moved behind him, a foot back, he judged, in a bid to ambush him. He wasn't deceived, but he kept that to himself. He raised his arm as if to throw sideways, faked the toss, then abruptly whirled his entire body and dove against Venus.

The water acted as a cushion for their descent; even so, Sanford reflexively braced her with his arm around her slim waist. No sooner had they doubled over, he forward, she backward, and their heads submerged, than he whisked her above the surface.

Venus immediately clutched his shoulder and gasped

from the dunking. Sanford's left hand remained poised above his head, his purpose to spread the scoop of mire over her face the instant she caught her breath.

But the longer he stood with her in his embrace, her slick, feminine curves connected to his manlier proportions, the harder it became to recollect just what the hell he'd meant to do.

His rapid pantings diminished to unsteady intakes and the scent of Venus filled him. Earthy elegance. Saturated silk. Liquid lace.

She stared at him. He felt her lively eyes on his face, felt her irregular breathing in harmony with his. What did she think when she looked at him? Did she think him handsome? It was not a matter he placed much importance on, and yet, she was so tiny compared to him, so perfect, quite probably the beauty she claimed to be, that the matter of his own looks suddenly concerned him. He hoped to complement her appearance and wasn't sure he did. After all, he hadn't shaved in weeks and his clothes left much to be desired. But he knew he was healthy and toned and wondered if his build might impress her.

Hers he found more than satisfactory. It was downright desirable! Even the damn contraptions she stuffed herself into every day didn't disguise the lushness of her breasts pressing against his chest, or the natural womanly shape of her waist and hips.

Did she experience the same stirrings of lust as he when their bodies touched? Did her blood surge and her eyelids grow heavy?

Did she yearn to be a part of him as he yearned to be a part of her?

They were crazy thoughts to have for a lady partner he'd never wanted in the first place and he knew it. Yet he was as powerless against their invasion as he was powerless to move from her, this high-society-lady-innocent-maiden mixture.

"What are you doing, princess?" he asked hoarsely, in a vain attempt to separate confusion from reality.

She caressed the plane of his cheekbone under his eye

and a nerve twitched. "I do believe I'm inviting you, Sanford."

Nothing she said could have surprised him more. Inviting him? To what? Kiss her as he longed to do? Make love to her as his body demanded? Give the desire rushing through his veins free rein? Treat her as he would any other willing woman and spend a few hours of physical bliss with her?

And then what? he silently questioned. Live like a normal man?

To have one of Venus's caliber as his own . . .

For him, that was pure fiction. A dashed dream. A hollow hope. A withered wish.

Caught up in the moment, apparently she had forgotten what he could not. He wasn't a regular man. He was a blind one.

His arms dropped to his sides; mud slid through his fingers. Sanford trembled as he finally let her go and retreated.

Concealing his regret, he said, "I decline, Venus. That's not what I brought you along for." The words came out flat and unemotional, colder than he'd intended. But even though her sudden withdrawal cut him to the core, he could not take them back.

It was for the best, he told himself. She'd only hurt him in the end anyway. Once she discovered he could not provide for her like a normal man, she'd leave. Find someone else with a body in full working order. Someone who could protect her from errant fires and wayward bullets and swollen rivers.

Yer skeared, boy. Yer plumb fearful ya cain't keep her safe.

Youthful vitality drained from Sanford at the piercing memory of his uncle's words and he told Venus, "Game's over. We have work to do."

Then, gripping Ranger's bridle, he was led back to dry land.

It was the second time he'd made a fool of her.

Land's sake, Venus thought, wading out behind man and beast, how many times did he have to spurn her before she finally got it through her head that he was not interested?

Not that she was interested in him, either, she insisted silently, but that had no bearing. To have her spontaneous wish so blatantly rejected, why, that simply did not happen to her!

Very seldom was she refused anything and never by men. Venus was at a loss as to how to deal with this uncommon occurrence.

C.J. had once called her a tease. Venus remembered replying saucily, "I know, isn't it grand?" Well, now that she was on the receiving end, it didn't seem grand at all. In fact, it was downright frustrating! And it made her kind of feel sorry for all the beaus she'd tempted only to walk away with a spring of conquest in her step and a song of victory on her lips.

But the man had walked away this time. From her.

She reached the bank and her high-button boots sloshed with water. Glancing down to watch her footing on the slippery ground, she came to an abrupt stop. Her mouth twisted in a horrified frown.

Spreading her limp skirts, Venus took in the sight of her once-elegant gown with its soaked and muddy panels, and the clumps of slop clinging to the lace at her cuffs and bodice.

She rushed to the sorrel grazing nearby and retrieved her mirror.

A sob caught in her throat. No wonder Sanford hadn't been captivated by her; she looked a fright! Like something a mutt dragged through a barnyard then spat out. Her hair bore no semblance to the crowning glory she took great pains to keep silky and pale. Instead, it was strands of a rag mop dipped in an axle-grease barrel!

And her face, oh, land's sake, her face . . . under all the moist grime she glimpsed a spattering of horrid freckles and the tone of her skin looked suspiciously *tanned*!

Near tears, Venus beat a hasty path back to the water's edge and dunked her head into the tumbling depths, raking her fingers through the mess, freeing the mud clods from her beautiful tresses.

Land's sake, she almost wailed, what had possessed her to engage in such foolish behavior! Participating in a mud fight? That she was even capable of such unseemly behavior . . . how disturbing. Worse, that she had enjoyed it, however briefly . . . how positively *shameful!* A sob caught in her throat.

If anybody had seen her . . . could see her now . . . Venus shuddered. She'd simply *die* of humiliation!

I swear, if Sanford ever whispers a word of my scandalous behavior, I'll deny it to my last breath!

She flipped the sopping mass over her head and rested on her calves, fighting tears and frustration and misery.

This is all Sanford's fault! If he hadn't been trying to kill her then she wouldn't have been furious enough to throw something at him. He had started it, the juvenile game of dodge-the-mud-ball, and given her a glimpse of carefree play someone of her station just did not partake in! And in the process, he had awakened a wanton's need inside her, then doused it with his curt response.

She shot a scathing look toward where he'd gone behind a tree to change. All traces of previous cravings for his touch and kiss fled. The memory of those heated muscles under her cold fingertips persisted, though, tingling through the digits of both her hands, and Venus became angrier.

What was the point in practicing—even perfecting—ladylike qualities and social decorum when, at any moment, a pair of brooding eyes and a mischievous grin could shatter her control?

Then again, Venus reflected, wringing out her hair, she had lost control of her entire life the day she'd turned twenty and unwrapped Grandma's box.

It flitted across her mind that if she abandoned the labor given her, she might salvage whatever dregs of dignity she had left. The idea dissolved as soon as it formed. She'd carry the label of disgrace around with her forever. The labor entailed much more than the prize; its fulfillment was a source of honor. If she returned home without completing it, she'd be a disappointment to the entire family.

No, she sighed despairingly, she could no more return to Paradise Plains and admit to Grandma she'd failed the task than she could catch a rainbow. Her pride and the family name forbade it.

So what was she to do, then? she wondered. Continue living like a wild animal? Bear with the sun and sweat and exhaustion for the next three hundred and fifty plus days and nights? Consent to Sanford's pulling her strings as though she were a puppet?

Venus refused to accept that existence as her destiny. She hadn't yet figured out why Grandma had chosen this labor for her but she did know she was sick to death of Sanford and his underhanded tutoring methods.

Venus scrambled to her feet. She had to put a stop to his torture. Take charge of her life again. Show that blessed bookworm that Venus Daltry was not one to tangle with.

Keep on trying to kill me, you blessed maverick, she dared him in her mind. But she'd never let him manipulate her emotions again. Never let him make her feel a woman's yearnings again.

No, she was going to see that Sanford paid for every ounce of degradation he heaped on her.

She just had to figure out how.

Zeb's accusation continued to trouble Sanford while he changed into dry denims and a soft cotton shirt. At the time he had taken it as a slur to his character. But now he admitted that maybe it *was* a major factor in why he had rebelled against bringing Venus on this trip.

He listened to her complaints as she bemoaned her soggy tresses, swearing she'd never rid her scalp of river filth, and if she couldn't wash out the red film in her hair he'd wake up one morning without his because she'd shave him bald.

Sanford shook his head and tucked in the tails of his shirt. Yes, she was okay; she hadn't been hurt by her fall. But what about tomorrow? Or the day after?

The potential for danger and hazardous situations existed every day, everywhere around them. The last thing he wanted was to explain to her family that she'd gotten killed or maimed while entrusted to him for this trip. But it was more than that. If anything happened to Venus, he'd carry a burden of guilt for the rest of his life.

Who was he fooling? Something almost *had* happened to her. Today. Because of him. *He'd* been the one to cause her horse to bolt. Been the perpetrator of her tumble.

He'd been taught that men were supposed to care for the gentler sex at any cost and he'd gone and flaunted the unwritten code without a thought to the outcome. In all honesty, that obligation had made him uncomfortable ever since he'd lost his sight, which was why he'd avoided involvements with women, period. It was less risky to remain unattached.

And yet, he was stuck with Venus, bound to her by a promise made to a conniving old schemer to whom he owed his life. He had no choice but to accept this responsibility and this particular involvement.

But it was more than a commitment to his word now; there was something about Venus, her vibrancy maybe, that he found irresistible. Almost as if an unseen force tied their contrasting spirits together. For all the aggravation she caused him, all the inconvenience, he sensed a zest for adventure in her that, once tapped, matched his own.

And that awareness scared him, the possibility that he might start appreciating some of her qualities. They were business partners—nothing more. And if the lady in Venus made him forget the boundaries of their relationship, then he'd just have to remember all the grief she caused him. And as soon as this book was finished, he'd wash his hands of the troublesome baggage.

If by some stroke of fate Zeb wished to stay longer in Paradise Plains, then Sanford would have to find another partner. One who wasn't so damn distracting.

And one who didn't arouse feelings he'd stored away long ago. He trusted he could cope with the desire she stirred in him. He was well accustomed to quelling his lustful nature.

It was his increasing urge to protect Venus that had him worried. Today's events showed how difficult it would be for him to do so. Had the river been a little deeper, a little wilder . . . the thought of what could have happened chilled him to the quick.

He'd hoped never to experience the kind of terror he'd faced at age thirteen. Today had surpassed it.

His goal had been to make her self-sufficient so there'd *be* no call to shield her. To protect her. To keep her safe from harm.

But, apparently, he had failed.

No, better to stick to the original agreement. Keep his distance and still teach Venus to rely on herself. Let her think he was out to murder her, he told himself. It made no difference.

At least it would buy her a few more years of life.

Nine

LASSO WAS THE MOST PITIFUL EXCUSE FOR A TOWN THAT EVEN
calling it one was undeserved praise, Venus thought. Not
much more than a few boards slapped together with spit,
the buildings lined a dry gulch. Jagged boards had been
nailed onto a post stuck in the ground. One board stated
the town's name with an arrow charcoaled below it pointing west, the other pointed opposite toward the gulch,
Mustang Draw.

They had come across a number of these crude com-
munities, established on the assumption that the railroad
would cut through this stretch of prarie land and bring
prosperity. But most—like Lasso—wound up as mere watering holes set in the heart of rangelands.

Venus took the kerchief she had taken to wearing
around her neck and raised it over her nose and mouth
like Sanford to avoid breathing in the mild cyclone of
dust swirling to her left. The cheese-colored cloth was a
gaudy accessory to her already dreadful-looking outfit,
but in this case, necessity overruled fashion.

"Is there anyplace to grab a room for the night?" Sanford inquired.

One of the disadvantages of traveling with someone

who could not see was that they could not be punished with the silent treatment. So for three days, even though she loathed speaking to the tyrant, she'd had to carry on fragments of conversation with him. And as if he were aware of how much it irked her to talk to him while she was mad, Sanford pestered her with more questions than normal.

She was sick and tired of describing settlements and people, cattle that looked all the same to her, and the habits of armadillos. And he was especially interested in the landscape of the treeless plains, where all that existed was grass and a few sturdy mesquite and shin oaks sprouting from the sandy soil.

But with no other recourse, unless she wanted to find herself sent back home before the year was up, she told him of every herd of sheep, every windmill twirling in the breeze, the depth and width of every flat-floored playa they passed by, while she scrawled the mundane information in a journal and speckled her dress with indelible black ink.

She made sure he knew how it annoyed her, though. Her description of Lasso was especially sarcastic.

"Let's see," she drawled, studying the conglomeration of shacks. "There's a saloon, a saloon, and . . . why, Sanford, there's a saloon!"

He chuckled. "I take it there are a number of saloons."

"Five in all if you count Amazin' Grace's Dance Hall and Gamblin' Parlor."

"No wonder it smells like a distillery here." He tugged on the brim of his hat. "I'm not looking forward to being kept awake all night with drunken revelry so I think it's best if we replace our supplies and leave."

"Oh, goodie," Venus jeered. "I'd hate for the insects that reside in my bedroll to miss me."

"We'll find another town soon—one with a respectable hotel where we can rent rooms. Meanwhile, your bedbugs will have your charming company for a little longer."

"I want a bath, Buchanan. Whiskey town or not, I won't leave until I've scrubbed every inch of filth and freckles from my body." Crossly, she added, "And if you can't accept that, then you can go straight to Hades."

"I'm probably going to regret saying this, but I agree with you. I'm smelling pretty fragrant myself and a copper tub sounds too inviting to pass up."

Venus stared at him, astonished. *Bless my soul, Sanford and I actually* agree *on something? What is the world coming to?*

"Close your mouth, princess, before a horsefly swoops in. Now, where do you suppose we can find someplace clean and private?"

Grimacing at the thought of one of those disgusting black insects darting down her throat, Venus looked at their options. "Other than the saloons, there is a blacksmith's. And there is some sort of a general store in the middle of the block. I know that back home, Hank and Maybelle's Mercantile has a small room behind a curtain where ladies may be fitted for clothes or can try on dresses. Perhaps that store has one we can borrow."

"It's worth a shot."

Before heading forward, Venus and Sanford began their little rituals to prepare themselves for public appearances. Had she not been annoyed with him, she might have thought this performance amusing. While she adjusted her shabby straw hat with its crumbling dried flowers, he tipped his low, and while she straightened her spine and tugged on the jacket of her sole wearable outfit, Sanford's shoulders slumped into a casual pose.

Whenever they had to encounter unfamiliar people, the ceremony was the same.

With uncanny perception, each sensed the other's readiness, and they moved simultaneously toward Lasso. Venus discovered that Saturday evenings brought out revelers here as they did in Paradise Plains, but of a more worldly nature that she found revolting. The street—if the narrow dirt pathway could be considered one—bustled with ranch hands eager to binge on drink and cards and women after a long week of toil.

From what she could see, they'd not find a shortage of any of the three in this place. Nearly every saloon adver-

tised debauchery. Through the windows she spied men
seated around tables and along bars, hovering over cards
and amber-filled glasses. And the shady ladies who
weren't draped across male laps lounged at stair bases
inside, or hung suggestively out of upper-story windows,
luring in customers with flagrant displays of cleavage and
vocal enticements.

This was Venus's first glimpse of true soiled doves ply-
ing their trade and she came to one conclusion: they were
in dire need of cosmetic tips.

Sanford received his share of lurid propositions, and
hearing them, Venus veered the sorrel closer to him, unaware of her possessive gesture.

In front of the store, they lined the horses side by side
along the cross section of one of the large spits erected to
act as a hitching rail. Save for a meager speck of light, the
store was dark, and it took a good five minutes of pounding on the door to rouse the proprietor.

A crusty-looking man wearing a stained apron over his
opulent stomach and garters on his flannel sleeves appeared at the door.

It wound up costing a fortune, but Sanford haggled for
the use of a storeroom around back where Venus could
bathe in seclusion. To the waddling clerk they may have
appeared a loving couple, for Sanford's rough hand was
clasped in hers. Only the two of them knew she played his
guide as they skirted the potbellied stove near the entrance, cold now in deference to the warmth of the sea-
son, and strolled between rows of canned goods on one
side, kettles and crockery on the other, through a cur-
tained doorway leading out back.

And any remorse Venus felt for rousing him after-
hours disappeared the moment she laid eyes on the de-
crepit shack he directed them to.

Venus glanced about the room hardly bigger than an
outhouse, her lips pursed in distaste at the signs of neglect. Cobwebs hung around crates stacked along three
walls and in the corners of the sloping shack's roof. Wide
cracks above admitted dusty streams of moonlight and

the lantern in Sanford's hand cast an eerie beacon across the warped floor.

"It feels gloomy in here," he commented.

"Well, it's not the most elegant place I've wandered into, but as long as there's a bathtub with my name on it, I'll suffer." She was getting pretty darn good at that. She let her saddlebags drop to the dirt floor and, shedding her modesty, began to unfasten the buttons of her jacket.

"That boy we ran into outside should be bringing in water from the well any minute. While you bathe, I'm going to order our supplies and take the horses to the blacksmith's for a thorough grooming."

A sliver of concern coursed through Venus. For nearly two weeks, Sanford had been her constant companion, never straying far. But at the onset of their trip he'd dictated that she not coddle him. She supposed that if he felt confident enough to roam through Lasso on his own then she should not object.

"I'll be back in a half hour," he said. "While I'm gone, lock this door."

Alone after he left, she felt just that—alone. And a bit vulnerable. There wasn't a locking device on the door, but she found a ladder-back chair hidden under a pile of canvas and propped it under the knob.

While waiting for the water to fill the empty tub in the center of the shack, Venus peered out a plate-size hole in the ceiling at the galaxy. Unerringly, she picked out the three bright stars of Orion the Hunter's belt, and the three fainter stars resembling the sword below and beside the belt.

The blinded hunter of myths. Sanford. *No, Orion,* Venus corrected. Orion the mythological hunter. Powerful. Mighty. Wearing the skin of a lion and carrying a club. Blinded for the loathsome act of trying to gain possession of his lady-love Merope by violence when her father, Oenopion, withheld his consent to bless their marriage.

The two might be similar both physically and in their arrogant manner, but there the resemblance ended. Sanford would not take possession of any woman with violence; he not only thought too little of them, but he'd had plenty of opportunity to take her by force and hadn't.

It was simpler just to kill her.

The knock on the door startled Venus, but when the boy with the water identified himself, she removed the chair. The crowded cubicle filled with steam as the tow-headed youth combined hot water with tepid, then placed a pile of clothing Sanford must have supplied on top of a slatted crate. Venus smiled gently at him when he gawked at her, and after he finished emptying the buckets, she pressed a nickel into his palm for his trouble.

Venus stripped out of her soiled union-blue skirt and dingy blouse. Good riddance, she thought, dropping the garments. With a blissful sigh, she sank into the tub.

For a few moments, she gave in to the pleasure of relaxing. Tension and anxiety seeped from her body. Languidly, she thought of Sanford and hoped he fared well on his errands, then wondered why she spared an ounce of concern for the tyrant.

He certainly spared none for her.

Since the river incident, she had vowed to make him pay for his perpetual abuse. He did not allow her much idle time to plan, as he kept her busy from sunup to sundown learning his endless list of survival skills.

And though she'd wear trousers before admitting it to him, his lessons were paying off. She had graduated from the rifle to the revolver he kept strapped to his side, could tell directions on a cloudy day by noticing where moss grew on trees, gallop at full speed without falling off the sorrel, and distinguish the wide arch of his footprints from her own slender tracks. She was also very adept at packing her gear in one minute flat and judging the chances of rain by the condition of the grass in the morning; if dew was present, the chances were slight, but the absence of dew was almost a certain sign they needed to find shelter by nightfall.

Not that any of those achievements would serve her once she resumed her life in Paradise Plains, but at least she had secured her right to travel with him and carry out her labor.

Even so, her efforts didn't seem to impress Sanford. He was still the insensitive lout he always had been, and—if possible—more coldhearted than before they'd crossed the Colorado. Her resolve to strike back, to show him no man mastered her life, gained momentum every miserable hour.

Between his tiresome lessons she earnestly plotted her revenge. She thought to garner some satisfaction with the little pranks she'd been pulling on him.

While observing Sanford, she'd noticed the meticulous order of his saddlebags. So she switched around every item in his packs. Discovering her mischief, he merely hung his head and sighed, then reorganized the gear to his liking.

Another time, she moved the fire pit when he was grooming the horses so when he returned to camp, his step-count was off and he walked straight into flames and singed his pant legs. He didn't bat a lash, to her dismay, just swatted at the embers and went on as if nothing out of the ordinary had happened.

Then there was the night she moved his horse. She'd thought it such a brilliant ruse—until he woke the next morning and whistled. The ornery beast ruined her game by trotting obediently to his master.

The blessed beast botched a second prank as well, for on the day she relocated the entire camp while Sanford laundered his clothes in a pond, Ranger nickered and gave away the new spot. If not for him, Sanford would still be scratching his head in confusion in a vacant field.

Not only was nothing working, she acknowledged with a depressed sigh, but she had run out of ideas.

Venus fished a cloth and soap from her saddlebags, pondering where she was going wrong in her strategy. Oh, Sanford was aware of her pranks. He just wasn't responding to them.

She dipped the rag into the water and absently dragged it over her bosom. *It's time to resort to drastic measures,* she thought, her brows meeting together in contemplation. She needed to devise a plan so subtle, so clever, that even Sanford, with all his mind-reading insight, would never suspect what she was up to.

At the same time, though, it had to be something that would return her to power again.

But what? *What?*

Sanford rolled the back of his head against the shack wall, listening to the sounds of Venus bathing. Why was he dawdling outside her door tormenting himself? Lately, she had proven her grit in adjusting to all manner of hardship—to his astonishment—by countering each of his instructions with a bold prank meant to antagonize. Getting all riled up, though, benefitted no one. He just wore himself out and she just ignored him. But in truth, he found her mischief more amusing than enraging.

He wondered where she'd gotten the idea to change the contents of his saddlebags; it had been quite ingenious for Venus—whom he never would have credited with such deviousness, except she'd been the only one around at the time. Sanford refrained from reacting to her pranks; his reward was hearing her huffs of frustration when he acted aloof. But inwardly, he was pleased to learn that Venus had more talents than face-painting. Under all that frivolity, she possessed a quick mind.

Yes, she was certainly adapting well to her situation. Better than he ever imagined.

And yet, from the moment they'd entered Lasso, he couldn't shake his sense of unease. After placing his order with the surly store owner, he'd felt compelled to stand guard over Venus against a town filled with rowdy men. Not that he'd pose much of a deterrent for trouble, but he might slow them down.

Except that the last thing on his mind now was the erratic temperament of roughneck cowpunchers on a drinking spree. All he could think of was the temptation she evoked in him.

Sanford pushed away from the splintered boards, snorting in disgust at his behavior. Hell, he was worse than an adolescent virgin boy peeping into a young maiden's bedchamber. Although what his eyes could not see, his mind conjured up—perky, velvet-soft breasts beneath a froth of suds, lithe legs emerging from the water like a gentle ballad from a soprano's mouth.

Sanford paused with his hand braced against the wall and his head bent while he composed himself. Why was he afflicted with this condition so often around Venus? It seemed everything she did aroused him. When she talked in that affected Southern drawl or walked with that petticoat-rustling sashay or looked at him with what he was sure was hostile challenge—no matter what she did, he felt seduced.

And, when she touched him . . .

His discipline just evaporated. It took every ounce of strength he could summon not to devour her on the spot.

Not a single other female of his acquaintance managed to cause him this amount of turmoil, this degree of physical hunger. And by damned, he didn't understand how a prissy, conceited, the-universe-revolves-around-me belle could stir the dead ashes of his affections.

It should have been simple: collect the aide filling in for Zeb while he and Minerva renewed an old courtship.

But from the day they passed under that Circle D sign, nothing had been simple.

With a vulgar curse, Sanford shook his head and forced one foot ahead of the other. Lasso was a bit too untamed for comfort, and though Venus was as safe as possible locked in the shed, his unease was not going to abate until they were well away from this den of ill-repute. With the supply order already being filled, he only had to feed the horses their oats, inspect them for saddle sores or stones lodged in their hooves, and have that front shoe replaced on the pack horse. The sooner he completed the errand, the sooner he and Venus would be out of here.

Within thirty minutes, he left their curried mounts nosing buckets of grain in the blacksmith's at the end of town. Sanford stuck close to the buildings, trailing his fingers along the warped clapboards as he headed back to the general store to take his turn in the makeshift bathhouse.

More than once, the Saturday press of humanity

bumped into him, offsetting his balance. Sanford refused
to let a mounting panic override his senses, though. He'd
been doing just fine on his own so far. No use in getting
all worked up because he lost touch of the walls now and
then, he lectured himself.

He passed establishments one after another, identify-
ing each by noise and smell. The saloons were easy: ribald
laughter, whiskey and tobacco odors, stale perfume more
pungent than any Venus saturated herself with, the me-
tallic chink of coins.

From the barbershop he detected faint whiffs of lather
and after-shave and could almost hear the tales of story-
tellers lingering, though it was hours past closing time.

The dance hall emitted a succession of lively notes
from a well-tuned piano, the sliding scale of a harmonica,
and the rapid tapping of wooden heels on a raised platform.

A drunkard's song filtered mournfully from an alley,
and the briny aroma of pickled eggs from the fourth
building caused Sanford's tongue to tingle and his stomach to tighten with hunger pangs. He decided he'd do the
cooking this evening instead of forcing himself to digest
Venus's less-than-edible attempts.

Two more buildings to go before he veered down the
alley to where he hoped that Venus was waiting.

Then, all hell broke loose.

A cluster of leather-clad shoulders knocked into him
just as he reached the entrance to another saloon. Sanford felt himself propelled backward. His hand lashed
out, grappling for the security of a wall.

Again, muscle-bound bodies rammed into him, spinning him in the other direction.

"Hey, watch where you're goin', slicker!"

"Too much cactus juice, pardner?"

Sanford ignored the comments. He fought the disori-
entation clouding his judgment . . . struggled to collect
his scattered bearings . . .

Weaving, feeling the dregs of paranoia slip into his
thinking, Sanford stretched his arms out in a search of a

post, a wall, anything. As long as it was still and sturdy and he could hold on to it.

There was nothing but emptiness and the damned darkness that made his life a living hell.

Venus!

Her name was a silent scream, a plea. The saddlebags fell from his shoulder and he found them only by tripping over them. He stumbled, and in gaining his footing, flailed out his hand.

His knuckles smacked flesh and bone.

A lady screamed.

"I'm sor—" A fist landed in Sanford's gut, cutting off his apology, stealing the wind from his lungs. He doubled over with the gripping pain.

"That'll teach ya to hit my wife, ya sorry son of a bitch!"

Sanford sank to his knees beside the saddlebags, clutching his burning midsection. Under different circumstances, no man would have gotten away with insulting his long-deceased mother, and yet, the man must have believed he had just cause for the remark.

Again, Sanford tried to clear up the misunderstanding by gasping his regret, but another do-gooder cuffed him in the head. His hat sailed in the air, his ears buzzed . . .

"Throw that drunk in the tank with Elmer till he sobers up!"

"A man that cain't hold his liquor ain't no man a'tall."

A fist curled into Sanford's collar, ripping the worn fabric, and he was lifted to his feet.

Sanford decided he'd had enough of this abuse. He hadn't struck the woman intentionally! But since no one seemed willing to listen to reason, he had a right to defend himself.

He thrust his fist forward and met with a chest so solid, it felt as though his bones slammed into brick. A familiar whoosh to his right warned him of another incoming punch and he reared back. The next one didn't miss. Sanford's neck snapped back from the force of the blow to his chin. Glittering specks swirled in his head, like the stars of his childhood.

So this boisterous bunch was looking for a fight, were they?

Though it was against his nature to brawl, he knew there was no avoiding this battle. Self-preservation and manly pride demanded he protect himself.

Sanford spat blood, ridding his mouth of the coppery taste collecting on his split tongue. Then he rolled onto the balls of his feet and readied his fists for combat.

Uncle Zeb had taught him well. *Listen fer the wind ta break. Beware of pauses 'cuz that means they're about ta swing. Keep movin', boy! Stand in one place an' yer a easy target! That's it, Buck—dance!*

Two opponents were introduced to his knuckles up close before a third interloper snatched the back of his vest and spun him around.

"I'm gonna teach you some Lasso manners, stranger."

It was the voice of the outraged husband, foul and threatening.

But it was the voice that followed in its wake that made Sanford's head drop onto his shoulder.

High and mighty, it rang through the air: "You will do no such thing!"

Ah, hell. This is all I need. Venus to my rescue.

Venus was so angry with Sanford she declared she could rip his rock of a heart out with her bare hands. But she'd get her revenge in her own way, in her own time, not give this unruly pack of dogs the glory.

Her spine erect to the point of snapping, she strode through the crowd gathered around him, daring anyone to bar her path.

Though she knew she had drawn the attention of every male in attendance, she had eyes only for Sanford. The sight of blood caught in his beard provoked a fury unlike anything she'd ever experienced.

"Unhand him this instant!" she ordered in a tone crisp as a starched petticoat.

The paunchy fellow at Sanford's back tightened his hold on Sanford's shirt in a show of defiance. Though they were equal in height, the bully outweighed her partner by a good thirty pounds, and from the looks of his stomach under a plaid vest, most of the weight could be attributed to overeating. Long salt-and-pepper sideburns framed a sneering mouth and pug nose, and a pair of black marble eyes nearly made Venus eat her bravado.

"Sooo," he jeered. "The woman beater is also a yellow-bellied coward who has to hide behind a woman's skirts, hah?"

"Venus," Sanford ground out. "Get out of here. You're making matters worse."

"What do you suggest I do? Leave you to the gentle hands of the good folks of Lasso?"

"I was doing fine on my own!" he insisted.

"Fine getting beat up!" Then she whirled on the irate vermin clutching Sanford's shirt. "You, sir, have no call to judge anyone. For you are nothing but a yella-bellied coward yourself if attacking this man gives you satisfaction. Can't you see he's—"

"Venus, don't!"

The urgency in Sanford's voice commanded her attention and the rest of her sentence died on her lips. She sensed his whole body tense, and glancing at him, she saw his head tilted at a proud angle. He wore a grim expression, his face taut, his nostrils flaring, his hooded eyes nearly shut by the lowering of his brows.

Then her gaze swept their audience. Some of the cowboys seemed eager for more violence and were clearly disgruntled because she had broken up the action. And soiled doves glared at her with hostility as though they perceived her as a threat to their livelihood. Why, Venus couldn't fathom, for she'd been in the process of buttoning a gaudy orange shirtwaist that had gone out of fashion in the seventies and gave her complexion a florid hue. Her disparaging reflections as to the storekeeper's poor taste had ceased abruptly when a premonition of foreboding assaulted every nerve in her body. She'd raced out of the shack without bothering to don her heelless boots or brush her damp, unruly locks. Looking like Medusa come to life, she doubted she could give any of these jaded women a run for their money, but they obviously thought the opposite.

Still, not one spectator among them gave any indication they'd noticed Sanford's blindness. And *he* wanted his secret kept at all costs. Was his pride that great? Or his shame that deep?

Either way, intuition told Venus that revealing his impairment to these strangers would publicly humiliate him.

Venus smiled wickedly to herself. Oh, how flavorful power tasted!

Then her smile flattened. Though the temptation nearly killed her, a softening in her heart wouldn't allow her such cruel retribution.

Oh, she wanted him to pay for treating her so horridly. For pushing her beyond her limits. For tossing her beautiful clothes in a pit. For—she choked on a helpless sob—for rejecting her . . .

But not like this. Not by unmanning him in front of a bloodthirsty horde. Not by declaring his blindness to idiots too stupid to figure it out for themselves.

Of course, he did hide it well; even she had not noticed it when they'd first met.

No, she decided, she wouldn't use his lack of sight against him. She'd rather extract her revenge personally, privately. She didn't know how yet; she'd think of something later.

Right now she had to get Sanford out of this mess while his secret was still a secret and his skin was still intact.

She wet her lips with her tongue and said, "All right, Sanford. I won't tell them who you are. But what, then, do you suggest?"

As intended, curious anticipation rippled through the crowd.

He lifted one thick brow. "If you're so smart, you think of something."

She did. She thought of the crew's reaction when Lee introduced her partner at the roundup camp. If he was well-known there, then it was possible this illiterate

bunch had heard of his stories here, too. If not, well . . .
then Sanford could think of something on his own.

"Buchanan—" she stressed his name—"I'm not the
one always boasting of brains. You're the one with the
imagination—what would a character in your dime novels
do?"

Slick Drayson, judging by his progress in chapter two,
would simply shoot his way out and suffer the consequences later. But it didn't matter to Venus what the
imaginary hero of *Race to Destiny* did. She only cared
about what Sanford would do with the inspiration she'd
offered.

She wasn't disappointed.

She swore a glimmer reached his vacant eyes as he
craned his neck toward the man holding him by his shirt.
"Look, mister, I beg your pardon for running into your
ravishing wife—"

Venus almost choked on her laughter at such an exag-
geration. The lady in mention was homely as mincemeat
pie; flat-faced, sharp-nosed, pinch-mouthed, and wearing
more ruffles on her pea-green gown than Lavender, who
designed Venus's hats back home, could ever compete
with.

"—but I was despairing of ever finding a suitable hero
for my next book . . ."

The man's fleshy jaw went slack and very slowly he
released his hold on Sanford's collar. "You're him. Buck
Buchanan, the author . . ."

"Why, yes I am," Sanford replied, feigning surprised
pleasure.

Of course, Venus wouldn't go so far as to calling him
an *author*. Land's sake, he was just a lowly dime novelist,
in no way comparable to Shakespeare or Plato or Horace.
But in perusing the crowd, she saw Sanford's pen name
had clout. The aggressive gathering whispered amongst
themselves while their avid gazes locked on Sanford. No
longer did they appear anxious to stake him up on the
closest ant hill; instead they seemed to be considering
building a pedestal for the adventure king.

Venus suddenly felt terribly dowdy and insignificant.

"And I have been searching for a man to represent the lead character in a story I am creating," Sanford continued. "I have in mind someone who owns a vast amount of land but does not get the recognition he deserves. Someone who aspires to a reputation equal to John Chisholm or Charles Loving, who have paved the way to success in the cattle industry. But not someone with substandard morals . . . You don't by chance, know of anyone who fits this criteria, do you?"

Good Zeus, Venus thought, the man looked as though he'd just been injected with a dose of hot air and was about to float away! She rolled her eyes. What flattery will do to *some* people!

"I certainly do!" he asserted, tugging on his coat.

"Well now—may I impose upon you to make the introductions?" Sanford queried. "I am eager to make his acquaintance!"

"You just have, my good man!" The hand once holding Sanford prisoner seized Sanford's hand as if it were a spigot handle and pumped it up and down as though he were trying to bring forth water. "Eustace P. Fairport, at your service!"

Forgotten was the insult to his wife as the prospect of fame beckoned.

"Eustace P. Fairport," Sanford echoed. "Well, Mr. Fairport, I'd be honored if we could arrange an interview . . ."

"I am free now—"

With a charming grin, Sanford shook his head. "I'm afraid I am in no condition to conduct one at present. I have been traveling for some time now, and have engagements with a bathtub and a lady—in that order. Perhaps tomorrow, say . . . noon?"

Mr. Fairport's crestfallen expression changed to one of eager agreement. He rambled off directions to a ranch fifteen miles out of town while Sanford committed it to memory.

In spite of her ire, Venus shared a relieved exhale of breath with Sanford when Fairport guided his very displeased wife toward a waiting buggy. They'd come through the crisis unscathed.

But as they stood at the mouth of the saloon, waving goodbye, both were oblivious to the fact that a Pandora's box of another kind was just opening.

Ten

HURRICANE HENDERSON GUZZLED THE LAST INCH OF SHARP-
tasting whiskey and wiped the back of his hand across his
mouth. Beating the tumbler against the plank bar held up
with two flour barrels on either end, he shouted, "Fill me
again, Bart!"

The rotund barkeep tilted a long-necked brown bottle,
topping another customer's glass. "I'll fill you, Hurry.
With buckshot if you don't git your scraggly butt outta my
bar. You can't pay for the two drinks you already downed
and I ain't runnin' no charity house here."

Hurricane felt a hot flush rise into his lean cheeks. Old
sowbelly *had* to remind him of his sorry financial state,
didn't he? Well, he'd show the beanhead he wasn't always
poor. Hurricane dug deep into his broadcloth pockets
and brought out the two lint-covered nickels from within,
then slammed them on the counter next to the empty
glass. "I got money, ya garter-totin' whoreson!"

Bart swelled up with outrage, his thick chest nearly
popping the buttons of his white shirt, his pudgy face
turning the color of a ripe turnip. "Watch who you're
calling whoreson, boy. I had your mama as much as every

other man in Lasso." A taunting glint lit his dreary eyes. "Could be *I'm* your pappy."

"You couldn't get that lucky, beetle-brain," Hurricane jeered. "More like you're the walkin' disease what kilt her."

The air in the Rotgut Saloon came close to sizzling. Hurricane watched the veins in Bart's squat neck pump and bulge and shame washed through him. Not many folks in this piddly town gave a care for a dead harlot's bastard. In fact, most of them never let him forget his low beginnings. But Bart had been the closest thing to a friend Hurricane ever had, getting him hired at the smithy's and finding him a place to live in the loft when Sally sold out to Crane Fullard and Hurricane'd lost his job and room. And when his ma died from the clap last week, it had been Bart who bought the pine for her coffin. Not that she had deserved it, but she had been his only blood kin, and he felt he owed her something.

With the exception of Bart, Hurricane didn't give two hoots for any person in Lasso. In general, the townfolk gave horse dung more notice than him, in spite of the many, sometimes reckless, attempts he made to earn their respect.

Long ago he had decided that someday he was going to make something of himself. Something so notorious, so impressive, that folks would hang their heads for the way they'd always treated him.

He still regretted not joining up with the Silverton gang when they'd passed through here in '79. They were almost as legendary as Billy the Kid or the Clantons. But when they discovered he had an aversion to keeping bullets in his gun and revoked their offer, Hurricane decided that robbing stagecoaches and banks wasn't his style anyway. It was probably for the best, though. They wound up hanging in Dodge last year.

Hurricane wanted to be a living legend, not a dead one, so he could come back to his birthplace and flaunt his success in all the mealy-mouthed faces that ever stuck their noses up at him.

The problem was, he never earned enough money running errands to finance his dream.

So he was stuck here, in a town he detested, with people he detested. But he figured that until the opportunity arrived when he'd amount to more than "Linelle's accident," he'd best keep on Bart's good side.

"Shoot, Bart, you take things too seriously." It was the nearest Hurricane could come to an apology. "Now, give me my ten cents' worth of that fire you call whiskey."

"I already did," Bart hurled back, swatting at the bar with a soiled rag.

Hurry heaved a disgruntled sigh, then jerked toward the sound of the double doors swinging open. He closed his eyes and groaned.

"Dammit, Hurry!" Bart hollered. "If I told ya once I told ya a dozen times that she ain't allowed in here!"

Hurricane slid off the stool and addressed the willful female horse swaying bold as brass up to the bar between two drunks near the window. "Daisy, I told you I'd be home soon. You were supposed to wait for me there."

He didn't expect an answer and didn't get one, either. She peered at him through lazy black eyes and defiantly wedged her thick body between two befuddled drovers near the window. With brazen purpose, Daisy wrapped her full lips around an untended glass, then tossed the contents down her throat.

Hurry's reflexes were slowed by the whiskey he'd consumed, and she managed to swipe two more drinks before he ambled to her side, Bart's cussing ringing in his ears.

Daisy belched, then made a move for the bottle sitting on the bar, but Hurricane threw one arm around her neck, grasped her matted mane with his free hand, and swerved her away.

"Now you owe me fifteen cents, Hurry. And don't come back till you got it, either!" To stress his point, Bart tore the shotgun off its wall rack behind the bar.

"Look what you done, girl! Got me kicked out." With a firm hold, Hurricane guided her toward the exit. "Don't know why I even keep you. You cause me more trouble than a damn mule. Liquor'll kill you, haven't you figured that out yet?"

Daisy nickered in protest. Hurricane whispered in her pert ear but until she sashayed out the door with him, he wasn't sure she'd heard him above Bart's curses.

With each step, the whiskey she'd drunk kicked in with a little more force. Hurricane supported the intoxicated mare as best he could, considering she outweighed him by half a ton and he was feeling pretty drunk himself.

He didn't imbibe Bart's sauce much, aware that his system had little tolerance for its potency, but the past week had been hell. First his ma's death, then losing his room and job, and the discouragement he felt thinking that he might not ever realize his dreams for a respectable future . . .

Pure hell.

Halfway down the road, his steps slowed and he looked curiously at the crowd of folks milling about, mumbling to themselves. Nothing exciting ever happened in Lasso, so the action caught his notice. Hurricane got the feeling he'd met with the tail end of an important event, but getting an explanation from his fellow town-dwellers was like scratching an itch between shoulder blades: frustrating and hard to reach. And he just didn't have the energy or patience to deal with their snubs today.

Once Bart's temper cooled, he'd ask him.

Hurricane tugged on Daisy's halter and managed to guide the mare to the blacksmith's shop. The place echoed with emptiness. No hammers rang on anvils, no coals burned in the huge cast-iron table, but a singed odor lingered in the darkness as if someone had recently left.

Hurricane struck a match and ignited the wick of a lantern hanging inside the double doors. His thin lips pressed into a scowl as he noticed the disorder: pliers and mallets and clippers had been thrown onto the workbench instead of replaced on the hooks, tethers tangled around his heels and nails skittered across the dirt floor with every step, soot-coated bellows lay half buried in the dead coals, and the water tub stank of scalded iron. Hurricane reckoned Big John must have stayed at the shop late tonight, for the owner of the smithy never tidied up; that's what he hired Hurricane to do, he claimed. It sure looked like Hurricane was going to earn every penny of his monthly wage, too.

Four stalls had been constructed at the rear of the shop and from there, a faint whinny broke the stillness. Hurricane gave it little regard, for Big John occasionally boarded horses.

"Long as he didn't use your stall, Daisy. I didn't agree to no three dollars a month taken out of my pay so you could bed down in the paddock outside."

Three of the stalls housed animals, one a fine gray stallion Hurricane admired for a moment, but Daisy's stall awaited her. And the instant she recognized "home," her knobby forelegs crumpled beneath her and she collapsed onto the mangy hay then commenced snoring.

"Damn critter," Hurricane whispered to the incoherent mare, stroking her blond mane. "Shoulda named you Hurricane Number Two. Did I ever tell you why my ma called me Hurricane? She said I was about as useful as one, that's why. And you . . . marching into Bart's like you own the place and swiping those whiskeys. Costing me money I ain't got. Don't know why I keep you. You're old as dirt, got rotten breath, and have a disposition more cantankerous than a hermit. No wonder that farmer wanted rid of you."

The farmer not only wanted rid of her, though, he wanted her carted off to the glue factory. And in spite of all the fuss the horse gave him, Hurricane fostered no regrets for rescuing Daisy, old nag that she was.

Two things he owned outright: the pearl-handled pistol Linelle claimed belonged to his daddy, and this delicate-footed roan. Both he held on to fiercely. The gun was a symbol of where he'd come from, the horse a symbol of where he planned to go—which was out of this stinking hole. And Daisy . . . she was his wings.

Hurricane rose from his crouched position and dragged a moth-eaten saddle blanket from the stall divider. With a flick of his wrists, the blanket fluttered over the animal's supine body.

He stretched then wished he hadn't, for the blood rushed to his head and the livery seemed to be spinning in circles. Hurricane pushed a froth of black hair from his eyes as he weaved in place. Maybe it was time to bunk down himself, he reckoned, feeling a lid-heavy drowsiness consume him. The whiskey had whooped him out, too.

The floor kept shifting under his feet as he moved toward the ladder leading to the loft. The rungs creaked as he ascended. At the top, he heaved himself over the ledge—and the seam of his trousers gave out.

Hurricane hooked his finger in the torn seat of his pants and groaned a curse. *Just dandy,* he thought, *now I gotta walk around with my shorts flashing.* There'd be no money for a new pair of pants until the end of the month, and these had been mended so many times before that an inch of cotton already showed through the threads.

He was distracted by a faint but feral clicking carrying across the loft. A noise much like the hammer of a gun being drawn back.

Instantly wary, Hurricane grasped the pistol jammed into the back waistband of his trousers and aimed his empty weapon toward the far corner. The hollow chambers were a running joke in Lasso, but if he was dealing with a stranger he might get away with it. If the horses down below were new to these parts, then the riders might be, too, he concluded. And outsiders didn't usually take time to wonder if a gun was loaded or not.

He peered across bales of hay stacked over a bedding of loose straw. His vision swam, yet Hurricane made out a single form outlined in the open hatch at the front of the building.

That looks like Charley Dane.

His sparse brows puckering in curious speculation, Hurricane watched the tender of the Drowned Sorrows saloon for a moment. *What's Charley doing in my loft with a rifle?*

Whatever it was, Hurricane sensed the scrawny man was up to no good. A man didn't just kneel against an upper-story hatch-frame aiming a gun without some foul deed in mind.

The low, slanted rafters forced Hurricane into a hunched position as he skulked toward Charley, his footsteps muffled by the cushion of hay. "Boo!" Hurricane yelled directly behind Charley.

Charley jumped. His balding head rocketed upward and cracked against the indrawn shutter held open by a rope.

Hurricane held his flat stomach against the spasms of laughter wracking his body.

"Damn you, Hurry!" Charley whispered harshly. "What are you doin' up here?"

"I live here. What are *you* doing up here?"

Charley seized the rifle that had fallen into his lap and said, "None of yer business. Now go away. Yer botherin' me."

That wasn't unusual, Hurricane thought. He bothered everybody. Even so, he hunkered down and set his jaw. "I'm not going nowhere until you tell me what you're doing sneaking around my bedroom." He gestured toward the blanket and bundle containing all his worldly possessions not two feet away.

"If you gotta know, I'm takin' aim."

Hurricane looked out the hatch. The crowd was still there, gathered around the prettiest woman he'd ever laid eyes on. She was easy to spot, even though she was little, because her light hair shone brighter than the lamp lit overhead, like a beacon in the pitch-black night. And the sight of her dainty face lit a fire inside Hurricane, warming him faster than any rotgut. So fast that sweat ran down his temples.

"Who *is* that?"

Charley propped one hand under the rifle muzzle and cocked his head to the side, bringing some elusive target into view. "Buck Buchanan," he answered with an evil smile.

Hurricane thought that an awful strong name for such an itty-bitty lady but kept his opinion to himself. "You guarding her?"

"No, you dimwit! I done said I'm taking aim!"

"At what?"

"At Buck Buchanan!"

"You're aiming at a lady?"

"Dammit, Hurry, which saloon did you leave your brains in this week? Buck Buchanan's the big, dark one standing next to her."

Hurricane's gaze settled on a tall man talking with a local rancher but swiftly returned to the vision in the orange shirt and brown skirt. Absently, he asked, "Who the hell is Buck Buchanan?"

"He's the bastard that ruined my life. He wrote about me in one of his books. Tole the whole gol-danged world I done robbed a bank in Antsbed an' I didn't. But no one believes me, and now no one sets foot in my drinkin' house."

So that's why the Drowned Sorrows had been empty for months. Hurricane just reckoned Charley had quit the business.

His fuzzy mind sorted out the information Charley sent it. There was no question that Charley intended to snuff out Buck Buchanan's candle, and all because of a book . . .

He felt something like a charge of lightning strike him and he sobered instantly. "He's a book writer?" Hurricane quizzed. "He wrote a book about you? Used your name and everything?"

Charley lowered the gun an inch. "Well, not exactly. He called me Charley Dawson. But everybody thinks it was me, and that some Texas Ranger caught me and had me sent to prison for a couple years. Just because I don't like talkin' 'bout my past don't mean I'm a criminal. Lotsa folks keep to themselves."

Hurricane was barely listening, though, nor was he interested in the woman any longer. He licked his lips. *Buck Buchanan, a book writer.* Just because he couldn't read so good didn't mean he was stupid. He understood enough to know that people in books were famous. They were talked about and treated special—especially if they were heroes. And if they were heroes—they were admired and never forgotten. Like Billy the Kid and Buffalo Bill. Didn't matter none that Billy the Kid was an outlaw.

Once people heard his name and read books about him, he became famous.

And Buck Buchanan, he'd written a book about Charley . . . "That means *you're* famous, Charley!" Hurricane stared at the barkeep with amazement.

"I never wanted to be famous," Charley countered. "I jist wanted to live in peace—and did till that man stuck me in one of his dime novels."

A dime novel, Hurricane thought, awed. His thoughts chased each other in his head. *He* wanted to be famous, though. Wanted folks to see *him* through different eyes. Open doors for him instead of slamming them in his face. Call him "sir" instead of "whore's brat."

And if he could get Buck Buchanan to write about him . . . make him a hero . . . everything he'd ever dreamed of would come true! Hurricane could tell Buck all about his life! Tell him of all the troubles he'd suffered and all the scrapes he'd escaped from—like the time he'd found that dynamite and blown up Gizzard's outhouse, nearly getting splattered all over the chicken coop in the process!

Yeah, he said to himself, he had stories worth telling!

"Hey, Charley?" Hurricane prodded. "If Buck Buchanan wrote about you, think he'd write about me, too, so I could be famous like you?"

"Nope."

Hurricane narrowed his eyes. "And why the hell not?"

" 'Cause I'm gonna kill the polecat and dead men can't write."

The instant Venus guided him away from the ragtag group, her imitation smile withered. With a firm grip on his arm, she ushered him down the street.

"I can't believe you were brawling in the street—step down. I can't even be separated from you—don't crack your shin against the horse trough—for a half hour to take a bath in peace—pardon our way, please—without you getting yourself into some kind of fix."

Sanford never said a word, just followed her quick pace with a silly grin on his face.

But it didn't stop Venus from ranting the entire way to the bathhouse. "And now we're going to be stuck here—step up, there's two feet of boardwalk here—until you interview that puffed-up peacock—" Then, Venus gasped with swift comprehension and pulled up short. "You can't mean to model Slick Drayson after that . . . that ambitious bully! His hands are softer than the underside of a snake! And his eyes—I've seen tar hold more appeal!"

"I thought that was the type of man you fancied for a husband. Ambitious and soft-handed."

Her lips clamped shut at the blatant reminder of her contrived reason for embarking on this westward journey. "Maybe so. But he must also be passably fine of form and face—not to outshine my own stunning looks, mind you—" Venus poofed her hair vainly, then frowned at its snarled condition. Tossing her head in dismissal, she continued, "And he must have at least a modicum of intelligence. The mere thought of *that* man as a model for Slick Drayson is about as deplorable as me attending the Governor's ball in a gunny sack!"

"What's got you worked up about Slick Drayson all of a sudden?"

Venus stared at him in disbelief. "Worked up about . . . Look, Buchanan. Mr. Fairport uses force and intimidation to achieve his means, even at the cost of another man's honor. Slick Drayson is no pompous egomaniac. He is clever and confident and fair."

"He's also a figment of my imagination. Too bad, though, isn't it? You could abandon your husband-hunting venture, marry him, and never have to lie in the dirt again."

Venus swore bitterness laced his comment, but for what reason?

"Don't go get all upset now, Venus. I wouldn't want you giving yourself wrinkles over something that isn't going to happen."

Her brow furrowed. "What do you mean?"

"I mean I have no intention of using Fairport as a character in any of my books. We'll be gone before he knows it, and other than bruised pride, he will be none the worse for wear."

"You *lied*?"

"I *bluffed*. Isn't that what Slick would do? Isn't that what you advised?"

Once this soaked in, Venus beamed. "You actually listened to me? You used one of my ideas?"

Sanford started her down the alley between the saloon and the general store, toward the bathing shack, and without being aware of it she continued to warn him of obstacles.

"I would have been a fool not to. You noticed something from an objective point of view, Venus. That's what I brought you along for."

Her mouth fell open at the offhand compliment. "Bless my soul, Buchanan. Did you take a blow to the head or something? I could swear I heard you say two nice things to me in a row!"

He shrugged off her comment with a helpless flick of his brows, but at the shed, he stunned her again.

He cupped her jaw with his hand.

Venus froze, gazing at him in wide-eyed wonder as goose bumps peppered her arms and her spine went all prickly. She had no control over the way her blood ran hot and cold simultaneously. Caught off guard by his unexpected touch and the queer sensations it produced, words failed her. She could only stare at him. At his scrubby jaw. At his finely curved lips, moist and inviting, and at the narrow bridge of his nose. At those cozy-fire and cupid-arrow eyes of his . . .

Stiffening, she resisted him. Resisted his magnetic pull, his rugged attractiveness. But more, she resisted herself. And it caused her an almost mortal pain, holding back the impulse to lay her cheek to his heartbeat, to feel comforted and loved.

But Sanford didn't love. She knew that well. He owned and drove and provoked. He degraded and disparaged and demoralized.

And he made her question herself. Her sanity, her desires, her expectations . . .

Oh, how she loathed his ability to turn her inside out!

Then, as if her emotions weren't in enough turmoil, he added to the maelstrom.

He pressed his lips to her forehead and whispered, "Thank you."

She blinked and he was gone, had disappeared inside the dim doorway to the luxury of a thorough cleansing.

Venus sank against the flimsy wall. Her breath came in fast pants, her heart hammered in her chest, and her corset seemed tighter than it had a minute ago.

Feeling hazy-headed and loose-limbed, she gawked at the shut door a long while before turning her bewildered gaze to the narrow line of dark prairie meeting even darker sky.

Venus brought her fingers to the spot he'd kissed, certain she'd feel a raised blister from the scorching heat of his lips.

Thank you.

She never would have believed those two words a part of his vocabulary if she hadn't heard them with her own two ears! But it wasn't just the words, it was the voluntary show of fondness. Not an accident but a true-blue deliberate gesture of kindness from the stoneman.

For what? For an objective opinion? Her opinions hadn't held any merit before—and she'd offered plenty! Why now?

Mystifying. Venus shook her head in eye-misting confusion. That's what Sanford was. One moment he loathed her and everything she stood for, the next he treated her with the gentleness of a lover.

So, who was the real Sanford "Buck" Buchanan?

And who was the real Venus Daltry? Surely not the reckless hoyden, the wanton woman, the saddle tramp's possession.

She used to be elegant and fashionable. A slave to decorum and social obligation. But her actions of late would have her banned from respectable circles, and no longer would mamas be urging their sons to court her, no longer would she be the most sought-after lady in the state.

She'd be alone and scorned, more so than she was by Sanford, who had never liked her to begin with.

Her lips curved in a sad smile she could not explain. Land's sake, she must be lonely! It was pitiful that she actually craved even a small sign of a dime novelist's esteem, if for no other reason than to make working with him easier.

It would be funny, though, if Sanford did like her, she mused. Especially when he was so adamantly opposed to her.

Then she giggled as an outrageous thought seeped into her conscience. What would be even *funnier* was if he fell in *love* with her.

Of course, the chances of that happening were as slim as walking on the moon. He barely tolerated her. No matter what she did—

Her head snapped upward, her melancholy vanished. *That's it!* She'd get Sanford to fall in love with her!

Venus did a little jig of glee as the idea took hold. Honestly, sometimes her own brilliance frightened even her! If she could get him to fall hopelessly and helplessly in love with her—she squealed in delight—then she'd drop him like a hot potato!

Not only would it teach Sanford not to fool with her, but she'd also regain her self-respect! Because if there was anything Venus knew she could do—and do well once she put her mind to it—it was steal a man's affections.

It was true he'd shown no interest in her thus far, but that was because she'd been handling him all wrong!

Sanford might be sightless, but he was still a man, with a man's pride.

And instead of appealing to Sanford the man, she'd been fighting Sanford the savage at every turn! She'd been rebellious and disobedient, asserting her independence, then attacking him at every turn when all else had failed.

But she hadn't done that in the crowd and had earned herself a glimmer of respect.

Why not employ the same tactic when they were alone?

Stop using his blindness against him by playing pranks on him?

Venus began to nibble on a chipped nail, pacing the area while a cool May breeze caressed her damp tresses.

And if he had a man's pride, then—under that tough exterior—he must also have a man's weaknesses. But she'd been so busy trying to discover what they were and where they hid that she'd forgotten *she* could be a man's weakness!

No, rather than searching for Sanford's vulnerable spot, she needed to look at her own strengths. Her ability to charm and bewitch. Until now, giving him the full force of her charm had seemed a waste and a bore. But if she melted that granite heart of his, got him to trust her, the rest of this year was going to be an easy ride to success.

Venus grew more jubilant as her plan developed. Instead of giving him guff as Lee accused her of, she'd be nice till her teeth hurt! Considerate . . . cooperative . . . and yet delicately helpless. Men needed to feel empowered and invincible. What better way to promote their feelings of masculinity than to regard them as gods?

Yes, she had agreed to learn survival tactics—she'd had little choice in that matter—but she could do so with less resistance. She could pretend to be awed by his frontier knowledge. Smother him with flattery and praise. Feed his ego, as rankling as it might be.

But, it *was* for a good cause.

A shiver of anticipation skated up her spine as she heard the shed door creak open. Venus nearly skipped toward Sanford and had to force herself to remain calm. Sanford was a very astute person and the tiniest slipup would make him suspicious.

Oh, why hadn't she thought of this plan before? It would have saved her hours of misfortune. So simple, yet so elusive . . .

Well, no matter, Venus consoled herself, taming her eager pace. Better late than never. The result would be the same.

She'd have the satisfaction of ultimate revenge—*and* she'd get her prize!

Eleven

AH, HELL, WHAT'S SHE UP TO NOW? THE TOWEL HE'D BEEN DRYING his hair with drooped in his hand as Sanford leaned against the open door. As if today's events hadn't made him weary enough, now there was Venus to contend with again.

He didn't need eyes to know she was plotting more mischief; he *felt* her calculating grin as she neared him.

"Did you enjoy your bath?" she asked with underlying sweetness. It clinched his suspicions. Well, his clothes hadn't been stolen, nor had his saddlebags been tampered with, so whatever misbehavior she intended must be outside the shed. The little imp sure didn't give him much time to recover before she attacked.

He pushed away from the door and slung both sets of saddlebags over his shoulder. "My pores can breathe now that they aren't clogged with dirt."

"Good. The next time you scold me about 'luxuries' I'm going to remind you of those words."

She wound her fingers around his thumb and tugged him out to open land, away from the security of buildings. "Where are you leading me, Venus?" Probably through a thistle patch, he figured, or someplace equally prickly.

"We still have another twenty minutes to kill before the supplies are ready, so you are going to brush my hair."

Sanford's brows shot upward. "I am, huh?"

"Yes, you are. And I don't want to hear any arguments. If I am to be forced to give up the comforts of a bed tonight just so you can appease your fetish for the great outdoors, then you can do me a favor in return."

Touching Venus in any way went against all wisdom, and yet, Sanford couldn't find the heart to refuse this one request. He had been overly cautious since they'd met, therefore had pressed her into learning twice as much in half the amount of time he would have a male partner. She'd held up well . . . considering her flighty upbringing. Maybe she had earned a concession or two.

Besides, she had him curious about her motives for being so all-of-a-sudden friendly. He didn't expect to get any straight answers questioning her, but if he played along for a while, she'd give herself away. Then he'd know he hadn't stepped into some unwritten chapter.

Venus stumbled, pulling him from his musings, and the quick reflexes of his hands prevented her from falling. Preoccupied, Sanford's toe caught on the same obstacle and he pitched forward. Venus braced him with her shoulder and he caught a generous whiff of delicate perfume before righting himself.

"Sorry," she said. "The dumb root jumped in my path so fast I didn't see it."

And Sanford gaped at her. *What, no snickers? No,* poor *darlings?* His lips quirked sardonically. "Things are prone to do that."

She settled down beside a hardy tree Sanford believed to be an oak and he lowered himself against the trunk.

"You didn't think to bring the lantern, did you?"

Sanford tensed and felt his face grow warm. "I don't . . . I didn't consider . . ."

"Never mind. There's nothing out here to see anyway."

"It's just that Uncle Zeb usually . . ."

She shushed him with her fingers to his wrist. "Please don't explain. I'm embarrassed enough for mentioning it as it is." She placed the brush in his hand. "Let's forget I said anything."

He tried, but he felt awkward and self-conscious now, and was afraid he'd do something worse than trip over a tree root or forget Venus needed her way lighted.

Venus ignored his reluctance, though, and guided his other hand to the back of her head. A wealth of matted hair tumbled down her back. Her shirt was damp in spots and her shoulder blades jutted out beneath the crisp fabric. Sanford was reminded of her petite frame. Of the demands he'd heaped upon her. Of how steady she remained in spite of him.

"I've never brushed a lady's hair," he confessed.

"Just gather it in your hands and work the tangles out of the ends first, then work your way up to my scalp. A full one hundred strokes is required nightly to keep it healthy and manageable."

She made it sound easier than it turned out to be. She had thick hair with tangled knots. He took extra care so he wouldn't jerk the strands out by the roots. But once the toughest clumps became smooth threads of fine silk, he began to relax.

Counting strokes also gave his wary mind a rest. Even if he wasn't overreacting, and Venus did have a trick up her sleeve, he wouldn't know what it was until she pulled it out. And by tomorrow morning, she'd probably be back to her former do-things-my-way self. So he decided to simply enjoy these few minutes of leisure before they returned to business as usual.

In truth, it was pleasant sitting with Venus under a tree in the evening stillness. From afar, the night's ribaldry disturbed the peace, and yet, alone here, with her, he experienced an enjoyable detachment. Nearby and above, a blackbird cawed softly, cicadas competed with crickets in song, and the lush grasses whispered a welcome.

Venus's head lolled back on her shoulders and her airy sigh touched a neglected piece of his soul. Her scent meandered up to his nose, pure yet womanly, innocent yet desirable. He searched his memory for the name of her pleasing fragrance. Whatever it was, she hadn't worn it before tonight, and he wondered why. It suited her well. "What is that you're wearing?"

She moved and said, "Some godawful orange tent that makes me look like a tomata."

He chuckled, partly because of her way of speech, partly because she had misunderstood. "No, your perfume."

"It's soap, Sanford," she replied wryly.

"No soap I've ever used smelled so . . ." *Arousing. Delicious. Edible.* "Tangy."

"It's scented. My mama adores flowers. She has a beautiful garden growing in front of our house where she cultivates different varieties for their unusual essence and beauty. She calls this soap 'oraposies'—orange blossoms, apple blossoms, and roses—tiny fluted buds with heart-shaped petals. It's my favorite."

Unconsciously, Sanford stored the information away.

Then she inquired after a pause, "Does your mama like flowers?"

"I don't know. She died when I was three."

"I'm sorry for you."

He shrugged and continued stroking her hair, the outer layer, then underneath. "I think it was harder on my father."

"He never remarried?"

Sanford wished he would have. Maybe he wouldn't have gone off to fight then. Wouldn't have gotten killed. "He was very fond of her."

"Oh. He still grieves for her then."

The line of discussion was making him uncomfortable. Bringing together too many memories of a time best forgotten. "Not anymore. They're together now."

And as if sensing he'd closed the subject, Venus did not pursue it further. Instead, she moaned, "I think I'm going to con you into brushing my hair more often, Sanford. I declare I'm turning to liquid."

Hell, he was turning to fire! Every nerve, every muscle had been kindled the minute he sat down behind her. And with each moan she issued, each flex of her small frame between his flanking legs, each curling waft of her soap, the flame licked a bit higher.

"If I ask you a question, will you give me an honest answer?"

If he could find the ability to talk! He nodded curtly.

"I'm confused about something."

You and me both, Sanford thought. He didn't understand how it was possible to desire someone he resented. And yet, he admitted to himself, he didn't quite resent her as much as he had in the beginning. In fact, she was sort of growing on him. But she still wasn't the sort a man desired. She was the sort he married. Squired around to balls. Hired maids for and drove around in velvet-cushioned buggies. She was high-bred lady through and through.

Unaware of his thoughts, she went on. "I'm not trying to pry into your business—I know how sensitive you can get—but I can't help but wonder . . ."

He knew what her next words would be without her saying them. "Why I wanted you to keep quiet earlier about my blindness?"

She hesitated, then nodded.

Without thought to the action, he lifted a skein of her hair to his nose and inhaled deeply. "I've been in enough of these makeshift towns in my travels to have gotten to know something about the residents. You want to husband-hunt"—Sanford's sentence broke for a second and he tamped down the quick sword of jealousy lancing his chest—"then look elsewhere." He cleared his throat of hoarseness. "Most of the men in places like Lasso are just a bunch of randy mavericks on the lookout for fresh fruit ripe for the plucking. Do you understand what I'm saying?"

Venus nodded again. "I've known my share of disreputable rogues. Lee and C.J. take care of them right off, too."

"Well, I may not be the deterrent your brothers are, but I'm all you've got. Imagine what might happen if word leaked out that your partner couldn't see the broad side of a barn door unless it smacked him in the face?"

She swung around to face him. "That's not true! I know I came in at the end of the scuffle, but I saw you sluggin' a few of those bullies before they even knew what hit them!"

The brush drifted down to land in Sanford's lap. She sounded as if she were defending him against himself! Severely, he countered, "Don't fool yourself, Venus. You either didn't see or are forgetting the ones I missed." He hadn't, though. And it would probably be wise to avoid spicy food until his tongue healed from that punch to his mouth.

She averted her body again. "Certainly not all those men had unscrupulous intentions."

He wondered if a particular one had caught her eye but didn't ask. He might not like the answer. "Maybe not. But are you willing to take the risk?"

"I guess not." She fell silent as the brush swept through her mane. Her slim neck bent backward, forward, backward, forward . . . a provocative rhythm that Sanford wished he could ignore.

At length, she remarked, "I like it when you explain your lessons to me, Sanford."

It was hard to believe they were exchanging polite conversation. Sanford had always found words flowed without effort in story form, but personal communication was difficult for him. He had trouble making sentences, was reserved with his private thoughts. He supposed his uncle's manner had rubbed off.

But strangely, he found Venus easy to talk to. Interesting to listen to—as long as he didn't need her describing things for him. She was a lousy set of eyes—vague with details and dismally general with appearances, unless, of course, they were discussing her wardrobe.

People like Venus baffled him. They had eyes but *didn't* use them; He had eyes but *couldn't* use them.

What a damned waste.

With Venus, it seemed more of a disappointment for she was brighter and more imaginative than she portrayed. And if she'd only let it loose, there was a fun-loving nymph trapped in that proper lady's shell.

Not that he cared to explore that hidden side of her . . . warning bells pealed inside him to leave well enough alone. To hold to their business pact.

But this close to her and in such a calm atmosphere, business was the last thing he thought of. Neither was a story clamoring to be written.

Rather, each brush stroke only stimulated his imagination further. And surrounded by fresh-washed femininity and mewling sounds of contentment, his iron-clad control slipped a notch further. The woman in her called out to the man in him. The man in him was responding. Furiously.

"Your hair's about dry and the supplies should be waiting—"

She halted his roughly spoken statement with her hand to his thigh. "It has to be braided, Sanford. I am well past the acceptable age of wearing it down."

His denims were no barrier to the searing heat of her slender fingers and supple palm. Kindling desire flared in an instant and Sanford lurched to his feet. "I can't braid," he croaked, knowing it was a lie. He'd been plaiting leather halters for years.

"Then tie it back with a ribbon." She pressed a frayed strip of silk against his chest.

Sanford shifted from one foot to the other, fighting the urge to bolt. If he refused, he'd look like a coward. And by damned, he had never run from anything before; he wasn't going to start by running from Venus.

Gritting his teeth, he gathered her tresses at her collar and wound the ribbon, securing it with knot and bow. Then he jumped back. "If you're done primping . . ."

"Sanford?"

He closed his eyes against the shaft of bittersweet pain. "What now, Venus?"

She stood on tiptoe and kissed his chin. "Thank you for the respite."

He nearly exploded.

The first step of her plan had gone pretty darn well. Venus mentally toasted herself as she led Sanford through the grasses behind the buildings. The idea of his brushing her hair had spawned from the fact that, since he was unable to see, she must employ other methods to make him aware of her. In her experience, men were attracted through physical means, then snared with an emotional connection.

Obviously captivating Sanford with her outward beauty was impossible. Therefore, she had decided to tantalize his other senses: touch, smell, hearing, and taste. This was the long route to his heart, but it wasn't as if she had anything better to do for the next year. And as long as she kept three things uppermost in her mind—the revenge, the prize, and the challenge—the thrill of winning all would outweigh the inconvenience.

Thankfully, the folks of Lasso were milling about a pair of men lying in the street and gave her and Sanford little notice as they rounded the smithy building.

Her curiosity piqued by the activity, Venus craned her neck to see, but a wall of people blocked her view. She did catch snatches of conversation, though.

"I think old Charley's gonna be good as new once his arm and leg heals up," someone informed the others. "Broked both of 'em."

Another man snidely commented, "Lucky he didn't break his fool neck fallin' out the hatch."

"Looks like Hurry's comin' round. If anybody's got some powders, better fork 'em over 'cuz he's gonna have a whoppin' headache."

"Anybody know what happened?" came the question from a slouchy old-timer wearing a twill newsboy hat.

"Two hotheads in a second-story window?" the first man rejoined. "That shouldn't be too hard to figure out even for you, Breadbutter."

"That's *Leadbetter,* ya wag-wit!"

Her interest waned as they neared the entrance of the blacksmith's building. Once inside the shop they could barely hear lively discussion going on outside. Venus spied the lad who had brought her bathwater setting down sacks that looked twice his weight near Ranger's stall.

The horse nickered, and Sanford, turning to the sound, nearly stuck his foot in a dented pail. Venus reflexively snatched it from his way before either he or the boy realized it as Sanford made a direct line for Ranger.

They spent the next few minutes saddling and cinching and loading in companionable accord, the boy lending his help with the pack horse. Venus paused more than once to watch Sanford's hands skim over the straps and oiled seat, again marveling at his deftness. His gentleness.

Her brow furrowed and she touched her hair, absently rubbing a rebellious curl between her thumb and forefinger. Her stomach roiled and tumbled with a combination of eagerness to move forward with her plan and guilt for concocting it.

How would he cope when she jilted him? With morose gloom? Righteous affront? Passionate anger?

It's not too late to forget this foolhardy notion, her conscience warned.

Defiantly, Venus flipped the draping lock over her shoulder. She had nothing to feel guilty about. Sanford deserved a lesson of his own. And if his feelings got hurt or his pride was bruised, well then, he'd have a taste of what she'd been suffering the past couple weeks.

Besides, once they arrived in Nevada and he'd written his book, neither of them needed to see the other ever again. He could go on seeking another adventure and she could go on romancing another barrage of admirers.

They'd both be happy in their separate lives.

The thought did not cheer her as much as she had expected.

"Whaddya mean they're gone?" Hurricane regretted yelling at the kid but he told himself it was because his brains were about to burst from his head, not because the boy was cowering in the alley.

If there was anything he'd learned in twenty-two years of living by his own wits it was that the streets spared no room for weaklings. Therefore he had little tolerance for those who showed promise of becoming one. Especially orphans like himself; he'd considered himself an orphan long before Linelle's number came up.

Hurricane massaged the soft, egg-sized knot at the back of his skull and studied the boy. He wanted to shout at him to quit curling up like a baby, to toughen up if he wanted to see his thirteenth birthday, but the scolding refused to surface.

Oh, who cares anyway? This kid will learn just like I had to—the hard way.

Besides, he had more important things to do than waste time giving free advice to dullards. He had a future to chase—as soon as he could get information on when it had left and where it was going. "How long ago did they leave?"

" 'B-bout t-ten minutes . . ."

"In a wagon? On foot? On horses?"

"H-horses. Three."

Hurricane recalled the horses he'd seen near Daisy's stall. "Was one a big gray stallion?"

The boy nodded mutely.

So that was Buck Buchanan's stallion! Damn, if he woulda known, maybe he coulda hid it. Slowed them down some.

Well, they were only ten minutes ahead. If he hurried, he could still catch up . . . "Which way did he go?"

The boy pointed toward Mustang Draw and Hurricane took off toward the smithy shop, his normal swagger more of a stagger thanks to his scuffle with Charley Dane. But at least he'd stopped Charley from killing Buck. And Bart had told him that Charley was going to be out of service for a while since he'd busted a couple bones. That meant Charley wouldn't be on Buck's trail.

That eased Hurricane's mind. As long as Buck stayed alive he had a chance of becoming a hero in one of those dime books.

Hurricane halted. *Yeah! Now I'll really be a hero!* Once he caught up to Buck, he'd tell him all about Charley's trying to kill him and how he'd saved his life! 'Course, he'd stretch the truth a bit. Instead of telling Buck that when he'd grabbed Charley's rifle, they had fallen out of

the loft, he'd tell him there was a gunfight in the street.
Yeah. And he'd been quick on the draw . . . yeah! And
the silver bullet he kept in his chamber had pierced Charley's heart and the villain had toppled face first in the
dirt. And when the gunsmoke had cleared and the folks
of Lasso saw what he'd done, they'd cheered him!

Hurricane thrust out his chest and pulled his gun from
the back of his pants, blowing imaginary smoke from the
barrel. "Aw, shucks," he told the empty shop with deep,
drawling modesty. "It's all in a day's work. Now I gotta
track down more bad men so the world can be safe for
decent folk."

And the people threw flowers and money at him as he
rode boldly out of town on a coal-black steed.

Yeah. That's what he'd tell Buck.

Consumed with renewed energy, Hurricane advanced
to the rear of the building and raced up the ladder. He
threw his few belongings in a large kerchief and tied the
four corners together. Returning to the horse stalls, he
headed straight for Daisy . . .

And stopped short at her gate.

Hurricane's temporarily banished headache resumed
with full force as he spied the old nag lying in the straw.

He wasn't going nowhere till Daisy sobered up.

Twelve

SANFORD EASED HIS BACK AGAINST THE WALL OF ROCK ABOVE the arroyo where they had made camp and listened to Venus inventory the supplies he had purchased for her in Lasso.

"Jerky, matches, canteen . . . One thing is certain. My supplies were more colorful. Everything you bought is *brown*."

He smiled to himself. He realized he'd been doing quite a bit of that lately. Venus was more of a nuisance than he had counted on but traveling with her was not dull. In truth, her prissy ways had become entertaining during the long hours of riding and researching. And since the day she'd gotten a bee in her bonnet and had begun pulling shenanigans left and right, she'd kept him on his toes.

Sanford shook his head tolerantly and reached into his saddlebags for the shirt torn in the mobbing in town. From a small housewife kit, he withdrew a needle and thread and proceeded to repair the shoulder seam. At least he didn't have to worry about the fire pit mysteriously moving itself. They had no fire tonight. It seemed wise given their recent trouble. In the event Eustace P.

Fairport got wind of their departure and came looking for him, the lack of a blaze would make them harder to spot.

To his surprise Venus hadn't complained. In fact, now that he thought on it she'd been awful quiet altogether. Usually she had plenty to say about his decisions regarding where they camped, what they ate, when they bathed, how hot the weather had turned . . . Jesus, he knew of every speck of soil that stained her clothes, how many times a weed poked her tender skin, when her hair frizzed after a rain . . .

Her hair.

No, he wouldn't awaken that memory. He'd just put it to rest, having finally regained feeling in his numb fingertips from brushing that luxuriant mass of curls.

He returned to the task at hand. Just as he bit off the finishing knot, Venus moved her pallet next to his. Her petticoats swished and he felt her warmth as she settled down beside him. Then she took the shirt he held. "Not bad."

"That surprises you?"

"Everything you do surprises me."

At his quizzical look, she said, "You don't mind if I sleep by you tonight, do you? It's kind of unnerving way over there by myself."

"Afraid of the dark, princess?"

Venus ignored the scathing comment and shucked her outer clothing, then her corset and bustle. She wasn't afraid of the dark; she'd simply taken advantage of it to get closer to him. But once in her thin chemise and petticoat she wondered if she hadn't erred in judgment. Suddenly she was acutely aware of the man next to her.

Quietly and with a hint of sadness he told her, "Don't worry. You get used to it."

Venus felt her color heighten. She hoped he was referring to the darkness and hadn't read her mind again.

Sitting on her quilt with her arms looped around her updrawn knees, Venus covered a yawn. She wasn't ready to sleep, though, despite it being close to midnight. Neither had Sanford dozed off yet.

"Do you want me to write for you tonight, Sanford?"

"I thought you'd be too tired."

"I think I'm too wound up."

"Used to staying up late wearing holes in your slippers, huh?"

Venus smiled with nostalgia. "Those nights seem so long ago."

"You'll dance again, Venus." He toyed with the weaving of his blanket a moment then sighed. "All right. I suppose there won't be any harm in lighting a candle. Ranger will alert me if we have any unwelcome guests. There should be a taper in your packs, along with a small metal container holding matches."

"Notes or story?"

"Notes first, I guess. We'll get down the day's events and observations while they're fresh. Then, if you're up to it, we'll work on the story. We need to get the first draft finished, then we'll go through our notes and fill in the details."

An odd warmth filled Venus at his choice of words. He said *we* and *our,* as if his book were truly a joint project. Not that she was especially thrilled to write a dime novel, but at least it was binding him to her.

After igniting the candlewick, she withdrew the journals. Sanford reclined comfortably with his hands clasped behind his head while dictating his perceptions of Lasso. Then she switched to the booklet marked *Story* and read yesterday's entry for chapter four. Her voice slid over him like a fuzzy blanket, soft as down, the inflection of pitches like wrinkles in the material.

" '. . . The animal crouched before him, hackles raised, fangs bared, growls vibrating deep in his throat. Slick's legs tingled with the need to stretch, yet budging from the hunched position meant instant death.

" 'In front of him he faced menace: a crazed wolf out for blood. Behind him menace trailed at a distance, no less hungry, but much more dangerous for its cunning: man.' "

Abruptly, Venus closed the journal, marking the page with her thumb. "Is he going to shoot the wolf?"

He wore a pensive frown. "Can't. The report of his

pistol will alert Gunns Murphy to his location. And he can't run, or the wolf will attack."

"Well, he can't just sit there, either. If you ask me, he should have been watching where he was going instead of pondering over why Gunns Murphy wanted the saloon back so bad. Then he wouldn't have happened upon the wild dog feasting on the armadillo."

"If I can't figure a way to get Slick away from the wolf, then I'll just change it to something workable. That happens sometimes. I get into a plot device, but can't get out of it and have to abandon the idea." He shrugged. "It's all part of the process."

"Seems to me it's just a waste of time and energy. Didn't you ever want to do anything else with your life?"

He paused and Venus hoped she hadn't made him angry. She was trying to make him fall in love with her, not alienate him.

But Sanford found himself ready to talk. Maybe it was the stillness of the night compelling him, or the impression that she truly seemed interested; regardless, the words flowed freely and felt good being spoken. "I used to want to be an equine doctor. Me and my father trained horses before the war and from that livelihood stemmed my love for the animals."

"That explains why Ranger is so manageable."

"I worked with him for three years. His sire came from good Arabian stock, and his mare was a pure-bred Morgan. The combination makes Ranger a fast steed with quality stamina, although his crossed bloodlines lessen his monetary value."

All Venus saw when she looked at the gray was a smelly beast. Sanford's high respect didn't change her opinion much. "Well, what stopped you from becoming a horse doctor?"

His lips twisted skeptically. "Whoever heard of a blind veterinarian?"

"I never heard of a blind dime novelist either, but you managed that."

He chuckled. "I wish you'd tell me honestly why you are so opposed to what I write."

Venus considered her reply. No one in her circle of friends touched the paperbacks. In the Literary Club, the ladies occasionally discussed classic works between community gossip, and the topic of books never arose with her suitors. Usually they remarked on how her eyes shimmered with diamond dust or declared they would be the envy of every male attending the Harvest Festival if she chose them to escort her. Cultural things.

So far, those she'd met who recognized Sanford's pen name did not appear to have an ounce of intelligence in their heads, nor a hint of refinement. That was reason enough to disdain Sanford's books. She was not of his readers' class!

At length she said, "Dime novels do not reflect education . . ."

"Are you saying I am not educated because I love adventure and excitement?" His voice trembled with laughter. He braced the flat of his hand on his thigh and cocked his head. "What would you say, then, if I told you I attended one of the finest schools in Boston?"

"I'd say I'm not that gullible. Schools teach people to read and write. And if you could do those things then you wouldn't need me."

"For your information, Miss Smarty-petticoats, my certificate of graduation from the Perkins School in Boston, Massachusetts, and my degree in business are proof that you *are* gullible!"

Venus stared at him in astonishment. *Sanford* held a certificate of graduation? A degree in business? She could not credit it! Not this woolly follow-my-tracks-and-shoot-my-gun dictator! "But . . . but *how*?"

"I studied. Next you'll ask me why I 'waste my time' having lurid tales of gamblers and outlaws published."

Again, he read her thoughts correctly.

"Well, I'll tell you why. Because I wasn't the only sightless student bored to tears with the textbooks available to us. I wanted to read something gritty and gripping. I wanted to lose myself in fiction that portrayed good pitted against evil, and good won. I wanted to live in other times, in other places, and wanted to believe for a few hours that I could do anything.

"Before and after he sent me off to school for those two years, Uncle Zeb spent our days together teaching me to hunt and fish and take notice of life around me. But every night we camped in the wide open, he took me to the realms of imaginary worlds. He would read popular novels by Anthony Trollope and Wilkie Collins and Herman Melville until I could recite their works by heart." Grinning, Sanford bowed his head and it shook back and forth. Moonlight reflected off the damp strands, making them appear more white than brown. "*Then* . . . then he picked up one of Ned Buntline's dime novels. I was so captivated by the characters, the outlaws and lawmen and cowboys and Indians . . . After I'd soaked in every dime novel he could get his hands on, I started making up my own stories, never knowing he wrote my words down and submitted them to an editor until the day I received an offer from the New York Publishing House wanting to buy them."

He wasn't going to stop *now,* was he? She hungered to know so many things about him, but he hoarded details of his life so carefully that he was as much a mystery to her now as he had been the first time she'd seen him. Venus pushed his shoulder. "*Then* what happened?!" Sitting on the edge of her quilt, she waited with unsuppressed fascination.

"*Then* nothing." Sanford shrugged. "I was seventeen years old the first time I sold one. Then I sold another, and another. Soon I had a name built for myself without the stigma of being blind attached to it. I had accomplished something I loved based on talent, not sympathy."

"And now that you have, what do you plan on doing with it?"

He shrugged again. "Keep creating. And eventually I will have just the right story written and send it to the American Printing House to have it published in Braille. Give those without sight a variety of reading material that I did not have."

"Is Braille anywhere near Nevada?" she couldn't refrain from asking.

His hearty laugh took her by surprise. Venus scowled. "What's so funny?"

"Braille isn't a place. It's a style of print for the blind . . . here. Let me show you." Sanford leaned over and retrieved a large book from his saddlebag. Venus had seen it when she had fiddled with his belongings but hadn't given it any notice in her haste to finish the chore before he caught her.

Sanford laid it in her lap and opened the cover. His arm slanted across her back as he propped his weight against the ground, and his other hand grasped hers.

Then he glided her fingers over a series of tiny bumps on the page. The cream she applied kept her skin soft and Sanford was conscious of his own hardened calluses pressing on such delicate fingers. His hold gentled. "Exploring India. That's what those raised dots spell."

Venus wrinkled her forehead. "How can a bunch of dots spell anything?"

"Each group of point type ranges from one to six dots and represents a letter of the alphabet. The school teaches people like me to train their fingertips to read each letter, then each word, then each sentence, and so on. Just like a schoolmarm teaches sighted children to read primers."

Venus scanned a couple pages with her fingertips while Sanford followed, telling her what the contents said. "How fascinating! You *can* read, then!"

"I never said I couldn't. That was *your* assumption."

"Can you write, too?"

"With a special tablet grooved in small squares. But it is slow, tedious work and I find my thoughts run faster than I can put them to paper. That's why I dictate my stories to an assistant—in this case, you—and have them retold to me. That system also helps me notice a detail I might have missed in the story or one I want to do away with."

While he talked, the candle sputtered, then extinguished in a pool of wax. Sanford didn't notice, but Venus experienced the intimacy of darkness.

Sanford's tutorial position seemed more of an embrace, his voice a caress. His hair tickled her cheek and his manly, leather scent surrounded her as tangibly as his arms.

She turned to watch his lips move, but could not hear the words he spoke. She only saw the lines on his lips, and flashes of even white teeth, and the fringe of whiskers framing his mouth.

She realized he had stopped talking when he veered toward her and their faces were inches apart. His breath fanned her lashes, warm and dewy and minty. And her traitorous body reacted. It yearned for the taste of him. Those lips, that breath.

His dark lashes lowered and his breathing quickened to match the accelerated beat of her heart.

Venus waited with hopeful expectation that once, just once, he would appease her curiosity. Give her a meager taste of what his lips offered and what hers desired. And not pull back . . . please don't pull back . . .

His arm tensed at her back, his muscles flexed, the hand covering her own squeezed the fingers resting on the open page. Venus wished he would read the goose bumps along her arm like he read the Braille print—with a faint touch.

His face drifted down, hers raised slowly . . .

He bared his teeth and growled like the wolf in Slick's story; then he whipped his body away from her. "Damn you, Venus, go to sleep!"

Venus sat, stunned.

So close, so close . . .

Where had the resolve not to let him affect her gone? Not to let him stir forbidden desires?

Venus tried to remember the importance of making herself irresistible to him and yet there were times he made her feel like a little girl dressing up in her mama's clothes. Other times he made her feel like . . . well, she didn't know what he made her feel like, but it wasn't a little girl.

Lying down, she curled into a ball, hugging the empty ache inside her.

It wasn't a lady, either.

Hurricane shut his eyes and cursed. It figured. Of all the horses he could have bought, he'd picked the sorriest damn critter in the lot.

"Don't do this to me, Daisy," he pleaded to the stalled horse. Of course, she didn't listen to him. Daisy did as she pleased. And at this moment, it pleased her to sleep.

Hurricane's body swayed backward as the mare lowered her front, then swayed forward as she dropped her back end. She didn't seem to care that she was not in a stall, but smack in the middle of the wagon-rut road ten miles outside of town, and that it wasn't nighttime, but the middle of the day.

Hurricane's feet were flat to the ground even though he was still mounted. "Get up, Daisy."

She bared her yellow teeth at him, then settled her head upon her folded front legs.

He couldn't believe he'd wasted five dollars on this creature.

Hurricane stood and swung his leg over her back, then looked down at her. "I should have let that old man melt your hooves, you know that? If I thought I'd find another fool to take you off my hands, I'd trade you in a second!"

The threats had never worked on her before, though. She just ignored them.

Hurricane moved to grab her bridle and she nipped at him. He withdrew his arm in the nick of time. "Damn you, you ill-tempered old nag!"

With a discouraged sigh, he crouched down to Daisy's level—a safe distance from those formidable chompers. "Look, Daisy, it's like this. We're less than a day behind our fortune. But the longer we sit here, the farther ahead they're gonna get, and the longer it's gonna take us to catch up. We've already lost a whole night while you slept off your drunkenness, and part of this morning while you recovered from a hangover. We can't afford to lose more time!

"They're heading northwest, and I've heard those deserts in New Mexico Territory can be pretty brutal. You don't wanna have to cross those hot white sands, do you, honey? So why don't you get up, get moving, and get us to Buck Buchanan? I promise, once we reach him, and he makes us rich and famous, you'll never have to carry nobody's weight again. I'll buy you your very own pasture with the sweetest clover ever grown and I'll hire somebody to carry you to your bed so you don't even have to walk if you don't want to. But you gotta stop stopping every few miles to sleep. You hear that, honey?"

The sleeping animal didn't hear a word.

Hurricane cussed in disgust and sprang up. Turning his back on the lazy animal, he started following the ruts gouged into the dirt by the passages of wagons hauling supplies to various ranches in the area.

If he had to walk the whole distance, he'd catch up to Buck Buchanan. No way was he gonna let some stubborn old horse deprive him of making something special of himself. If Daisy wanted to share in his success, then she could just follow behind *his* trail.

Damn ornery female. She was just like his mother. Selfish and mean and spiteful. And fickle, too. Damn ornery fickle female.

This was the thanks he got for taking care of her? For cleaning her stalls and stealing oats for her and using his own comb to curry her?

He hoped the coyotes picked her scrawny bones clean.

Hurricane halted in his tracks. *Coyotes?* With another curse, he spun around, and headed back toward his horse.

Damn his own soft heart.

Venus had no idea how long she had lain awake, nor how much sleep she had finally been able to obtain last night, but it hadn't been enough.

As much as she yearned to seize a few more minutes of slumber, a habit of waking at dawn had formed, and her body would not allow her the luxury she once took for granted.

Besides, Sanford's bedroll had already been removed,

indicating he was up and probably working with Ranger as he did in the mornings while she set their coffee to brewing and attended her toilet. But since they had forgone a fire the previous night, she assumed they'd also postpone the customary cup of brew.

Oddly enough, she had grown used to spending those few moments sipping coffee with him, watching the sun rise, watching him. Sometimes he would stand with one hand hidden in his pocket and his feet scuffling against the ground and she would know he was deep in thought. Other times, he would stoop low with the tin vessel cupped in his hands, a thin column of steam clouding his features as he discussed their course for the day.

The deviation in their routine left her feeling . . . incomplete.

Much like she had felt last night.

Venus shook free of the whimsy and rolled off her quilt. If she had come to any conclusions in these wee hours, it had been to stop fancying herself attracted to him. To stop reacting so strongly to his nearness. *He* was the one who should be feeling like bubbling butter and ice cream—hot and cold and ready to melt—the instant they touched. Not her!

The memory returned with a vengeance, though, when she spied Sanford in the near distance. As she had guessed he would be, he stood beside the gray. Ranger was nuzzling Sanford's side. The animal retreated, Sanford's pistol clamped in his mouth. Venus had seen this remarkable animal perform often but his feats never ceased to amaze her.

Master rewarded beast with a loving scratching of ears and a pat to the neck.

Her lips set in a grim line, Venus wadded the thick blanket into a ball. She wasn't jealous of a smelly, four-legged creature, she told herself. So what if Sanford gave that animal more affection, more praise than he ever had or would give her. She wanted no tender fondness from him—she wanted a deep and passionate love—something so intense that when she jilted him, he'd feel the effects for years to come.

She wanted revenge.

"I did something real stupid last night, Ranger. I told Venus things about myself I've never told another soul—except you, boy." Sanford laid his forehead against his friend's warm coat and purged his thoughts. "Not even Zeb knows that I want to submit my work to the American Printing House. Why did I tell her?"

He took the gun from the horse's mouth, wiped it off with his kerchief, and shoved the weapon back in the holster. Then he reached into his pocket and gave Ranger a sugar cube. "I wanted to kiss her," Sanford confessed. "But I didn't want to stop there. I wanted to hold her in my arms. I wanted to see her face with my hands. Is she as pretty as Uncle Zeb described?"

Ranger's head bobbed up and down as if to say yes.

Sanford released a pent-up breath. "Well, it doesn't matter whether she is or isn't. You know looks have never been important to me. She could be Aphrodite in the flesh and it wouldn't change my feelings where she is concerned. Where any woman is concerned. I have this hunch that if I ever allowed myself to think of Venus as anything other than a business partner, my whole world would be turned upside down. And you know how lost I get when things aren't straight up." Adjusting his tilted hat, Sanford reminded the patient animal, "Besides, like every other woman I've met, Venus is afraid of the dark."

Or maybe he was just reminding himself.

Thirteen

HURRICANE BALLED HIS HANDS AND GROUND THEM INTO HIS eyes, then gaped ahead.

"Is it them, Daisy?"

Chewing her grass, Daisy swerved her head to look at him. Her doleful brown eyes and lazy manner implied that she cared little one way or the other. Hurricane hardly noticed. His adrenaline gushed like water spilling from a broken dam at the faint sight of three horses' behinds on the horizon, one a massive gray with a darker gray tail swishing to and fro. He barely discerned the two mounted figures, but those horses were unmistakable.

"It *is* them, honey, I just know it!" Hurricane bounced in the shabby saddle, unable to contain his enthusiasm. "I can't believe we finally caught up to them! As many times as you stopped . . . Then when we almost got strung up for filchin' those eggs from that henhouse, I was beginning to think they'd be so far ahead that we'd never find them . . . and there they are! Like they just dropped out of the sky in front of us!"

He jabbed his heels into Daisy's bulging sides. "Gid-up, girl. At a run, we'll meet up with them in ten minutes—less if you run fast!"

Daisy's head dropped and she pulled another mouthful of grama with her teeth.

"Gid-up, girl! What are you waiting for?" Hurricane pointed earnestly. "They're *right there*!"

Her jaw worked the grass in uncaring circles.

"Awww, damn you!" Hurricane jumped to the ground and stared at the disappearing specks, his thin brows wrinkled with worry and his breath coming in hard, panicked pants. "They're getting away . . . They're so close I can almost touch them, but now they're getting away . . ." He swung to the insolent brown form. Hurricane raised his fist as if to bop her good, but one glimpse of those sorrowful eyes and the temptation deserted him.

He yelled at her instead. "What the hell are you doing? Don't you understand that while you're standing here having a snack, I'm eating the dust of my future? My fame? Don't you care—" Hurricane abruptly clamped his mouth shut. He was wasting his breath anyway.

Scanning the now-empty stretch of range, he realized he was also wasting time. If he stood around waiting for Daisy to finish grazing, he'd be here till doomsday.

His eyes riveted to the distance, his feet started moving before his brain gave the command. Without thinking, he told the mare, "Just stay here, girl. I'll come back for you."

His feet moved faster and Hurricane broke into a run. Long years of escaping from the irate folks he'd played pranks on, or had stolen food from so he could eat, or swiped clothes off their lines, made him swift as the wind. But those days of escaping and stealing were about to end, he thought, racing toward his destiny. The flat land gave way to rocky rises and it was the one straight ahead that his attention remained glued to. Buck Buchanan had just disappeared behind it. Hurricane pumped his legs furiously. The loose sole of his boot flapped in time and his lungs strained for air. But he did not stop. A stitch developed in his side, but he did not stop. He stumbled twice, scrambling over rocks on the hillside, stabbed his palm on a blooming thistle, and extended the tear in the seat of his britches, but did not stop.

Until he reached the top of the mound.

There, Hurricane bent over with his hands braced on his knees, wheezing and gasping, his darting eyes scanning the vast range below. A few head of russet beeves grazed in the open pasture. Stunted mesquite granted shade for those lying in the grass beneath the twisted branches while others basked in the afternoon sun.

And there, at the far western corner of the prairie, were three walking horses and two riders. One wore a dark hat. The other wore a bright reddish-orange shirt.

Buck Buchanan and his lady fair!

He laughed breathlessly. At last! He was finally gonna catch up with the famous writer! Finally gonna have his name printed in one of those books everybody read. Finally gonna have the respect and admiration denied him since birth.

He was finally gonna be a hero!

Hurricane sprinted down the incline, one hand holding the shock of thick black hair out of his eyes. He had gone halfway across the pasture when, from the corner of his eye, he spied a sight that made his heart freeze.

The biggest, meanest, ugliest-looking bull ever put on the face of the earth had his sights beaded on the departing writer and his lady.

The bull lowered his massive horns and began to paw the ground. Hurricane tried to holler a warning but his throat closed and the alarm came out in a squeak. He increased his pace even though his lungs threatened to burst already. If that bull charged, there was no way Buck Buchanan would know it until it was too late, for the fierce animal was to their backs.

As Hurricane dashed across the field, he wasn't sure what he was gonna do. But he knew he couldn't let that maniac beast attack Buchanan.

He couldn't seem to make his legs run fast enough. *Why don't Buck see the danger? And why the hell did he cross this plot of land anyway?* Everyone knew how contrary bulls were. How territorial. Especially with a herd of cows close by. And the woman was wearing that bright orange color . . .

Hurricane concluded that Buck Buchanan had to be the boldest, most fearless man he'd ever heard of. Braver than Jim Bowie facing a renegade tribe of Apaches. More daring than Sam Houston taking on the entire Mexican army.

For the man to stroll through the territory of this formidable bull, he had to be bigger than life!

Hurricane's admiration for the writer knew no bounds.

And it gave him the will to keep running—until his legs fell off if that's what it took!

He spared a second to gauge the bull's actions. Desperation wrenched his vitals. The animal was now snorting and tearing up the dirt and Hurricane knew the creature was about to charge. And there was nothing he could do. He'd never reach the animal in time. Five hundred feet still separated them, and his sides were splitting. He curled his arm around his waist to stem the cramps and felt something crunch in his vest pocket. Slimy fluid from the eggs he had heisted earlier soaked through to his shirt.

And suddenly, Hurricane knew a glimmer of hope. If he could distract the bull, then he'd lose interest in Buck Buchanan—at least long enough for him and the lady to get away.

His pace slowed marginally as he dug in both pockets. Two eggs were intact. He clutched them like balls and heaved them in succession, using all the might his lean body retained.

And he had a good idea where the term *bulls-eye* came from. One of the eggs splattered right between the bull's eyes while the other got caught on his horn, the shell dangling on the white bone, yolk and white dripping to the ground.

The bull started, then swung his triangular head to the side. Hurricane skidded to a halt as the animal pinned him with a menacing glare. Then, that huge head lowered, and those hooves pawed, and Hurricane's mouth fell open. "Uh-oh-ohhhh!" He wasted not a moment beating a hasty retreat as the bull, wild and furious, leaped into a gallop straight for him.

*   *   *

"This poor ole hat. Honestly, Sanford, I declare it's in worse shape than yours." Venus continued fiddling with the wreath of flowers she had been weaving to pass the time while they rode. She had hoped the bright reds and yellows would spruce up the tattered remnants of straw crown and brim, but it didn't look as though anything could save her mama's creation now.

As she tied the ivory bow beneath her chin, Ranger sidestepped into the sorrel and issued a nervous whinny. "What's the matter, boy?" she heard Sanford ask. "Venus, what's got my horse spooked?"

In answer, the ground beneath thundered, and together, Venus and Sanford jerked around.

"What the hell is going on?" Sanford's voice echoed her alarm.

Then, Venus relaxed. "Nothing to worry about. It's just a cow chasing a cowboy across the pasture. Oops, there he goes, up a tree."

"The cow or the cowboy?" he inquired with mock seriousness.

"Why, Sanford, you made a joke! Land's sakes, I didn't know you had it in you!"

"We all have our faults."

Some more than others. Venus frowned. It had been seven days since she'd come up with her plan and she was no closer to her goal than when she'd started. Honestly, coming up with ways to make Sanford fall in love with her was a labor in itself! Brushing against him at every opportunity to tempt him with the whiffs of soap he'd expressed mild interest in was about as effective as cuddling up to a canyon wall. And each night she arranged for him to give her hair its hundred strokes, she had no way of knowing whether he fancied her soft curls piled atop her head or gathered loose at her neck. His opinions—if he had any —were never revealed.

Her hopes that he might find her acts of helplessness were also dashed. Passing him buckets of water and requiring his expertise in fashioning knots she deliberately botched provided excuses for her fingers to linger along his sensitive hands, but did little to dent the armor around his heart. And she feared asking him to supply meat for supper or pretending to need his help skinning the wild game too often for he might begin questioning her motives.

That, she was well aware, must be prevented at all costs. This was a daring sort of manipulation. If Sanford ever learned she planned to use then abuse his heart, he'd leave her for buzzard bait, she was certain. She might as well consider her prize history then!

Oddly enough, evading discovery made her quest all the more exciting. Even if there was an easier route to his affections, Venus was in no hurry to pursue it. Perhaps, she thought, there was a bit of adventurer in her after all!

The morning wore on and the heat increased, baking land and bleaching sky. Venus felt as arid as the bands of rocky hills they followed but she held on to her optimism, and withheld her complaints.

While Sanford quizzed her about the patterns of venomous snakes she must watch for, Venus attempted to screen her complexion from the sun's brutal rays with beauty aids. Smoothing cream into her cheeks, she answered, "The coral snake has wide, alternating stripes, a rattlesnake bears distinctive brown or red diamonds on its back, and a smaller version of the rattlesnake with a pair of horns over its eyes is called a sidewinder."

"And what measures are taken in the event of a rattlesnake bite?"

"Find a pine tree and build a coffin," Venus quipped, dusting white powder across her sunburned nose. Pursing her mouth at her reflection in the mirror, she traded the powder puff for the tube of lip coloring in her bag. Upon removing the cap, she found a liquefied mess of red and wailed, "Darn it, my lipstick melted!"

"Venus, put your paint away and listen carefully! In case of a rattlesnake bite, the whiskey bottle is the first thing to grab. Drink until your teeth float. It dulls the pain and slows the heart rate, which also slows the spread of poison into the bloodstream. Then treat the bite." He mimed on his arm a remedy while they rode.

Venus pulled her attention from the blood-hued wax on her hands to Sanford. She watched with fascination as he used the tip of his knife to scratch a circle around a nonexistent bite, the white mark defined on his dry, tanned skin. He then pretended to suck the venom and spit it out.

"Some folks cut an X over the fang marks rather than cutting around the bite. I've also heard a poultice of kerosene and sliced onions over the bite draws out the poison. When the onion turns black, replace it with another slice. Burning the area with a hot knife is another method. I haven't tried those cures, but I've known men still alive because they have."

Venus plucked rags from her saddlebags and wiped off her hands, then bound the tube in cloth and stuffed it back into her cosmetic pouch. She heard his words but the prospect of actually cutting into someone's skin and sucking out venom made her shudder with nausea.

Thereafter, Venus combined Sanford's sensory perceptions and her own visual observations of the barren landscape in her notebook. She did not share his fixation with rocks and mesas and chaparral thickets, but writing kept boredom at bay and her mind off reptiles.

An hour before the sun reached its zenith, Sanford leaned over Ranger's neck; the horse halted. Although these frequent rest stops lengthened the time it would take to reach their destination, they were necessary to preserve the animals' endurance. Sanford dismounted, and as always, Venus envied his body's lazy grace as he swung his leg over the cantle and kicked his other foot free of the stirrup. Buckskin strained with the bunching muscles of his thighs; his vest stretched across his back; his shirtsleeves molded around corded biceps.

Entranced, Venus swallowed with difficulty. For all his experience, Sanford seemed completely innocent of his own magnetism. His manly appeal.

Venus wished she were as immune. Her body continuously betrayed the vow she had made not to react to this rugged tyrant. He was supposed to hunger for her, not the other way around! But too easily he distracted her from her plans of retaliation; too easily just the sight of him awakened yearnings she had sworn she would not feel, but did. Intensely. She imagined Sanford holding her, cherishing her with his lips and his hands . . . taking her to heights she had always longed to climb but had never reached.

Her thoughts venturing into forbidden territory, a moment passed before she realized Sanford was speaking to her. Venus's head snapped upward. "What did you say?"

He scowled in annoyance. "I *said* Lincoln is about forty miles or so west of here. I think we'll stay there for a couple days and let the horses rest up. This heat is sapping their strength."

"Should I plan on bunking in a livery with them?"

"Suit yourself," he replied nonchalantly. "But I'm getting a room at the hotel."

"A hotel?" Venus gasped. "Dare I hope a restaurant, too?"

Sanford's mouth twisted into a semblance of a smile. "Everything your greedy heart desires, princess."

The news filled Venus with elation. *Civilization. Two days on stable ground. Real food, beds, and baths!* It didn't matter that his reason for a break in travel was to give the horses a rest—she nearly wept with the wonder of it all, anyway! "How long will it take us?" Venus queried, unable to hide her eagerness.

"Two, three days." Sanford shrugged, uncapping his canteen and taking a deep drink. Then he poured tepid water into his hat and allowed Ranger to quench his thirst. "Depends. As hot as it's been, I don't want to press the animals or we'll be walking."

Venus didn't much care if she had to row a skiff through desert sands and if it took a week! Land's sake, it was all she could do to restrain herself from planting a big, fat kiss of gratitude smack on Sanford's lips! A mischievous giggle escaped. Wouldn't that shock him down to his toenails!

Of course, she'd never commit such a brazen act, but then again, lately she was doing lots of things she'd never thought she'd do.

And maybe a bit of reckless behavior would serve her in good stead. She wouldn't kiss him, no—he'd refused that offer twice already—but there were other ways . . .

As he passed by her on his way to the pack horse, she called his name. He wheeled in her direction. At his inquiring expression, she put every ounce of sweet Southern inflection into her voice. "Would ya mind helping me down?"

When he hesitated, she rushed on. "I know I'm supposed to be fending for myself, but I'm purely exhausted from this heat . . . why, I fear I'll swoon without your aid."

He seemed to battle with indecision so Venus pressed a bit further. "Please, Sanford?"

He gave her one of the scowls she had come to expect but reached for her. With a calculating grin that she knew he could not see she floated into his arms, purposely sliding her body down the solid length of his. She ignored the delicious tingle curling through her nerves. Once her feet touched the ground, she squeezed the biceps she'd been admiring earlier, barely putting a dent in the taut flesh. "My, you have strong arms. Did you know that firm muscles are a sign of a good provider?"

He released her instantly and stalked off.

Venus quelled her disappointment. After all, it had been like this all week. For each compliment she issued, he made a face, then put as much distance between them as possible. Capturing his devotion was harder work than she had anticipated.

Venus loosened the feed bucket from the saddle ring and poured water into it for the sorrel. Absently she combed the gelding's tangled blond forelock with her fingers.

Well, she wasn't going to let her spirits plummet. They were heading for a genuine settlement with respectable inhabitants. The name Lincoln rang a bell. Venus couldn't place where she'd heard it but just knowing they were going there filled her with anticipation. Maybe if Sanford-the-stoneman got a gander at other men's reactions to her, he might regard her in a new light. Sometimes all it took to bring a man to his knees were the attentions of another man. And Zeus knew she'd run into a shortage of *them* lately!

The horse drank his fill, and Venus, returning to her packs to give the beast his ration of oats, faltered at the sight beyond.

There stood Sanford beside the last horse, his left arm bent at the elbow and his hand in the air. A sudden bubble of laughter rose in her throat.

Using his right hand, he tested his flexing biceps.

Venus smothered sounds of delight with her hand and shook her head in pity. *Oh, Buchanan. One of these days you're going to realize you don't have a snowball's chance in July against me.*

Venus's eyes were trained on the castle rising from the dust in the distance. Of course, it wasn't a real castle, just a bunch of false-fronted frame buildings, but to her, Lincoln of the New Mexico Territory looked like something out of a fairy tale.

"Why is the name of this place so *familiar?*" Venus voiced aloud the question that had been nagging at her the past three days.

Sanford fiddled with the brim of his hat. "Maybe because it's the site of the most ruthless and violent land wars this country has seen to date."

Venus shook her head. "No, I don't pay much attention to wars, especially those over a patch of dirt."

"The Lincoln County War concerned more than land rights and hostilities between cattlemen and merchants," Sanford corrected. "It was primarily a conflict over political control and injustice, and derived from long enmity between the English and Irish. Range wars and cattle-rustling stemmed from those conflicts."

"Sounds like a plot for one of your books, Sanford."

"Not mine, but a score of other writers cashed in on the killing, and more jumped on the literary bandwagon after Lincoln's corrupt sheriff, William Brady, was gunned down by a cocky young desperado named William Bonney. You might know the outlaw better as Billy the Kid."

Venus's eyes widened. "That's where I know the town's name from!"

"I don't think there's a soul alive who isn't acquainted with the Kid's involvement in the Lincoln County War. But tales of his deeds have been grossly exaggerated—he wasn't the hero avenging his merchant boss's murder like the papers made him out to be but an Eastern-born hothead who used his charm to get him out of trouble. And when his charm failed, he used his Colt revolver."

"Actually, I don't give much credence to newspapers, either. If I believed everything they printed, then I'd have to accept that Rebecca Porter is the most popular girl in Paradise Plains and everyone knows what hogwash that is because *I* am the most popular girl in Paradise!"

"If they don't, I'm sure you inform them."

Venus splayed her hand to study her nails. "Of course." Zeus, she was long overdue for a decent manicure. "I cannot have people being deceived, now can I?"

He nodded seriously. "That would be a sin."

Venus let her hand fall to her lap. "Yes, it would. But I don't recall Lincoln because of the outlaw; the town stands out in my memory because one of my old beaus bragged about carrying the same name as the Lincoln lawman that finally shot Billy the Kid—Garrett. Ironic, isn't it?"

"I'll sleep better nights with that sacred confession."

Venus ignored his sarcasm. Instead she focused on distinct features of the infamous town the closer they approached. "Oh, Sanford! I see ladies! *Real* ladies, strolling down real boardwalks, shading their heads with real parasols! And their gowns . . ." Venus broke off, aghast. "Oh, land's sakes, I can't be seen like this!"

In a vain attempt to save herself from utter humiliation, Venus fluffed the lank curls hanging down her back and brushed at her blouse. *Oh, it's no use!* The outfit was years out of fashion and stained beyond redemption. She felt about as ravishing as a tumbleweed with her trade-store clothes and freckled face.

Part of her longed to escape, to return to the unfet-
tered comfort of being with Sanford alone on the trail.
Around him, she did not feel so conspicuous. But
amongst people for whom first impressions were lasting
ones, one glimpse of her in this pitiful condition and the
elite would see her banned from their circle. Even the
Daltry name would not influence them.

"Quick, let me borrow your long coat," Venus demanded of Sanford.

"Venus, it's eighty-five degrees out here! You'll faint in
this heat!"

"I don't care! I'd rather collapse in a swoon than be
seen in these rags."

Sanford sighed, but lent her his duster. He was right,
she did swelter under the canvas, but at least the coat hid
her atrocious outfit.

It also earned her a number of baffled stares as she and
Sanford wended their way down the main street that was
broken by several side avenues and alleys. Calvarymen
from some military outpost squired cultured ladies to various shops to purchase merchandise, or send telegraphs,
or attend to business at the bank.

Tailor-suited cattle barons riding in luxurious black
coaches paused in conversation to gawk at her, no doubt
wondering whether she belonged in this respectable section of town or with the disreputable populace opposite
the sophisticated establishments. Venus pretended not to
notice the insult; even so, her eyes darted back and forth
and she imitated one of Sanford's habits by tugging on
the rim of her hat.

Passing the wide glass windows of a land agent's office,
Venus spied an odd-looking grate below the steps of an
unidentifiable building. "Sanford, there is a pit dug in the
street near the courthouse, with a top door of wooden
bars—an underground cage. What is it used for?"

"Bad men. Criminals thrive in the West, and some
towns believe if men act like predatory animals, then they
should be treated as such. That cage is used to hold
wanted men until they appear in court—or until a vigi-
lante team beats the law to deciding their fates."

Venus's eyes widened. From all she had seen thus far, she wouldn't have expected the fine citizenry of Lincoln capable of such barbaric inhumanity.

In front of an elegant, two-story hotel with glaring white railings circling each level, both Venus and Sanford started on hearing his pen name being shouted from across the street. Whipping around, Venus spied a dashing soldier in a crisp blue uniform rushing between pedestrians toward them. His short blond hair was trimmed above his ears and stylish sideburns softened the severe cut of his jaw. His eyes were the color of slate and lit up at the sight of Sanford sitting stiff and wary in the saddle.

"Buck! I didn't expect to see you again so soon. Don't tell me you missed our maggot stew?"

Venus's face scrunched up. Soldiers didn't really eat such disgusting fare, did they? If so, she'd have a talk with Sanford. Convince him to restock their food supply and take their meals someplace else. Her opinion of Lincoln was sinking lower every minute.

As though secure with the voice, Sanford's rigid bearing slackened and he returned the hearty handshake. "Truthfully, I didn't expect to be back so soon."

Venus hadn't known he'd visited here before. Then again, there was a lot she didn't know about Sanford.

"Did you need more information on that book you were writing?" the soldier asked.

"No, I finished it last year. I gave my editor instructions to send you a copy, so expect one on the mail coach in the next couple months."

"The captain will be relieved. He's been awaiting your next book . . . pesters me about it all the time."

"I also used the title you suggested."

"You called it *March of the Thunder Sticks*?"

"I thought it apt, considering the Indians always heard your rifles before they saw your blue coats."

"You told the truth, didn't you?" He seemed genuinely concerned. "You talked to the Apache and heard their side along with the Army's?"

"I contacted a brave at the reservation south of here

who rode alongside Quanah Parker," Sanford assured the soldier. "His name was Great Hands and he—"

"Ahem," Venus finally interrupted. Although she was a bit stunned that such an obviously educated man revered Sanford for his work, she was weary of the talk, sweating under the duster, and vexed at being ignored.

The soldier turned abruptly in her direction and his generous mouth dropped open. Then he smiled. "Why, Buck you old dog. When did you get hitched?"

"She isn't—"

"And to such a pretty filly, too!" His eyes never leaving her, the soldier advanced, his shoulders square. "Mrs. Buchanan, it's a pleasure to meet you. I am Sergeant Phillips. Theodore Phillips, and I am at your service."

He clasped her hand within his and kissed her knuckles. Venus experienced the urge to yank her hand away and wipe the moist mark off on her skirt. The impulse mystified her, for Sergeant Phillips was an extraordinarily handsome man and exhibited the conduct befitting an officer and a gentleman, even if she did look the part of a hoyden at present.

"Ted, this is Miss Venus Daltry, my assistant," Sanford corrected.

Phillips sent Sanford a startled glance. "Your . . . then she's not . . . I beg your pardon, Miss Daltry. But I am pleased to hear the title preceding your name, as will be every unattached gentleman in Lincoln County. Rarely are we treated to the presence of such a beautiful lady. You will remain with us—at least for a short while—won't you?"

"Just for a couple days," Sanford rudely cut in. "We'll be taking rooms at the hotel, then hit the trail again on Monday."

"Let's get you settled, then. You must rest up for the dance tonight."

Her interest piqued, Venus momentarily forgot her state of disarray. "Dance?"

"Every last Friday of the month a dance is held. Officers from nearby Fort Stanton bring their wives for a holiday weekend. It's nothing fancy but it satisfies their taste for social integration and relieves their boredom."

A dance! Now *there* was a way to get Sanford to touch her! And she'd have a grand time in the bargain!

The inquiring glance she sent Sanford earned her a speculative look from the sergeant that she ignored. "Will we be attending? If so, I must buy new clothes." Venus plucked at her brown wool skirt peeking from the duster. "Fancy or not, my outfit is on its last thread."

"You'd look ravishing in a potato sack, Miss Daltry."

"You'll have new clothes, Venus," Sanford promised, his voice caressing her from inside out. It was exactly what she needed to hear—compassion for her haggard appearance, not platitudes from a stranger who knew nothing about her.

Ted Phillips clapped his hands and rubbed them against each other. "Well, then. Let's find you a room so you can refresh yourself. Buck and I will go shopping and return with a gown fit for a princess. Is that agreeable with you, Miss Daltry?"

Again, Venus looked at Sanford. He had dismounted and was walking toward her, his face tight. She knew what he was thinking; she felt the same irritation. It had been just the two of them for so long that having someone else step in and make decisions for them grated on their nerves.

He stopped near her knee, and reached for her at the same time as the soldier. Venus didn't think twice. She rested her hands on Sanford's shoulder and allowed *him* to guide her off the sorrel. "Is that agreeable with *you*?" she whispered against his collar. Although what she really wanted was to be assured that he felt comfortable with Phillips. She feared a repeat of the Lasso episode.

Sanford squeezed her waist and nodded curtly. "Ted's okay."

She searched his brim-shaded face. Not that Sanford would lie to her, but sometimes his pride ruled his actions. Other than showing mild annoyance, his features remained calm, confident.

The flash of a wan smile between his whiskers eased

her mind. Venus patted his arm and he released her. Together they stepped onto the boardwalk, Ted Phillips
forgotten until he pushed past them to open the glass-
fronted door of the hotel. "Ladies first."

From a doorway to the left, dishes clinked together as
unseen workers labored in the first-floor restaurant. A
diversity of tantalizing aromas, from rich coffee to freshly
baked cinnamon rolls, hovered in air lightly scented with
lavender.

Venus waited while Sanford spoke with a tiny woman,
not much older than herself, about renting rooms. She
was quite lovely in a prim mauve gown that comple-
mented her sable hair. Natural color stained her cheeks a
delicate pink and her pleasant smile made Venus all the
more aware of her own dishevelment.

Self-consciously, Venus tugged the edges of Sanford's
coat close to her neck and glanced around the lobby.
Feminine touches were obvious: plump settees with inlaid
cherrywood arms lent the spacious area modest refinement, fragile figurines of serene ladies and sophisticated
men adorned round tables clothed in tatted doilies, helio-
trope velvet drapes descended from brass rods to polished oak floors, and transparent curtains underneath the
velvet allowed morning light to filter through the tall windows.

Venus silently praised the woman for her elegant taste.
At the same time, she wished Sanford would hurry with
the keys. Once bathed and suitably attired, she wouldn't
feel like a beggar in a tycoon's parlor.

"I'm sorry, Mr. Buchanan, there are no rooms available. Folks are doubling up as it is," the woman explained
from behind a purple-skirted reception desk. "Many of
the area ranchers have planned to stay at least the night
due to travel distance and have reserved their rooms in
advance. Even the Army has been forced to pitch tents
outside town."

"I have a room, Buck," Ted Phillips cut in. "You can
bunk with me—just like old times—and Miss Daltry can
share a room with another lady if she has no objections."

Venus laid her hand on Sanford's arm, stalling any objections he might have voiced. "Accept the offer. After the dance, I'll be so tired I could sleep in a horse trough and be content."

In a short time, Venus had mounted a banistered stairwell and entered a second-story room genteelly decorated in muted browns and roses. Passing between two brass beds, she headed straight for the window overlooking the street below and parted the sheer curtains. She picked out Sanford's husky form instantly from among the milling residents. He dragged his hand along building fronts while his soldier friend walked at his side.

"You'd best see no harm comes to him, Sergeant Theodore Phillips," Venus warned, watching the pair. "Or you'll have the Daltrys to deal with. And no one who incurs the wrath of Mount Olympus escapes unscathed!"

Fourteen

"WHERE DID YOU FIND A GODDESS LIKE THAT, BUCK? I thought you had sworn off women."

Sanford clenched his jaw and pushed at the door of the merchandise store. It had once been owned by Lawrence Murphy, one of the chief players in the Lincoln County War, before his death and the subsequent sale of the property. "I told you, she's my assistant."

"There's got to be more to it than that. I thought you had sworn off women. And what happened to Zeb?"

"He's taking a holiday in Texas."

"Convenient," Ted remarked.

Sanford seized Ted's arm and spun him around. "What's that supposed to mean?"

Ted shrugged off Sanford's hand and there was a grin in his voice. "Only that your Miss Daltry appears quite a warm fire on a cold winter's night."

"Venus is a lady," Sanford hissed.

"I never said she wasn't." His tenor voice faded as he walked away.

Sanford followed the sound of his footsteps toward the front of the store. Ted whistled an idle tune as he slid garment holders along a wooden rod. Sanford fingered bolts of cotton, trying to make sense of this sudden possessiveness for Venus. Ted was a decent fellow, he was capable of providing for a wife. And he sure seemed smitten with Sanford's partner.

Venus. Would she also find Ted to her liking?

Sanford snorted in disgust. What the hell did he care, anyway?

"Hey, Buck! In a gown like this, we'd have to cage all the men in Lincoln to keep them off Miss Daltry."

Sanford curled his lip, but fingered the material. "It's soft as spring water."

"But?"

Gauging the low-cut bodice, he pictured Venus's bosom spilling from the scanty design, and half the men in the territory panting at the sight of her lush globes. He snapped, "Venus doesn't need anything that revealing. She needs something more—"

"Spinsterish?" Ted countered.

Sanford shouldered past his old acquaintance and sorted through the meager selection of gowns on the rack. His hands roved over backs and fronts and pleats and frills. Finally, he settled on a soft cotton one and brought it forth. "What color is this?"

"It's . . . like a ripe blueberry pie. Sweet and dark."

Sanford shoved the gown against Ted's chest. "Have it wrapped while I find her a couple outfits for riding."

Shortly after Sanford delivered a paper-bound package then left, Venus's roommate arrived. Venus had just untied the string when the door opened, and blue gazes collided. Venus stared at the plump-figured girl standing in the doorway. She looked about Allie's age. Her face was rounder, though, almost plain if not for her striking robin's-egg eyes and lush mouth. A straw floradora banded in silk orchids and peacock feathers perched upon hair the color of an afternoon sun, and one long curl lay against the tight-fitting bodice of her mint-green morning gown.

The door clicked quietly shut. "Margaret, the lady downstairs, told me I'd been given a roommate."

Venus lifted a pair of wrist-length white gloves lying atop the pile. "There weren't any rooms left."

"I know," the girl said, moving toward the empty bed. She set her reticule on the pale red coverlet and removed the hatpin from her floradora. "My father had to pull strings to procure ours."

"He has influence, then?"

"Oh, yes. He's a captain at Fort Stanton and has done favors for the governor, who is also in Lincoln for the weekend."

Tossing her hat beside her reticule, she turned as Venus lifted out the gown Sanford had chosen for her and both let out simultaneous gasps. The material was a vibrant blue that matched her eyes perfectly. It had tight sleeves down to the wrists, a sheer panel of ivory netting over the low-necked bosom, and a dipping waist. The attached skirt was unadorned and slimly cut. It drew up in the back to reveal frothy tiers of ivory lace, had a sewn-in padded bustle to sit over her bottom, and a flattened ivory bow that lay across the bustle.

Strangely, the creation reminded her of a combination of the three gowns he had buried. Stroking the row of tiny pearl buttons running down the back opening, Venus wondered if the thought had occurred to him too, and that was why he had chosen it. Of course, it was highly improbable that Sanford could be that considerate, but still . . . Venus wondered.

"It's lovely," the girl breathed.

Clutching the gown to her breast, Venus settled her misty gaze on her awestruck features. "It is, isn't it?"

"A gift?"

"Recompense, I think." Venus freed one hand and held it out to the girl. "I'm Venus Daltry."

"Rosemary Weston of the Galveston Westons," she formally replied, clasping Venus's hand.

"Texas?" Venus cried. "Me, too! Of the Paradise Plains Daltrys!"

They giggled, then plopped down on Venus's bed. "What's a nice girl like you doing in no-man's land?" Rosemary queried.

Venus pondered the question. "I'm . . . sort of helping a friend."

"Must be a special friend if you're willing to brave the heat and desolation of this territory."

She'd never thought of Sanford as a friend. Their relationship was far more complicated. "I guess he is."

"He?"

"Well, yes." Venus tried to conceal her blush and failed. "He's a writer, and I'm helping him with a book."

Rosemary shot to a sitting position. "Oh, how exciting! What does he write?"

"Dime novels," Venus whispered.

"Oh, now that is *truly* exciting! Don't ever tell my father, but I have a whole collection hidden in my trunks!" Rosemary confided, "He thinks they'll corrupt my morals."

"You read dime novels?" Venus exclaimed. She wouldn't have imagined it! Why, Rosemary and she came from the same circles; it was easy to tell from her speech and dress and manners!

"Oh, yes!" She flopped back onto the mattress. "My heart's greatest desire is to meet a man as dashing and courageous and romantic as the ones I've read about!"

"What of the violence and bloodshed, though? What of the lack of cultural interests and respectability?"

"Oh, Venus. Not all the novels are like that. But in the ones that are, I look beyond those things, into the soul of the hero. And I imagine that if I ever find my own hero, I'll know just how to treat him. I'll have a better understanding of him. Dime novels are like windows into a man's inner spirit. They tell you what they think and how they feel and why they react as they do . . . fiction cannot be that much different from real life, can it? I mean, the words on the pages must come from somewhere, and men are the primary writers of the stories, right?"

Rosemary practically echoed what Sanford had told her so long ago and the realization stunned Venus. Thinking back, though, she had compared him to Slick Drayson in a fashion. Just as Rosemary pointed out, Slick was dashing and courageous and romantic, much like Sanford—when he wanted to be.

"Oh, drat!" Rosemary startled her from her thoughts. "I completely forgot that my father is waiting in the lobby. My mother passed on about five years ago and ever since then he won't let me out of his sight. It's almost as if he's afraid I'll leave him, too." Collecting her hat and reticule, she shrugged and grinned. "Oh, well. He's taking me shopping then out to lunch. I don't suppose the day will be too dull."

Venus grinned back, truly finding Rosemary Weston of the Galveston Westons a breath of fresh air.

For the rest of the day after she and Rosemary separated, Venus pampered herself as she had not done in nearly a month. She scrubbed her body until every inch was a healthy pink, then rubbed her skin with moisturizers. She could do little for the tan lines on her wrists or the smattering of freckles on her face without lemon, but powder did make them less noticeable. She washed her hair three times, and while she had the damp locks wrapped around rags to produce bouncier curls, she soaked her nails in soapy water, then shaped them.

During the hottest part of the day she napped for a couple hours, and when she awoke, she discovered Rosemary had returned from her father-daughter outing. Together they spent the rest of the afternoon hours applying makeup and fussing over their hair and helping each other into their party gowns, all the while reminiscing about dances they had attended in their respective hometowns.

By the time Sanford arrived to take her downstairs to dinner Venus felt like her old self. And yet, she felt like a new person, too. A few strokes with a brush dipped into her melted tube of lipstick added vibrant coral color to her lips. She smiled at her sparkling reflection in the framed mirror above a carved washstand and gave the cascade of curls tumbling down her back a final pat. *Oh, if he could see me now!* If he wasn't already blind, her beauty this night would surely do the trick!

He knocked on the door for the second time. "Are you ready, Venus? The food is going to mold!"

"Is that your writer?" Rosemary asked.

Nodding, Venus skipped across the room and plucked a gossamer shawl from a thick-cushioned armchair near the door. "I'm so hungry I could eat maggot"—she flung the door open and the last word faded like the last ray of sunset—"stew. Oh, land's sakes, who *is* this god on my doorstep . . . ?"

It was Sanford, she knew, but not the Sanford she'd ridden with and fought with and made the target of her revenge. Standing before her with all the dignity of a Roman warrior was a man who stretched the realms of her imagination.

She had envisioned him handsome, but those visions did not do the real model justice. He had shaved. Other than a small nick on his chin his face was pure perfection with his chin and jaw sharply angled. His gold-tipped lashes acted as shutters for sloping eyes that stared right through her, and his mouth . . . Land's sake, those ruddy lips practically begged to be savored. Remembering all the times he'd pulled away before she'd sampled them left Venus feeling a keen emptiness.

Even his wavy hair sported a tamer refinement. Though not short, it was trimmed neatly and he'd parted the rebellious mass on the right side. Still-damp strands wound around his ears and flirted with the prominent cords of his neck.

And he wore a handsome brown coat over a white pleated shirt that opened at the throat, and modest-fitting nankeen trousers with creases so crisp, surely they'd pare the skin off her fingers if she traced the vertical lines. Only the sorry hat he clutched against his stomach with one hand assured her that this was indeed the Sanford she recognized.

Finally Venus whispered in a voice she did not recognize as her own, "You must have the wrong room, sir. I am awaiting my wild and woolly partner to escort me to supper." She'd meant for the words to come out in playful banter, but a frog's croaking sounded more enchant-

ing. "I don't think he'd be very pleased if I deserted him
for a handsome and dashing gentleman such as yourself."

Sanford bowed his head. His complexion reddened as
if embarrassed that she should remark on his improved
looks. "I . . ." He cleared his throat and reached into
the pocket of his frock coat. "This is for you."

Venus's eyes widened. "You got me a present? I *love*
presents!" Her gloved hands made little noise when she
clapped them together. But spying a small brown bottle
emerging from his pocket, her smile drooped. "What is
it?"

"Perfume. Well, not perfume exactly, but the closest
thing to it."

Holding the bottle as though it were fragile crystal,
Venus smelled it dubiously. "Vanilla?"

Sanford's head tilted at a proud slant. "It's not an import from Paris but it's all the store had to offer. Your
horse won't know the difference."

Ashamed of what he no doubt perceived as ingratitude,
Venus inhaled deeply of the sweet aroma. Truthfully, the
simple fragrance seemed more charming, more delicate,
more *honest* than the most expensive fragrance ever
bought for her. But what touched her most was that she
hadn't solicited the gift; Sanford had given it to her for no
reason other than he knew she'd run out. And part of her
hung on to the belief that he'd given it to her because he
wanted to.

Clutching the vanilla to her breast, Venus declared, "I
adore your present, Sanford. No one has ever . . ." Her
throat blocked and she could say no more. She blinked
rapidly against the tears gathering and smiled brilliantly
as she dabbed the essence to the pulse points at her wrists
and neck. "We'd best leave before Buck Buchanan comes
for me. He might set me to scouring pots or carving ar-
rowheads or something."

"A man that crass should be shot," Sanford avowed.

"Tonight, I'd be the first to fire the weapon. I learned
from the best, you know."

"I'll keep that in mind."

He offered his arm, and Venus slid her hand through

the bend of his elbow. Then she turned to her new friend.
"I hope you find your heart's desire tonight, Rosemary."

"You, too, Venus."

Venus glanced at Sanford, then mouthed over her
shoulder, *I think I already did!*

Sanford stood against the corner of a building at the
end of town, his scowl making his face hurt. The cheery
music and stomping of feet coming from the center platform mocked his sour mood. The baked trout he'd eaten
earlier had settled like a grease pool in his stomach,
churning around the two glasses of liquor-diluted punch
he'd had soon after the band struck up. The fish hadn't
been bad, though, nor did his innards rebel against such a
scant amount of liquor. It was the sickening thought of
other men holding Venus in their arms and whisking her
around the dance floor that had him ready to retch.

He should have known buying Venus that cheap imitation of a perfume was a mistake, should have known her
appreciative stuttering was a pretense. She had probably
dumped the stupid bottle in the nearest trash bin first
chance she got.

Why had he thought she'd be pleased to wear a food
flavoring, when at the snap of her fingers, any of the men
dancing with her could provide the exotic fragrances she
was accustomed to? But that wasn't all they could provide, and he knew it. He'd been aware of that since the
first day he'd met her. It wasn't his job to cater to her. But
he loathed the limits of his own body that prevented him
from ensuring she'd have anything she wanted or needed.

Jesus, he couldn't even swing her around in time to
banjos and harmonicas and horns.

"That face of yours would scare the hide off a buffalo,
Buck. What's got you so down in the mouth?"

Sanford didn't flinch at Ted's sudden arrival. Nor did
he bother answering a question that was nobody's business but his own. "You got a cigarette, Ted?"

"I thought you gave that habit up in school."

"I don't need a lecture. You got makings or not?"

"Sure, friend." Sanford wrapped his hand around the

hide pouch Ted offered. With rusty groping, Sanford rolled the thin rectangle of paper over a plug of tobacco, spilling more than he folded. Then he shoved a twisted end of the pungent taper into his mouth. The flame of Ted's lucifer nipped at his nose. The first couple of pulls on the cigarette made him cough, and in a sense, he felt like a boy in his teens again, sneaking away from school to steal a smoke with Ted.

Sanford supposed if he did have a friend in the world, Ted would be it. If not for Sanford's reluctance to make lasting bonds with people other than Zeb, they might have been confidants. But their relationship had remained in a neutral zone, confined to boyhood mischief, companionship for studying, and occasional moral support. They had met through Ted's brother, blind since birth, who attended Perkins School for the Blind in the same class as Sanford. Over the years, fate had thrown Ted and him together, as it had two years ago in Lincoln County, as it had now—in Lincoln County.

Casually reliving a moment from the past, neither man spoke. A round of applause signaled the attendees' approval for the band's horn rendition of "Listen to the Mockingbird."

When the strains of a waltz began to croon to the balmy night, he felt his gut wring. Who would she be dancing with now? Who would be holding her curves against his body, surrounding himself with the frivolous melody of her laughter, basking in her youthful freshness?

Who would be doing with Venus what he might dream of doing if he was the type to dream?

Sanford sensed Venus's approach before the breeze carried her scent to him and before he actually heard the swish of her gown. But he was unwilling to believe that she might waste a turn around the floor to spare a few moments for him.

Ted straightened beside him. "Miss Daltry, might I say you are the epitome of loveliness?"

"Yes, you may. Thank you, Sergeant Phillips."

"Please call me Ted. All my friends do. And I hope I may consider you a friend."

Sanford nearly gagged. Ted always had been one to lay it on thick.

The sudden touch of Venus's lace-clad fingers lighting upon his wrist jolted him. "I saved a line on my dance card for you, partner," she invited coyly.

Sanford steeled himself against her sweet, drawling voice. Just as he figured. He could take the belle out of society, but not society out of the belle. "Best let someone else fill it, Venus," Sanford said with a hint of disdain. "I don't dance."

Her physical withdrawal couldn't hold a candle to her mental withdrawal. "I see," she said stiffly. "Apparently when you promised I would dance again, you hadn't meant dance with you."

What, and make a fool of himself for all the world to witness? Humiliate Venus with his clumsy feet and groping hands? "I don't believe I included myself in the statement, no."

Venus inhaled a shuddering breath but refused to let the hurtful words destroy the evening's enjoyment. "Well, then." She gave the blond officer next to Sanford a tremulous smile. "Sergeant Phillips?" Pointedly, she did not accept the informal use of his name. Where the reserve stemmed from, she had no answer, other than an instinct that she did not wish a relationship with this man beyond impersonal kindness. But a dance . . . she needed something to salvage her dignity.

"*I* would be honored, miss." With a searing glance at Sanford, Ted led her across the street. The festivity was in full swing at the edge of town, between a solitary A-frame house and the business sector. A bonfire near the band stage and lanterns attached to the front posts of buildings illuminated the area designated for dancing. At the fringes of the waltzing crowd stood soldiers and cowboys, grim-faced fathers and diligent mothers, and under the eaves a group of men passed a bottle amongst themselves.

"A Rose in Summer" was in its second stanza when the sergeant's hand clasped hers and he placed the other at her waist. They circled the earthen floor with a dozen other couples dressed in vibrant costumes of silk and taffeta and fine wool. Gay laughter joined animated conversation and accelerating notes of the musical instruments.

Finally, Venus could no longer refrain from inquiring, "Have you known him for long, Sergeant Phillips?"

"Twelve years, off and on," Ted replied, knowing of whom she spoke. "My brother and he went to school together."

Her eyes never leaving Sanford's shadowy form, Venus set free the question hounding her all evening. "Why has he been glowering at me for the past two hours?"

"Because he's a horse's—uh, rear."

Venus returned the sergeant's bashful grin. "I already knew that. But, earlier at dinner he wasn't this . . . morose. Quiet, yes. That's nothing new. But if glares were pins, my cushion would be filled. And I don't understand—" Venus broke off in midsentence. Oh, land's sake, she was going to start blubbering all over the gold banner slanted across the sergeant's snappy blue uniform! With great effort, Venus swallowed the tears clogging her voice and blurring her vision.

Sanford was *not* going to ruin these few hours of social entertainment for her! If he wanted to stand apart from the rest of the crowd, smoking odious tobacco and being his old obnoxious self, then fine. The men she'd danced with thus far had appreciated a lady. And if they became a bit overzealous with their adulation, and their pawing grew tiresome, well, they could hardly be faulted. After all, she was decked out in her finest. Sanford might be oblivious to the extra care she had taken with her appearance, but the rest of the male population of Lincoln certainly had noticed!

She pretended the sting of his refusal had vanished, that the hurt did not remain a wound to her soul. And she convinced herself that it had not been for Sanford that she had gussied up, hoping to gain an ounce of affection. Invitation glittered in the eyes of every man dancing on the platform, including the man now squiring her. That was to be expected. She always had that effect among men and it bolstered her vanity.

If she could grant them a memory to brighten their mundane days then she had done her duty. That was what she had been born for—to brighten their lives.

Venus closed her eyes in an attempt to recapture the bliss she used to feel being the belle of the ball. But the image that came to her mind was not the one she desired.

She saw only Sanford. She saw him disturbingly handsome as he rode his big gray horse, his hair ravaged by the wind. She saw the bunching of sinew as he lifted his saddle. She saw that flash of defiant vulnerability when he'd been molested on the street of Lasso . . . And she saw him as he had been before dinner, standing so tall and clean, his head dipping shyly as he handed her a bottle of vanilla . . .

She clenched her eyes tightly against those persistent tears. What was happening to her? She could not recall a single other admirer with such profound clarity: not Garrett, not Andrew, not the Gemini Twins, not any of the numerous young men who had kissed her hems and bathed her in compliments and lavished her with expensive gifts.

None of them had caused her loss of sleep or chaotic confusion. And none of them had had the power to make her cry.

Venus shook her head with determination. Neither would a slave-driving, frontier-loving, pen-wielding ten-cent writer reduce her to tears. *If I have nothing else, I have my dignity.*

No, she swore, *I have been a victim of mockery and battery and humiliation for as long as I'm going to be. If it's the last thing I ever do, I'll make him rue the day he thought to control my life.*

Venus started as Ted tipped her head up with his thumb to her chin. "He doesn't see you the way every other man in this town sees you."

Venus shied away from his sympathetic eyes and choked on a humorless laugh.

"It really bothers you that he cannot see you, doesn't it?"

"Yes. No. I don't know!" Venus paused, aware that she should not be talking about her personal affairs with a total stranger. But the sergeant's kindness, his perceptiveness, compelled her to try and explain. To maybe make sense of her own confusion. "He's different. His blindness doesn't repel me . . . and yet, all my life I've been worth something because of my beauty. He can't see it, and I don't know where I stand with him." Venus looked at Sanford once more. He was so hardened, so callous. "Why is he the way he is?"

Ted whirled her gently to the music. Mistaking her meaning, he answered softly. "I only know because he told me one night after we'd imbibed heavily, and I can't guarantee he even remembers confessing, so you must not repeat this. Yankees stormed his family's farm and stole his horses. In the melee, one of the animals kicked him in the head. I don't think he ever really recovered from losing his sight, although he puts up a good front."

"He puts up a solid brick wall," Venus contended.

"That, too. But if anyone can tear it down, I am confident you can."

"Sergeant Phillips"—her smile was dangerously sweet—"you can bet money on that." Oh, yes. She was going to make the tyrant fall in love with her if it was the last thing she ever did.

"You should have danced with her."

"Mind your own business."

"You hurt her feelings."

Sanford jerked his hands from his pockets and shoved away from the wall. "Lay off, Phillips."

"I won't lay off, Buchanan! Someone has to drill it into that thick skull of yours—that lady is needing you . . ."

"She doesn't need me! She never will. I am making damn sure of that, teaching her everything there is to know about being independent—"

"All right, so she might not need you, but it doesn't take eyes to see that that lady is in love with you!"

Sanford's chest constricted. Love him? Venus didn't love him—she was too busy loving herself and her status.

"Right now, she's looking at you. In fact, she hasn't stopped looking at you."

"She's afraid I'll leave her behind," Sanford countered. "She came with me to find a husband before her next birthday—some stipulation to her inheritance. And if I send her back unmarried, she'll lose the bundle of money her grandmother plans to bequeath on her."

"It seems awful funny that she has rejected three proposals tonight if she's so desperate to marry, then."

"She wants someone with money and position and a respectable job," Sanford said, sneering.

"If that's the case, then she would have accepted my proposal. I have a fortune in the bank, I'm a noncommissioned officer up for promotion in the U.S. army, and I am respected in every circle."

But Sanford was still reeling from Ted's first sentence to listen to his self-acclaim. "*You* proposed?" he whispered menacingly. Jesus, when had loyalty ceased to exist?

"Damn right! My mother didn't raise a fool. When I find a treasure I'm not about to squander it!"

Sanford displayed a ready fist. "Unless you want this plowed into your face, Phillips, get the hell away from me." Whether his anger stemmed from the insult to his heritage or Ted's gall at trespassing into unmarked territory, Sanford could not discern.

"Let me give you a warning of my own," Ted threatened. "If you don't claim that lady as your own, you're going to lose her to someone else. And if I have my way, that someone else will be me."

As in the war, two friends, a Yankee and a Rebel, faced one another over a battle line, on opposite sides of an issue. And Sanford knew that he had about as much chance of winning as his Southern compatriots.

But it wasn't his youth hindering participation in this

conflict; he was a prisoner of darkness, chained more securely by his own limits and his own failures than if iron manacles shackled him to a wall.

"I can't lose what I don't have, can I, Ted?"

Fifteen

THE WASHERWOMAN IN CHECKED CALICO UNCLIPPED THE
clothespins from another pair of blue canvas-lined trousers. Dropping the pants into the basket filled with sun-
dried uniforms, she lifted the basket. She walked toward
a one-room house at the edge of camp, her burden
perched on her hip.

Hurricane bided his time until her ample form disappeared through the open doorway, then he sprinted bow-
backed toward the three ropes stretched between
T-poles. Faded blue wool and flannel shirts flapped
against his face as he fought the wind to unclasp a soldier's uniform from the clothesline. Pocketing the pins,
Hurricane raced behind the laundress's house just as she
returned to collect another batch.

Hurricane's heart pounded in his chest as he shucked
his tattered clothes and donned the calvary uniform. His
own pants were about done for. Hopefully no one would
question him about his brown boots, or look too closely
at the nonregulation belt he buckled around his stomach.
If they did they'd know right off he was an imposter.

He sure hadn't expected being famous would take this
much work, or include so many dangers. First he nearly

killed himself stopping Charley Dane from shooting Buck
Buchanan, then narrowly missed being gored by a bull,
spent roughly two days trapped in a tree, got eaten up by
ants, and now he was risking prison by posing as an en-
listed army man.

But, he acknowledged, a hero had to do what a hero
had to do.

And right now, he needed to find out if anybody here
at Fort Stanton had seen Buck. He was a damn good
eavesdropper, and Buck's lady had made a big impression
on a couple of cowboys during some party in Lincoln a
couple nights back. He'd heard a pair of them whining
about some hulking brute stealing away a pretty blond
and breaking their hearts. Hurricane put two and two
together, then picked up their trail at the west edge of
town. The horse tracks were heading straight for Fort
Stanton. Even though one of those peculiar rain showers
—the kind that flooded one side of the road but didn't
touch the other—had wiped out every trace of them
about ten miles outside Lincoln, Hurricane reckoned
they must have come this way.

Folks back home could say what they wanted—he used
his noggin. He wouldn't have gotten this far if his head
was empty, now, would he? And someday after he was
famous, he'd throw a big shindig like that one in Lincoln—right in Lasso—and make sure to invite everyone
who had ever stuck their noses up at him. They'd eat
their words, too. All those who'd told him most of his life
that he'd never amount to anything more than a whore's
son would soon be laying out a red carpet—like he was a
king. And if they were lucky, he wouldn't order them
beheaded. *If* they were lucky.

He'd be famous a lot sooner, though, if Buck would
just stay in one place for a while. Give him a chance to
tell the peckful of tales he'd been saving up. He could
even tell Buck all about the bull. 'Course he wouldn't tell
him that he'd been chased up a scrub oak! That didn't
sound very heroic.

Hurricane buttoned the two rows of brass buttons on
the oversized wool jacket, pondering what he *would* tell

the writer. No, instead of being treed, he . . . he'd
flashed a kerchief! Yeah! A big red one, brighter than the
shirt the lady had been wearing. Bloodred. Yeah. And
when the bull caught sight of it, he blew a cloud of smoke
out his ringed nose. And it wasn't no little ring in his
nose, it was a huge one. The size of a . . . of a barrel
band! Yeah. But instead of running away, Hurricane decided, he had just stood there, waving the bloodred
kerchief, while two thousand—no, three—no *five* thousand pounds of maddened flesh rushed toward him. And
when that bull was about to spear him with his ten-foot-
wide horns, Hurricane stepped to the side, then reached
out and grabbed one of his horns and . . . and flipped
him over! And the bull was so stunned, when he rolled to
his feet, he skedaddled in the other direction like a
whipped puppy. Yeah, that's what he'd tell Buck!

Settled on his story, Hurricane pulled the pant legs
down around his boots, then tiptoed along the back of the
laundress's house in the direction of the fort. No one
seemed to pay any attention as he left the protection of
the building. Acting as if he belonged, he whistled an
aimless tune while scanning for Buck or the horses or
even the pretty blond lady. For all his outward calm,
though, he worried that someone might hear his knees
knocking. A couple soldiers passed by him without glancing, and a dozen others were assembling in the center
square. Long straps of leather bags slanted across their
uniform fronts, the pouches heavy against their hips, and
rifles were gripped in their gloved hands. From the looks
of it, a march detail was forming, maybe a hunting party.

Busy watching the activity in the center court, Hurricane didn't see the tall blond officer exit the barracks. But
he felt solid muscle crash into his shoulder as they
bumped into one another. Hurricane was spun halfway
around and stumbled. "Hey! Watch—" He bit his tongue
in the nick of time, remembering he was supposed to be a
low man on the totem pole. He snapped to attention and
gave the officer an insolent salute. "Sir, sorry, sir!" he
cried, recalling how soldiers once passing through Lasso
had spoken to their commander.

"At ease, Private."

Hurricane remained stiff and saluting while the man with brass stripes on his upper arm band inspected him a little too closely for comfort. His inquisitive eyes bored into Hurricane and he asked in a commanding tone, "Are you one of the new transfers, Private?"

Hurricane's eyes shifted nervously. "Ah . . . yessir . . ." Seemed a good enough reason to be wandering aimlessly about, he figured. "Just arrived."

The sergeant glanced at a piece of paper in his hand. "Name?"

"Uh, Smith. Henry Smith."

Scanning the list, his brow furrowed. "I don't see it on this roster . . . wait—I have a Hiram Smith . . ."

"That's it!" Hurricane rushed to explain, "My birth name, I mean. Folks been calling me Henry for so long I almost forgot . . ."

"Private Smith, you have been assigned to fatigue detail."

"Yessir." Not sure if he should move, Hurricane stood still, two of his fingers curled above his eyebrow.

"I advise you to carry on."

"Yessir!" Hurricane forced his feet to follow the rest of him as he seized the chance to flee.

"Private!" The officer's bark halted him after two steps. Turning, the sense of foreboding was poison in his bloodstream. He shoulda known that officer was too astute to be fooled!

"Yessir?" Hurricane asked, his mind conjuring a picture of himself rotting behind bars.

He jerked his thumb in the opposite direction. "Fatigue detail is that way."

Hurricane glanced toward the group of men the blond officer pointed to, digging a trench some distance from the barracks. His eyes darted about, searching for an avenue of escape. Spying a set of enclosed stalls ahead, inspiration seized him. "I, uh, need to use the outhouse."

Seeming to accept the excuse, the officer told him, "Well, make it quick. I want that drainage ditch behind the mess hall shoveled out by the end of the day. We have no room for laggers in this outfit."

Hurricane's relief nearly melted him on the spot. "Yessir." He raced toward the outhouses, feeling an immediate need to use them after all. Once safe inside, he sank onto the wooden box with a hole cut in the center and buried his face in his hands. *Damn, that had been close!*

'Course, the way his luck was running, it wouldn't have surprised him to spend a few nights locked up. Every time he got to within a few feet of Buck Buchanan, something happened to detain him and Buck just slipped through his fingers.

Hurricane suddenly raised his head at the sound of voices outside. Two men were involved in a heated debate. Hurricane might not have paid any attention if he hadn't heard the one using broken English say something about a yellow-haired woman. Buck Buchanan was traveling with a yellow-haired woman, he thought.

"We can both have her, then!" the second man barked. "But what are we gonna do about Buchanan?"

Hurricane waited, his suspicions confirmed.

"Kanan be no trouble," said the other. "Kanan no see nothing. We go after, we wait. When time right, Bent Nose attack big man. Eller steal woman, hide. Easy!"

"All right, then. Phillips assigned me to march, so I gotta get back before bugle call. After inspection, we'll head out. I heard we're gonna relieve the detail guarding the 'Pache Reservation. You tell Phillips you're gonna scout ahead and I'll volunteer to ride along. He won't think nothin' if we're gone half the day. He knows the men don't wanna be around him; he's been in a pissy mood ever since he got back from Lincoln. But instead of headin' south, we'll go west. Buchanan and the lady can't have gone too far since they only left a couple hours ago, so we should be able to catch up with them. We'll take care of Buchanan, have the woman, then rejoin the troop, and Phillips won't know a thing."

Phillips might not know anything, Hurricane thought, but he sure knew plenty! He knew the two men plotted to destroy his one chance at becoming famous! Damn, he couldn't let them stalk Buchanan then kill him just to get to that blond lady!

While the men joked about the vulgar things they wanted to do to Buchanan's lady, he racked his brains for a way to stop the foul deed without the two being aware he'd heard their plans. Recalling a trick he'd played on Bart years back, Hurricane cracked the door to the outhouse open.

The coast was clear. The corral housed a remuda of horses and he spied two stocked saddles roosting on the fence. Attached to both were coils of rope. That's all he needed.

Hurricane dashed to the corral, grabbed the rope, then approached the outhouse as if it were his first trip—except this time, he wasn't quiet. Hurricane purposely issued a bounty of noises: loud footsteps, pained groans, crude grunts . . .

And again inside the necessary, his noises continued. During short pauses, he listened for signs of their leaving, but heard none. After a few seconds, he emitted a great sigh.

Still, the two culprits remained; he could almost picture them looking at one another, wondering if he'd heard their plans. A few seconds later, Hurricane let out a booming curse and flung the door open. He acted as though he'd happened upon them by chance when he stormed around to the other side of the outhouse. "Boy, am I glad you two came along!"

A flat-faced, crooked-nosed, mixed-blood Indian wearing cavalry pants with a fringed buckskin shirt, and a goateed infantryman with pockmarks on his cheeks stared at him.

"I done dropped a hunnerd-dollar bill down the hole!" Hurricane lied. "Either one of you fellows got a rope on ya? Or somethin' else to git it out? It's all the damn money I got!"

When they continued to stare at him, Hurricane rushed on. "I'll pay ya! Split the money fifty-fifty with either one of ya who can help me git it out . . ."

Hurricane's shoulders slumped with true disappointment. Bart had fallen for the ruse, but neither the Indian nor the infantryman appeared interested in fetching money from a sewer hole. Maybe he shoulda told them he dropped a five-hundred-dollar bill, but since he wasn't sure one actually existed, he had settled on a hundred, which was still a fortune. Hell, it would take the infantryman almost a whole year to earn that much! If it was the truth, Hurricane would have been tempted to dive for it himself.

Dejected, Hurricane turned and left the men. 'Course, he wasn't sure where he should go now. If he returned to the main grounds, he risked recognition by the officer. But he couldn't very well stand around an outhouse all day, either. He had to stop these two from ambushing Buck.

Reaching the first set of barracks, he paused and acted as if he'd gotten something in his boot. It was when he was bent over that he noticed the men peering inside the outhouse.

Not wasting a moment, Hurricane raced toward them, shoved them inside from behind, and pulled the string through the peephole on the door. He leaned against the door and grinned while they rattled and cursed and shook the whole shack with their outrage. Hurricane hoped the thing wouldn't fall over from the force!

Swiftly he retrieved the rope from the back of his pants and wrapped first one, then the other around the outhouse as double security against their breaking the door open.

He reckoned that if they didn't break out of their prison themselves, sooner or later someone would find them and set them free. But for his own good, not to mention Buck's, he sure hoped it was later and not sooner.

"Sanford, these buttons are the dickens to reach. Would you mind?"

His throat closed on him and the gulp of coffee stuck in his mouth. Dexterity drained from his fingers and he set his cup on the ground before he dropped it. His hands were clumsy as they traitorously reached for Venus's back. Tiny buttons, too many, studded the cotton of the shirtwaist he had bought her to replace her wardrobe. As Sanford closed the gaping edges, his knuckles brushed the boning of the corset she persisted in wearing despite his advice to the contrary. If only he could be so lucky as to conform to Venus's figure in the same fashion . . .

The sensitive nerves in his fingers deadened at the swell of her buttocks. An incorrigible impulse seized him, to cup her bottom in both his large hands, to knead the supple flesh, to grind himself against her softness.

Ah, hell. Sanford fastened the last five buttons with haste and spun on his heel. His long abstinence induced nastier thoughts each passing day. He wasn't going to shoulder all the blame, though. Venus was just as responsible . . . flaunting herself around him at every turn. Laying on that sappy Southern voice so thick he felt mired in it. Arousing him to the extent that his self-discipline seemed only a nebulous memory. And there was no way of predicting how much longer he'd last before his iron-clad composure shattered and he just attacked her like an animal.

He scraped his short nails along his jaw then grimaced at the welts left behind on the bare skin. He missed the familiar, abrasive stubble he'd become obsessed with shaving off. His beard was hot, he excused, feeling more comfortable with that reasoning than the truth. That maybe a certain sought-after Texas belle would look more favorably on a civilized professional than on a scruffy saddle tramp.

Yet, toning down his wild appearance did nothing to master the beast raging within. So much for convincing himself that his and Venus's relationship went no further than student-teacher. Hell, he'd be satisfied if he could just remember they were business partners.

Business—hah! Sanford scoffed. Concentrating on his book was an impossible feat when Venus made the lady in her so obvious! A decent story scene hadn't developed since he'd hooked up with the bit of fluff! He'd heard of writers getting stumped while creating a book, but in fifteen years, with seventeen successful novels to his name, never once had it happened to him.

Until Venus Daltry sashayed into his ordered life.

Ideas that had in the past flowed so freely were now barred by images of skin fragile as clouds and hair thick enough to sink his teeth into. A vein of gentle persuasion sliced through her spirited demands, confusing him, frustrating him. He was drawn to her fire but loathed his craving for her heat.

He retrieved the tin mug from the ground and flung the contents into the thirsty sand. Sanford cursed his lustful appetite and he cursed the sway of that tatted-lace voice Venus used to get him to do what she wanted. Momentarily he wondered if she sensed his guilt for not remaining in Lincoln for the promised two days and was taking advantage of it. He just couldn't bring himself to stay there, listening to other men ply her with compliments and lavish her with attention. And Phillips was the worst one—playing the polished Easterner to gain stature in Venus's eyes. He didn't want to think about the insane jealousy that had gnawed at his vitals when Ted offered to escort them as far as Fort Stanton and Venus accepted. Nor did he acknowledge his fear that if they tarried in the company of his school pal Phillips might have gotten his perfidious claws into Venus, for that meant that Venus meant more to him than he was willing to admit.

But no, he reminded himself as he shoved the cup into his pack. His normally strong will had been losing its potency prior to Lincoln, prior to Ted Phillips's threat, and prior to their quick departure from the fort. Venus had managed to wrangle services from him since they'd deserted the whiskey town in Texas. It startled him to realize just how often Venus pitted his resolve against his desires. Lately he seemed to have no command over his own actions. Whatever her request, he found himself complying, then condemning himself for giving in. Sometimes she didn't even have to say anything. He instinctively knew what would make her happy and what annoyed her, and an inborn gentleman's honor surfaced to promote the first and banish the second.

Turning around, he listened to Venus hum as she finished her morning dressing and grooming. Sanford sucked in a deep breath. Dry air filled his lungs. The scent of dehydrated earth and zesty sage surrounded him, but all he smelled was sunshine and prim calico.

When had this compulsive need to prove himself to Venus begun? It was almost as if he'd become addicted to feeling manly and useful to her. The more she asked of him the more powerful he became. Sanford wished he knew how she was accomplishing it. More importantly, why? What did she hope to gain? They had so little in common, save a mission to venture West, and even that was for two different purposes. She wanted a husband that suited her; he wanted his book completed to his satisfaction. It didn't look as though either of them were getting what they sought.

At least Venus had options. She simply chose to reject them. His choices were limited, courtesy of a negligent and foolhardy promise. Like it or not, he was stuck with Venus as his associate. Yet when it came down to his writing, she was utterly useless.

Maybe it was about time he accepted the very real possibility that this book would never be written. Black cows. Flat land. Dusty cowboys. Hell, one of these days he would discover himself tramping through a nest of scorpions and she'd describe them as "a bunch of bugs." The general terms she used reaffirmed his opinion that she still maintained a narrow view of the world.

And when she looked at him, no doubt she saw just a blind ten-cent writer. Not a success in his literary field. Not a provider of adventure and excitement. Not a person who felt and aspired and craved.

Not a man.

Would she ever see more than what her limited view of the world allowed? And why the hell did he even care?

His mood soured further. "Check the pack horse," Sanford ordered gruffly, grabbing his saddlebags and bedroll. "Make sure those straps are tight. We're heading for higher elevations again and we can't afford to lose any gear."

"We're crossing *more* mountains?"

Sanford's mouth twisted. "We've hardly *begun* crossing them." He buckled the rolled blanket to the cantle. "You're so damned determined to shackle yourself to me—well, get used to mountains. That's all you're going to see the farther west we go."

"I just thought . . . well, I just assumed we'd go around."

"That's what you get for thinking. If we go around, we lose time going south, then we would have desert to contend with—which means little if any water. I told you before I don't have a hankering to die."

"But . . . they look so . . . high!"

"High," he said flatly, his hands stilling.

"Well . . . yes. Even from this distance I can tell they're imposing."

Sanford whirled and searched for Venus by ear and instinct. If he asked her what she was wearing there wouldn't be enough hours in the day for her explanation.

But descriptions of what interested him? She could hardly be bothered to spare a word or two!

Something inside him snapped. The spark of temper he'd kept banked, flared rather than dimmed. That's *it*! Sanford flung the saddlebags to the ground. "You're making me crazy, do you know that?" His boot heels kicked up thick clods of dirt as he paced in a circle. Tripping over the pouches, he kicked the offending objects. His clumsiness made him angrier, ashamed. More so than it ever had because it only made his body's disorder more obvious in front of Venus. Venus, who was so damned perfect. Venus, so much a lady.

He hated her for making him feel less of a man and he wanted her for making him feel so much a man. And he hated wanting her as he had never wanted another woman in his life, in spite of her ignorance.

He lashed out at her. "As much as it galls me, I rely on you. My mind is a blackboard, you are my chalk. Your job is to draw me pictures of my surroundings. But all you draw are big blots of nothing!"

"I'm doing the best I can!" she returned, astonished. "What more do you want from me?"

Venus probably thought him crazed. He felt her eyes boring into him as he stood in the middle of God only knew where, his fists clenched, his chest heaving. But he didn't care what she thought, he told himself for the hundredth time. Let her think what she wanted; it was her fault anyway! For being such a damned innocent temptress. For riling him, not just physically—but emotionally . . .

What did he want from her? He wanted a damn fight! That's what he wanted! He wanted to vent his frustration, purge his confusion, release his passions . . .

"I want you to understand!" he yelled spontaneously. "I want you to understand what it's like for me . . . this damned darkness I must live with."

"How can I? I am not blind!"

"Try, Venus. For once in your self-centered life, put yourself in someone else's shoes!"

"You'd wish your fate on me?"

"Not forever. Not on you. But for a moment, if you just glimpsed into my life, maybe you could comprehend how important, how necessary verbal paintings are to me. Are you willing? Do you dare? Or does the darkness frighten you so much that you'd prefer to exist in ignorance and prejudice?"

She marched forward and captured the edges of his vest. "I told you once not to call me ignorant, but calling me prejudiced is going way too far."

Sanford grabbed her shoulders, spun her around, and ripped his kerchief from his neck. He wound it around her head and over her eyes. In a voice tight with pent-up rage, he said, "This is the dark, Venus. The difference between me and you is that your blindfold can come off. Mine can't. I woke up one day, my skull feeling as if it had been split in two after I was kicked in the head by a horse. At first, I was scared."

Venus brought her hands to the knot at the back of her head. Sanford wrestled her arms to her side and pinned them there with tempered strength. Her body trembled in his unyielding embrace. "Feel it? The fear? The helplessness? The fury? I can feel you feeling it and remember it myself. Thirteen years old, my father away fighting in a war we really didn't understand, but giving his loyalty to the South, for a home he'd not live long enough to see again. And in his absence the battles came closer, surrounding me. Sometimes the cannons shot so close, and the guns volleyed across our land, that days would pass before the air didn't stink of gunpowder. Can you smell it? The acrid smoke? The death and pain?" Venus struggled, but Sanford could not discern if she wanted free of his hold or his past.

"Yankees and Confederates alike were doing their best to swipe horses that I, and my father before me, had trained and sold to survive. I fended the troops off as best I could, but one day, a band of Yanks caught me by surprise and stole every last one of my animals. I couldn't stop them any more than I could stop those horses from panicking, or stop the bloodshed between our country's men."

Venus remained tense, but ceased fighting. Sanford's tone went gruff with emotions he could no longer suppress. His lips moved against her ear. "There was no sun, Venus. Only a light that grew dimmer and dimmer and a great pain in my head and in my soul. Finally, pure black. And over the years, even the memory of colors deserted me. They became cloudy and harder to bring into focus, like the face of a loved one who has died." Sanford's fingers splayed over Venus's ears, holding her head still when she attempted to turn it. "The feeling was there, how good and sometimes dangerous red felt, or how light, sometimes sad, blue felt. That's when my fear turned to bitterness. Can you taste that bitterness, Venus? That sharp sorrow of a boy condemned to a life of shadows and hostility? The curdling anguish of a boy uprooted from everything he held dear and safe?"

She gulped and bowed her face. Sanford desperately longed to read her mind right now. Was she rejecting the images? Was she receiving them? They were not the silks and perfumes of her fanciful existence, but the harsh reality that bred loneliness and detachment.

He held her securely, unconsciously lending her strength and shelter from words he'd dammed up inside but which now spilled forth through widening cracks in the fortifications. "After becoming blind, I used to wish that I had never been able to see at all. Then I wouldn't know what I was missing. I could not miss what I'd never had, would not grieve for what could never be returned. I guess I still feel that way. Other times, I'm glad for those years of vision so I can remember the things I saw. That isn't always good either, though. When faces aren't clear anymore and colors have faded so I can't quite recall their exact shades, it's like losing my eyes all over again. But word pictures, and writing, they bring what I've lost into focus. They give me something to look at besides the darkness."

Venus stood still and silent as he loosened the knot and let the bandanna fall. She shaded her eyes against the sudden brightness of the daylight he'd withheld. Sanford settled his hands on her frail shoulders, and after giving her a moment to adjust to the glare, he gently demanded, "Now, look at them; at those mountains, at that land, at the sky. Tell me what you see. Bring it to life for me."

She hesitated for a long while as though studying the vista. "It's not easy to find words to tell you what things look like. They are just mountains . . ."

He knew how difficult it could be. His whole body screamed for Venus to try, though. To latch onto one word, one nuance . . .

Timidly, she said, "I suppose they are kind of like rock knuckles . . . like a giant fist sitting on a table, in silhouette. And above them float clouds . . ." She suddenly gasped, "Why, I do declare. They look as scrumptiously fluffy as the inside of Persy's fresh home-baked bread. If you could eat them, they'd taste as warm and light, too!"

Relieved beyond comprehension, Sanford rested his forehead upon the back of Venus's head and smiled. It wasn't much, but it was a beginning. "*That's* what I brought you along for."

Sixteen

VENUS, IN THE MANTLE OF SANFORD'S ARMS, RESISTED THE compulsion to weep. She had come a hairsbreadth away from acknowledging defeat, from finally admitting that whatever progress she had made getting Sanford to fall in love with her, or at least make him aware of her as something besides his slave, had been destroyed the night of the dance.

For three days following the party she endured his cold hostility. Venus couldn't imagine where she'd gone wrong. Originally, she assumed Sanford was simply jealous because she'd spent the evening pairing off with other men. It wasn't the first time one of her escorts had succumbed to a fit of jealousy. And, after all, that had been her intention, to confront him with rivals and pressure him into declaring his undying devotion.

But it hadn't happened. Instead, he'd practically shoved her into other men's arms. And the only declaration he'd made was a silent warning: she'd crossed the invisible line of their relationship. And as if that had not been enough, he'd reneged on his promised weekend rest, jarring her awake the next morning with orders to pack up, they were leaving Lincoln. Why, she'd barely had time to send off a terse report to Grandma Minerva and say goodbye to Rosemary! The one time she had asked for an explanation, his biting reply nearly drew blood. He'd said, "Only a fool beds down with snakes." Venus had no idea how to interpret that but an ache lingered in her breast, almost a palpable wound.

In spite of his insensitive words and actions Venus had ignored his forbidding attitude, testing his limits with sweet requests and provocative touches. Conversations with Rosemary replayed in her mind. Beneath her flighty innocence, Rosemary was quite astute about men. Time and persistence, she had advised, would open a closed spirit. The other girl's counsel motivated Venus to redouble her efforts, even when she continuously rammed her head against the stone wall barricading his emotions.

It wasn't a stone wall holding her now, though. It was a flesh-and-blood man. A heart *did* pump under all the rigid muscle and taut flesh. She felt it hammer against her shoulder blade, alive, hungry, filling her own dejected heart with new hope.

Sanford wasn't as hard as he wanted everyone to believe. Proud, yes. Maybe too proud, a product of the trials he had faced as a young boy, and perhaps still encountered.

That pride, his defense against pain and scorn, was a greater obstacle than his blindness had ever been.

That he confided in her at all stunned her. Seldom did he divulge anything about his past; even more rare was a passionate display of emotion. She'd even begun to allow the possibility that he wasn't capable of love or desire—at least, not for her—and that the fruits of her labors might be for naught.

She *had* reached him, though. Venus slumped against his chest, blinking back tears of delirium. Finally, after so many days and so many failures, she'd finally hit on a missing piece of the puzzle.

All he desired was simple understanding. Oh, Venus wanted more, much more, but if that was the key to unlocking his heart, then she'd oblige. She'd give him the pictures he longed for. Seduce him with them. Maybe lively and descriptive conversation would impress him. Combined with physical temptation, surely she'd win his love.

Except, Venus was no longer sure just why winning meant so much.

They continued on a northwesterly course toward the Rio Grande River, braving extremities of heat and red dust and often a scarcity of water. In spite of the arduous trek, Venus's hopes that she was having some effect on Sanford's reserved isolated personality grew by leaps and bounds. Patiently, he taught her the medicinal and edible qualities of the flowering cacti, root plants, and wildlife. Venus learned to appreciate the knowledge instead of disparaging it, for at any given moment it might mean the difference between life and death.

And each day, his armor dented a bit deeper as she searched for words to tell him of sights she had always taken for granted: grass was no longer light green, but whispering lushness; clouds in the sky now looked like kittens skittering across a smooth carpet, rock formations became pompous profiles of foreheads and noses and receding chins rather than hunks of rusty lava or sandstone, and she used the opportunities to take his hands in hers, and make the shapes in the air, so he could imagine what they looked like.

Sometimes descriptions came easily to Venus. Other times she had to study the land for a while before she found just the right comparison. But she reveled in the challenge, and came to see the surrounding countryside as much more than the boring wasteland it first appeared.

There were moments when her blundering attempts at new and unique terms provoked a chuckle from him, as when they came upon that mesa she described as a humpbacked camel with a severe case of hives. Venus had gazed at his broad, quaking shoulders, filled with immense pleasure that she could make him laugh as well as frown. In her mind, they seemed to have reached a turning point in their relationship, and as they climbed into higher elevations, she pursued his sense of humor with

the persistence of Bellerophon obsessed with catching the
winged horse, Pegasus.

Venus had no golden bridle from the goddess Athena
to help her capture the beast, but that didn't deter her.
She was learning that chasing Sanford only made him feel
hunted, wild for freedom, just as Pegasus must have felt
when Bellerophon stalked.

Likewise, Sanford panicked at surprise attacks. The
clues had all been laid out for her, too: the cowboys at
Lee's camp mobbing him, the crowd pouncing on him in
Lasso, his withdrawal when she became too ardent with
her demands.

She just hadn't seen those clues clearly until Rosemary
shed light on them with her objectivity, and Sanford
brought them into focus by exposing his past.

Both had removed her blindfold.

"You know something, Sanford? I never would have
guessed I had a hidden talent. But I'm not half bad at
painting pictures, am I?"

"Not half," he conceded. "Although I can't recall having a ledge equated with a plucked eyebrow before."

"Well? They're both slender and curved . . ." Venus
gripped the reins tighter as the sorrel dislodged a loose
rock. Leaning in the saddle, she watched it tumble down
the mountainside. "Honestly, it's a good thing the horses
are so surefooted. From up here, the treetops look like a
bed of mossy nails waiting for us to topple over the edge
and stick us like meat on a spit!"

"Don't tell me you're afraid of heights as well as the
dark."

Venus swerved at the waist to look at Sanford. "I'm not
afraid of the dark."

She only sidled up to him each night because she could
not resist his body, he thought with a twinge of resentment. And when he'd tied the bandanna around her eyes,
she had trembled with desire. Sanford's lips quirked.
Right. He knew better.

"I'm not afraid of heights, either," she added, facing
forward again. "Now, my mama—she's the one not par-
tial to high places. One time, Daddy was building a bal-

cony outside my bedroom window. He took Mama out on it and barely got her back in the house, she was so petrified with fright. But me?" Venus shrugged. "Probably the only thing that scares me is aging."

Sanford pressed his lips together to stem his amusement. "Growing older isn't the end of the world, Venus. It's a natural process. Only death stops it."

"Creams and powders sure slow it down."

"Maybe the wrinkles, not the years."

"Well, it's the wrinkles that I worry about."

"You still think beauty and wisdom are competitors?"

"Petronius once said 'Beauty and wisdom are rarely conjoined,' " Venus haughtily retorted.

Venus negotiated the path ahead of him. Sanford gawked in astonishment, imagining from her tone a spine stiff as a starched collar. Not that he thought Venus was empty-headed, but he hadn't expected her to be a philosopher! Recovering, he settled back in the saddle, trusting Ranger to keep his balance on the uneven shelf as they veered left. "Margaret Wolfe Hungerford said a few years back that 'beauty is in the eye of the beholder.' "

"Lord George Lyttelton: 'Where none admire, 'tis useless to excel; Where none are beaux, 'tis vain to be a belle.' "

He lifted his brows, further perplexed. " 'The perception of beauty is a moral test.' Henry Thoreau."

"Shakespeare!" Venus proclaimed, sounding as invigorated by their debate as he felt. " 'Beauty itself doth of itself persuade the eyes of men without an orator'!"

"Plato: 'Beloved Pan . . . give me beauty in the inward soul; and may the outward and inward man be at one.' " Sanford tilted his head. "In this case, woman."

" 'A woman's time for opportunity is short, and if she doesn't seize it, no one wants to marry her, and she sits watching for omens.' Aristophanes. My inward soul won't get me a husband."

"A husband snared with beauty won't have an ounce of substance."

"Who said that?"

"I did." Grinning, Sanford exhaled loudly. "Damn, that

felt good. It's been ages since my intellect has been stimulated."

Venus glanced back at him, almost blurting out it wasn't his intellect she hoped to stimulate. She caught herself, and instead asked quizzically, "Where'd you get the idea I was afraid of the dark, anyway?"

"*All* women are afraid of the dark."

Venus snorted. "I swear, Sanford Buchanan, you've been meeting the wrong women! You're a feather short of a plump pillow if you think—"

"A *what*?" He choked on his laughter.

"A feather short—you know. Daft."

"I figured that's what you meant. I just haven't heard it defined in those terms before."

A blush stole into Venus's cheeks. "I guess I picked up a few of my grandfather's phrases."

"Give me another one."

"Why? Do you like being called senseless?"

"No—I'd like to use a couple in this book, with your permission. Slick Drayson needs more personality and depth. A few catchy phrases will give the story an original twist, and identify his point of view without me having to spell it out."

Venus had no idea what Sanford was talking about when he spoke of the technicalities of writing nor was she especially interested. What she did find hard to digest was that he had requested her permission for something— least of all an idea! "You want to use an expression of *mine* in your book?"

"Do you object?"

"No! I mean, it's fine . . . I just can't think . . ." Usually her late grandpa's idioms popped from her mouth without conscious thought. Now that she wanted to quote one, she had to struggle for recollection! "Well, there's 'a pickle short of a full peck,' 'a hinge missing on the barn door,' 'a wick shy in the candlestick' . . ."

"I like that one."

Venus preened at his approval. "I'll give you more as I remember them."

"If it's no trouble, jot them down in the note journal in

case I need to freshen my memory after we've parted company."

His reminder was a bucket of ice water on her warm mood. A month ago she loathed the thought of trekking anywhere with him, and two weeks ago, she had been consumed with the need to escape his presence with her life.

She clutched the reins with her bare hands as the sorrel rounded another treacherous curve in the Manzano Mountains. But now . . . now they were getting along! She didn't fear waking to the next sunrise, didn't dread what lessons he had in store for her, didn't worry that he'd send her back home before she'd fulfilled her labor.

The labor. In her preoccupation with punishing Sanford for his deeds, she'd almost forgotten what had thrown them together in the first place! She had less than eleven months before she needed to return home, *with* the task completed, or the prize was lost.

And yet, nowhere in the rules did it state the labor could not be completed before the year was up; the time frame was a deadline—not a requirement. If she and Sanford made the trip to Nevada, and wrote the book, and returned by April 30, 1885, she would have fulfilled the terms—providing he never learned the truth of why she was helping him.

Therefore, just because she had eleven months to perform the labor didn't mean she had eleven months to have an impact on Sanford's life, change his as he had forever changed hers. At the most, she figured there were six months left. Land's sake, that wasn't long at all given the fact that he hadn't even succumbed to kissing her yet! At the rate things were progressing, it would take six years!

Oh, Venus groaned, maybe she should just forget about stealing Sanford's heart. Concentrate on surviving the task, then go home and collect the prize. After all, the trials she had endured would eventually be forgotten. And Sanford, he'd toss away this time with her like a plot device gone awry.

She stiffened at that realization, every fiber in her body

rebelling against simply becoming another page in a Buck Buchanan novel. She wanted to mean more to him than that. *Needed* to mean more to him than that!

But now that she had less time . . . How was she ever going to attain her desires? No, not desires, Venus adamantly corrected. *Revenge.* She must not lose sight of the importance of making him fall in love with her. She meant to jilt him. To punish him for being such a tyrant toward her. To prove to him that she could not be controlled or dominated or disposed of.

Venus swore she wasn't going to feel guilt or remorse or sorrow for breaking his heart. And someday, she'd forget she'd ever been attracted to him.

"You're quiet all of a sudden, Venus."

Her head snapped up. "I was musing to myself."

The ledge widened and Ranger scrambled up beside the sorrel. Sanford dragged his hand along the wall of rock to his left. "I've been having a few doubts, too, almost a sense of something missing."

Venus shut her eyes and bit her lower lip. *Don't do this, Buchanan. Don't make me change my mind about you. Or question myself. You'll only hurt me again, and this time, I'll break. I swear I will . . .*

"I mean, Slick is on an adventure. He's running for his life from Gunns Murphy, the original owner of the saloon. Obviously that saloon is valuable or Gunns wouldn't care less about losing it in the card game."

Oh, thank Zeus! She was afraid Sanford had sensed the tumult raging inside her. Profound relief allowed Venus's breathing to return to normal. When she felt confident enough to speak in normal tones, she returned to their discussion—anything to free her mind of its plaguing confusion. "Why is Slick running from him in the first place?" she asked, satisfied when she sounded casual. But in the future, she could not be so careless, lest he read her mind. "Wouldn't a confrontation solve his problem? In a gunfight, he could just kill Gunns Murphy and claim the saloon without interference. After all, he outwitted the wolf by tossing him a piece of meat to divert his attention."

"You know, Venus, you may have something there. But not a gunfight. Gunns Murphy didn't earn his name for nothing—he's the best draw in the West."

"Better than Slick Drayson?"

"Even Slick Drayson has his deficiencies. Besides, killing isn't his style—even if he could outshoot Murphy." Sanford pondered the plot for a second. "No, he lives by his wits. But like the wolf, maybe he could dangle a piece of meat in front of Murphy. And Murphy wants the saloon. Why not use it as bait?"

"What if Slick Drayson sends Gunns Murphy a challenge? Another card game?"

Sanford's face broke out in a smile and Venus experienced the same queasy feeling she'd felt ever since the first time he smiled. She couldn't blame it on the heat anymore, or on her perfume, for both had tamed considerably.

"A challenge to a card game, huh?" he said. "I think that'll work. He knows Gunns is tracking him and surmises that his days are numbered. He could really throw Murphy for a loop and scratch a note on a rock!"

"The camel or the profile?"

Sanford only laughed. "Let's make camp early tonight and get all this on paper before the idea is lost."

Before sunset, Venus found a flat area nestled between two jagged sandstone escarpments. A twisted Douglas fir resembling a claw shaded a small pool of clear water. They unsaddled the horses, hobbled them under the tree, then slipped nosebags of oats over their heads. Soon after, Venus set about gathering chunks of wood while Sanford unrolled their bedding.

In between bites of warmed-over beans and bacon, and biscuits she had made herself in the coals of the fire she had also built, Venus recorded Slick Drayson's progress. The words flew from Sanford's mouth and it was all her fingers could do to keep up with them. Often when an idea hit him, he spoke so rapidly, and with such energy, that it left her in awe. Sanford brought Slick Drayson and Gunns Murphy to life with his prose and dialogue. Venus saw them in her mind and gradually they had become almost real to her. The story had come to captivate her. She worried about how Slick was ever going to be free of the menace of Murphy, and wondered why in Hades a saloon could rule the actions of two men who were equally ambitious but of opposing morals.

But it didn't look as though she'd find the answers to the unfolding mystery—not by the end of chapter eight, anyway.

Closing the journal, her gaze sought the story's creator. Finished with his own meal, Sanford had picked his way over loose rocks to remove the horses' feed bags. He was running his hands down the tendons of the sorrel's legs. His fingers probed the crevice of each hoof with the same tenderness he always used on the animals.

That darn horse doesn't know how lucky he is, Venus thought, picking up a stick. He didn't have to overcome obstacles to earn Sanford's affection. He receives it freely.

Using the stick, Venus drew circles in the dirt. Land's sake, she missed being touched with that sort of gentleness. She'd been raised on affection. Daddy had always greeted her with a warm hug. Grandma Minerva patted her hands. Mama would cup her cheek. Even the boys tousled her hair affectionately, Venus remembered with a sad smile. She had scolded them for messing up her curls, of course, but she regretted it now.

Venus cocked her head, absently adding lines atop the flattened circles. She missed the touches of her suitors more, though. Strong fingers laced with hers. Her cheek caressed, her lips kissed. Formerly, a day wouldn't pass without one of her beaus stealing a chaste liberty, for she didn't allow anything bolder. They could not help themselves, she'd always been told. Her beauty bewitched them and they could not resist touching her—if only to make sure she was real and not a mirage.

The praises were never-ending. Sighing, Venus supposed she'd taken it for granted that as long as she retained her beauty, those attentions would never cease. But Sanford was right—her beauty would fade one day, and then where would she be?

Alone, that's where.

If only, Venus thought wistfully, if only there was a man out there who didn't see her as just a pretty prize to boost his ego in front of his friends or adorn his arm to gain social standing or make others envious of his conquest.

Sanford appeared at her side then, and without thinking, Venus scooted over on the rock to make room for his large frame.

"The sorrel had a stone in his hoof," he said. "He seems okay, but we'll ride easy tomorrow. If he shows any signs of limping or weakening, we'll have to stop. Give him a couple days to mend."

Glancing down, she noticed the drawing in the dirt and frowned. Eyes. A pair of them, curved down at the outer corners, with short, dense lashes, very much like Sanford's. Land's sake, she'd been so deep in thought she hadn't realized what she'd drawn! With her foot, she erased the picture, even though he couldn't see it. "What if he gets worse and doesn't heal?"

Reluctantly, Sanford said, "He'll have to be put down."

"I'll be extra gentle with him. I never thought I'd say this, but I'm getting sort of attached to that beast."

"Animals have a way of working their way under your skin—smelly or not."

"Like Ranger got under yours?"

"Yeah." Sanford chuckled. "He's shown me more loyalty in three years than I've received in a lifetime."

Venus stared at the darkening skyline between the gap in the mountains. "Loyalty is important to you, then."

"I depend on it. It's more than important—it's vital."

The question slipped out before Venus could stop it. "What about love? Have you ever been in love, Sanford?"

"Like—with a woman?" He tilted his head.

Venus nodded and Sanford grinned wickedly. "Not for longer than an hour."

Venus's entire face went crimson. "I didn't mean . . . I wasn't referring—"

"I *know* what you meant." He sprang to his feet and scratched the back of his neck. "Why the curiosity?"

Venus shrugged. He'd brought up a good point. Why *was* she so curious? To judge her chances of winning his heart for revenge? Or for more personal motives?

Tilting her face, she watched Sanford duck his head and shift his hat brim back and forth as he paced. She took note of his agitation, of the habitual sign of discomfort, as if love and women and his blindness were connected.

Was that it? Venus marveled. Did he think his blindness made him unworthy of the love of a woman? But . . . that was preposterous! His eyesight—or lack of it—in no way detracted from his manliness! Why, he was as much of a man as any of the sighted fellas she'd ever known. He possessed the same scent . . . of dusk and dreams . . . and his touch was just as stimulating, like wind and candlewax. And his voice was sometimes like bullets, sometimes like butterflies . . .

Her eyes widened and her mouth dropped open with the wonder of understanding. She gripped the stick tight. No, he wasn't like any man. He was as different from all the others as night was from day. For only he could propel her into a world of midnight and feeling, only he could make her think in terms of sensation rather than sight.

And she knew then, knew with frightening clarity what was happening to her. How could *she* have been so blind? How could she have let her thoughts become so obsessed with revenge that she could not see what had been so obvious all along? And why had she wasted so much time fooling herself?

But everything made sense now. Her intensifying attraction, her willing obedience to his rules, her sensitivity to his emotions . . . and her diminishing zest for revenge. She could no more punish Sanford than she could hold a rainbow.

Yes, he was different. He was the first one she'd ever begun falling in love with.

Falling in love with . . .

Oh, land's sake, she was falling in love with him.

Honest to goodness breathe-the-same-air, sleep-in-the-same-bed-till-death-do-us-part love. The kind she'd searched for in so many faces but had never found.

Somewhere down a road between Paradise and Hades, she'd begun thinking of him as more than a saddle tramp. That was why he invaded her thoughts so often, why she couldn't tear her eyes from him, why his rejections stung so viciously.

But when? Venus pondered the question. She'd always believed that when she finally did fall in love, it would be sudden and jolting. Weren't two people supposed to spy each other across a crowded room and feel the pierce of Cupid's arrow? It wasn't that way at all—not in her case. What she felt for Sanford had crept up on her like a thief in the night and, over a period of weeks, robbed her of the will to fight it.

And land's sake, now that she had just experienced the most profound revelation of her entire life, what should she do about it? An alarm vibrated through Venus's body, warning her that if she blurted out her feelings, she risked the very high possibility of Sanford bolting. Not literally, of course. He needed her, even if he wouldn't admit it. But emotionally, her declaration might cause him to withdraw so far into himself she'd never reach him again.

No, Venus decided, best to keep quiet for now. Test the waters, in a manner of speaking, and see how Sanford would react. Besides, her discovery was still too fresh, too raw . . . she needed a little time to get accustomed to it.

Finally answering his question, she said, "I suppose I was wondering what makes you drift from place to place." She skirted the issue uppermost in her mind. "You remind me a lot of Slick Drayson because he has never settled down, either."

Quiet for a moment, Sanford shoved his hands into his pockets and jutted his hip. Then he said, "Not everyone is obsessed with putting down roots. Slick's home has always been any flat piece of ground, and any firepit is his hearth. Why should he settle down when there's a whole wide world out there to explore?"

"Doesn't he ever get lonely?"

"He cures his loneliness with a couple dollars and a saloon girl."

"But . . . what if one of those saloon girls were willing to go to the ends of the earth with him?" she pondered aloud. "What if he found love with her?"

Sanford jerked his head toward her. "He can't find what he isn't looking for."

"Sometimes a person doesn't have to look to find love," Venus contended. "Sometimes love finds a person when they aren't watching. Take the saloon girl, for instance. The last thing she imagined waiting for her at that gambling table was love, but there it was."

"You lost me, Venus. What saloon girl? What gambling table?"

"The one Slick Drayson was sitting at in Lincoln. No gambler I've ever heard of has been able to resist the lure of shuffling cards. But the minute he sat down at that table, and the girl brought him a drink, she knew."

Sanford shook his head in absolute confusion.

Venus exhaled loudly. "She knew she was falling in love!"

Then Sanford laughed. "You're really getting into this story, aren't you, Venus?" He stepped back and searched for the rock with his hand, then lowered himself beside her again. "All right, does Slick wind up in this saloon before or after he leaves the message on the rock for Gunns?"

Sanford seemed to actually consider her wild suggestion.

"Before. He's running low on supplies and needs to win money to buy more. That's when he meets the saloon girl. She's the one who gives him the idea. Slick never learned to read or write, so she marks the message on the camel rock's side with a chunk of sandstone."

"She's traveling with him?"

"Of course! He saved her from some bad men who escaped from the pit—remember the pit they used to imprison men in Lincoln? These bad men were attracted by her beauty and were hiding in her upstairs room, waiting to have their way with her. They didn't count on Slick feeling a little"—a fleeting blush heated Venus's cheeks but she forged on—"*lonely* after playing cards. So when he goes to meet her in her room, he finds the bad men holding her against her will. Slick punches them out and steals her away in the nick of time!" Venus leaned close and whispered as though the mountains had ears. "He's got a soft heart when it comes to a lady in distress."

"Does Slick even know the name of this lady in distress?"

"Why, it's Venus, of course!"

Sanford threw back his head and roared his amusement. Venus hadn't intended to become so involved with his story, but as the idea of Slick finding love planted itself in her mind, the words simply poured from her mouth. And who knew? Maybe Sanford would follow his character's example and find love, too!

Sanford's hearty laughter dwindled to intermittent chuckles. "Where'd you come up with this, Venus?"

"Well, you keep saying your story is missing something and I figured that that something was a bit of the romance all those dime-novel readers crave. Who better to give them that romance but a goddess and a gambler? After all, you wouldn't be deceiving your readers by adding a little love to the plot. Everyone's interested in love, Sanford." Venus patted his hand consolingly. "Except you, of course."

"I hate to disappoint you, but Slick Drayson isn't interested in anything more than staying alive to claim Gunns Murphy's saloon. Besides," Sanford added sardonically, "he thinks love is for dreamers."

"A dreamer's dreams come true if they wish hard enough."

"Wishes don't come true, either."

"Land's sake, it's just Venus's luck to care for a cynical man," Venus wailed. "Someone needs to tell Slick that maybe he's been wishing for the wrong things!"

"Oh? What does 'Venus' wish for?"

She replied hesitantly, "For someone to care enough for her to look beneath her outward appearance. No one's ever explored below the surface of her artfully painted face and silk costumes. And before she met Slick, she never really cared, either. It was easier to give folks what they expected than to be disappointed if they didn't accept her as herself. But Slick, well, she saw something in him that made her want to risk everything for his love."

"So she wishes for love?"

"No, she hopes for love. There's a big difference."

Ducking his head, Sanford rubbed the knuckles of one hand with his thumb. "What does all that have to do with him?"

"She doesn't want to be just a saloon girl to him," Venus stated boldly, pinning Sanford with a solemn, steady gaze. "Maybe she wants to be everything that has been missing in Slick's life—maybe she wants to be his woman."

Venus was learning to read Sanford's expressions quite accurately but the one on his face now left her puzzled. He looked terrified.

Seventeen

SANFORD SLID HIS HANDS INTO HIS DENIM POCKETS AND LEANED his shoulder against the fir tree. He curled his bare toes around gritty pebbles and evergreen needles and an errant breeze wrapped the open tails of shirt around his wrists. Dawn whispered softly against his face and exposed chest yet did little to calm the turbulence inside him.

All last night one haunting phrase had deprived him of rest. *Maybe she wants to be his woman.* Tossing and turning into the wee hours, he had tried to banish the image of Venus brought on by those Southern-tinged words. Venus, as a woman. Touchable. Resilient. Courageous. Doing her damnedest to learn all the ways of the frontier in her spirited fashion. She had traded her fancy silks for durable calico, her lace gloves for kidskin, her fancy meals for gamey fare. Slowly she'd gone from braving his contempt and resentment to earning his admiration and his respect.

At the same time she retained a unique softness that set her apart from other women he'd known in his life. She didn't make him feel tied down, she gave him wings. Made him feel limitless, as though he could dive off this

mountainside and not drop but soar. She was like an ad-
diction, dangerous yet irresistible, and under her influence he craved nothing but making her his.

But Sanford kept coming back to the same conclusion—she'd never consent to being *his* woman. Though
she had adapted, he wasn't sure she would ever be satisfied with the constancy of the life he had to offer. One of
dust and danger. Of saddle sores and inkstains. Of un-
blazed trails and unpredictable calamities. The sort of life
that required regular protection.

Neither could he abide living in her upper-crust world.
All those people whose importance was measured by material possessions and for whom a man's worth was based
on his ability to provide. Of claustrophobic rooms and
social restrictions. Of constantly being thrust into public
scrutiny. If people weren't so narrow-minded and self-
righteous about the physically impaired, he might not
have such negative opinions of them. Experience was a
hell of an educator, though. And all of his experiences
made it perfectly clear that a blind man had little or no
worth—as a protector or a provider.

Yer skeared, boy.

Damn right. Sanford scuffed the sole of his boot along
the ledge. He was scared. And he could finally admit he
was scared. For himself and for Venus. He had failed
himself more times than he cared to remember. He had
the scars to prove it. If he failed Venus, though, he risked
a lot more than puncture holes in his foot and a couple of
knocks on the head. He risked having his heart ripped
from his chest when he disappointed her. And eventually,
he would disappoint her.

An event nineteen years ago had seen to that.

His life might be lonely at times, Sanford reflected with
a bit of regret, but it was his and his alone. No one de-
pended on him; no one expected things from him he
couldn't possibly provide. He preferred it that way. *At
least they both were safer.*

Then Sanford wondered why in the hell his thoughts
were so consumed with Venus as his woman, anyway.
They'd only been acting out a scene, exploring character

motivation and plot possibilities. Thinking that an invention of their imaginations could be reality was pure folly. Venus had been born a lady, was bred a lady, and would die a lady. Anything less she considered beneath her. If she sounded a lot like the saloon girl, and he sounded a lot like Slick, then it was mere coincidence.

So why couldn't he shake the gut-deep feeling that fiction had somehow crossed into the real world? That he and Venus, in their make-believe world, had made some sort of connection?

Honestly, nothing was making any sense anymore.

He heard Venus stir, then rise from her quilted pallet. Her footsteps were faint as she approached him. Sanford acknowledged her presence with a brief inclination of his head.

Venus curled her arm around his and laid her cheek intimately against his shoulder. He did not pull away. She often touched him, and he wondered if he hadn't been waiting for her.

"It's peaceful here," she observed softly. "The sun is splashing the scrubland with firestorms and blood, and the shadows around the brush are like pools of tar. To the left, lava beds ride across the land, like a scab over an open wound."

"Sounds so tragic . . ." Sanford whispered back. "But I can almost see the beauty in the sorrow, the oranges and reds, and the steep ridges . . ." His musings drifted off. "Have you ever tried fitting a square block into a round hole, Venus?"

Venus tilted her chin and gazed at his face with mute inquiry. His hat was a permanent fixture on his head, even when he slept, shading his eyes and upper cheeks.

Not quite certain what he meant with this question, she murmured, "No," and shook her head. The end of her braid bobbed up and down along his belly. Sanford shifted, drawing her attention to his half-naked torso. His rumpled white shirt acted as drapery for a thickly muscled chest. Venus's fingernails cut into her palm as she restrained the impulse to pet the sprinkle of brown hair across the powerful breadth. Just cuddling up to him was a bold act on her part, a gamble. He could have easily rejected her nearness as he had repeatedly in the past.

But seeing him this morning, a dark silhouette against the pink-streaked sky . . . well, not a canyon between them could have stopped her from walking to his side. He had looked so lonesome and vulnerable beside the bent tree, and yet so masculine it had made her pulses leap just watching him. And perhaps she'd been a little awed, too, that a man of his arrogance would require comfort.

She was here for him, though. Whenever and however he needed her. She sensed he needed to talk.

"When I was younger," Sanford began after a moment's silence, "Uncle Zeb made a board for me. He was teaching me to differentiate between textures and shapes, and to build speed in my hands. The board had shapes cut out of it. I had to choose which shape belonged to which cut. Just when I became skilled at filling the board one way he'd turn it around. The day I filled it, no matter which way he turned it, I felt this overwhelming pride in my ability. I foolishly thought he'd share my pride."

Sanford stared at the nothingness and spoke evenly. "He got angry with me. He told me to never count on that board staying the same, to only count on the shapes I held in my hands staying the same. Then he made me a new board and repositioned all the cuts. I had to learn the pattern all over again. I remember feeling such impotent rage as I held a square block, and tried fitting it into a round hole. I slammed it against the board over and over again, but no matter how hard I forced it, it resisted."

Venus squeezed his arm, encouraging him to continue.

He swallowed with difficulty. "The change frustrated me, and rather than take the time to let myself adjust to the change and accept it, I tossed that damned board away." Sanford removed his hands from his pockets and unfolded Venus's fingers from his arm. Tracing the slender knuckles, he said, "I have done the same thing with you. From the first moment I met you, I tried forcing you into a slot. You were either going to be the type of female who scorned me for my blindness or the kind that babied me because of it. Those were the only two sorts of women I'd ever known. But from the very beginning you set out to destroy my convictions. You demanded I wait on you, you challenged my authority, and you dared me to test my independence. Not once did you baby me.

"And just when I thought I had you pegged, you went and changed on me. You stood up for me in public, defended me against myself, and took a mild— if sometimes opposing—interest in my career. But you didn't scorn my lack of sight.

"It still wasn't good enough, though. I blew up at you for not being blind. Then you went and changed again and every day I've spent with you since has been an adventure. You make me laugh with your similes, make me examine my work more closely, and make me . . . make me see things more clearly than I've ever seen them before."

Venus stared at him, her mouth slack, her eyes wide. "Well, bless my soul! Sanford Buchanan, are you apologizing to me?"

His shy grin was his answer and Venus's knees went weak. But whether her limpness was caused by that charming curve of his lips or from his unexpected confession or the fact that he stood before her, blessing her with this first glimpse of his bared body, she could not decide. Perhaps it was the three combined.

She glanced at their hands, his mighty and capable, hers meek and compliant. Together, entwined, he strengthened her hands, and she gentled his. Such a chaste fusion, yet so poignant that tears stung her eyes. She almost felt sorry for Sanford. He was falling in love with her too, and didn't even realize it.

He would, though, Venus promised herself. Before they reached Nevada, he'd be just as aware that he could no more live without her than she could exist a day without him.

Communication. That was her key.

"Maybe I have tried forcing some people into slots that didn't fit them," Venus confided. *Maybe that had been her problem with Sanford all along.* Although knowing he was like no other man of her acquaintance, she had treated him as if he were just another of her beaus. She had stepped on his monumental pride, taken for granted that, with a little persistence and a lot of conniving, he'd kiss her hems like every man preceding him.

But Sanford wasn't the first one she'd made mistakes in judgment with. "My sister Persy made her debut in New York society five years ago. I remember being green as a stagnant pond with envy. I was only fifteen, but I didn't think it was fair that she see the world when I was stuck on the ranch—"

"With a bunch of smelly cows."

Venus grinned bashfully. "Exactly. In my mind, the ranch was where Persy belonged, and New York was where I belonged. But in her letters, she raved about the glamour and excitement of balls and teas and charity functions, so I thought that maybe Persy did belong in the big city. Then she came back—married to a *saloon* owner —and settled down in a little house on the ranch with Jake."

"But you had trouble accepting that she'd give up the city she claimed to love, to live a quiet life."

Venus nodded. "With a *saloon* owner! I thought I knew my sister, but she kept changing on me. I sure like her a lot better now that she's found her cozy niche. And she seems much happier." Venus studied Sanford's meditative profile then ventured, "Is that what's troubling you? That I'm changing?"

Sanford released her and fell back against the tree. "I don't know, Venus," he replied evasively. But it was a lie. Venus troubled him. She and all the new, conflicting emotions she aroused. "I'm a cautious man. In my life, surprises are something to be wary of and to prepare for." He turned his head toward the sunrise. "You're right, it is peaceful here. But I have this odd premonition that the peace won't last. It's as if something is out there, lurking. I want to be ready for it, but damned if I know what *it* is."

Venus smiled secretively.

High in the mountains of New Mexico Territory, the

last thing either of them was prepared for was a hurricane.

Hurricane had considered calling off his quest a dozen times already. The only thing working in his favor was Buck Buchanan's slow pace. If he had any idea where Buck was going, he might find a shortcut to head him off. But Hurricane hadn't stopped to think he might travel so far; he hadn't figured on it taking so long to catch up with the writer! Even if he wanted to quit, he couldn't. He'd wind up lost. Lasso wasn't much, but it was home and familiar. Out here, in mountains and wilderness, he was completely out of his element. And though he'd always thought of himself as self-sufficient, crossing through valleys and over peaks, he now realized how truly dependent he was.

Buck had started with a two-hour lead out of Fort Stanton and that had grown to five hours, then eight hours. He'd lost Buck's trail twice crossing the rocky buttes and arroyos. Locating the tracks cost him hours of good daylight. Hunting for sporadic suppers consumed more time since Daisy scared off most of the wildlife with her mournful whinnies, and area ranches where he might swipe a few eggs or a chicken or a pie cooling in the window were few and far apart. He'd had a helluva scare too when Daisy was resting near that Indian burial ground. One minute, there wasn't a soul in sight for miles, and the next, a line of redskins stretched across the top of a mesa. Still garbed in borrowed soldier's clothes, Hurricane thought for sure his scalp would be flapping in the breeze on some warrior's spear. But all they did was watch him for half the afternoon while the sun baked his face a blistering scarlet. Hurricane reckoned they just wanted to convince him not to disturb their sacred cemetery. He'd been convinced.

Then, six days after leaving the fort, he and Daisy came upon the Rio Grande River where he met with another delay. 'Course, Daisy was to blame for it, as usual. Sensitive of hoof, she refused to cross the strip of water some fool had stuck between him and Buck. Hurricane had been patient the first time she'd plopped on her rear at the bank of the Pecos River, but at least the level had been low enough to bare a sandbar for her to pick her way over.

No such luck at the Rio Grande. No amount of threats or bribery would coerce her into crossing even the shallowest point. He'd even gotten down on his knees, for the first time in his life, and begged the mare to take pity on him. But Daisy's hooves dug deeper into the rock-littered banks. So he was stuck wasting more hours looking for a route heading around the churning flow. Even with his limited education Hurricane understood who was the true master in their relationship. And he thought it pretty damn pitiful that a four-legged, foul-breathed critter could rule his actions.

"I shoulda traded you in for one of those horses at Fort Stanton," Hurricane grumbled to the contrary creature as she plodded alongside the eastern bank of the Rio, unperturbed. "Woulda saved me a whole helluva lot of agger-vation. At least on an army horse, I might have already caught up to Buck. And at least then, when I got hanged for being a horse thief, I woulda died a hero."

Recalling the fort, Hurricane felt his spirits lift. He kind of wished the two bumblebrains had escaped from the outhouse and come after Buck Buchanan as they had planned. Nothing like a little excitement to take his mind off his problems. Hurricane chuckled, imagining the looks on their faces when the noise they made inside the necessary alerted the troop.

It was another good story to tell Buck, too. 'Course, two villains trapped in a privy sounded a bit doltish. Hurricane amused himself with a variety of spruced-up exaggerations and decided to merge the burial-ground incident and the fort incident into one tale. He'd look a lot more like a hero if he saved Buck and the lady from a band of hostiles instead of a pair of mallet-heads. Yeah, numbers were good. A dozen—no, two dozen 'Pache warriors. And all those mean black eyes were focused on Buck's lady, their plans for her so foul, a person had to plug their nose against the stench. And the tortures they had in mind for Buck . . . staking him out on an ant-hill—no, torching him alive. No, cutting open his gut and letting the big black flies feast in his innards. Yeah.

'Course, Buck wouldn't see the Indians when he passed by 'cause they'd be hiding behind the rocks. But Hurricane would know they were there 'cause he'd be down below in the burial grounds. Yeah, that sounded good. Then, just as those Indians were about to charge down the sides of the butte, Hurricane pictured himself coming to Buck's rescue in the nick of time. He'd rise up from the burial grounds, waving a tomahawk, and make the 'Paches think he was the ghost of some long-dead relative angered by their plans. Since everybody knew how superstitious Indians were, he reckoned Buck would believe him if he said they fled screaming in fear and hightailed it in the other direction.

Yeah. That's what he'd tell Buck. *If he ever caught up with the son of a bitch.*

Venus dreaded high noon on barren plateaus and plains, for the late June temperatures scaled into the eighties and nineties and sweltered well past nightfall. Her layers of petticoats and sundry undergarments trapped dry heat and perspiration against her skin. Not even the essence of vanilla she dabbed on disguised the musky odor she found mysteriously appealing on Sanford, but offensive on herself. The diet of salty foods Sanford insisted they eat to retain body water and prevent dehydration only made her sweat more. And she never wanted to see a piece of fried pork, brine-soaked bean, or tasteless biscuit as long as she lived.

But even the negative aspects of travel didn't seem as loathsome as they once had. Sanford kept her occupied with lessons in survival. Never enter a canyon of no escape, don't walk blindly into caves, beware of buzzards circling overhead, and so on and so on . . .

And while they rode, parallel to each other, she often talked of her family and upbringing. She confided that she believed her grandmother's candlewick might be

burning a bit short as she grew older, to which he replied
that Minerva and Zeb should get along famously, then,
for the grease was drying up in his uncle's bearings, too.
In turn, he also confessed that growing up as an only
child on a Mississippi farm, he'd often longed for the
companionship of brothers or sisters. Venus told him a
day or two spent with her boisterous siblings would cure
that notion. Little by little he opened up to her, and she
found herself amused by the tales of his extensive travels
and the novels they inspired.

Mostly, though, they worked on Slick Drayson's story.
Together, they expanded on Venus's idea of the saloon
girl. Yes, she'd been flippant when suggesting he add romance to the plot, but it had been the only way she could
think of to slowly reveal her true feelings. At first, she
worried that he might guess at the truth behind the mes-
sages she was sending him via the imaginary "Venus" and
run in the opposite direction. Why, just the hint of a serious involvement between his *characters* had practically
sent him bolting when she had first introduced the idea!
But when Sanford decided to change the saloon girl's
name to "Mara" to avoid confusion, Venus found it much
easier to reveal the love blossoming fuller in her heart
each day without him making the connection between
herself and the character. Instinct told her it was still too
soon to reveal her feelings to Sanford.

Constantly painting pictures of their surroundings also
helped stave off boredome and discomfort. They were
approaching the forested ranges of the New Mexico and
Arizona Territories now. Settling dusk washed out the
vibrant hues of daylight, and as Venus kept an eye out for
a suitable campsite, she scribbled an observation in the
note journal. "The hills are in repose, like a sleeping
woman."

"Is she naked?"

At Sanford's impertinent question, a forbidden thrill
curled around Venus's spine even as a blush suffused her
cheeks. His talent for reading her mind could really be a
nuisance. Tipping her nose, Venus hoped to conceal her

mortification with a saucy retort. "She's wearing wicked velvet, and a halo of fire circles her head."

"Sounds dangerously delightful." His eyebrows wiggled lecherously. "A sultry, mature woman, well versed in satisfying the demands of a man?" He sighed in bliss.

"That type of woman appeals to you?"

"That type of woman would wear me out in fifteen minutes," he countered.

Crimson heat soared from Venus's neck to her scalp. Although she remained properly innocent of details, she knew passions of that degree involved bare skin and body parts.

"You once told me to feel free to ask you anything. Does that offer still stand?" Sanford said.

A combination of joy and anxiety replaced her embarrassment. Curiosity was a good sign, but she'd made that proclamation before she'd had anything to hide. And considering the topic they'd been discussing, Venus wasn't sure his question would be appropriate! "What is it you want to ask?"

Sanford hesitated. "I . . . well, it's your voice, Venus."

She shot him a surprised glance. "My voice?"

"Actually, your speech. I've noticed how you taper your consonants—no one in your family that I've met talks like you, and I guess I'd always wondered why you talk with a Southern-belle accent instead of a Texan's drawl."

"You know, I'd always wondered—you hailing from Mississippi—why you talked like a Yank."

"My father was raised in Ohio. What's your excuse?"

"Maybelle was from Georgia."

He arced his head and mocked, "Well, that answers my question. Maybelle is from Georgia so you talk with a southeastern dialect. Is Maybelle, by chance, some relative I didn't meet?"

"Oh, no. She and her husband, Hank, own the mercantile back home. When they first moved to Paradise Plains, all the gentlemen in town hung on to her every word because it sounded so genteel and ladylike. I noticed how enamored they were with her way of speaking, so I asked her to teach me to talk like a Southern belle. I've been talking like her for so long, it comes natural."

"And did all the gentlemen of Paradise Plains find your mode of speech as enamoring as you'd hoped?"

"Among other things, yes. Of course, poor Meredith cringed every time she heard me lose my *r*'s or use slang."

"Meredith?"

"My sister-in-law, Lee's wife. She's the town school-marm, very proper. She has a fiery side too, but only Lee sees it." Venus paused with her forefinger to her chin. "Except the year he stole her school away. All of Paradise witnessed that hidden side of her then."

"Lee stole the school?" Sanford chuckled.

"Well, not the whole school, just her class for a year. She had arrived in Paradise to fill the teaching position, but when she got there, she discovered that Lee had taken over her job. She was very angry with him. Of course, she has long since forgiven him."

"I can't imagine the Lee I met teaching children anything but how to herd cattle."

"Oh, he didn't want to, not at first. But it was his la— his destiny," Venus quickly amended. "He fell in love with Meredith that year. Once they were married, she took over the school, but he still helps her out when a student is having trouble. His first love is the ranch, though. He tends his cows, and him and C.J. and Atlas manage Daddy's herd too, because Daddy much prefers building things to working the ranch."

"Then why does your father own a ranch if he doesn't like working one?"

"Grandma Minerva gave it to him as a reward. I think so he'd have something to build on, a legacy to pass down to us."

Yet, her near slipup about Lee's labor reminded her of her own. And of the rules that went along with fulfilling it.

She hadn't thought about her task or home in so long. Sanford had occupied all her thoughts, first those of revenge, and now those of love . . . Suddenly, she realized her grandmother wasn't named for the goddess of wisdom for nothing. Had Grandma known she would find love in this labor? Had she known, somehow, that what had been important to her two months ago paled in comparison to what was important to her now? Had Grandma known that by the end of the term, she would long for a greater prize than one the Daltry wealth could buy?

"Your father shows foresight."

"Maybe when you get too old for traveling, you'll want a few acres to raise your family on," Venus hinted, hoping to plant a seed in his mind. Although she had no plans to bear children now, the idea of having a few strapping, sepia-haired, whiskey-eyed sons in Sanford's likeness, and a couple of dainty, blond-haired, blue-eyed little girls like herself in the future sounded quite delightful.

"If I ever get the chance to raise my own family, I'd make sure they never had to worry about having their home destroyed by cannons or their lands being taken by a tax collector."

"Sanford, I'm sure your father never meant for any of that to happen to you."

"He should have considered those consequences before he left me and the farm to fight in a war he didn't even believe in."

"Maybe he did believe in it. Perhaps not the issues, but maybe he saw it as a way to protect your future."

"Well, it backfired on him, didn't it? I wound up losing everything—the farm, him, and my eyes."

"But look at all you gained." Land's sakes, Venus thought to herself. She was beginning to sound like Persy! "You found an uncle who taught you self-sufficiency; you gained an education out of reach for most people; you've been places and met people and made a success of yourself doing what you love. I think you're an awful lucky man, Buck Buchanan."

"Venus," he told her with a grin, "you'd best watch yourself. You're gaining a bit of wisdom, and together with your beauty, you'll wind up a package no man can resist."

That's what I'm counting on, Buchanan!

She would willingly forfeit any reward Grandma planned to give if Sanford was the man who could not resist her.

Eighteen

SQUATTING BESIDE VENUS, SANFORD SHOOK HER SHOULDER AS another rumble vibrated through the night. "Wake up, Venus."

She mumbled unintelligibly, flung her arm around his hip, and her supple body rolled onto his lap. Her head nestled in the crux of his thighs and Sanford froze.

"Venus . . ." he croaked. "Princess, we have to move. There's a storm brewing . . ."

"Darling, it can't storm," she argued in her sleep. "I just fixed my hair."

Sanford shook his head with amused exasperation. "I'll help you repair any damage once we find someplace safer."

At that moment, a sharp clap of thunder jolted Venus wide awake. She shot upward in alarm and scrambled fully into his lap. "Good Zeus!" she cried, as she put a death grip around his throat and shoved her bosom against his chin. "That sounded like the world just cracked open and is going to suck us into Hades! Why didn't you tell me there was a storm on top of us?"

Sanford tried disentangling the collection of arms and

legs from around his waist and neck. "I've been trying to warn you . . ."

"What should we do?"

"Get dressed and pack up," he answered, submitting to Venus's choking hold. "Find shelter—a cave, a copse of trees, anything to protect us from the elements."

"But it's the middle of the night!"

"We have no choice; we can't wait until morning. Shallow though it is, in this canyon we risk being swept away to China by a flash flood or struck down by a bolt of lightning."

"Sanford, I swear I didn't know we were in for a storm." Her head swung back and forth vigorously. "I never would have picked such an open spot to camp if I'd seen a single black cloud yesterday."

Her sweet breath caressed his ear and the scent of vanilla clung to her skin and undergarments and her lyrical voice was doing crazy things to his insides. Sanford gritted his teeth against the pleasure-pain of holding her, her breasts clamping his chin in their plump fold, and not touching her in a forward manner. But all he wanted to do was touch her in a forward manner. He had in his dreams, before the thunder and Ranger's blowing whinny woke him. "I know, Venus," he assured her, spanning her back with his hands. It was as much as he dared. It sure wasn't enough, though. "You've done very well judging the weather. Sometimes it just changes out of the blue. I've been caught unawares before."

Her voice went soft as goosedown and her grip relaxed. "You really think I've done well judging the weather? What else do you think I've done well?"

"Can we discuss this later? Any second now, the heavens are going to open and those pretty ears of yours won't hear a word I have to say."

"Ohhh, Sanford," she cooed, pulling away. "You think my ears are pretty!"

For the first time in his life, Sanford ignored caution, laughed in danger's face. He slid his hands up the ridges of her spine and cupped the back of her head tenderly. "I think all of you is pretty, Venus. In fact, you're the most beautiful lady I've ever known."

Venus threw herself against him, knocking him backward. Above the thunder rolling overhead, Sanford thought he heard her repeating, "I knew it, I knew it, I knew it . . ."

He had no idea what she was referring to but at the moment nature required his immediate attention. "Venus, we have to get out of this canyon."

She sprang off him. "You're right. I'll gather our gear while you saddle the horses. Land's sake, there's nothing like natural fireworks to ring in the Fourth of July, is there, Sanford?"

"I don't recall ever seeing fireworks."

"Well." She paused. "Imagine a star exploding, then parts of it showering down but never touching you. Except, there are colors—*shattered* colors in every hue of the rainbow . . . Oh, I'm not explaining it right. Sometimes it's hard telling you what things look like when you can't see them or touch them or hear them or smell them."

Sanford furrowed his brow as he tugged on the cinches of Ranger's saddle. He knew what Venus looked like, though, and he'd never seen her—not with his eyes, anyway. And he'd never asked her to describe herself—hell, there were only so many hours in the day!

Yet, he knew. He knew she had mellow sweet-butter hair with untamable curls that bounced all the way down to her backside when he brushed it. And he knew she had wide, clear eyes that flashed with lightning heat when she was angry and sang the ballad of a nightingale when she was content. And he knew she had more curves than a mountain pass, just as treacherous and just as awe-inspiring . . . and that touching them made the adrenaline rush through his veins faster and with more force than a wall of water crashing through a canyon chasm . . .

Sanford shook his head to dispel the images and the sensations. If they didn't get the hell out of *this* canyon, he'd never smell vanilla again.

Working quickly together, Venus had their packs strapped on the nervously shifting horses almost before Sanford finished securing the saddles.

Mounting with haste, Venus took the lead, with the pack horse tied behind her and Sanford following. Just as they made the ascension up the steep ridge, a furious deluge of rain pelted their slickers. The horses virtually sprouted wings as they galloped across the plains, cutting through the wind and rain for the safety of the ponderosa pines looming in mountains above the foothills.

The malevolence of the storm and the speed of the animal beneath her filled Venus with a power and reckless abandon she had previously felt only when shooting a weapon. *The same wild surrender she felt while in Sanford's arms.*

She lifted her face to the slashing rain. The land was a blur behind the watery sheet, and unable to focus, Venus gave her full trust to the sorrel gelding who now followed Sanford's magnificent stallion.

For nearly five miles, the horses maintained their pace but Venus knew if they were pressed much farther, they'd collapse. She slowed the sorrel to a lope, and the other two steeds heeded, blowing and heaving, foaming from the mouth. After another mile, Venus leaned over and yanked on Sanford's sleeve. She cupped her hand over her upper lip to project her voice and shouted, "We're at the base of the mountain!"

He nodded, rain streaming from the brim of his hat, down his neck. He spurred Ranger forward, and regal head bowed with exhaustion, the stallion forged over bramble and branches into the sparse growth of evergreen trees. High, needled branches scarcely shielded the rain and the ground shuddered with thunder that sounded like longhorns stampeding.

It appeared out of nowhere, the crumbling shack with only three sides still standing, and an eave that might have been a porch at one time before weather and neglect had taken their toll. Venus would have mistaken it for just another pile of dead branches and broken trees if Ranger hadn't swerved toward it.

Again she pulled on Sanford's arm at the same moment the horses pulled up short. "It's a shed of some sort," she hollered over the wind. As both dismounted, Venus immediately reached for Sanford's elbow under his rubber slicker. "Watch your step. The ground is littered with sharp rocks and rotten limbs."

At the yawning entrance to the shack, Sanford quickly assessed the damage with his hands. "It's open to the weather. It needs to be blocked, or we might as well stand out here."

"I'm going to put the horses under the overhang and stow our things inside."

"Grab the ax off the pack horse. We'll probably need it."

Once Venus returned to Sanford's side after attending to the horses, she noticed he had collected a pile of loose branches. She shoved into his arms several lengths of rope and rawhide she'd braided herself during their travels. His smile told her he was pleased with her foresight.

Soon, cut and stripped boughs were lashed together with lengths of rawhide to form a lopsided but fairly sturdy wall. She and Sanford attached it to the shanty, threading the rope between wide cracks in the original structure and around the temporary blockade. Soaked to the bone, they slipped between broken planks in the side. It was a perilous shelter to say the least, but it protected them from the wind and muted the heavy cascade of rain pounding upon the earth outside.

The few semidry logs Venus had brought inside with her made a clatter as she dropped them onto the floor. They raised a cloud of gagging dust and the musty smell of decay. Venus unclasped her slicker, and taking Sanford's also, tossed them into a corner since there were no pegs on which to hang them. She wiped her hands down her skirt, more to rid them of grime than to dry them off, for her clothes were drenched through every layer.

"Are you comfortable, Venus?"

"Snug as a bug." She shucked off the sopping wool and four petticoats but left on her clinging pantalettes. "Now

I can add constructing lean-tos to my list of accomplishments!"

"I'm surprised we haven't had more storms before this one. It's as if the territory's suffering a drought." Sanford gave the branches a firm shake, testing their security. "Long as it stops raining apples, we should be safe enough until this blows over."

"Speaking of blowing, that wind sounds congested. Hear the way it wheezes through the trees?"

"I'm amazed that you managed to find this shack."

"Give your horse credit, not me." Venus reached behind her neck, unbuttoning the top two buttons of her blouse, and pulled it over her head. Unclasping the front of her corset, she glanced at him. "Sanford, why are you setting a basin outside?"

"In case you haven't noticed, I need a shave. It feels like there are things crawling in my beard." As if to support his claim, he scratched at the two-days growth of bristles.

Venus giggled, knowing how he felt. In spite of the shower they'd received, dust and grime had imbedded itself in her skin too, and the tingling was annoying. Oh, what she wouldn't give for some of Mama's scented hair soap!

She dug out Sanford's bedroll from among their belongings and laid it over the dirt floor in the farthest corner of the shack. Then she propped the saddles lugged in earlier against the flimsy wall to use as headrests.

A brief scrape, then the smell of sulphur mingled with the rot and rain as Sanford set a match to the mound of damp wood. A weak flame caught. A thin column of smoke plumed out a gaping hole in what passed for a roof. At the prospect of heat, Venus suddenly realized how chilled she'd become in her damp underclothes, and she shivered. Sanford brought in the basin, and while he used his bandanna to wash his face, Venus delved into her packs for her brush and worked out the snarls in her hair.

A gentle smile rested on her lips as she studied him while he lathered his face. She'd grown used to his beard and mustache, but she much preferred the sight of his bare jaw. He had a strong bone structure, and weather-worn skin. With each swipe of the blade ridding him of those whiskers, he rewarded her with an unimpeded view of his mouth.

Following a sudden strike of thunder, a curse sliced through the shack and Sanford's hand shot to his chin. Venus suppressed a giggle. That was three times already he'd nicked himself.

Venus dropped her brush on the blanket and padded to his side. "May I?"

She took note of his reluctance. A streak of lightning brought his face into stark relief. His jaw was taut, stubborn, as if he were using every effort to restrain from voicing his independence.

"You ever shaved a man before?" His voice rumbled with the thunder.

"No, but I've always wanted to." Venus took the foam-speckled razor from his unprotesting hand and rinsed it off in the water. "Trust me, Sanford. I can't carve up your face any worse than you're doing."

"That remains to be seen."

"First, you need to get rid of this dumb thing." She whisked his hat off his head and tossed it onto the floor. "I don't know why you hide beneath it anyway. You have a handsome face."

Sanford held himself stiff and defensive. "Maybe for the same reason you hide beneath your cosmetics," he criticized. "So no one can disapprove of the real you."

Shocked, Venus stared at him, the straight blade poised against the vein beneath Sanford's jaw. "Is that what you think I've been doing?" she choked out. Venus let the razor fall then whirled away, suddenly unable to bear touching him. Her hands trembled so badly she might wind up slicing him from ear to ear. And she didn't know why. She only knew the camaraderie, the partnership she'd felt working at his side as they repaired the shelter had been eroded.

"Venus, wait . . ." He groped for her wrist. She

evaded his hand. "That was an uncalled-for remark and I . . . I shouldn't have said it."

"But it's what you think," she accused, rounding on him. "That I'm a coward. And when you told me I was the most beautiful lady you'd ever known . . . it was a lie, wasn't it!"

"I don't lie! I meant what I said. You *are* the most beautiful lady I've ever known—"

"How in Hades do *you* know? You can't see me! You're too busy hiding behind that wide brim!"

"All I ever wanted was to be normal," he growled, rising to his full height, towering above her.

"And all I ever wanted was to hold on to my beauty! If I don't have it, I am nothing."

"Who the hell planted that notion into your head?"

It wasn't just a notion, it was the truth. At least, the truth according to how she had been treated for twenty years. That her beauty made her special. Made her lovable.

"Cosmetics don't make you beautiful," he cut in harshly. "They just enhance the outer shell. And when you become obsessed with them, you are just hiding your true beauty. The kind that glows from inside out, the kind you don't fake. *That's* how I know you're beautiful. I don't have to see it." He slammed his fist against his chest. "I can feel it."

Trapped, Venus lashed out. "Fine. You want me to swallow that nonsense, then taste this—*you aren't normal. You never will be.*" He sucked in his breath. Venus knew she had hurt him. She hadn't meant to sound so cruel, and yet she was sick to death of tiptoeing around his blindness. It was an indisputable fact, and maybe this was what he needed—to get it out in the open. To accept it. Just as he expected her to accept her own insecurities. "You aren't normal because you *can't* be."

Her voice softened, hoarse with emotion. "You're far better than normal, you're *you.* You're strong and smart and competent. Normal is dull, do you hear me? It's everyday, and it's ordinary. But you've been so mired in your own black, self-pitying depths that you can't reach the light beaming down on your head."

A long, tense silence followed as their gazes collided, his cloudy darkness, hers misty blue. The thunder had stilled for the moment but the rain unceasingly pummeled the shanty roof and the wind continued to wheeze its congested breaths through the pines.

Finally, he asked her softly, "Where is the light, Venus?"

Her lips trembled with a tender smile and a sob caught in her throat. Venus held out her hand. "It's right here, Sanford."

Venus waited, her palm outstretched. She knew he couldn't see the gesture. She intended it that way. To find what she offered, he would have to reach out, climb that mountain of pride of his. And when he did, they'd have a funeral. They'd bury that blessed hat of his—alongside her cosmetics—and face the world together. Naked and exposed, but accepted by each other in spite of—or perhaps because of—their flaws.

She saw the hunger etched into his shadowed, fire-kissed features, the yearning . . . a spark of hope.

And then, he turned from her to squat beside the basin and finish butchering his face with the razor.

Dropping her hand to her side, she blinked back her tears. Perhaps the purpose of her labor was to teach her patience. If so, she was earning her prize in spades. "What do we do now?" she asked, lifting her chin. "We're stuck here together, and hollering at each other is only going to make a miserable situation even more miserable."

"I never wanted to make you miserable, Venus. I only wanted you safe."

"Well?" She slapped her thinly clad thighs. "I'm safe as anybody can be in this mortal world." She grabbed her quilt and settled against one of the saddles. "I'm also cold. That fire isn't big enough to bake a worm, and from the way it's sputtering it won't last very long. So hurry up and shave, then get out of those wet clothes and lie next to me so I can borrow some of your heat."

He took another gouge out of his chin and hissed. "That's not a good idea, Venus. Not tonight."

"Why not tonight? We've been lying next to each other every night for a month. And right now my teeth are ready to chatter their way out of my mouth if I don't get warm."

He sighed. Using his bandanna, he sponged off the remnants of lather then unfolded his body from its bent position. "Because I'm not feeling very strong or smart or competent tonight. I'm feeling very, very ancient."

"What would make you feel young again?"

His teeth flashed white in the dimness. "An adventure."

"Well, if you can't go on an adventure, then an adventure should come to you." Venus gathered her pens and ink and journals and arranged them on her quilted lap. She flipped through the pages. "All right, Slick and Mara have just left the message on the rock telling Gunns Murphy to meet them at the saloon on July first—winner takes all. But now they must make certain they arrive there on the designated date, too. And since we haven't yet explored the territory of Arizona, we can't fill in the details of their journey. But you don't want them there until the very last moment, anyway. How long until they reach Nevada?"

"Venus, what are you doing?"

"Helping you write your adventure. Isn't that what you brought me along for?"

Venus didn't understand the look of sadness that washed over his face. She'd given him the opportunity for wishes and hopes and dreams and he'd refused it. She hadn't admitted defeat, yet—she still had time to wait for him to come around—but neither was she about to back him into a corner. Nor was she going to waste time pouting and moping over something she couldn't change.

"You're right. I did bring you along to help me with my story."

"Well, let's get to work then! How long till all of us get to Nevada?"

He wandered over to the blanket and sat with his knees raised and his hands dangling over them. "A couple weeks, I figure."

"If you're going to sit here, you have to get your wet clothes off and crawl under the quilt. I told you, I'm cold, and I don't see any reason why you should catch a chill from being ornery."

One side of his lip quirked. Venus tore her gaze away from the gradual unveiling of his chest as he slipped his shirt buttons free of their holes. "Two weeks, then. That means we have to come up with delays. Any suggestions?"

He rolled first one brawny shoulder, then the other, divesting himself of the transparent linen. A thunderclap made him glance roofward. "I guess that's a suggestion. Might as well start working on a storm scene. Although I just hate using scenes I've used before, and I had storms in both *Boot Hill Avenger* and *Whiskey for Gold Dust.*"

Venus rubbed the blunt end of the pen along her lips and sneaked sideways glances at Sanford. "A storm," she repeated. Land's sake, the man had so much chest she figured two formal place settings could be laid on the surface and still leave room for half another one!

Next, he yanked off one boot, nearly kicking himself in the head with it, removed the other, then he unrolled white socks bearing dark marks on the toes from wearing his boots. She'd never given much consideration to men's feet before, but she found herself fascinated with Sanford's. Especially his right foot. She noticed two old teardrop-shaped marks at the base of his long toes. "What are those scars from?"

"Pitchfork."

Venus cringed. "Ouch."

"It was a long time ago." He shrugged. "I got used to getting injured. As long as I wasn't distracted, though, I wasn't hurt."

"It must have been tough at first." They both knew she referred to his sight loss.

His hands cupped his knees. "Yes, princess. It was tough. Sometimes, it still is."

After he set aside his gunbelt, Sanford lifted himself off the blanket and wriggled his soaked trousers down the length of his solid trunk. Noticing he wore cotton long underwear beneath, Venus released a breath.

"Where were we?" he asked.

Venus was well on her way to drooling over his firm, lean flanks! "Distractions." Suddenly, she thrust the pen away from her mouth. "I mean, delays!"

Why was she pretending their argument hadn't happened? Sanford pondered. She had probed the very bowels of his soul, found his secret vulnerability, and bared it. She made him confront the enemy he thought he had vanquished. Before, he had accused her of fearing the dark. Yet, he'd been the one who was afraid. At any other time, he would have faced that fear head-on. Yet now, all he wished—Sanford swallowed heavily—was to be consoled. Held. Like a damned baby. No, like a man.

Damn her for making him wish again.

But maybe Venus had the right idea. Forget the violation of impersonal boundaries and concentrate on the business end of their relationship.

Clutching that decision, he built on the plot from where they'd left off the night before, bringing Slick and Mara to a mountain shack much like the one he and Venus shared. The familiar smell of ink being scribbled on parchment as Venus wrote beckoned him to a world of make-believe. He reclined against the saddle, his damp, bare back sticking to the leather. A thousand horses' hooves thundered across the sky above. ". . . Pungent wet earth and foliage," he dictated, crossing his arms over his chest, "mingled with the steady pounding of rain saturating wood pulp—"

"That's good!" Venus exclaimed, scrawling furiously. "Those are exactly the smells and sounds of the storm!"

"Slick struck a match to the pile of moist pine. Mara huddled close to the struggling flame, her fingers tight around the coarse blanket circling her throat. Peeling off his clothes, Slick stretched out on the earthen floor behind her. Mara lowered herself against his length, and together they stared at the dance of feeble flames while the storm raged all around them." Sanford gulped over the pressure in his windpipe. In a husky voice, he told Venus, "That's enough. We'll work on this later."

"But if we wait till later we'll lose the impact of the scene!"

"I don't feel like working. I'm tired, Venus."

"Sanford, you are always telling me that if the words are coming, you have to get them down before the idea leaves you."

"They aren't coming anymore."

"Oh, pooh. You were just gaining momentum. Now, Slick is alone in a broken-down shanty with Mara. What's he going to do next?"

"Roll over and go to sleep."

He heard the pen slap against paper. "Wrong!" Venus cried.

"Wro-ong! It's my story, how can it be wrong?"

"The Slick Drayson I know wouldn't roll over and ignore the opportunity practically whacking him in the face!"

"Meaning?"

"Why, there's a beautiful woman lying beside him, stripped down to her bare essentials! The last thing he's going to do is roll over and go to sleep!"

It was an innocent enough remark, but the image in Sanford's mind wasn't innocent at all. Venus, stripped down to her bare essentials, sharing his body warmth . . . No, he corrected vehemently, it was *Mara* clothed in transparent cotton underclothes, lying beside Slick!

Yet, Mara didn't carry the faint scent of vanilla and rain and rawhide. "He's tired, Venus," Sanford ground out. "If I say he'll roll over and go to sleep, then that's what he'll do!"

"And I say he'll pull her into his arms and kiss her!"

"Why?" Sanford challenged.

"Why?" Venus echoed. "Well, because he cares for

her, silly! And when a man cares for a woman, the natural thing to do is kiss her!"

"Does she care for him?"

Venus stared directly at him. Quietly, she said, "With every beat of her heart."

Sanford squirmed on the blanket. "Then why doesn't she kiss him?"

Venus huffed with exasperation. "Because it wouldn't be proper. Mara might be a saloon girl, but she is no harlot."

"Is that why she hasn't kissed him before now?"

"Partly," Venus conceded. "She's been waiting for him to stop denying his feelings for her, yes. But I think she's more afraid he will reject her again."

"Well, maybe he's been wanting her secretly for so long that he's afraid he won't be able to stop with just a kiss."

Breathless, Venus answered. "Maybe once he starts kissing, she won't want him to stop."

Sanford's racing heart stumbled. "She won't feel like a harlot?"

And when Venus cupped his jaw with her tiny hand, his heart stopped beating altogether. "She'd feel like his most precious treasure."

Sanford absorbed the softness of her hand against his own rough skin. He closed his eyes, seeing not the enemy of darkness, but the promise of light. Imagined his lips fusing with Venus's, his hands exploring every valley and swell of her body with painstaking slowness, so that her figure would be forever stamped in his memory . . .

"All right! You win! Write down that he kissed her."

Her hand fell away from his face. "That's all you want me to write? *He kissed her?* Land's sake, Sanford, I think your readers will be sorely disappointed!"

"Then what do *you* suggest?" he barked.

"You always say a writer should experience scenes for himself. It makes the story more plausible." She hesitated, then said, "I suppose . . . you could . . . experience the scene with me."

"I should kiss you?"

"Well, yes." Her voice contained the impression of a blush. "I mean, you cannot disappoint your readers."

"No," Sanford whispered, reaching over to drag a strand of her damp hair through his fingers. "I cannot have my readers disappointed."

Venus did not move her gaze from Sanford as his lips descended toward hers. One thought skittered through her mind: *It's about darn time.*

Then she could think no more. Their lips met. Pure sensation consumed Venus. Of paradise. Of home. Of belonging and beauty and bliss. So tender, his kiss. Tremulous and timid. Seeking and seeing. It was sprinkling rain and flashes of lightning.

He tugged on her wild curls, fitted his mouth fully over her lips. Venus went limp. His arm wound around her back and his chest burned her arm. She swiveled and slipped her hands between them. Her palms flattened on a plane of bulky muscle, his heart galloped under her fingers. She dug her nails into the unyielding flesh, wishing she could snatch his heart and hold it forever. "Wait," she whimpered. "Who are you? If you are Slick, please don't touch me. I cannot even pretend to belong to another man. I cannot pretend to be another woman."

"I . . . am Sanford Joseph Buchanan," he rasped.

Venus clenched her eyes shut. "And who are you kissing, Sanford Joseph Buchanan?"

"A goddess."

In spite of her efforts, a tear trickled from beneath her closed lids, down her cheek.

"One of unsurpassed beauty and undisputed victory."

Another tear fell.

"You've won, Venus . . . princess . . . goddess. I surrender." While he craned his neck for another kiss, she opened her eyes and saw the strained greed in his dusky features. Saw a glaze over his blank brown eyes.

Venus pressed him down, onto the saddle. "I want to see you, Sanford. As you see me, I want to see you." She untied the bandanna still around her neck and twined it about her eyes. Then she brought his hands to her face. Encountering the strip of cloth, she felt him tense, felt his

chest tighten, and knew deep, deep in her soul that he
was touched by her action.

Venus gripped his fingers. Slowly she guided them
along the sides of her jaw. Her own hands blindly
searched for his face. His brows were thick as she remembered, and curved over his down-tilted eyes. She combed
her fingers through the waves of his hair, soft and sleek
with raindrops, then around the shell of his ears. With the
tip of her finger she traced the half-circle scar at the side
of his head. "Is this the scar? The one that caused you so
much pain?"

His thumbs stroked her cheekbones. "Not anymore."

She was pulled roughly against his body. His lips
against hers were not gentle this time, but ravenous. His
tongue plundered her mouth, his hands questioned every
inch of her body, hungry for all her secrets. Outside, nature vented her wrath. Inside, a storm of passion erupted,
of hot thunder, of wicked bolts.

In the world of shadows Venus entered with Sanford,
her senses became as acute as his. Her breasts swelled
and were sorely sensitive against his chest. The fine linen
of her chemise chafed.

His mouth assaulted hers, and she matched the force,
forgetting how a lady might act or feel. She was no lady;
she was Sanford's woman, and eager to have him claim
her. His hands were everywhere upon her body, leaving
not an inch neglected. His callused palms raised the hem
of her chemise. Bare hands roamed naked flesh, leaving
behind a trail of goose bumps. Then they slipped inside
the band of her pantalettes and molded to her bottom.
Tearing her mouth from his, she gasped and bucked on
top of him, his arousal solid and throbbing at the juncture
of her thighs.

Instantly, he stilled, removed his hands from her bottom, and wrapped them around her back. "I . . . am an
honorable man. A Buchanan. I cannot, and will not take
you. Just . . . let me hold you . . . awhile. Let me sa-
vor your light."

Venus moaned in agony, her body empty and aching

and hungry. "Please, Sanford," she begged against his
neck. "I hurt . . . for you."

His heart thumped so furiously, Venus felt it in her
own chest. And he smelled of raw man, of earth and
musk and leather. Wild, untamed. How could she ever
have preferred cologne and sophistication? Beneath her
lay a warrior, half-god, half-mortal.

"I hurt for you, Venus. But I've met my limit. Just lie
still, or you'll understand the true extent of lonely." With
shaking fingers he sought her face. "Damn, you are so
very beautiful. So delicate. So innocent."

He should have been more cautious. Should have put
up more resistance against his building hungers. Should
have been strong enough to combat the weaknesses Venus brought out in him and more alert to the danger she
represented. And he for damn sure should have had
more control over his emotions.

But it was too late for him now. Venus had become a
part of him he could not live without—his heart, his soul.
His every dream and wish and hope, all come to life from
the grave he'd buried them in so long ago.

Yes, it was too late for him now.

But it wasn't too late for her.

"I think I've fallen helplessly in love with you, Sanford."

He shut his eyes in anguish. She said that now, but
what about when she wanted to dance, and he trod upon
her feet? Or when the words no longer came, and he lost
his good name, his income, his way of life? Would she still
love him when she was hungry and poor and without
status? And what about when she cried his name and he
couldn't find her? Would she still love him when she realized he was only half a man?

He opened his eyes and saw . . . nothing. Just black
despair. "You should get dressed. I need to check on the
horses."

Venus whipped the blindfold from her eyes and stared
at Sanford. His face registered a bleakness she'd never
seen before. She clasped his cheeks between her hands.
"Did you hear me, Buchanan? I said I think—"

He turned his face away. "I heard you." He slid from beneath her. Her blood ran cold. He stood, and looked down at her, the line of his vision only slightly off. Then he said without malice, "Spare us both, princess. Don't think."

Dumbly, she accepted his help rising. Just as she made it to her feet, the wall to the shack was torn down, and the scruffiest-looking character Venus had ever seen stood panting in the portal.

Nineteen

"VENUS, WHAT'S HAPPENING?" SANFORD DEMANDED, SHIELDING her behind his back.

"I don't know. A fella has come and ripped our wall off. He's about my age, whipcord lean, and with anxious eyes the bitter green of a tornado sky."

"You ain't got no idea how glad I am to finally catch up to you," the panting young intruder said, flipping his soggy hair from his eyes.

Raindrops swooped out to spray Sanford's naked chest with icy dribbles. He was keenly conscious that he'd been caught unawares in his underwear.

"The name's Hurricane. Hurricane Henderson. And I'm a hero."

"A hero?" Sanford repeated in confusion.

"Yeah. You know, for those books you write!"

"Sanford, maybe he got caught in the storm like we did and he's looking for shelter," Venus suggested as she quickly slipped her skirt over her hips.

Hurricane had been so busy introducing himself to Buck Buchanan that he hardly paid any mind to Buck's lady until she spoke. Spying her across the fire, though, he understood what had driven the half-breed and the soldier to want her bad enough to kill Buck to get her. Up close, she was even prettier than from a distance. All hair and eyes and pink skin under that skimpy top. The same rot-gut type of fire he'd felt first seeing her on the street of Lasso warmed his innards now. "Yeah, this is one helluva storm, ain't it? Me and Daisy was standing at the rim of a basin when it hit. Never woulda seen yous racing toward these hills if not for the lightning." Hurricane thrust his scrawny chest out proudly. "But me and Daisy managed to follow you two anyways. Just took us a little longer 'cause Daisy can't run fast as your horses."

Sanford felt the skin at his nape prickle. "You were following us? Why? And who is Daisy?"

"I told you, 'cause you're gonna put me in one of your books and make me a famous hero! And Daisy's my horse. I put her 'round back with the others and fed her some of the oats from your sacks. She ain't been eating too good."

Well, this was all he needed. Another hopeful hero dogging his every step. In the past, Zeb had been the one to fend off any solicitors. Now he had to rely on his own wits. "I'm sorry, Henderson." Sanford shook his head. "I'm not looking for any heroes at present." Venus shoved his denims into his hands. Sanford thrust his feet into the pant legs, grateful that she had noticed his vulnerable state. He'd feel a damn sight more comfortable with his piece strapped to his hip, though, too. "But you're welcome to share our fire," he invited, stalling. "And we have food in our packs that we can prepare." Behind his back, he motioned to Venus to follow his lead. "Meanwhile, if you'll excuse us, we need to check on the horses ourselves."

Buck took the lady's arm and stepped forward, making to leave. Hurricane blocked their path. "But I'm a hero!"

"I'm sure you are. I am just not in need of a hero right now."

Hurricane never reckoned Buck wouldn't be interested in writing about him! He figured that once he tracked Buck down, and told him all his stories, he'd finally gain himself all the fame and riches he'd always dreamed of.

Make all the folks in Lasso look at him as more than Linette's bastard. It wasn't supposed to end like this!

And by damn, it *wasn't* gonna!

Hurricane spread his arms wide, nearly touching the walls of the shack, oblivious of the jagged streaks of lightning behind him and the rain pummeling his back. "I've been to hell and back trying to catch up to you! And I've collected all kinds of adventures along the way. And I ain't gonna let you outta my sight till you hear me out. Even when I get you in my sight, you always manage to slip away." His voice rose to a squeaking pitch with each desperate word but he could see he was having no effect on Buck.

Taking drastic action, Hurricane pulled his treasured, pearl-handled pistol from the back of his pants and leveled it at the pair. "I can't let you go nowhere, Buck Buchanan."

"Sanford, he has a gun."

"Now you and the lady just sit down there so I can tell you all about my adventures and you can make me a rich and famous hero in one of your books."

Sanford clasped Venus's clammy hand in his. "Do what he says, Venus." Sanford swallowed the impotent rage consuming him and took two backward steps, then lowered himself onto the blanket with Venus reluctantly following suit.

"That's better," Hurricane said. "Now, I ain't fixin' to hurt no one but I can't let you get away from me, neither." With his gun trained on them, he reached for the coil of rope hanging from a saddle at Buck's back. After binding Buck's hands, he turned to the lady. Damn, she had pretty eyes. Big blue ones.

Hurricane jerked back when she fluttered her lashes at him. He didn't have a lot of use for women, but Buck could sure pick pretty ones. "You his?"

Venus lowered her face and peered at the young man coyly. "He doesn't have a claim on me, if that's what you're asking."

Sanford spun toward her, a look of shock on his face. Venus squeezed his fingers reassuringly. He might not understand what she was up to now, but he would thank her later, she told herself.

Hurricane's mouth went dry. He couldn't never remember a girl this pretty making eyes at him. Most of them told him to bugger off, or called him names.

They wouldn't no more, though. He'd finally caught up to Buck. He was gonna go home to Lasso a hero. And maybe a lady as pretty as Buck's would take a shine to him. Hurricane cleared his throat and dropped his gaze to the leftover section of rope. "You too, lady. Put yer hands behind your back."

"Don't you hurt her," Sanford threatened. Blind or not, if this intruder harmed one silken hair on Venus's head, he'd kill him with his bare hands.

"I told you I ain't fixin' to hurt no one, long as you both listen."

Venus obeyed, shivering from both the cold, moist drafts blowing into the shanty and the reckless way the boy waved his gun around. If she didn't listen to him, he might cause damage to something much more important than the shack! Obviously, he was missing a few furnishings in his upper story to have followed them through a storm, just so Sanford could make him the subject of a book. But the knowledge might come in quite handy. That, and the fact that her charms were already whittling away at his tough composure.

"Uh . . . you got any of that grub still? I got me a powerful hunger."

"There's a slab of smoked beef in our supplies," Venus said. Then she graced Hurricane with her most dazzling, dimpled smile. "If you'll untie me, I'll get it for you."

He seemed to weigh the consequences of freeing her. Apparently deciding that she posed no danger, he removed the rope he'd just tied around her wrists. Venus gave her hips an exaggerated, provocative swivel as she sashayed toward the packs and withdrew the paper-wrapped hunk of meat, then resumed her place beside Sanford.

Hurricane's manners left much to be desired. He talked about his horse and the storm as he chewed, tell-

ing them how a bolt of lightning had frightened poor old
Daisy. She had tumbled halfway down the mountain,
landing less than twenty yards from this shack. When
Hurricane heard the other horses nicker, he knew Daisy
had located Buck Buchanan for him. No one rode a big
gray horse like Buck's. Throughout the narration, Venus
summoned all her practiced ladylike deportment to appear engrossed in his tale. Often one of her old beaus
would go on for hours about a topic she cared little
about. Venus simply batted her lashes as though every
word fascinated her. She was glad to discover that some
behaviors still came naturally.

When Hurricane finished devouring the meat, he
smacked his lips together and stared at the couple watching him. Now that he and Buck Buchanan were finally in
the same room, he wasn't sure what to do. The writer
looked like that bull did just before he charged. Meaty
chest bulging out, brown head lowered, and eyes scowling
until they were mere slits of pure meanness. Hurricane
wiped his greasy hands on his filthy trouser legs then
dabbed at the nervous sweat collecting on his neck. "Like
I said, I got all kinds of stories. So you'd best be ready to
sit for a spell while I tell them to you."

Venus wanted to smack Sanford over the head when he
snapped, "What are you going to do if I don't?" Was the
man determined to ruin all she'd accomplished?

Hurricane glanced at the gun in his hand, then brought
it even with Buck's nose. "Well . . ." He licked his lips
and darted a look at Venus before focusing on Sanford
again. "I reckon I'll have to shoot you."

The blood in her veins turned to ice. "But if you shoot
him, he can't write about you!" Venus exclaimed.

Hurricane pondered that for a second. "Well, then I'll
just make sure I aim low. He don't need his leg to write."

Venus absorbed that truth, then wondered if Hurricane
even understood that Sanford didn't use anything but his
imagination and that it was she who wrote. So far, it
didn't appear Hurricane realized Sanford was blind. If
they could keep up the pretense . . . "You know, Sanford, I think maybe he's right. He is a hero, and just

perfect for that book you were planning to write. Remember that place . . ." Venus waggled her finger, struggling to recollect the name of the mountain Red O'Ryan had told him about. "Babyhead! That's it."

"Venus, what the hell . . ." Venus jabbed him in the arm with her elbow. "Uh, yeah," he amended with a curious frown. "The Babyhead book."

"You know, Mr. Henderson"—Venus tilted her head in an adorable manner—"we were just discussing heroes and such. Why, a big, strong young man like yourself? I think you'd fit the role just perfect."

His Adam's apple bobbed up and down. "You don't have to call me mister. Just Hurricane. Or Hurry."

"Hurricane. What a powerful name for a hero."

Hurricane puffed up like a rooster prepared to crow his virility. "Never thought it powerful. Ma just called me that 'cause I was about as useful as one."

"Oh, but it is powerful! It conjures up an image of speed and forcefulness and might! Why, I declare, Mr. Buchanan would be honored to include you in his book!"

Hurricane narrowed his wide-spaced eyes. "He don't look honored."

"That's because he's thinking," Venus excused, noting the stubborn set of Sanford's jaw. "He grinds his teeth when he wants to write and can't."

"Why can't he write?"

"Because you have him bound. If you want him to write a story about you, you must untie his hands so he can take notes."

"Oh, yeah. I didn't think about that." Hurricane leaped to his feet and removed the rope from Sanford's wrist. Venus's hopes that it would enable Sanford to retrieve the holster were quickly dashed when Hurricane snatched up the revolver. "Just in case he gets any notions into his thinking head."

Venus maintained the smile that had melted so many hearts as she handed Sanford her journal and pen. The ink bottle had spilled, but she hoped that the black-stained sides of the jar would hide its emptiness from Hurricane's eyes.

Sanford had no idea what Venus was up to, but with no other recourse until a better plan formed, he grasped the pen and slanted the paper for writing. "Start with your birth and childhood background."

"Ah, well, I was borned in the summer of '61 to a who—uh, to a hatmaker. Yeah, that's right. And she was a real fine lady, too. Moved around a lot 'cause folks liked her hats so much. Yeah. Around my tenth summer we settled in Lasso—"

Venus and Sanford jerked their heads up in unison. "Lasso!"

"Yeah. That's where I first saw the two of yous. You were talkin' to Fairport on the street."

"You've been following us across New Mexico Territory?" Sanford cried.

Hurricane wore a pleased look. "That's right. And damned if I didn't save your butts plen-ty of times!" he crowed. "But that's for later telling. Where was I? Oh yeah, my ma the hatmaker. Anyways . . ."

Venus smothered her astonishment. If Hurricane had been following them all this way, he was more desperate than she had imagined. And, perhaps, more dangerous. It made her wonder if he would be as easy to shake as she first assumed. He might seem inexperienced and gullible, but he'd kept his pursuit a mystery from them—from Sanford! And Sanford was usually so astute!

She summoned every detail of the lessons he had taught her. This situation called for control, and the only control she figured would deter Hurricane Henderson was that of a weapon; he had two pistols, his and Sanford's, and the rifle was still with the horses.

She needed to get her hands on a gun! Yet, he wouldn't let either her or Sanford out of his sight. That meant she had to somehow get a hold of the guns in his possession. Venus studied him carefully. Sanford's Colt lay at Hurricane's side, and the other, Venus suspected, had been returned to the waistband of his pants. If she could manage to get close enough to him, she trusted her honed reflexes would enable her to grab both in one swift motion.

"Hurry," she purred, interrupting his speech. "Would you care for a beverage?"

"Uh, no thanks. But if you got something to drink, that would be fine. My throat's a mite parched."

Venus reached into Sanford's saddlebags, the one containing his medical kit. Her fingers grazed the familiar glass of a whiskey bottle he kept for medicinal purposes. Rising, Venus lifted her skirts to give Hurricane an eyeful of her trim ankles and calves. He stumbled over his life's story to gape at the wanton display of leg. Venus knelt beside him, covering Sanford's gun with her flowing skirt. As Hurricane took the bottle, she allowed her fingers to graze the back of his broad hand. "You've led quite a fascinating life," she whispered against his jaw. Then she trailed one finger down his skinny neck, dipping into the banded collar of a soldier's shirt he wore. "Men who've led fascinating lives? Why, they purely fascinate *me*."

The pen stopped scratching and Sanford growled.

Venus trailed the same finger up Hurricane's neck again, then over his bony shoulder, then down his spine. "I just adore adventure and excitement. It's so . . . dangerously romantic." *A few more inches* . . . "Don't you think so, Hurry?" Reaching the band of his pants, she simultaneously clamped her teeth onto his earlobe and seized his pearl-handled gun.

Hurricane yowled in pain; Venus scrambled backward, fishing under her skirts for Sanford's Colt.

"It's empty! It's empty!" Hurricane shouted, throwing his hands into the air in a gesture of surrender.

Sanford sprang up, yelling, "What the hell are you doing, woman!"

Venus glanced at Hurricane's gun. She checked the chamber for bullets and found it hollow. Then she whipped out Sanford's gun and cocked it. "This one isn't empty."

Picture the blood, the guts, all the gory details . . . there is time for remorse after the deed.

Yet all Venus saw was wide green eyes and a young boy's face and she couldn't bring herself to shoot Hurricane. Even so, he didn't know that, so she kept her aim.

"Sanford, get the rope." Her voice was amazingly calm. "It's right beside you, and Hurricane is four paces straight ahead of you."

"What the hell are you doing, woman?" Sanford repeated.

"I'm saving your ungrateful carcass, Buchanan. Now do what I said!"

"I don't need saving! Damn it, don't you trust me enough to protect you?"

Venus's gaze shifted for an instant from Hurricane to Sanford then back again. "It has nothing to do with trust. I saw a way out of this mess, and I took it. Isn't that what you have been preparing me for? Survival? Now, damn you, tie him up! This gun is heavy!"

Sanford stomped the four paces with rope in hand and quickly trussed up Hurricane. Swinging toward Venus, he ground out, "*This* is why I've rejected you! Why I've avoided women all my life! Jesus, I can't even protect you from a bumbling fool holding us captive. How competent can I be if our lives are truly in jeopardy?"

With Hurricane disabled and watching them intently, Venus felt safe enough to lower her trembling arms. "You *have* protected me, Sanford!" she countered. "You have spent every single day teaching me how to defend myself, how to assess conditions, and how to best proceed. In teaching me to survive under any circumstances you have armed me with the best protection—wisdom. If not for your tutoring, I never would have thought to steal this fella's gun, nor would I have had the knowledge to use it."

"So you took it upon yourself to put yourself in a dangerous predicament to save us? Great!" He threw his hands wide. "I've sunk to the deepest of depths. Because I am blind, I have to rely on a high-society princess to defend me!"

"You're blind?" Hurricane piped in.

"Shut up," Venus and Sanford both ordered.

Sanford raked his fingers through his hair. It made him sick to think of Venus putting herself in danger for him, to think of how his own damned darkness had prevented him from shielding her from possible harm. And their journey wasn't even half completed yet. How many more times would he have to suffer her interference? Her lack of faith? His own incompetence?

None, he decided.

He was sending her home.

"Venus, you cannot stay cooped up here forever," Minerva gently chided. "Your beaus have been stopping by every day all month to welcome you home. I cannot keep sending them away. They will only return again and again, and I have better things to do with my time than answer the door."

Venus stared out the rear window of her bedroom, recognizing the winding, tree-lined banks of the creek yet not truly seeing them. Not when she hungered for the sight of craggy mountains and endless plains. "I don't wish to see any callers."

"This is not like you, child. You used to drive everyone in this house mad with your exuberance! Now, why don't you don one of your gowns—Atalanta took her responsibility of them very seriously, going so far as to have Atlas record each of them—and come downstairs?"

The concern in her grandmother's voice touched a chord of remorse. Venus turned to the old woman, who did not seem as old as she had six months ago. Venus suspected Zeb's continuing courtship had a great deal to do with the stardust in Minerva's eyes and the high color in her plump cheeks.

Oh, it hurt to even think of *his* uncle staying here, let alone seeing him every day. And though Venus always waited with bated breath for news of Sanford, it seemed that not even Zeb would oblige her.

She told herself she didn't care. Sanford had rejected her for the last time, tossed her love—the only true love she had ever felt for a man—back in her face.

And all because of his stupid pride.

"I am not the same girl anymore, Grandma. He changed me. Or perhaps I changed myself. What I once

wanted seems so . . . trivial now. Unimportant. Do you
know that I don't even care about those clothes anymore?
Or my jewels? I'd trade them all if only he would . . ."

"Come to you?"

"No." She shook her head sadly. "It has been three
months since we said goodbye already. He will not come.
If only he would admit he loved me . . . even for a time.
That would be enough. But he denied it, up to the last
day when I boarded the stagecoach at Fort Apache, he
denied it."

Venus spilled her heart's secrets to Minerva. Of how
she wished she would've remained silent, not told Sanford of her feelings. At the stage depot where she was to
catch the stagecoach that would take her to the train station bound for Paradise, she had declared her love for
him and begged him not to send her home. Her reasons
had nothing to do with having to abandon her labor. She
wanted only to make him understand why she had been
compelled to protect him, that she couldn't have gone on
another day if Hurricane Henderson had killed him. But
as she had dreaded, he'd distanced himself further from
her than ever before.

Part of her was angry with Sanford, angry that he
couldn't have been manipulated into giving his heart to
her. She respected that trait, and yet, because of it, because of his stubborn blasted pride, he couldn't accept,
would not allow, someone to get so close to him.

Another part of her, the lonesome, hungry part, felt
such wrenching anguish she could hardly bear it. *It just
isn't fair.* The one man who had finally touched something
deep inside her, who perceived her moods, gave her special and unexpected gifts, delighted in her triumphs and
encouraged her when she was ready to quit . . . well, he
thought of her as a means to an end. A nuisance.

A lady.

At one time, she had been proud of that title. Superior
with the knowledge that she could wangle affection out of
even the most stubborn man and not feel the need for a
lifelong attachment or physical yearnings or a restless de-

sire to see more of the world than Paradise Plains or New
York or any big glamorous city.

But Sanford had awakened all those things in her to
such an intense degree that she could not deny them—
not to herself. Not to him. She craved the world he had
opened up to her—of adventure and romance and unpre-
dictability. She'd been bluntly honest with him. No arti-
fice, no pretense, just naked honesty.

And look where it had gotten her.

Passionately, Venus seized her grandmother's hand. "I
don't understand him! I don't understand why! He is not
a coward! He never was, he never will be! He is courageous and daring and smart! And he has dreams, although he denies them, too!"

Venus choked on a sob. "But he is proud. Too proud
for his own good. And I . . . failed him, myself, you, the
whole family. The most important task I've ever per-
formed in my life, and I failed. I could not even decipher
your riddle that was to explain why you chose my labor in
the first place."

The door inched open and Venus's mother peeked inside. "Sweetheart, there's someone here to see you."

"Please, Mama, send him away." It was probably just
another of her old beaus, hoping to renew a courtship.

"He said the strangest thing, though. He said to tell
you that Slick Drayson humbly begs the light of Mara—"

Venus dashed out the door, nearly running down her
mother. At the second-floor landing Venus came to an
abrupt halt, smoothed tears from her cheeks, patted the
simple coil of her hair, then descended the last flight of
stairs with haughty grace. Reaching the base of the stairwell, she drank in the sight of him. He stood tall and
powerful in his buckskins, clutching his hat to his stomach. Beside him, Hurry Henderson shifted from one foot
to the other, then cast her a shy glance. It didn't surprise
Venus to see the boy with Sanford. After the storm had
abated and they continued on to Fort Apache, Hurry had
talked nonstop of his life. Sanford had felt grateful to the
boy for safeguarding them against evils they hadn't even

known about, and decided to reward him by writing the book about him after all. The concession had pierced Venus to the core. For having saved him, she had received only scorn. But he had felt compelled to reward Hurricane. Venus didn't share Sanford's gratitude; it was easier to blame Hurricane Henderson for Sanford's final rejection. Had it not been for Hurricane taking Sanford hostage, Venus wouldn't have come to his rescue, and earned his contempt.

Coolly, she asked, "What brings the pair of you to Mount Olympus? And if you're supposed to be Slick, who's Hurry supposed to be? The ass you rode in on?"

Sanford shifted his weight from one leg to the other. "I know you're angry, Venus, but can you put aside your hostility for a minute to hear me out?"

"I believe you said everything there was to say when you ousted me from your life."

The hat became a mangled wad of felt in his hands. "Slick and Mara . . . I couldn't finish . . . Hell, they never claimed the saloon!"

Venus crossed her arms over her bosom and lifted one brow. "Hurry could've helped you write the words, as long as you spoke slowly."

"He doesn't have a lady's sensibilities," Sanford returned lamely.

"Then that should suit you just fine. You never had much use for a lady." Venus spun on her heel.

Sanford raised his voice. "The truth is . . . it was too dark, princess."

Venus froze.

"After you left, it was too dark."

"I didn't leave willingly, Sanford. You sent me away."

"And it was the biggest mistake I've ever made in my life. I couldn't think, I was always distracted, and I tried to write you but the words wouldn't come."

With his head bowed, Sanford closed the gap between them. He reached out and encountered her stiff back, then rested his hands on her shoulders. "And I found myself so lonely, and so alone, that I knew only you could fill the void. It took only a couple of days for me to realize that you and me were partners. Partners watch out for one another, defend one another. You were only acting as my partner, not testing my ability to keep you safe. If you had been a man, and not the lady I had fallen in love with, I wouldn't have been offended."

Venus whirled in his loose embrace. "Say that again."

"I wouldn't have been offended."

"No, the lady part."

"That I had fallen in love with?"

"What took you so long?"

"Adventures follow Hurricane like a plague. The train we took was wrecked so we had to take the stage and it got robbed outside Sweetwater."

"No, silly! To realize you loved me?" Then she reared back. "And land's sake, Sanford! Whatever happened to your acute senses?"

"Remember I once told you that sometimes it's easier to cope without something you'd never had, than to have it and lose it?"

Venus nodded.

"When I let you get away from me, I lost something— my heart, my senses . . . you took them with you. I had to come for you. Beg you if I had to, to give me another chance. Venus, can you forgive me for being such a fool?"

Venus curled her arms around his back and smiled with mischief. "You'll have to spend the rest of your life making it up to me. Marry me, Sanford Buchanan. Be everything that's been missing in my life and give me my heart's desire all the rest of my earthly days. Maybe then I'll forgive you."

"I love you, Venus Daltry. I never want you to be disappointed in me."

"The only way I'd ever be disappointed in you, darlin', is if you deny yourself the freedom to dream."

"Never again, princess." Sanford lowered his head.

Venus felt more than heard Jane and Minerva appear on the landing. Odie was in the barn carving the cradle headboard for the baby Persy was expecting, Atlas had gone to Paradise to Lee's library, and Allie was no doubt in the corral with Hal, ogling the new mustang colt C.J. had brought over yesterday.

As her lips sealed with Sanford's, she forgot the existence of her family, forgot Hurricane's presence, and gave herself over to finally tasting love's wine again.

Epilogue

EVERYONE IN PARADISE PLAINS, TEXAS, KNEW WHAT APRIL 30, 1885, was. Venus Daltry Buchanan made sure of it.

Therefore it came as no surprise to Minerva Daltry when she found her gazebo teeming with grieving beaus and ecstatic maidens. Her granddaughter's former suitors sobbed into their kerchiefs as Venus exchanged vows with Sanford Joseph "Buck" Buchanan, and the maidens gave very unladylike whoops when the preacher pronounced her a missus. Now they would finally have their chance to mend all the broken hearts Venus left behind.

The invitations had been sent two months ago, shortly after Sanford and Venus returned from Nevada to finish the book they'd started, and the ranch had been in an uproar ever since. Banners were strung around the gazebo columns; saws grated and hammers banged as the Daltry menfolk hurriedly constructed benches; the kitchen was an inferno as Persy cooked on the ranch oven by day and on her own oven by night; Jane frantically pored over her horticulture books to find the right combination of pollens and seeds for her daughter's bridal bouquet; and Atlas kept all the workers in line by posting lists of duties on every available wall.

Compounding the hectic activity of preparing for Venus's wedding was the fact that she had chosen to marry on her twenty-first birthday.

But it had been worth the exhausting efforts. The crowded gazebo reflected taste and dignity—if one discounted the bawling ensemble of scorned suitors and yipping gals—and the aromas of twenty-five various culinary delights wafted in the spring breeze.

And watching the ceremony, Minerva thought her beautiful granddaughter had never looked more lovely than she did on this day. She wore a simple ivory linen toga Minerva had stored in a trunk for ages, with a halo of Jane's spring blossoms crowning her flowing blond curls. And Sanford was dressed all in a black suit, with a sprig of vanilla leaves pinned to his lapel. *He so dark and rugged, she so fair and dainty.*

"Almost don't recognize my nephew without his hat," Zeb whispered beside her as the newly wedded pair strolled down the aisle.

"And I cannot recall seeing my granddaughter without her cosmetics in years," Minerva confided. "Zebuelan, dear, would you mind walking with me to the library? I have a bit of business to attend to before the reception."

Zeb escorted her to the family library then disappeared. Minerva lowered herself to her rocking chair. One by one, her grandchildren filed in. Lee with Meredith on his arm, and their children, Jimmy, Jupiter, and Cynthia, crowded onto the window seat. Jake aided a burgeoning Persy, who was expecting a brother or sister for their little Diana, to a chair then took up a protective post behind his ladies. C.J. held a squirming Thalia in his arms but the child soon escaped, her wobbly steps taking her to her mother's side. Atlas entered with Allie, Odie with Jane, and soon, all were present except the birthday bride and her groom.

Out on the front porch, Venus applied pressure on Sanford's arm, delaying him from joining the rest of the family. "Darling," she began nervously. "Remember when I told you my grandmother is a bit—"

"Short of salt in the shaker?"

She gave her new husband a wavering grin. "Yes. Well, she has this tradition she follows every time a Daltry turns twenty years old. She assigns a labor to be completed in a year's time. If it is successfully accomplished by the twenty-first birthday, she rewards the Daltry with a wonderful prize."

Venus released his arm and turned to watch the wedding guests gather in Mama's garden. Perfume of dozens of colorful blooms mingled with stuffy cologne and expensive fragrances. Two dozen tables had been set up, two alone for the feast Persy had spent a week preparing, and one for the three-tiered heart-shaped cake. "I know I should have told you about it sooner but it was in the rules that I couldn't. And after I fell in love with you, it no longer seemed important."

He wrapped his arms around her waist and rested his chin on top of her head. "But it's important now?"

"I don't want our new life marred with secrets." She grabbed his left hand and kissed the shiny gold band on the third finger. "Before I tell you, I want you to know how very much I love you. I never expected to—"

"Tell me, Venus. Nothing you can say will make me love you any less."

"Do you promise? On your name, do you promise?"

"On *our* name."

Venus sought the safety of his embrace and cupped his cheeks in her palms. "I was given my labor one year ago today. It was to accompany a dime novelist to Nevada and help him write his books."

He digested her news. "Has Lee completed a labor?"

"Yes. It was to teach the children for one year. Persy made her debut in New York, and C.J. found a husband for Lizzie Colepepper—himself. Allie will have her turn next year, then Atlas after her."

"You had no idea—"

"None," Venus interrupted, her belly twisting with dread. "Grandma keeps the labor she chooses a secret until the twentieth birthday. It's a matter of honor that we accept it, along with all the rules."

To her surprise, he grinned. "I suppose this dime novel-ist was me."

Venus laid her head on his chest and nodded.

"Was that why she wanted my uncle to visit?"

"No. She told me she hadn't conceived my labor until after he told her he could not leave you to fend for your-self. She had hoped to prod him into coming with the offer, and at the same time present me with a task she knew would be a challenge. Grandma never does things the easy way."

"Then it's a good thing I'm a dime novelist. I'd hate to have lost you to Ned Buntline."

Venus jerked back. "You aren't angry?"

"*I* am the luckiest ten-cent writer ever born. If it took your grandmother and a labor to make me find the light missing in my life, then I owe her a debt I can never repay."

Venus's smiled burned brighter than the sun. "I love you, Buchanan."

"Not half as much as I love you, princess." His face dipped, and Venus met his kiss halfway.

Breaking for air, he said, "Well, you went to Nevada, helped me write about Slick winning not only a saloon sitting on a silver mine, but also winning Mara, and re-turned before your twenty-first birthday . . ."

"*And* got Hurry a job here at the ranch until we finish his book so he can return to Lasso a hero!" Venus in-serted pointedly.

"Yes, and found it in your heart to forgive Hurricane," Sanford agreed. "So does that mean you have success-fully accomplished your labor?"

She paused, then said, "For the most part."

"There's more?"

"Well, Grandma also gave me a riddle to puzzle out. I don't think I've put all the pieces together, so I don't know if I'll get my prize. But it doesn't matter. No prize is worth more than the one you have given me."

"And what is that?"

"Your heart."

"It's yours always, Venus." His head once again lowered.

A full ten minutes later, Venus guided her husband down the hallway to the library where her family was assembled. "I'm sorry for keeping everyone waitin'." Venus's high color and swollen lips bore evidence that her tardiness had nothing to do with primping over her hair or gown. And yet, no amount of inward change prevented Venus from gliding to the settee and, once seated beside her husband, arranging her skirt.

The good-natured banter dwindled. Even the children seemed to understand the magnitude of the moment and hushed.

"Venus," Minerva began, folding her lined hands loosely in her lap. "You have fulfilled the terms of your labor but have you solved the riddle? Discovered my reasons for choosing Hercules's twelfth labor?"

Everyone waited in suspense. Venus squeezed Sanford's hand. He squeezed it back for encouragement. "Well, Hercules had to go into the lower world and bring the three-headed dog Cerberus back to Hades, god of the dead, without using any weapons."

Venus replayed the events of the last year in her mind.

Suddenly, she knew. She knew what lesson she'd been expected to learn. With a beaming smile, she answered, "Wisdom. You wanted me to learn wisdom. The goddess Venus represented light and love. The lower world was the darkness and Hades was the possessor of the darkness. Cerberus—" She elbowed Sanford gently. "That's you, darlin'." Addressing Minerva again, Venus continued. "Cerberus was a mystery, his three heads signifying hopes, dreams, and wishes. He needed to face his darkness and conquer it in order to find his way to the light." She leaned against Sanford's arm. "That's me, darlin', and I'm shining brighter now that I'm with you again."

A round of boisterous applause met the last sentence. Once the rowdy noise died down, Minerva queried, "And what was the weapon?"

Without hesitation, Venus replied, "The weapon was my own beauty. I had used it as a tool of manipulation and control. And, perhaps, as a defense against rejection. But physical beauty is useless in the dark. I needed wisdom to lure Cerberus. Sometimes wisdom must come from within. Of course, I had a little help."

"Venus." Minerva's voice cracked. "I am proud of you. And of you, Sanford. This ordeal could not have been easy for you, either. So to reward you both . . ." Minerva handed Venus a small, wrapped box. "Open it. I know how you adore presents."

Venus tore off the paper. She lifted a vellum card and read, " 'To my darlin' granddaughter, Venus. For successfully completing your labor, I award you the prize of a trip to India, so you and your husband may continue your adventures.' "

Venus's eyes watered. To Sanford she said, "You always wanted to visit faraway places. How does India sound?"

Sanford's face registered his astonishment. "How does it sound to you?"

"Like a very exotic, romantic honeymoon!"

"You'd be willing to go to India on our honeymoon?"

Venus tossed the box; it landed in Atlas's lap. "For you, Buchanan, I would go anywhere, do anything. I'd even walk through a mud puddle for you."

"That's the nicest thing you've ever said to me, princess."

"I love you," she whispered against his lips.

Well, Sanford amended with a grin, *the second nicest thing*.

If you enjoyed this book, take advantage of this special offer. Subscribe now and get a

FREE
Historical
Romance

No Obligation (a $4.50 value)

Each month the editors of True Value select the four *very best* novels from America's leading publishers of romantic fiction. Preview them in your home *Free* for 10 days. With the first four books you receive, we'll send you a FREE book as our introductory gift. No Obligation!

If for any reason you decide not to keep them, just return them and owe nothing. If you like them as much as we think you will, you'll pay just $4.00 each and save at *least* $.50 each off the cover price. (Your savings are *guaranteed* to be at least $2.00 each month.) There is NO postage and handling – or other hidden charges. There are no minimum number of books to buy and you may cancel at any time.

Send in the Coupon Below

To get your FREE historical romance fill out the coupon below and mail it today. As soon as we receive it we'll send you your FREE Book along with your first month's selections.
